W9-CFB-235

INTIMATE
STRANGERS

Intimate Strangers

Alexandra Thorne

DOUBLEDAY

New York   London   Toronto   Sydney   Auckland

Loveswept®

PUBLISHED BY DOUBLEDAY
a division of Bantam Doubleday Dell Publishing Group, Inc.
666 Fifth Avenue, New York, New York 10103

Doubleday and the portrayal of an anchor with a dolphin
and the word Loveswept and the portrayal of the wave device
are trademarks of Doubleday, a division of
Bantam Doubleday Dell Publishing Group, Inc.

Library of Congress Cataloging-in-Publication Data
Thorne, Alexandra, 1934–
    Intimate strangers / Alexandra Thorne. — 1st ed.
    p.   cm.
    I. Title.
PS3570.H64975P37   1992
813'.54—dc20   91-22795
                                                        CIP

ISBN 0-385-42291-1
Copyright © 1992 by Alexandra Thorne
All Rights Reserved
Printed in the United States of America
April 1992

1   3   5   7   9   10   8   6   4   2

FIRST EDITION

In memory of my father,
Alexander Hope Jablow,
who showed me the way through the shipop.

ACKNOWLEDGMENTS

Every book is a collaborative effort. This book would not have been possible without the guidance and encouragement of my indefatigable editors, Elizabeth Barrett and Nita Taublib. Thanks are also due Carolyn Nichols, Beth de Guzman, Susann Brailey, Richard Curtis, the staffs of La Fonda Hotel, the *Santa Fe New Mexican*, the Heard Museum, and the Santa Fe Museum of Art for their patience and help, as well as to the pueblos of Acoma and San Ildefonso. My gratitude also goes to Thelma Scott, Shirley Estes, Lawrence Lee, and Mary Wyant.

PROLOGUE

The smoke-laden air burned Jade Howard's lungs and throat. She gasped, fighting for breath. Get out. She had to get out. But she was completely disoriented. The searing heat at her back propelled her forward. She stumbled and fell to her knees, paralyzed by a mortal dread that jellied her bones.

Then she felt herself lifted by a strong pair of hands. "The door is straight ahead," a man said from behind her.

She saw a rectangle of moonlight and staggered toward it. Under her bare feet, the wooden floor changed to the softer feel of grass. Fifty feet from the burning building, she turned and looked back. Greedy tongues of red and gold licked the adobe walls, sending pyrotechnic jets of flame into the black night sky.

She saw the man through a large window. He was still inside. God. She thought he'd been right behind her.

The fire roared like a hungry beast of prey, drowning out all other sounds. The flames burst through the roof. The ceiling, oh no, the massive vigas, the log rafters, were coming down. She tried to scream a warning—and that's when she woke up.

Every time.

CHAPTER 1

Malibu
May 13, 1989

The dream. She'd had the dream again, the nightmare that had plagued her since childhood. There were no spectral monsters, nothing that went bump in the night—just an escape from a burning building that left her trembling and sick with loss. She'd never even been near a life-threatening fire, yet there was always something so familiar about the scene. . . .

"Damn," she muttered, brushing a few tousled curls from her eyes. With an important meeting that afternoon, she had counted on getting eight hours of sleep. The clock on the nightstand read four. The sun wouldn't rise for a couple of hours, and neither would she if she could help it.

Outside her Malibu beachfront house, the Pacific Ocean murmured ceaselessly, its serried ranks of combers caressing the shore. Seeking the warm place her body had left on the sheets, she curled into a fetal position and concentrated on the sound, willing herself to sleep again. But her mind refused to cooperate. The aftereffect of the nightmare lingered on, as oppressive as Los Angeles smog, and she decided just to get up. She had a busy day ahead.

Jade should have realized that a day so badly begun was unlikely to have a happy finish. But she'd been born with an optimistic mind-set and had cultivated the philosophy that everything happened for a reason. In the past it had helped her survive the death of her parents and, later, being jilted by her college sweetheart just weeks before their wedding.

Forget the damn nightmare, she told herself, and got out of bed, heading for the kitchen to make a pot of coffee.

When the telephone rang at eight-thirty in the morning, she sent a hopeful prayer skyward. Please, God let it be Ira Max calling from New York—not someone soliciting a donation she couldn't afford to give.

"Jade Howard here," she said.

Her prayer had been answered. It was Ira. Although her literary agent usually got straight to the point, he began by asking after her health, chatting about the weather, talking about anything and everything except the new novel she had Express Mailed to his office a couple of weeks ago.

"Please don't keep me in suspense," she said, interrupting the smooth flow of his chitchat. "What did you think of *Power Play?*"

Her heart pounded while silence stretched the moment taut.

"I had a few problems with it."

"And?" she prompted anxiously.

"There are places where the writing is brilliant, especially in the descriptive passages."

"And?" she said again, a premonitory chill icing her skin.

He cleared his throat. "Your heroine . . . She, ah, well, she's terribly brittle. The truth is, I didn't really care for her. In fact, I didn't like any of the protagonists."

Jade felt as if she'd been sucker-punched. As with all writers, her characters were extensions of her own personality, dredged up from the sunny or the dark side of her mind. Hearing Ira say he didn't like any of them made her feel raw inside. She had to force herself to speak. "I admit my characters have a bizarre way of looking at things—who wouldn't, living in LaLaland?—but I thought they were intriguing."

"Jade, sweetheart, I don't have to tell you to give readers a character they can root for. You're a pro."

2

The underlying affection she heard in his voice didn't take the sting out of his words. "I used to be," she muttered. Her knuckles whitened as she gripped the phone harder. She had so much riding on *Power Play*.

A decade ago, after her first novel hit the best-seller lists, she wouldn't have believed it if someone had told her that her literary career was destined to be a classic case of diminishing returns. But ten years and four more books had transformed her from the critics' darling to their favorite target. Until now she had refused to heed the nagging voice in the back of her mind that had the temerity to suggest it might be her fault.

"Believe me," Ira continued, "I know how hard you worked on the project. And as I said, there are flashes of your old brilliance. But . . ."

He paused again. She knew it was going to be a huge *but*.

"I hate having to say this, *but* at this point in your career, I think showing the book to publishers would be a mistake. A big one. Hollywood novels don't sell all that well unless your name happens to be Jackie Collins. And yours . . . Well, you can't afford another loser. If you take my advice, you'll put the manuscript aside."

Her chest felt tight, and tears burned at the back of her eyes. Biting her lip, she knuckled them away. Tears weren't her style. "Are you sure?"

"Yes. Very." Finality rang in his voice. "I can't tell you how sorry I am. You're all right financially, aren't you?"

She had too much pride to tell him how small her bank account was. Besides, it was more than the money. Her writing was her salvation. When she was younger and the loss of her parents had threatened to overwhelm her, she'd turned to writing for emotional release.

She could still quote verbatim parts of her first published piece. She had been fifteen years old at the time, a confusing age at best and an utterly miserable one if your parents had died six months earlier and there were no relatives to take their place. She had written of their death in a collision with a drunk driver, a useless, horrible death. She had written about what had happened to her afterward, the anger, the anguish, the way other teenagers turned away as if there were something contagious about tragedy, the naked fear of being alone in the world.

Her English teacher had given the essay an A+ and convinced her to send it off to *Reader's Digest*. Having the piece published, seeing her words in print, had soothed her pain and made her feel as if her life had a purpose again. Before she knew it had happened, writing had become her reason for being—the one thing that validated her existence and made her feel worthwhile.

Things should have changed after Paul came into her life in college. He had been sweet, gentle, proud of her. But she had been so afraid some dreadful twist of fate would spirit him away, too, that the idea of risking her whole heart had been unthinkable.

What was it he said the day he broke their engagement? "I don't know you. You won't let me know you." Tears had been streaming down his face.

She had been dry eyed then and she was dry eyed now. She had failed at love long ago and now she had failed as a writer. But she wouldn't cry. Once she did, she might never stop.

There had been a time when she'd actually been afraid she wouldn't live long enough to write all the books that lived in her imagination. On this too-perfect spring morning she suddenly wasn't sure she would ever be able to summon up the courage to write another one.

"What do you think I ought to do?" she asked Ira.

He didn't respond at once. She waited, wondering what he would say, hoping . . . Hell, she didn't know what she hoped. Ira was a terrific agent—the best—and her dear friend, but he certainly didn't have a cure for what ailed her. Perhaps there wasn't one.

"You know," he said at last, "maybe it's not you. Maybe it's that plastic city you call home. Your first book had so much heart. You made readers laugh a little, cry a little. You still write like a dream, Jade. The words are all there. The heart isn't. But I don't see how anyone can keep in touch with reality in Tinsel Town."

She looked around her study with its trendy bleached-wood furniture and white raw-silk upholstery, the expensive art on the walls and the multimillion dollar view of the Pacific, and remembered how she'd bought the house in the first flush of her success. Spending all that money had been a defiant reaction to finding herself alone in the world when she had expected to be sharing her good fortune with Paul. But now the damn place was mortgaged to the hilt and she could barely make the payments.

By contrast she could imagine Ira in his cozy office, sitting in the deep leather chair behind his massive partners' desk, books and manuscripts piled high on shelves behind him, the walls hung with lovingly inscribed photographs of authors he represented. His was a room that said Welcome while the one she sat in suddenly seemed as sterile as a laboratory.

"Besides," Ira went on, "Los Angeles has been the setting for so many books that it's virtually impossible to come up with something new and fresh using it as a backdrop. Have you considered going away? A change of scene might be just what you need. I seem to recall you saying something about going back to the University of Iowa and visiting some of your old writing teachers."

"I don't think that would be productive right now."

"Well, I suggest you get out of town. A trip might help you get a little perspective on things."

"Ira, I know you mean well, but I'm not ready to make any plans."

"Think about it," he said, concern so evident in his voice that she felt guilty for putting it there.

"Don't worry about me. I've always been a survivor. Besides, there's still a chance the movie deal will go through." For Ira's sake, she tried to sound confident even though she knew there wasn't much chance of a famous producer-director like Harrison Denby being seriously interested in a book that wasn't hot off the best-seller list.

"When are you meeting Denby to talk about it?" Ira asked.

"This afternoon."

"If he wants to discuss the plot, go ahead. But don't talk money with him. I'm asking for a low six figures."

"That sounds great," Jade replied, although she knew Ira was being overly optimistic. Denby would undoubtedly spend six figures to option a best-seller. But her second book, *Better Than Sex*, had barely been an also-ran. Having him express any interest in it at all was an incredible stroke of luck.

"Call me after the meeting," Ira said. "You can get me at home if I've left the office."

"Sure thing."

After saying good-bye, she sat at her desk for a long time, trying to deal with the fact that *Power Play*—a book she'd spent two years writing—wasn't going to resurrect her career, put a dollar in her savings account, or rebuild her sagging self-esteem. The knowledge hurt. Badly. She hated disappointing Ira, hated what he had said about her book.

Most of all, she hated knowing he was right. In order to deal with this failure, she had to believe she had failed for a reason. One of these days, she might figure out what that reason was.

In the meantime she had to put herself into a more positive frame of mind for her lunch meeting with Denby. Although she had never met the man, she knew the type. He would be able to smell a loser a block away.

She spent the rest of the morning washing and polishing her leased Mercedes. Then, although clothes had never been important to her, she dressed with particular care in a green silk Dana Buchman suit that was three years old but so classic it didn't look dated —she hoped.

One o'clock in the afternoon found her turning her Mercedes left off Sunset onto the Beverly Hills Hotel's curving drive.

When she first moved to Hollywood, she'd rented the old Lionel Barrymore house on Summit Drive in the hills above Sunset. The Beverly Hills Hotel had been the closest place for a meal, and she'd become a regular.

It hadn't changed a bit, she thought, braking to a stop by the entrance. After handing her car keys to a valet, she headed up the canopied walk to the lobby, passing several people on the way. In the past she might have been greeted by one or two of them. But Hollywood was a tough town. After the critics had ravaged her last book like barbarians attacking a vestal virgin, her so-called friends had forgotten her phone number. The mail no longer brought invitations to the openings of trendy restaurants, art galleries, and boutiques. There were no frantic messages from publicists who wanted her to attend the screening of their studio's latest, megabuck, surefire hit. At thirty-two, she was a has-been. *Sic transit gloria mundi.*

Ten years earlier, when she had arrived with stars in her eyes, hope in her heart, and impossible dreams in her head, it would have mattered. But she had long since learned that beneath Hollywood's tinsel was simply more tinsel. And only children fell in love with tinsel.

She strode through the marble-floored lobby, heading for the Polo Lounge. Gilbert, the maitre d', wasn't at his station, so she paused in the entry, searching the lunch crowd for Denby.

"Can I help you?" a man asked, coming up to the maitre d's desk.

"I'm waiting for Gilbert to take me to my table."

"Gilbert doesn't work here anymore," the man replied, looking her up and down as if he was trying to decide if she merited his attention. He must be Gilbert's replacement, she thought.

She obviously met his criteria, because he again asked, "Can I help you?"

"I'm Jade Howard. I have a reservation for one-thirty."

He studied his reservations list with the same care that attorneys give to important briefs. His self-importance should have made her laugh, if only silently. But this afternoon, with her entire future on the line, she didn't even crack a smile.

Gilbert had always ushered her to her regular booth as if she were visiting royalty. What if Harrison Denby walked in now and saw her standing in line like a nobody? She needed to make the right impression on the producer-director, and this certainly wasn't the way.

"Ah," the maitre d' said, finally locating her name, "here we are. A table for two at one-thirty." He checked his watch. "I'm terribly sorry, Miss, ah . . ."

"Howard. Jade Howard," she said sharply.

"Howard, of course. Forgive me." The man scanned the crowded room. "You're a little early. We don't have a table right now. However, I'm sure one will be available in half an hour—if you don't mind waiting."

Jade fought to control her temper. She'd suggested the Polo Lounge as a meeting place because she'd been sure of getting a good table and even better service, and she'd been equally sure Harrison Denby would be the sort of man who cared about those things.

She drilled the maitre d' with a disdainful look. "I do mind waiting. I'm expecting Harrison Denby to join me."

The name registered instantly. "I understand perfectly," the maitre d' replied in an unctuous tone. "We wouldn't dream of making Mr. Denby wait. If you'll follow me."

He walked across the restaurant, then halted abruptly at a table in the middle of the room and pulled out one of the chairs.

"This won't do," Jade said. In the Polo Lounge hierarchy, such tables were relegated to unimportant guests. "When I made the reservation, I asked for my usual booth."

"I'm terribly sorry, Miss, ah . . ."

"Howard!" she said so loudly, a few diners looked her way.

"As you can see," the maitre d' continued, his smile as frosty as a Siberian winter, "this is the only table available. Of course, if you prefer, you can wait at the bar."

Tourists were sent into exile at the bar and sometimes sat there for hours without being seated. The only thing worse than sitting at the table, she concluded, would be making a scene about it. She hated playing mind games but she had no choice. She gave the maitre d' a brilliant, this-is-a-terrific-table-and-I'm-having-so-much-fun smile, ignored the chair he had pulled out, and sat down in the one facing the entrance.

After he left, she took a deep, calming breath and looked around the crowded room, hoping the serene green-and-peach decor would soothe her. The morning had taken its toll. She could feel a tiny muscle pulsing under her left eye, and her nerves were ragged.

Taking her compact from her purse, she gave her makeup a cursory glance. She didn't consider herself particularly good-looking, and generally ignored the admiring glances that came her way. The dark curls framing her oval face hadn't been styled for months. She looked pale and tired. Her eyes, a startling jungle green, frowned back at her, not liking what they saw.

She snapped the compact shut, then, straightening in her chair, tried to look as composed, confident, and successful as her fellow diners. Although she could have used a double anything, she asked for a Perrier when a waiter finally deigned to take her order.

At two-thirty, she checked her watch for the sixth time. The power players had long since returned to their offices, and half the nearby tables and booths were unoccupied. The few customers lingering over coffee spoke in the sepulchral tones usually reserved for funerals, as if they didn't want to disturb the Polo Lounge's midday quiet.

Jade had expected Denby to be a little late, but not this late. No matter how busy he was, he could have had his secretary page her to let her know he'd been delayed.

"Would you like another Perrier?" her waiter asked.

Not trusting herself to speak, she simply shook her head.

Across the room, the maitre d' looked her way, scorn in his eyes. He'd obviously concluded that she didn't know Denby and had used the name to get a table.

She stared back until he averted his gaze. Only then, in an act of pure bravado, did she take a twenty-dollar bill from her purse and drop it by her empty glass to cover her drink. She'd be damned if the supercilious man would be able to brand her a deadbeat as well as a liar. Squaring her shoulders, she got up and marched out of the restaurant, her head held high, her sunglasses hiding the sheen in her eyes.

Back in the lobby, she walked over to a phone and dialed Denby's office. "This is Jade Howard," she said when his secretary answered. "Mr. Denby and I had an appointment in the Polo Lounge at one-thirty, but he hasn't shown up."

"There must be some misunderstanding, Ms. Howard," the secretary replied. "Mr. Denby is out of town. Would you like to leave a message?"

Jade felt a flush reddening her cheeks. "Yes, I would," she said fervently. "You can tell him to go to hell."

By the time she pulled up in her drive an hour later, she knew Ira had been right. She had to get out of Lalaland before it swallowed her whole.

But she wasn't running away, not her, not Jade Howard, she thought as she began to pack her bags. She preferred to think of the trip as a personal quest, a journey down the Yellow Brick Road in search of her heart.

CHAPTER 2

Santa Fe
May 16, 1989

In the years to come, Jade would realize she had been drawn to Santa Fe as inexorably as a bee to its hive. But when she drove out of the Los Angeles basin the evening of May thirteenth, heading east, she had no destination. Three days later, while cruising along I-40 on the outskirts of Albuquerque, New Mexico, she saw a highway sign pointing to Santa Fe and simply turned her car north.

The sun had set by the time she reached the city. She drove along Cerrillos, the main road leading into town, passing dozens of brightly lit motels. Every time she decided to check into one, something about its appearance, its location, its ambiance, made her change her mind. She was being ridiculous, she told herself as she neared the center of the city. Any clean hotel room would do.

And then she saw the bulk of La Fonda looming out of the darkness like an ancient pueblo, and she knew she had reached the end of her journey.

Five minutes later, having left her car in the hotel lot, she stood at the front desk, her luggage neatly piled around her. "I'd like a single room, please," she said, holding out her MasterCard.

"I'm afraid we don't have any available," the desk clerk, a young Hispanic woman, replied. When she read Jade's name on the credit card, though, her expression brightened. "I believe you have a reservation, Miss Howard."

"I couldn't. I didn't even know I was going to stay here."

The clerk ignored Jade's reply and began going through the reservations list. "Ah, here it is," she said, triumphantly flourishing a piece of paper. "You asked for Suite 310."

"That's impossible. I didn't know La Fonda existed until five minutes ago. And I don't want a suite. All I want is a bed." Jade was too tired to get angry, and too embarrassed to confess that she couldn't afford to squander her money on a suite. "You must be expecting another Jade Howard."

The desk clerk shrugged. "It's hardly a common name. Furthermore, Miss Howard, all our singles are occupied. However, since we seem to have made the mistake, I'll give you the suite at the single-room rate."

Jade smiled her acceptance and thanked the woman. She took the key to the suite, sent a bellboy ahead with her luggage, and stayed in the lobby long enough to buy a newspaper and a Santa Fe guidebook before taking the elevator to the third floor.

Jade woke up refreshed by a deep and blessedly dreamless sleep. Eager to explore, she dressed hurriedly. Ten minutes later she left La Fonda by the San Francisco Street exit and looked around.

She saw a plaza on her left and a handsome cathedral a short distance to her right. As she gazed at the cathedral, a name, *St. Francis*, popped into her head. With it came an unsettling sense of déjà vu. She felt chilled, dizzy, and disoriented.

Must be the thin mountain air, she thought, thankful that the odd sensation ebbed as suddenly as it had arrived. She took the guidebook from her purse, paged through it, and saw that the cathedral was indeed named for St. Francis. She must have seen the name when she glanced through the book before she'd fallen asleep, she concluded as she headed for the plaza.

Santa Fe was like no other city she'd ever seen. It seemed to have sprung from the soil, to be an indigenous part of the landscape rather than an intruder upon it. The pueblo-style buildings were uniformly painted in warm earth tones. The precise geometry of their architecture was softened by gently rounded walls. Narrow streets invited a leisurely pace, and delightful vistas beckoned around every corner.

To the northeast, the Sangre de Cristo Mountains thrust pine-clad peaks into a sky as clear as a perfect diamond. The Jemez Mountains rose to the west, the Sandias to the south. The city sat between them on a high, rolling plain. Jade, who had grown accustomed to L.A.'s smog, breathed deeply, marveling at air she couldn't taste or see.

She spent the morning circumnavigating the plaza and the streets radiating from it before following the guidebook's directions to Canyon Road, a street noted for its many art galleries. It proved to be quite a hike under a fierce sun that wilted her desire for exploration. When she reached Canyon Road she slowed her pace and began looking for a place to have a cold drink. All she saw, though, were the galleries the guidebook had promised.

A few blocks farther on, she glanced down a tiny alley and saw a sign moving in the breeze. Its faded lettering read AURORA'S BOREALIS —Treasures from the Past. What an out-of-the-way place for a shop, she thought as she approached the building. Judging by the scabrous condition of the plastered adobe, it was a very old build-ing. Two high windows with wooden sashes so weatherworn the grain had separated flanked a wooden door bearing ghostly traces of turquoise paint. She was about to peer in the nearest window when the shop door opened with an audible creak.

An enormous woman, a good two hundred pounds and easily six feet tall, stood framed in the entrance. She fixed Jade with catlike amber eyes and said, "Good afternoon. I was hoping someone would come by today." Her voice, as breathy and delicate as a child's, belied her bulk.

"Won't you come in," she continued. "I don't get many custom-ers this time of year."

Feeling oddly uncertain about going into the shop, Jade glanced up, and was surprised to see that the sky seemed about to burst open like a ripe seedpod. How peculiar, she mused. A few minutes ear-lier, the sky had been cloud free. "From the look of the weather," she said, "I had better get back to my hotel."

The huge woman looked skyward too. "Oh dear. We're going to have one of our spring storms. You'd better come in and wait it out with me."

She opened the door wider, ushered Jade inside, and took a proprietorial stance behind a counter. An ancient cash register, its intricate brass work gleaming, squatted at the counter's far end. Beaded evening bags and what appeared to be estate jewelry were artfully displayed beneath the glass top. Jade blinked in awe. She'd seen enough expensive gems in Rodeo Drive's pricey shops to know the real thing. These elegantly set stones would have done credit to Tiffany's.

"Welcome to the Borealis," the woman said. "My name is Aurora. I'm the owner." She smiled again, and her eyes almost disappeared in the folds of fat surrounding them. She had even white teeth, a Cupid's-bow mouth, a delicate nose, and well-arched brows.

"And mine is Jade Howard," Jade replied, holding out her hand.

When their fingertips touched, a spark leaped between them. Aurora laughed merrily. "There's always static electricity in the air during a storm."

As if on cue, a loud thunderclap rattled the windows.

"You're perfectly safe," Aurora continued without missing a beat. "This house has been here for two hundred years and it will be here a hundred more. Do you know what the locals say about our weather?"

Jade shook her head.

"Exactly what they say almost every other place. If you don't like it—just wait a minute." Aurora's chortle made her abundant flesh shimmy. "Would you like a cup of tea?"

"No, thank you. I'll just look around if you don't mind."

Despite the building's external decay, Jade noted that the interior was meticulously neat and clean. At the end of the counter a large hall tree sprouted hats like so many spring flowers. Rows of shoes sat on the well-waxed wooden floor. Racks of clothing filled the room, turning the space into a maze of intriguing passageways. Another room opened off the one they were in, and she could see that it too overflowed with clothing.

"I have the finest antique garments west of the Mississippi." Aurora's breathy voice swelled with pride. "As long as you have to wait out the storm, I'd be happy to give you a guided tour."

"I'll just browse, if it's all right."

Aurora offered the freedom of the store with a sweeping gesture, then headed for the back of the building.

When she was gone, Jade walked to the front door, cracked it open, and looked out. The storm had gathered strength and clouds pressed against the rooftops. Wind blasted the sign above the shop, making it swing dementedly. Huge raindrops splatted on the unpaved alley, raising puffs of dust. For the moment, she was stranded.

She closed the door quietly and walked over to the nearest rack. A quick survey revealed that the clothing was systematically organized according to period. Each decade from the 1970s on down had a space of its own. The garments appeared to be in excellent condition, as clean and fresh as if their original owners had purchased them just the day before.

As she began thumbing through them she discovered that price tags were conspicuously absent. With good reason, she suspected. This was no ragtag collection of used clothing. The dresses, suits, and gowns bore labels such as Chanel, Balenciaga, Dior, Quant, Chapman, and Carnegie. She had stumbled onto a clothing collection that would do credit to a museum devoted to fashion history. Many of the dresses were so timelessly elegant, she felt tempted to try them on even though haute couture had never interested her before.

"Well, what do you think of my pretties?" Aurora asked, materializing out of the shadows.

"I'm impressed. How in the world did you manage to get so many designer fashions in a place like . . . ?"

"A place like Santa Fe?" Aurora completed Jade's question. "It's simple. I don't have to find the dresses. They find me. Now, have you decided on anything?"

What a peculiar answer, Jade thought. But then, nothing about Aurora's Borealis had been ordinary so far. The ancient building, the huge proprietress, the clothes themselves, were all extraordinary. She began looking for a Dior suit she had seen in the fifties section, a cream colored wool with a flaring skirt and peplumed jacket. Finding it, she took it from the rack and held it out. "I thought I'd try this on."

Aurora's expression soured, and Jade had the peculiar feeling she'd just failed an important test.

"Oh no, my dear. That's not for you. It would never do!" Aurora stepped back a few paces, her bulk filling the narrow aisle. "Hmmm. Let me see. You wouldn't be suited to anything as recent as the fifties." Indicating that Jade should follow, she headed toward the back of the building.

They passed through the second room and into a third. This one proved to be as crammed as the others, but the clothes were dramatically different. Feathered plumes and lush flowers festooned broad-brimmed hats. High-button shoes lined walls from which hoopskirts hung side by side with lacy petticoats. A quick glance assured Jade that she would never feel at home in such blatantly feminine things. They belonged on a Victorian society girl.

"I really liked that Dior suit," she protested.

Aurora shook her head. "Now just let me decide what's best. I've been in this business forever and a day and I have a sixth sense when it comes to matching my customers to the right era." For a minute, she seemed to be meditating. Then moving with surprising grace, she sorted through the racks, rejecting one garment after another.

"Ah, here we are," she said at last, pulling a jet-beaded black velvet Edwardian jacket and floor-length skirt from the jumble. "This is from the House of Paquin. Hold it up, dear, and let me see how it will look on you."

Jade grinned. This was turning out to be a very curious experience. The shop owners on Melrose Avenue would do well to emulate Aurora's unique approach to the plebeian act of selling used clothes.

As she took the hanger from Aurora's hands, light from an overhead fixture sparked iridescent fire in the jet beads. The jacket had a flowery scent, as if it had been packed in sachet, and the velvet felt seductively soft.

Aurora concentrated fiercely, her brow furrowing, her Cupid's-bow mouth turning down at the corners before she shook her head.

"I don't understand. I'm almost never wrong, but this just isn't right for you. In fact I don't think the turn of the century will be." She took the garment from Jade and hung it back up.

Jade laughed nervously. "Every time I've liked something, you decide it's not for me. If you're using some sort of reverse sales psychology, it's working."

Aurora looked wounded. "I'm much more interested in seeing my treasures find the right buyer than I am in making money."

"Forgive me. It's just that shopping makes me nervous. I'm not very good with clothes—or people either, to tell you the truth."

Aurora tsked loudly. "With that face and figure, you could be a model, even if you do dress like . . ." Her voice trailed off while her eyes took in Jade's faded jeans and her T-shirt with the Malibu 5 K Run logo silk-screened across the front. "However," she continued, "if you'll be patient, I think I can find something that will suit you perfectly."

Jade checked her watch. To her surprise, although she felt as if she had been in the shop only a few minutes, an hour had passed.

"Now." Aurora stepped back and sized her up again. "Where did I go wrong?"

She began meditating once more, and this time the silence grew uncomfortably long. Jade fidgeted, shifting her weight from foot to foot, wondering why in the world she was putting up with Aurora's outrageous sales technique.

Suddenly Aurora clapped her hands in delight. "I see it now!" she declared. "The image was hazy at first, that's why I got confused." She headed toward the front of the shop, halted in the second room, and began nimbly searching through the racks. "Ah, here it is," she said at last, waving a dress before Jade's eyes.

The first thing Jade saw was color—a magnificent geranium red.

"Yes, this is it. This is perfect," Aurora said.

"How can you be so sure? You haven't even asked my size."

"You wear a seven."

"How did you know?"

"Knowing is my business." Aurora continued holding the dress, gazing at it with satisfaction.

"May I look at it?"

"Of course." She pressed the hanger into Jade's hands. "Look all you like. You'll see how right I am."

Although the dress appeared to be ethereal and delicate, it proved quite heavy. The deep neckline was encrusted with crystal beads. The silk-chiffon fabric hung in a straight sweep to an abbreviated, above-the-knee hemline. Chevron-shaped swatches of fabric, also encrusted with crystal beads, were attached at midthigh and fell below the hem. A matching slip of softest silk underlay the semisheer garment.

"It's lovely," Jade said.

"It should be," Aurora said. "It's a Molyneux, purchased in Paris in 1929."

"Where in the world did you get it?"

"From a local. Megan Carlisle, the original owner, sold it to me last week."

"I can't imagine anyone keeping a dress that long. She must have loved it."

Aurora hesitated a moment, then said, "I got the impression that she didn't want to sell it at all. She kept on talking about how the dress had changed her life. Megan is a bit strange. People around here think she's eccentric, but there's nothing wrong with the old girl. She's as sharp as a tack, and each time she brings in a garment she drives a hard bargain."

Jade narrowed her eyes, trying to imagine the woman who had owned the dress. "She must be in her eighties."

"Eighty-nine. She's been selling me clothes for years. Poor thing. She's had a hard life since her husband passed away in the fire. But that's ancient history. Enough about Megan Carlisle. I think it's time you tried the dress on."

Retrieving the Molyneux from Jade's hands and holding it in front of her like a talisman, Aurora escorted Jade to a dressing room at the back of the shop. "I'll leave you now. Call me if you need any help."

Alone at last, Jade stripped down to her panties. Realizing the Top-Siders she'd put on that morning would look ridiculous with the magnificent creation, she stepped out of them as well. Barefoot and half nude, she took the slip from the hanger and pulled it over her head. A shiver followed its silken path down her body as it fell into place, and the unsettling feeling she'd experienced earlier that morning returned full force. Fortunately, it passed as quickly as it had the first time.

She reached for the dress and put it on. It floated down her arms and swirled around her torso as if it had a life force of its own. The dress fit so well, it seemed as if Molyneux himself had patterned it to her body. She took a step back to look at herself in the mirror and gasped.

She had been transformed. A glamorous, sensual-looking stranger stared back at her—a sophisticated, fashionable woman from a long-ago era. For a moment she surrendered to the fantasy of becoming that woman, of being anyone other than who she was—a failure at writing, a failure at life.

The dramatic red heightened her coloring, serving as a foil for her black hair and deep green eyes. The silk slip clung to her breasts, teasing her nipples erect. As she moved, turning from side to side to admire the fit, the chevrons flared out and their crystal embroidery caught the light.

For the first time in her thirty-two years, Jade found herself coveting an article of clothing. In view of her finances, she had no business buying a dress from Kmart, let alone one as expensive as this had to be, but she knew she had to have it.

"How are you doing back there?" Aurora's breathy voice called in the distance.

"Just fine."

Jade walked into the front room wearing the dress, and Aurora smiled with satisfaction. "You look lovely. But then I knew you would."

"You do have a talent for choosing clothes for strangers. I have just one question."

"Ah. You want to know the price."

"No. I'm going to buy it regardless of price," she said, ignoring the twinge of guilt. "I wanted to know why the dress is so heavy. It must weigh ten pounds."

"I could tell you something mystical, like it carries the weight of six decades. But the truth is the beads are made of real crystal. Today's plastic beading is nowhere near as heavy."

Jade smiled. "Can you wrap it in tissue and box it for me? I'm traveling, and I don't want to pack it with my other things."

"I won't hear of it," Aurora protested. "This dress doesn't belong in a box. It belongs on you. It *is* you. I'll just put it in a garment bag after you change. You may even want to wear it tonight. Would you like me to call a cab while you get dressed?"

Jade glanced out the window. The storm had ended and the newly washed sky had the clarity of blue topaz. "I think I'd like to walk back to my hotel."

"La Fonda," Aurora said, making it a statement rather than a question.

"How did you know?" Jade couldn't recall mentioning where she was staying.

"I can't imagine someone like you wanting to stay anyplace else. The woman who owned the Molyneux was one of La Fonda's original investors. Time was when La Fonda was the place to see and be seen in Santa Fe. Of course there are new hotels now, but La Fonda is still very special."

Jade nodded her agreement. There was something special about the old hotel, something that teased her mind with the promise of revelations to come.

CHAPTER 3

Santa Fe
May 17, 1929

Rudy Vallee's voice crooned from the Victrola, filling Megan Carlisle's bedroom with a soft nasal sound. She sat cross-legged on the
edge of the double bed, naked but for two coats of newly applied
scarlet nail polish, fanning her fingers through the air.

She had an oval face, ebony hair that capped her head as sleekly
as a seal's fur, full lips that seemed to invite a kiss, and a flawless
complexion. Her eyes, the color of green emeralds, were rimmed by
long lashes. Megan was well aware of her beauty and always made
the most of it—not that it mattered in the isolation of Rancho
Cielo. She looked around, frowning, oblivious to the charm of the
graceful adobe house and its tranquil wooded setting.

God, she was bored. Bored to death!

After her nails were dry, she undulated off the bed and padded to
the huge walk-in closet that held her clothes. When her husband,
Duncan, had built the house during the first year of their marriage,
the closet had caused quite a stir among the Indian and Mexican
workmen. They simply couldn't believe that anyone actually had

enough clothes to fill it, so they took to calling it *la pequeña alcoba*, the little bedroom.

Shelves overflowing with lingerie, shoes, and purses lined three walls. Floor-to-ceiling mirrors covered the fourth. Down the center, racks of dresses, gowns, suits, and coats hung from thick brass poles. Their labels—Paquin, Lanvin, Schiaparelli, Patou, Molyneux, and Chanel—reminded Megan of the exciting world beyond Santa Fe. But that reminder merely served to heighten her dissatisfaction.

Sighing heavily, she began sorting through the clothes. With her arms laden with satin-and-lace underthings, she returned to the bedroom and tossed them helter-skelter on the bed. A second trip added half a dozen dresses to the pile. Finally, covering her nakedness with a maribou-trimmed silk robe, she opened the bedroom door and walked into a wide, clay-tiled hall.

"Dulce," she called loudly, pronouncing it *Dull-see* rather than *Dool-say*, the way the locals did, "is my red dress back from the cleaners yet?"

Getting no response, she walked farther down the corridor. "Dulce, where the hell are you?"

"Coming, señora," a woman replied, appearing in the arch at the opposite end of the passageway.

Dulce Ortiz was a broad-shouldered, broad-hipped Hispanic woman in her mid-forties. She had been Duncan's housekeeper when Megan had arrived in Santa Fe as a bride. Although Megan had seen Dulce day in and day out for ten years, she still regarded the woman as a complete stranger. There was something alien and unknowable in the housekeeper's flat obsidian eyes.

For the life of her, Megan couldn't figure out why Duncan spent so many hours in the kitchen, chatting away in Spanish with Dulce and her husband, Jorge. But then, there were lots of things Megan couldn't understand about her husband, such as why he chose to live in a backwater ranch twenty miles from Santa Fe when, as one of America's most famous artists, he could be the toast of Manhattan.

"Did my red dress come back from the cleaners yet?" Megan asked.

"Which red dress?"

"Dammit, Dulce, why do you always act as if you don't know what I'm talking about? You must recall the dress I asked Jorge to take to the cleaners last week, the Molyneux I brought back from Paris in January."

"Sí. Jorge picked it up this morning when he drove to town to get supplies. It's hanging in the kitchen."

"I want to wear it at La Fonda tonight. You can pack it with the rest of the clothes on my bed."

"Sí, señora," Dulce replied. Her tone was as flat as the expression in her eyes. Never, by word, gesture, or deed, did she reveal what she thought of Megan. Megan felt her dislike just the same.

"Is that all, señora?"

Megan felt like shouting, no, that is not all! I want to get the hell out of this house and all it stands for. I want to get away from you and Jorge, away from Santa Fe—even from Duncan. Instead, she just turned on her heel and walked back into her bedroom, shutting the heavily carved oak door behind her. There wasn't any point in taking Dulce's head off. It wasn't the housekeeper's fault that Megan was mortally unhappy.

If only Leland Wylie III had come back from the war in one piece instead of minus his legs, she'd have married him the way they'd planned. Today she'd be lunching at the Palm Court, going to the theater, or shopping on Fifth Avenue instead of moping around her bedroom with nothing more important on her mind than spending a weekend at La Fonda. Would Duncan never finish painting so they could leave?

Marrying him and moving to Santa Fe had seemed terribly romantic when she was nineteen. Now, with her thirtieth birthday just around the corner, she felt as if life had passed her by. Pulling her robe closer, she walked to the bank of windows on the south wall and stared out, heedless of the stunning views of the Sandias as her mind ranged back to the night she'd seen Duncan Carlisle for the first time.

The winter of 1919 had been a season of parties, none more memorable than her own coming out. A year had elapsed since the Armistice and all the good-looking, eligible men were back from the war. She'd been the center of a social circle that included the sons and daughters of war profiteers as well as the offspring of old aristocratic families like her own.

New Yorkers had been in a festive mood despite the newly enacted Volstead Act. Even now, Megan giggled at how the idiotic Congressmen had firmly believed their silly law would stop people from drinking. Inside the city's finer restaurants and clubs, nouveaux riches arrivistes mingled with the Four Hundred, and all of them carried flasks of liquor.

That December night she had dined with a dozen friends. She'd worn a white satin Doeillet chemise that revealed the tops of her breasts—and a great deal more when she leaned over. They had just finished eating and were talking about going to the Cotton Club, when Paulette Vanderwyck suggested attending Duncan Carlisle's opening at the Max Gallery instead.

Megan had raised her brows at that. Paulette had never exhibited an interest in anything other than men, clothes, and parties—in that order. "Since when did you become an art lover?" Megan asked.

"Since I met Duncan Carlisle at the DeWitts' dinner three nights ago," Paulette replied, giving Megan an arch look. Her expression piqued Megan's interest. If Paulette was a connoisseur of anything, it was men.

Megan laughed. "Perhaps it is time we got a little culture. Think how pleased our parents will be when we tell them we spent the evening at an art exhibit instead of a speakeasy."

The Max Gallery was crowded when they arrived. While the others went off in search of food and drink, Paulette pulled Megan aside. "Let's find Carlisle," she said, a feral glitter in her eyes. "Believe me, he's even better looking than Douglas Fairbanks." Taking Megan by the elbow, Paulette began working her way through the throng as eagerly as a bird dog on the scent of a quail.

They were still searching for their quarry a few minutes later when the people to Megan's right shifted, and she found herself gazing at the most spectacular-looking man she had ever laid eyes on. He appeared to be in his mid thirties, and he was tall—over six feet she guessed—with magnificent shoulders that stretched the fabric of his tuxedo jacket taut. Even more arresting was his aura of virility that made every other man in the gallery seem effeminate by contrast. She was taking a hasty inventory of his rakishly long dark hair, his strong cheekbones and jaw, when he drilled her with an unforgettable pair of smoky eyes and she felt her knees weaken. Then he smiled straight at her, revealing the most adorable dimples, and she practically swooned.

While she stared at him, Paulette left her side and walked right up to the stranger. "How divine it is to see you again," she gushed.

The man gave Paulette a quizzical look that clearly said he didn't know who she was.

Paulette batted her sparse lashes. "I'm Paulette Vanderwyck. We met at the DeWitts'."

"How could I forget?" he replied graciously.

So that's Duncan Carlisle, Megan thought. He was absolutely the cat's pajamas. No wonder Paulette wanted to see him again. She stepped forward boldly. "I'm Paulette's friend, Megan Hayward."

Duncan Carlisle took her hand, and she felt as if an unspoken message passed between them. The look he gave her was as intimate and personal as if they were already lovers. When he brought her hand to his lips, the noise and the crowd receded. She felt his mouth on her bare skin, and something deep in her abdomen tightened with anticipation. She had to have him.

He looked deep into her eyes and said, "You and I have things to talk about, Megan Hayward."

And so began a whirlwind courtship that culminated in marriage just three weeks later. Now, as Megan gazed unseeing at the Sandia Mountains, all she could think about was what a mistake she'd made ten years ago.

Duncan Carlisle had been painting steadily all day. Now he stepped back from the canvas, a two-by-three-foot rendering of a hill outside of Truchas. The twisted, tormented figure of a crucified *penitente* dominated the lower right foreground. The colors— umbers and siennas—were dark and brooding, a reflection of his mood. It was, he realized, as dismal a scene as any he'd ever painted.

Once he had reveled in color, and every brilliantly hued canvas had conveyed the joy he found in life. He hated the man he had become, a bitter, cynical misanthrope who had learned to expect only the worst. But he couldn't find his way back to the man he had been. It was too late. He had given up all hope of being happy. Now he would settle for peace, quiet, and a modicum of serenity. After the mistake he had made, the pain he had caused himself and Megan, he deserved no more.

He glanced across the room to the painting hanging on the studio's far wall. Megan's portrait, completed ten years ago, was a startling contrast to the one on his easel. He'd painted her right after their honeymoon, and their sexual passion was evident in every brush stroke. Red, the color of life itself, dominated the work and provided a striking setting for her black hair and ivory skin.

How many times had they stopped to make love in the middle of a sitting? He'd never known such a need to possess and be possessed.

He'd give the world to feel that way again. But not with Megan. Never with Megan. Marrying her had been a tragic error—for both of them. He would never forget the day he had finally confronted that painful truth.

It had been mid April, the second year of their marriage. Spring had come late that year and Megan had been suffering from cabin fever. She was restless, bored, dissatisfied. Thinking she might be happier if she knew more about his work, he asked her to spend the day with him in his studio. She spent the first hour pacing back and forth, smoking one cigarette after another, barely paying attention to his explanation of technique.

He finally admitted that having her there was a distraction, and not a very pleasant one. "You're really bored, aren't you?" he asked.

"Darling," she said, "watching you paint is about as exciting as watching grass grow."

From then on, Megan didn't even pretend an interest in how he earned his living. She couldn't seem to grasp the fact that the man she bedded and the artist in the studio were one and the same.

He wasn't the first man to have mistaken lust for love, nor the only one to deceive himself into believing that physical perfection went hand in hand with intelligence and sensitivity.

Megan's beauty had trapped him. But, he thought with infinite regret, it had trapped her too. No matter how unsatisfactory their marriage was, he still had his work. She had nothing to fill her time —except for occasional weekends at La Fonda with friends like Malcolm Ashford and Hilary Delano.

Perhaps things would have been different if they'd had children. That Megan—the most sensual, fecund-looking woman he'd ever seen—should prove sterile, was incredibly ironic. There was no place to lay the blame except at God's feet—and Duncan had long since stopped believing in God.

Discomforted, he picked up a sable brush and resumed painting. The sorry state of his marriage continued to gnaw at him, though. Had they never met, Megan would have undoubtedly been one of the crown jewels of New York society—and he would have been free to find a woman who understood his need to paint. Sadly, Megan's concept of creativity was limited to her ability to choose the perfect accessories for a new outfit. The word "mismatched" was a polite description of their marriage.

It took an almost physical effort for Duncan to subjugate his unhappiness to the demands of his work. But soon he was thoroughly engrossed in the new canvas, building up layers of dark colors that matched his brooding intensity. Hearing a knock on the studio door, he called out, "Come."

Megan walked in, looking her usual elegant self in a striped jersey Chanel suit. "I've been waiting for you," she said in an angry tone.

He checked his watch. "I'm sorry. I guess the time got away from me."

"Dammit, Duncan, you said we'd leave for La Fonda at five and it's quarter to now. Malcolm and Hilary expect to meet us at seven, and I need time to unpack and dress for the evening. I know my happiness isn't very important to you anymore, but common courtesy should be." She pulled a pack of cigarettes from her purse, lit one, and puffed on it impatiently.

"I'll just be a few minutes." He put his brush in a jar of turpentine and began closing the tubes of paint he'd used that day. "As long as you're here, I think we ought to talk."

She arched an eyebrow. "Oh God, I hope you don't want to have another soul-searching discussion about the dismal state of our marriage. It's useless, you know. There isn't a damn thing we can do about it—unless you've reconsidered moving to New York?"

He shook his head. "You knew I lived in New Mexico when we married. It's never been an arbitrary choice. This is a special place for an artist. That's why so many of us live here."

Impatience thinned her lips. "Don't bother lecturing me about the quality of the light in Santa Fe. We're going to be late as it is."

"There is another solution."

"To what, darling?"

"Have you ever thought about getting a divorce?" he blurted out. He hadn't planned to discuss it today, but suddenly it seemed as good a time as any.

She paled under her artfully applied rouge. "That's absolutely out of the question!"

"Why?"

"Don't be dense." She stubbed out her cigarette and immediately lit another one. "Do I have to remind you that the only grounds for divorce in this state is adultery? If I let you divorce me, my parents would never forgive me. I'd be a pariah. Can you imagine what Paulette Vanderwyck would say? She'd tell everyone I was an adulteress before the ink dried on the legal papers."

"Then I'll supply the grounds, and you can divorce me."

She snorted. "I will not be cast as the scorned woman. Besides, we only know one woman who wouldn't object to the scandal of being named corespondent. In fact, Hilary Delano would probably like nothing better. She's always had the hots for you. But I'll fry in hell before I see you in *her* bed. So, my darling, this discussion is pointless."

"We can't go on the way we have been."

"You're probably right," she agreed, sounding surprisingly reasonable. "There are times when I'd sell my soul to have a second chance at life."

Unexpectedly, she gave him a radiant smile. For a moment, he felt the old, familiar lure of her beauty.

"But this isn't one of them," she went on. "I've been looking forward to this evening all week. Now, why don't you hurry up. I don't want to be late for our dinner date with Malcolm and Hilary." Her chuckle was throaty, sexy. "I'm going to wear the Molyneux tonight. Hilary's never seen it. I can hardly wait to see her face when she does. She'll be green with envy!"

CHAPTER 4

Santa Fe
May 17, 1989

By the time Jade had walked from Aurora's Borealis to La Fonda, she regretted not taking a cab. The red dress weighed heavily on her arm as she took the elevator up to her third-floor suite.

Late afternoon sunshine bathed the bedroom in soft pastels as she walked in. She hung the dress in the closet and closed the drapes, then sat on the bed, yawning prodigiously. She couldn't remember feeling more tired, not even in the final stages of writing a book, when she spent twelve and fourteen hours a day at her word processor. Dialing the desk clerk, she requested a wake-up call for six-thirty.

She could barely keep her eyes open. Must be the altitude and all the walking, she thought. She undressed quickly, snuggled into the pillows, and pulled up the covers. Tomorrow she'd have to make plans, serious plans for her future. But right now she was just too exhausted to think about anything.

An hour and a half later an intermittent ringing sound jerked her awake. For a moment, she didn't know where she was. Panic prickled her skin while she fumbled for a light switch in the dark room.

The sensation of being lost, adrift in an unfamiliar world, over-whelmed her as she swung her legs over the edge of the bed.

The instant before her feet hit the floor, it all came flooding back —Ira's phone call, her flight from Malibu, her arrival in Santa Fe. She switched the lamp on and the cozy comfort of the La Fonda bedroom enveloped her as she answered her wake-up call.

She hung up the phone, and her gaze strayed to the open closet. The red dress glowed inside it like a well-banked fire. When Aurora had suggested she wear it that night, it had seemed a ridiculous idea. After all, a dress like the Molyneux deserved an important occasion rather than a solitary dinner in a hotel restaurant. But she just couldn't resist its pull. Maybe she wasn't the sort of woman who normally would own such a dress and wear it with enviable panache, but for tonight she could pretend. She retrieved it from the closet and laid it out on the bed.

Hoping to catch the evening news, she walked into the sitting room and turned on the television. She flicked through the unfa-miliar channels, clicking past an "I Love Lucy" rerun, a Spanish-language show, and a couple of commercials before Tom Brokaw's face filled the screen. Turning up the sound, she returned to the bedroom.

The Molyneux caught her attention again and held it. The crys-tals seemed to trap the light and shimmer with internal fire. If only the dress could talk, she mused, easing a pair of pantyhose up her legs, what a story it might tell. She retrieved a sheer underwire bra from a dresser drawer and put it on.

Ordinarily she didn't bother with makeup. Her appearance had never been high on her list of priorities. She'd been a gawky, too-tall colt of a girl, all knees and elbows, her features too adult for a child's face—and after her parents' death, far too somber.

In her opinion growing up hadn't improved things. Her forehead was still too high, her lips too full, and her naturally curly hair had a mind of its own. But that night she sat down at the dressing table and applied her cosmetics with particular care, shading her eyes with shimmering emerald shadow and mascaraing her lashes until they looked exceptionally lush and thick. A dusting of blush across her cheekbones and an application of pale pink lip gloss completed the job.

She slipped into a pair of high-heeled sandals, gave her pantyhose a final tug, pulled the slip over her head, and picked the dress up. Suddenly a harsh burst of static obscured the newscast. She put the dress back down and headed for the sitting room. Although the picture was rolling when she reached the television, the static had stopped. She fiddled with the dials until Brokaw's face settled in place and turned up the volume.

Returning to the bedroom, she picked up the dress again. The television emitted an even louder burst of static. For an instant she was immobilized—torn between the need to put an end to the horrible noise and the desire to finish dressing. But the garment's weight tugged at her hands. Closing her eyes, she compressed her lips so the gloss wouldn't stain the fabric. Then she pulled the Molyneux over her head—and the universe tilted.

Her ears rang. A wave of nausea made her stagger. Seen through the semisheer chiffon, the bedroom shimmered and undulated, as if she were viewing it through a veil of her own blood. The lights dimmed. The air vibrated. Caught in the fabric's silken web, she fell to her knees. Her field of vision narrowed. She felt as if she were falling into an inward-spiraling tunnel.

Later she would remember every detail, every sensation. While it was actually happening she didn't have time to analyze the experience. Completely disoriented, she reached for the edge of the bed and clung to it with the desperation of a drowning woman clutching a piece of driftwood. The muscles in her jaw clenched involuntarily. Every nerve in her body seemed to spasm as she felt herself being sucked into a black vortex.

"No," she cried out. "No. No. No."

The sensation of speed increased. She was falling . . . falling . . . falling . . .

And then she hit bottom.

The dreadful sensations ebbed as unexpectedly as they began. She was suddenly aware of the rough carpet pressing on her knees, the bedspread clutched in her hands. Struggling to her feet, she sat on the edge of the bed. Her legs felt rubbery, the way they had when she'd had pneumonia as a child. Sitting forward, she lowered her head between her knees, forcing herself to breathe deeply until the pounding of her heart eased. As she began to calm down, she heard music coming from the living room, a funny syncopated sound she couldn't quite place. What the hell had happened to the evening news?

She stayed put until her stomach settled and the dizziness was totally gone. Perhaps, she thought hopefully, the only thing wrong with her was having gone too long without eating. Rising to her feet, she reached to get her purse from the dresser.

She blinked. Once. Twice.

The dresser wasn't where it ought to be.

In fact, as she gazed around she realized the entire room looked askew and off center. Even the beds didn't seem exactly where she remembered. And all of the furniture looked brightly new rather than cozily old.

She shook her head, trying to clear it of any residual vertigo, and walked into the living room. It had been transformed too. The television set was gone and an antique radio with a high, domed top stood on a table in its place. A large Chimayo rug hung on the wall where the Southwestern prints had been when she checked in.

What the hell was going on? Had she somehow gotten into someone else's suite? Utterly confused, she stood in the middle of the room. Think, dammit, think, she commanded herself. There had to be a reason, a rational explanation for the changes. She closed her eyes, counted to ten and opened them again, hoping against hope to find herself back in her suite.

It didn't work.

She drew a deep, settling breath and began going over her day, starting with the chorizo and eggs she'd had for breakfast in a little hole-in-the-wall coffee shop off the plaza. Could that be it? Had the sausage been spoiled? Was she suffering some weird form of food poisoning that made its victims hallucinate?

The fact that she was wearing the Molyneux offered incontrovertible proof of her visit to Aurora's Borealis. She clearly recalled coming back to the hotel and taking a nap. Either something was terribly wrong with her—or someone was playing a very unfunny practical joke. The hotel management was going to hear about this, she concluded angrily, and walked over to the phone.

It still sat on the desk, but this phone was very different from the sleek modern instrument that had been there earlier in the day.

This one looked like it belonged in a Noël Coward drawing-room comedy. Picking up the alien instrument and holding the receiver to her ear, she jiggled the disconnect lever impatiently, waiting for a dial tone.

"This is the hotel operator," a nasal female voice said. "May I help you?"

"I certainly hope so," Jade said.

Before she could get another word out, the door to the suite opened. She stood there slack jawed as a man walked in. Although he was a stranger, for one insane moment she felt a shock of recognition. He was tall and dressed in black trousers and a starched white shirt that was only half buttoned, revealing an aggressively masculine chest. He held an ice bucket in his hands.

He looked at her and frowned. "My God, Megan, what's wrong?"

"Who the hell are you?" Her voice was pitched so high, she barely recognized it as her own.

"For God's sake, they'll hear you next door if you don't calm down." Putting the ice bucket on the coffee table, he turned to shut the door.

She thought about trying to slip past him, but seeing the bulk of his shoulders and the athletic way he moved, she realized he could easily prevent her escape.

"Don't come any closer!" she warned, when he faced her again.

"You're white as a sheet. Did someone try to come in while I was getting the ice?"

She clutched the phone in trembling hands. "If you don't get out of here right now, I'll call the police."

"You'd better sit down before you fall down," he said, closing the distance between them and taking the phone.

Jade could almost taste the adrenaline that jolted through her body. Should she scream, run, both? She watched him, wondering what came next. Robbery? Rape?

He continued to study her, as if the encounter were an everyday occurrence. Finally, his self-assured expression changed to one of surprise. "What have you done to your hair?"

"My hair! Are you out of your mind? My hair isn't the problem. You are. I want you to leave. Now!"

For a moment he seemed as baffled as she, but his confusion

quickly faded. "I thought we were going to try to have a pleasant evening, Megan."

Megan. Where had she heard that name before? If only he would leave, she might be able to sort it all out.

Then it came to her. The dress—the Molyneux—had belonged to a woman named Megan. *Megan Carlisle.* Jade's knees almost buckled as relief washed over her. She'd always had a wild imagination, never more so than when she slept. That had to be it. She was having an elaborate nightmare, undoubtedly instigated by buying the dress and wishing, even for just a moment, she could be a different person.

Well, she knew how to deal with bad dreams. Years ago, she'd consulted a psychiatrist about her recurring nightmare. He had told her she had to surrender to the nightmare, enter into it fully and willingly in order to control it. Like handling a car in a skid, she had to steer with it before she could maneuver out of it. Her fire dream, unfortunately, always ended before she had the chance to test the theory.

This bizarre nightmare gave no sign of stopping, though. Enter into it. That's what she had to do.

"I was looking forward to the evening too," she said, giving the stranger her most ingratiating smile.

His expression became marginally less intimidating. "I'm running a bit late. Why don't you go downstairs and see if Hilary and Malcolm are there."

He made it sound more like a command than a suggestion. Not trusting herself to speak, she nodded and headed for the door, wondering what in the hell she would find on the other side.

CHAPTER 5

Santa Fe
May 17, 1929

Anger and concern vied for control of Duncan's emotions as he watched his wife leave their suite. He half expected her to turn back and say something, but she shut the door without a backward glance.

Something had happened while he was in the hall, something that still made the hair on the nape of his neck prickle. From the fear he'd seen on Megan's face and the bizarre way she'd just behaved, she must have felt it too. What the hell could it have been? A minor earthquake? Some strange perturbation in the atmosphere?

A few minutes earlier he'd been walking down the hallway, ice bucket in hand, when the lights had dimmed and he could have sworn the floor moved under his feet. The sensation had been so powerful, he'd dropped the bucket and cubes had spilled across the carpet. For a moment, he'd thought he was having a heart attack.

The sensation had passed so quickly, though, he'd discarded the idea. Then when he'd opened the door to the suite, Megan had seemed genuinely terrified. He was used to her moods, her unhappiness, her dissatisfaction. This had been different. She even looked different.

It was more than just her hair, although he had no idea how she had managed to curl it during his brief absence. The expression in her eyes had been a heart-stopping mixture of terror and vulnerability that, despite all their differences, had made him want to take her in his arms and tell her that everything was going to be all right.

Megan. His wife. His nemesis.

Perhaps she was just punishing him for wanting a divorce. Yes, he thought, that had to be it. Megan was a consummate game-player. God knew she had little else to occupy her time. Still, that didn't explain what he himself had experienced. He'd never endured anything even remotely like it.

What now? he wondered impatiently as the telephone's insistent ring roused him from his unhappy reverie.

"It's me, old chap," Malcolm Ashford said in his impeccably upper-class English accent. "I'm down in the lobby. Just thought I'd see if you and Megan were running on time."

"Megan's on her way down. I'll join you in a few minutes. Do me a favor and keep an eye on her."

"Is something wrong?"

"She was a little pale when she left." Duncan grimaced. Talk about understatements. She'd been as white as alabaster.

"I hope this doesn't mean you'll be cutting the weekend short," Malcolm said.

"I don't know. It's probably nothing."

"I'll be happy to keep an eye on her. Don't give it another thought."

Malcolm sounded remarkably cheerful, Duncan mused. If something had happened, and by now he was inclined to believe the whole thing had been a figment of his imagination, Malcolm didn't seem to have been touched by it.

After saying good-bye, Duncan walked into the bedroom and finished dressing, threading jet studs through his starched shirt-front, hand-knotting a black bow tie, and shrugging into a well-tailored tuxedo jacket.

The scent of Chanel No. 5, Megan's signature fragrance, lingered in the air. Despite her pallor, she had looked exceptionally lovely before she left their suite. There was something unusual about her this evening, something he couldn't quite put his finger on.

There were times, after he'd consumed just the right amount of liquor, when he still wanted her. He had to give the devil her due. If Megan had any talent at all, it was for the bed. They hadn't made love in a long time.

Perhaps tonight . . . ?

This had to be a dream, Jade thought as she waited for the elevator. A Technicolor dream so real that she not only saw and heard it, she tasted and smelled it. Her senses—sight, hearing, smell, touch—seemed heightened. She could clearly differentiate the odors of perfume and tobacco that permeated the corridor. The sound of laughter, drifting from behind closed doors, was painfully intimate. She was uncomfortably aware of the Molyneux's silken caress on her skin.

The shock of what had happened a scant fifteen minutes earlier still vibrated through her. She could only think of one alternative to her dream theory—she was going stark, staring mad. But despite the strain she'd been under since Ira's call, she didn't think she could ascribe her recent experiences to a nervous breakdown.

Her life had been founded on certain basic assumptions; the sky was blue, the earth round, and two and two always and unconditionally added up to four. She believed in cause and effect and took pride in her ability to think things through to their logical conclusion. But she couldn't manufacture a logical explanation for the altered appearance of her suite, or the arrival of a man who obviously thought she was his wife, Megan Carlisle.

If two and two still equaled four, she had to be trapped in a dream, a surreal nightmare where—as in Salvador Dali's paintings—time was out of whack. She pinched herself hard, hoping the pain would wake her. The only result was an angry red spot on her upper arm. This dream had the texture of reality. That was what made it so frightening.

The man in her room had been intimidating too. And astonishingly good-looking. Although he'd had one hell of an attitude, she'd been uncomfortably aware of his intense masculinity. He struck her as the sort of man—a little cold, perhaps even cruel—that misguided women tended to fall all over in the mistaken belief that they alone could thaw his winter-frost heart.

Suddenly, her lips parted in a nervous grin. Here she was thinking about him as if he were a flesh-and-blood human being instead of a figment of her subconscious mind. Trust her to conjure up someone like the men who peopled her books—utterly desirable, completely unapproachable, devoid of feeling, the sort of consummate bastards who . . .

Her musing was interrupted by the elevator's arrival. The doors opened to reveal a uniformed elevator man. He pulled aside a flexible metal gate that folded accordion style, the sort she recalled seeing in movies set in the twenties. "Going down?" he asked politely.

She took an involuntary step backward. A few hours earlier, La Fonda's elevators had been thoroughly modern, as well as self-service. Narrowing her eyes, she peered at him suspiciously. "How long have you been on duty?"

"All afternoon."

She had hoped he would tell her that La Fonda employed elevator operators to work the evening shift. But this man was obviously part of her dream—a chimera in a natty red uniform. Praying her legs wouldn't tremble, she marched stoically through the elevator's gaping doors.

"How long will you be staying with us this time?" the man asked as he closed the metal gate.

This time? Apparently—like the man in her suite—the elevator operator thought he knew her. "I'm not sure," she replied, thinking it was the understatement of a lifetime.

The elevator stopped at the second floor and a couple walked in. "I hope you didn't forget anything," the woman was saying to her companion, "because I'm never coming back. Talk about hick towns. You'd think passenger trains would get to Santa Fe. After all, this is the twentieth century. But no. We've got to take a bus to Lamy to catch the eastbound." She turned and looked at Jade as if she expected Jade to agree, but Jade kept her lips pressed together and her eyes front and center.

The elevator reached the ground floor, the gate and doors were opened, and the couple exited, trailing complaints.

"Tourists!" the elevator man said scathingly, giving Jade a look that clearly said he expected her to share his feelings.

"Tourists," she dutifully echoed. So far, her attempt to control the nightmare was turning out to be a dismal failure. Her palms were cold and sweaty, and she felt as if she'd left her stomach on the third floor. She hung back, trying to pull herself together.

"I don't mean to rush you, ma'am," the elevator man said, "but my lights are blinking." A nod of his head indicated a glowing panel by the door.

Jade forced herself to step forward. If the dream followed its own rational irrationality, she would find herself in the broad hall that opened into La Fonda's lobby. She was just as likely, though, to have arrived at the gates of hell.

Taking a deep breath, she left the elevator's relative safety. The doors shut quickly, leaving her stranded in alien territory. She took one cautious step and then another, her glance darting around. Nothing was the way she remembered it.

She spent the next few minutes wandering aimlessly, dazed by the changes she saw. The hotel's main entrance had been transported from the north side of the ground floor to the east. A large walled patio took up the space that had been occupied by a coffee shop that morning. The south-facing side of the building contained a flagstoned room with wide windows that opened onto another courtyard. The pricey shops and boutiques she had passed on her way out that morning had disappeared.

Following the sound of music, she walked into the space where the main lobby had been a few hours ago. The oak front desk had been replaced by a low rostrum, currently inhabited by a five-piece band. Chairs and sofas created inviting conversational groupings against the walls. Lamps glowed on low tables and several huge wrought-iron chandeliers were suspended from the ceiling. The only trace of the area's previous decor were the Saltillo tiles on the floor.

Most of the chairs were occupied and a few couples were dancing. Their clothing reminded Jade of a glamorous Busby Berkeley thirties movie she'd seen on late-night television. Hugging a wall in an effort to be as inconspicuous as possible, she watched people come and go. There were a few Hispanic faces in the crowd, but most were Anglo-Saxon. Although a few men were wearing business suits, the majority had on black tie. However, she saw none of the exotically colored cummerbunds, vests, scarves, and wild ties that were common at formal affairs in Hollywood.

Here, black tie meant just that. Jackets were double breasted and nipped in at the waist. Trousers were pleated, shirt collars were wing tipped, and patent leather shoes were definitely de rigueur for male evening attire.

The women were dressed in variations of her own gown, beautifully beaded chiffons or bias-cut velvets and silks that clung to the figure with a sensuality that the shortest miniskirt could never equal. In fact, she realized with dismay, all the women looked as if they too had shopped at Aurora's Borealis.

She wandered around scanning faces, half expecting her own deceased mother and father to be part of the elegant throng. A few people smiled at her, nodding as if they knew her and expected her to stop and chat. The seemingly random gathering had the vaguely incestuous feel of a typical film-industry party, where everyone knew everyone else, and at least half the people in the room had slept with each other at one time or other.

She returned the smiles but continued making her way to an alcove where she spied newspapers and magazines for sale. Picking up a copy of the *Santa Fe New Mexican*, she scanned the headlines.

GIANT GRAF ZEPPELIN BREAKS THREE MOTORS—Forced to Turn Back. FAMED GANGSTER GETS HIS FIRST JAIL SENTENCE—Scarface Al Capone Arrested and Sentenced in 12 Hours. GENERAL MOTORS BUYS FOKKER AIRCRAFT.

She could feel her pulse beating in her throat. Don't panic, she told herself, digging her nails into her palms. She must have read those headlines somewhere, perhaps while researching some long-forgotten history report back in school. They were just another facet of her fantasy.

Then she read the date.

May 17, 1929.

She could feel the blood draining from her face. An icy cold radiated from her stomach to her arms and legs.

"Are you all right, Megan?" A strong hand grasped her elbow.

She turned to see a pleasant-looking man in his mid thirties, dressed in black tie. An expression of concern warmed his hazel eyes.

"I'm a little dizzy," she replied truthfully.

"Duncan said you might not be feeling well. He asked me to look after you. Hilary's in the loo, but we don't need to wait for her. Let me take you to our table." He slipped his arm around her waist. "Really, my dear," he continued, "you're as white as a sheet. Have you been dieting again? I know breasts aren't in fashion, but you can't starve yours away."

She glanced sidelong at him. He was near her height, almost delicately built, with a long, intelligent face, pale skin, and black center-parted hair slicked back to expose an unusually high forehead. He was nowhere near as rugged or virile looking as the man she'd left upstairs, and he seemed infinitely more approachable. She found herself feeling grateful for his help.

The maitre d' hurried up to them as the stranger guided her toward La Plazuela, the one familiar landmark in the lobby's now alien territory. "Good evening, Madame Carlisle, Mr. Ashford. Your table is ready."

His arm still circling her waist supportively, the man nodded at the maitre d'. "Mr. Carlisle and Miss Delano will be joining us shortly."

"I'll bring them to you as soon as they arrive," the maitre d' replied, leading them to a table for four. He helped Jade into a plushly upholstered chair, and she couldn't help recalling how badly the maitre d' had treated her at the Polo Lounge a few days ago. Just the same, she fervently wished she were back there.

The man the maitre d' had called Mr. Ashford took a seat next to her. Leaning forward so that his lips were just a few inches from her ear, he asked, "Did you and Duncan have another row?"

She glanced at him, and his eyes probed hers. As he took his napkin from the table and placed it in his lap, she noted his long, elegant fingers and carefully buffed nails. Whoever he was, he certainly didn't do manual labor.

"Really, my dear," he said, "you know you can confide in me."

Before she could reply, a woman wearing a striking black velvet dress that emphasized her flawless ivory complexion walked up to the table. She had wide-set brown eyes, pencil-thin brows, pouting carmine lips, a sleek cap of platinum hair, and an aura of barely bridled sexuality that seemed to superheat the air around her.

"Malcolm, darling, so there you are. The least you could have done was wait for me."

"Now, Hilary," Malcolm said, "Megan was feeling faint."

So they were the Malcolm and Hilary she was supposed to meet, Jade thought. The maitre d' had called the man Mr. Ashford. *Malcolm Ashford.* Jade was so startled, she jumped to her feet. Malcolm Ashford had been a literary giant during the first half of the century, a writer whose early novels broke new ground with their frank sexuality. And the man in the suite had to be Duncan Carlisle, the famous painter who had helped put Santa Fe on the artistic map back in the twenties. Why hadn't she realized it before? She'd read about Carlisle in the guidebook, something about his home still standing on the outskirts of the city. Megan Carlisle, the original owner of the Molyneux, must have been his wife.

Now it all made sense. Of course she was having a dream. Her sleeping mind, fueled by her purchase of the dress, was creating an elaborate scenario from her newly acquired knowledge. Any minute now she'd wake up in bed in her suite.

She could hardly wait.

Hilary was gazing at her. "Megan, it's the man who's supposed to stand when a woman joins him. Sit down, darling."

"Are you all right?" Malcolm asked, rising and helping Jade back into her chair.

"Of course she's all right," Hilary said. "Just look at her. She's positively blooming. Where in the world did you get that divine dress?"

"At Aurora's Borealis," Jade blurted out.

"I've never heard of it. Have you been keeping secrets?" Hilary's glance was needle-sharp.

Avoiding Hilary's eyes, Jade struggled to think clearly, to pierce the veil of unreality that threatened to smother her.

Apparently sensing her discomfort, Malcolm came to her rescue. "You two can talk about clothes when I'm not here."

"Of course," Hilary agreed at once. "One of these days Megan and I are going to have a long, long talk—about clothes and other things." She turned her attention back to Jade. "There is something very different about you tonight, Megan dear. A certain . . . je ne sais quoi."

"I'm not feeling very well."

"I know what it is," Hilary crowed triumphantly. "It's your hair! Look at it, Malcolm. My God, she's had it marcelled like a shop-girl's. Curls are so déclassé."

"Leave her be!" Malcolm commanded. Favoring Jade with a gentle smile, he said, "Can I get you a drink?"

"I could use a martini—a double," she replied truthfully.

Hilary greeted the request with shrill laughter. "For heaven's sake, Megan!"

Malcolm frowned. "I'm afraid all I have in my flask is whisky. But it's the best Canadian."

"What's this about whisky?" Duncan Carlisle asked, arriving at their table.

Jade hadn't seen him approaching. Now she took a moment to study him more thoroughly. His features, but for what appeared to be a broken nose that had never been properly set, were ruggedly symmetrical. He had a powerful brow, well-defined cheekbones, and a square chin. His eyes, the blue-gray of newly forged steel, held a peculiar mixture of curiosity and disdain as he studied her too.

Fear spasmed in her chest. How could he look at her so closely and not realize she wasn't his wife? It took all her courage not to flee. It's only a dream, she reminded herself, a crazy dream.

"You know the hotel doesn't permit guests to drink," he was saying.

"How droll," Hilary said, and gave Duncan a challenging look. After emptying her water glass into a nearby potted palm, she took a silver flask from her evening bag and poured an inch of amber liquid into the glass. A white-jacketed waiter, who had just begun to pass out thick vellum menus, ignored what she was doing.

Hilary snickered. "You see? The waiter doesn't care if we have a little booze." Raising her glass in a toast, she added, "Here's to my bootlegger. May the G-men never catch him."

Jade felt as if she were on a roller coaster, careening down a precipitous incline. She needed a moment's respite, a chance to gather her wits. Burying her face in the menu, she ignored the chatter around her. No nouvelle cuisine tonight, she realized. The bill of fare offered items such as prime rib, filet mignon, and duck à l'orange, all heavily endowed with calories and cholesterol. To her surprise her mouth actually watered as she contemplated her order. Then she noticed the prices.

There wasn't an entree over two dollars.

She repressed an hysterical giggle as she became aware of the waiter's inquiring glance. "What would you like tonight, Madame Carlisle?"

She wanted to shout, *I'm not Madame Carlisle. I'm Jade Howard, and I wish all you people would get the hell out of my nightmare.* Instead, she handed him the menu and softly said, "I'll have the duck."

CHAPTER 6

The duck à l'orange was delicious—crisp skin, succulent meat, with a hint of Grand Marnier in the sauce. Jade surrendered to the sybaritic pleasure of every cholesterol-laden morsel. She still didn't know if she was having an elaborate nightmare, or if she'd gone completely mad. What she did know was that she'd been ravenous when she sat down at the table. Eating solved that problem. Her stomach no longer sent frantic "feed me" messages to her brain.

Under different circumstances she might actually have enjoyed herself. By the end of the meal she realized her companions were exceedingly bright as well as physically attractive. They were the sort of people she used to meet at the best Hollywood parties, the ones attended by the *doers* rather than the *hangers-on*. Malcolm, Duncan, and Hilary had carried the burden of the conversation while she made sure that she didn't say or do anything to arouse their suspicion. Malcolm's warmth and charm compensated for Duncan's more aloof demeanor. Hilary proved to be the most amusing of the three, a virtuoso of clever bitchery.

As Jade swallowed the last morsel of duck, Hilary was saying, "Have you heard Mabel Dodge raving about Georgia O'Keeffe coming out here this summer to paint the Southwest? You'd think

Georgia was about to invent Southwestern art when we all know"
—she turned her bold eyes on Duncan—"that you did, darling."

Duncan favored her with a frosty smile. "You give me too much credit. The Indians, the pueblos, the mountains, were all here long before Georgia and I arrived on the scene. No one invented them, unless you happen to believe in a higher power. As for painting them, have you forgotten that Joseph Sharp and Ernest Blumenschein were the first artists to settle in New Mexico?"

So he was Carlisle, the famous painter, Jade thought with a peculiar sense of satisfaction. It all made sense—sort of. If logic prevailed, the phone would ring soon, the hotel operator would tell her it was six-thirty, and she'd be back in her own world.

"You know," Hilary continued, staring at Duncan as if the two of them were alone at the table, "it really doesn't matter who came here first. You're the best of them all. One of these days, you simply must do my portrait." She reached across the table and ran a fingertip over Duncan's lips, then put the finger in her own mouth and sucked it.

Jade couldn't have been more startled if Hilary had invited him into her bed.

Malcolm broke the embarrassed silence that enveloped the little dinner party. "The band is playing your song," he said, getting to his feet and pulling Hilary to hers.

"No it's not," she objected.

"Every song is your song," he said, and led her away.

Jade decided that she liked Malcolm Ashford a great deal. Back at the University of Iowa where she had read his books in an undergraduate class, she had admired his daring, his sense of style, but she'd never thought she would meet him. And she hadn't now, she reminded herself angrily. Still, if she didn't wake up, if this nightmare had no end . . .

Shivering, she pushed the thought aside. She couldn't and wouldn't deal with the idea. Not yet anyway.

"You've been very quiet tonight," Duncan said, reclaiming her attention. "After the way you behaved in our suite, I was afraid you might make a scene during dinner."

For the first time that evening, she looked directly into his eyes. The experience was so intense, she felt herself redden from her hairline to the top of her dress. She had never been so attracted to a man, especially one she'd just met. Even if he was only a figment of her imagination, he disturbed her so thoroughly, she couldn't stop her instinctively defensive—and honest—response. "You don't understand a damn thing about me. I wonder how you'd act in my place."

"In your place? Are you talking about my suggesting a divorce?"

Divorce? This damn dream was getting much too real. Beneath his anger, she glimpsed a sadness, a loneliness that equaled her own. Under other circumstances, she might even have recognized him as a kindred soul. Eyes downcast, she toyed with her water glass. Its surface cold seemed to run up her fingers and radiate through her entire body.

Duncan's tone was even colder. "Your silences no longer bother me, Megan. I'm going upstairs." He pushed his chair back and got to his feet.

"What's this about going upstairs?" Malcolm asked, returning to the table alone. "It's early."

"It's been a long day," Duncan replied, biting off each word. "But my wife is welcome to stay as long as she likes."

Malcolm gave Jade a reassuring smile. "I'll look after her. Megan never needs to worry about being on her own while I'm around."

Duncan's expression grew even bleaker. "It's settled then." Pulling his wallet from his dinner jacket, he took out a ten-dollar bill and dropped it on the table. "Dinner's on me." Turning to Jade, he added, "I'll see you later. Don't hurry upstairs on my account."

"Well, he's a bit of a bear tonight," Malcolm remarked after Duncan had gone.

"Where's Hilary?" Jade asked.

"You know her. Ever the social butterfly. The band started playing the 'Black Bottom' and she just had to strut her stuff with the nearest admiring male." He reached for Jade's hand. "Lord, you're cold. Are you sure you're all right?"

She wanted to say, *No, I'm not. You're not here. I'm not here. None of this is happening.*

Despite his obvious concern, though, she couldn't trust him, couldn't trust anyone. The situation was so outrageous, so contrary to the orderly rules of the universe, that talking about it would undoubtedly result in her being committed to the nearest asylum. Unless she happened to wake up first, and right now she couldn't be sure she ever would.

"I'm just a little tired," she said, evading Malcolm's inquisitive glance.

He continued to hold her hand. "I'm glad to have a moment alone with you. I've never known you to be so quiet. Is it my fault? Have I said or done anything to offend you?"

She shook her head. "It's not you. It's . . ." Realizing how close she was to blurting out the truth, she stopped short. "It's Duncan," she improvised.

She didn't even notice the sympathy brimming in Malcolm's eyes. Somehow, she had to find a way to end this dream. Perhaps all she had to do was go upstairs and fall asleep again. Could it be that simple? She choked back a sob.

It had to be.

Jumping to her feet so quickly, her water glass overturned, she said, "I really must return to my room."

Malcolm dabbed ineffectually at the spreading fluid. "Duncan told you to take your time."

Jade didn't hear him. She was already halfway across the restaurant, her red dress swirling around her legs.

Duncan hung his jacket in the bedroom closet, took off his bow tie, and unbuttoned his collar. Returning to the parlor, he shook a cigarette from a pack of Lucky Strikes and sat down on the sofa to read the *Santa Fe New Mexican*.

According to the forecast it would be sunny and warm tomorrow, a pleasant day for an excursion. He wasn't looking forward to the one Hilary had planned, however. The thought of spending hours with Megan, Malcolm, and Hilary, dealing with Megan's moods while fending off Hilary's advances, soured his stomach.

He and Megan were obviously on a collision course. What game had she been playing during dinner, sitting so quietly, giving him anxious, worried glances when she thought he wasn't looking? She'd acted like a changed woman, a thoughtful, mature one. Could the mere mention of divorce have done that to her? Was she finally growing up? Did he care?

Sighing heavily, he stubbed out his cigarette and lit another. He knew men who made careers of if-onlys, who paraded their failures like icons. He wasn't about to fall into that trap. His wasn't the only marriage to fail. Now he had to find a way to end it before it destroyed them both.

His cigarette had burned to a smoldering stub that threatened to scorch his fingertips when he heard the door open. He hadn't expected Megan for hours. Knowing her, he'd been sure she would take the opportunity to drink, dance, and flirt to her heart's content.

Seeing the same stricken look on her face as she walked into the parlor that he'd seen earlier when they were dressing, he said, "Let's do each other a favor and try to go to bed without another scene."

Jade avoided Duncan's probing gaze. "That suits me fine," she replied. She'd been hoping to find him sound asleep.

The logistics of intimacy had always made her uncomfortable. In college, she'd felt awkward undressing in front of her roommate. And she had been horribly embarrassed the first time she disrobed in front of Paul. Now she was appalled by the realization that she would have to get ready for bed in the presence of a man who thought he was her husband, a man she found disturbingly attractive.

What if he wanted to make love? How the hell would she handle that?

Doing her level best to ignore his existence, she walked into the bedroom and began rummaging through the dresser that held Megan Carlisle's underthings, searching for pajamas. The lingerie included lace-trimmed tap pants, teddies, chemises, garter belts, and silk stockings that wouldn't reach above midthigh. To Jade's dismay, Megan's nightgowns were all sensually feminine, made of sheer fabrics that would reveal more than they concealed, or bias-cut silks that would cling to the body.

Jade chose the least seductive of them, a peach-colored floor-length crepe de chine with a matching dressing gown. Clutching the garments, she went into the bathroom and locked the door. As an added precaution she turned the water on in the sink so Duncan wouldn't hear her getting ready for bed.

She took off the red dress and slip, then removed her modern underwear and rolled it into a ball, which she hid beneath the dress. She pulled the nightgown on next, and like the Molyneux, it fit perfectly. Looking into the mirror over the sink, she saw the fashionable, sensual stranger looking back at her again. God. To think just a few hours ago she had wished to live this woman's life. She must have been crazy.

The gown clung to her breasts, revealing the outline of her nipples. She hurriedly pulled the robe around her and tied it firmly at her waist.

Duncan was in the bedroom when she walked back in. He'd taken off his shirt and was naked from the waist up. His chest was superbly masculine, with well-defined muscles and a dark mat of hair that narrowed to a tantalizing V as it approached his abdomen. He looked so strong, so primally powerful, that she had to fight the urge to seek shelter in his arms.

A cigarette dangled from his lips, the smoke obscuring his eyes. "There's something I've been meaning to ask you all night," he said.

"Be my guest." She turned her back and hid her underwear beneath Megan's.

"When did you have time to curl your hair?"

Thank heaven he couldn't see her face, she thought, as she tried to come up with an answer. If this was a dream, and she was becoming increasingly skeptical about that possibility, how she replied wouldn't matter. On the other hand, her life, her safety in this alien time might depend on her response. Continuing to rummage through the drawer, she said, "We women like to have a few secrets."

"You have more than your share." His voice had an angry edge.

She shut the drawer and turned, walking the few feet to the twin bed on her side of the room. She slipped beneath the covers, pulling them up to her chin even though it was quite warm in the room.

Before she could look away, Duncan took off his trousers with quick, economical movements. Underneath, he wore boxer shorts. His body would have done credit to a Malibu Beach volleyball star. Her own body grew warm as she realized that a part of her wanted to see all of him.

Glancing at her, he chuckled mirthlessly. "You don't need to sleep in your robe. I promise, I won't lay a hand on you if that's what you're worried about."

Sitting up abruptly, she untied the sash around her waist, slipped the negligee off, and tossed it to the foot of the bed. Then, turning off the light on her side of the night table, she lay down again—her back toward Duncan—and closed her eyes, trying to shut out his presence.

What if he slept in the nude?

She heard the bathroom door being opened and firmly closed. Still, it couldn't completely muffle the intimate sounds Duncan Carlisle made as he got ready for bed. Lying there, wondering what would happen next, was agony for Jade. The toilet flushed. The door opened. She heard his footsteps drawing closer. Every muscle in her body tensed as she anticipated his touch.

It never came.

She heard the rustle of covers and the creak of bedsprings as he got into the other twin bed, then the soft click of his light being turned off. Behind her closed eyelids, she felt the darkness. Within minutes, Duncan's even exhalations told her he must be asleep.

He'd opened one of the windows and left the drapes parted. She peeked over her shoulder and saw his powerful body silhouetted on the other bed, close enough to touch. Moonlight cast mysterious shadows on the walls. The smell of burning piñon pine drifted in as the night air grew cooler. The sounds of traffic slowly came to an end as she fought for sleep.

Malcolm lingered at the dinner table, quietly sipping a whisky-laced coffee. He had no desire to search out Hilary. She would find him after she quenched her thirst at the cup of masculine admiration. How many conquests would it be tonight? At least two, he decided. He'd always regarded Hil's predictability, her lack of pretense, as a virtue. She was what she was—an attractive, amusing, avaricious woman with an eye for the main chance.

He used to consider them ideally suited. He supplied the money; she supplied the sexual adventures. He wrote about them, earned still more money, and some of it wound up in her bank account. Quid pro quo.

When had he started wanting more? He couldn't pinpoint the exact day. The need had grown so quietly, he hadn't been aware of its existence until—like a bastard offspring—it appeared on his mental doorstep.

"So that's where you're hiding," Hilary said, appearing at his side and interrupting his reverie. "Where are Duncan and Megan?" She looked flushed, like a woman who had just left the dance floor—or the bed.

"They decided to retire early," he said, helping her into her chair.

"Don't look so put out," Hilary chided. "I assure you, they didn't rush off to make love."

"What makes you think I care?"

"This is me you're talking to, poopsie. You've had the hots for Megan for years. Not that I blame you. She may not have a brain in her head, but considering her looks, you probably never noticed." Hilary sat back and crossed her legs, swinging one sandal-shod foot in time to the music of a Charleston coming from the dance floor.

"Do I detect a green-eyed monster?" he asked.

"Don't be ridiculous. I wouldn't be in Megan's shoes for the world."

"Why?"

"Malcolm, darling, for all your literary brilliance, there are times when you can be dense. It's perfectly obvious that the Carlisle marriage is on the rocks. They were barely civil to each other tonight. I've never seen Megan so quiet. In fact, she was positively dull. And she ate like a stevedore. She'll lose her figure if she keeps it up." Hilary took a cigarette from her beaded purse and held it out for him to light.

He obliged automatically. "I thought Megan looked exceptionally lovely."

Hilary shook her head, sending her platinum bob flying. "You must be kidding! Those curls of hers belong on a French poodle. And she hardly had any makeup on. I never thought Megan was foolish enough to try a back-to-nature look. It may work for Georgia O'Keeffe, but Megan Carlisle hasn't got the intellect to carry it off."

"One of these days, that mouth of yours is going to get you in trouble."

Hilary's lips twisted in a spiteful smile. "You men are all alike. There isn't one of you who can see beyond a pair of big tits."

"Jealousy doesn't become you," he said, his tolerance coming to an end. "There was something fey and otherworldly about Megan tonight that I found incredibly intriguing."

"Fey, my ass!" Hilary hooted. "Megan is a party girl. The trouble is, you think there's a fascinating mind behind her gorgeous eyes. Trust me. If there was, I'd be the first to admit it. Now, I'm tired of talking about Megan Carlisle." She stubbed out her cigarette. "What will it be tonight—your house or mine?"

"Neither," Malcolm responded firmly.

He wanted to be alone to think about Megan. Hilary had been right about one thing. Megan hadn't been herself. Clearly, something was wrong—very wrong. And he intended to find out exactly what it was.

CHAPTER 7

Santa Fe
May 18, 1929

Duncan rose shortly after dawn, moving quietly so as not to wake Megan while he dressed. Although he'd left the window open the night before, the room seemed suffocatingly close. He had to get away from his wife, to breathe air that wasn't permeated with her exhalations or the perfumed scent of her femininity. He had to get far enough away to forget the urgent messages of his body, the need that had kept him tossing and turning much of the night.

He pulled on well-worn blue jeans and a sweater, and slipped into a pair of moccasins. As he left the bedroom, Megan cried out —a banshee wail that raised the hair on his neck. Pausing in midstride, he turned and looked at her.

She was still asleep, although she had kicked the covers aside. She lay on her back, her hands clenched as tightly as the Marys' in Grünewald's famous sixteenth-century Isenheim Altarpiece. She must be having one hell of a nightmare, he thought, moving closer.

Devoid of makeup, her bold features seemed more finely carved, with a delicacy he didn't remember. Her eyes moved under closed lids and her lower lip trembled, making her appear vulnerable and

53

childlike. For a second he felt as if he were gazing down at a stranger, a woman he'd just met.

Shaking his head angrily, he dismissed the idea as wishful thinking. Yes, Megan did look different this morning. He rarely saw her without makeup, though, and the new hair style certainly contributed to her altered appearance. Besides, he hadn't taken the time to look at her, really look at her, for years—any more than she bothered to look at him.

Just last month he'd shaved off the mustache he'd worn since his fortieth birthday, and days had passed before she'd even noticed. That was one of the sad things about marriages—theirs and most of the others he'd observed. Once the emotional and sexual honeymoon ended and habit took over, husbands and wives simply stopped paying attention to one another.

Certainly Megan looked different, her beauty even more startling than when they'd met. At nineteen she'd been an arresting mixture of sublime physical perfection and raw sensuality. Now he could almost swear he saw an even more compelling blend of innocence and intelligence on her face, along with a mature loveliness that took his breath away.

She'd been unnaturally quiet during dinner the night before, her glances guarded, her words carefully chosen. For the first time in years he had experienced the old tug of love and caring. He had fled the dinner party to escape that feeling.

But a man would have to be made of stone, he mused, gazing at the womanly form so easily discerned under the thin nightgown, not to respond to Megan. Heat flooded his groin and he felt himself harden as his gaze lingered, explored. Mesmerized, he watched her breasts rise and fall with every breath. Her nipples jutted against the semisheer fabric, inviting his touch. He could discern the dark triangle covering the mound of Venus between her thighs.

He groaned under his breath, remembering what it felt like to enter her, to drown reason and regret in the musky well of her womanhood. It had been so long and there she was for the taking. He reached forward, his fingertips tingling in anticipation of caressing that lovely flesh, his whole body yearning for fulfillment and release.

Startled by the intensity of his emotions, he forced himself to look away. He'd see himself in hell before he let lust lead him down the same old path. Sex had never been the cause of their marital problems, just as it wasn't the solution to them. If he had wanted Megan less when they met, or could be oblivious to her now, there wouldn't even be a problem. He'd be able to ignore her and get on with his life.

Again, he started to leave the room and she cried out once more. The sound stopped him in his tracks and he turned back one last time. Her cheeks were flushed and she trembled as if she had a fever. He returned to her side, pulling up the covers and tucking them around her shoulders. It was the only succor he could offer. Megan would have to deal with her demons alone, just as he would have to deal with his.

The cold light of an early spring day bathed Santa Fe in gossamer gold as he emerged from the hotel. He turned toward the plaza, deserted now but for a wood-laden burro being nudged along by a serape-clad man. Lost in thought, Duncan hunched his shoulders against the morning chill and veered left onto the Santa Fe Trail, his long purposeful stride taking him past the Loretto Chapel and the ancient adobes that crowded the narrow roadway.

He concentrated on walking, on making his muscles propel him forward, increasing his pace until it became punishing. He breathed deeply, cleansing his lungs of Megan's scent while he cleansed his mind of desire for her.

By the time he reached Carlos Vierra's house near where the Santa Fe and Pecos trails split, the walk had achieved its purpose. He had managed to push away the emotional overload that made rational thought impossible. True, Megan's behavior had been different last night. She had been so chastened by the talk of divorce that she seemed like a new woman. But he couldn't allow a single evening to change his mind about wanting his freedom. Not when they were so wrong for each other.

He didn't hate or even dislike Megan. Far from it. Deep down he supposed he felt sorry for her. She had gone from her father's luxurious Fifth Avenue mansion to her husband's rustic Santa Fe ranch without the slightest pause in between to grow up and become her own person. He could understand why, as a nineteen-year-old bride, she had looked to him for her happiness, her pleasure, all amusements, large and small.

Early in their marriage, he had tried to arouse her intellectual curiosity. But Megan had no intellectual curiosity to arouse. She cared nothing for politics, history, philosophy, literature. She was a grown woman, an adult who had no inner resources, no interests, nothing to live for. To Megan, life should be a perpetual dress-up party, free of all responsibility and concern other than what to wear, what to buy, and who to see.

Perhaps women would be encouraged to think for themselves someday, Duncan mused, to have careers and lives of their own. Megan had been born and raised only to marry well, to adorn the arm of a successful man. She would have been perfectly content if they lived in New York with a myriad of social engagements to fill her time. No wonder the thought of divorce, of having to meet life alone, terrified her.

Duncan stopped in midstride. Damn. Perhaps he had inadvertently found his way to the answer, the key to freeing them both. Megan had made it clear that she would never leave by herself. However, if she had a man waiting in the wings, a prominent individual who moved in all the right circles, she might want her freedom as much as he wanted his. And Duncan knew just the man. Malcolm Ashford was already half in love with Megan.

Duncan turned on his heel and headed back to La Fonda at an even brisker pace, certain he'd come up with the perfect everyone-gets-what-they-want solution. Starting that day, he'd encourage Megan and Malcolm to spend more time together. All he'd have to do then was sit back and watch nature run its course.

Jade couldn't tear her gaze from the burning building or the man struggling inside. The acrid, smoke-laden air filled her lungs. Shivering uncontrollably, she tried to scream a warning as the roof gave way—and then she woke up.

She'd had the dream again, so real this time that the odor of singed wood lingered in her nose and mouth like the aftertaste of a potent medicine. Coming fully awake, she realized the smell of burning wood was as real as the mattress under her body. She'd fallen asleep last night with that odor in her nostrils.

Her heart jolted in her chest. She bolted to her feet, ran to the window, and looked out. Santa Fe was coming to life. To her horror, it wasn't the modern Santa Fe of gallery-lined streets full of tourists. Three stories below, a horse-drawn milk wagon pulled up in front of the hotel and the driver got out, carrying metal containers of milk. Her legs gave way so unexpectedly, she found herself kneeling, clinging to the windowsill.

She had to face the truth. This was no dream. She had traveled through time to 1929.

The knowledge brought no comfort, and yet she couldn't go on denying the evidence of her senses. Lurching to her feet, she turned from the window and staggered back to the bed. Less than a week ago she'd been full of self-pity after Ira's call. Now she'd give anything she possessed to hear his voice giving her the bad news again.

Her skin felt clammy. Her hands shook. It took all her will not to cry out. Clenching her fists, she reined in her fear and forced herself to think. If she had accidentally found a way back in time, there had to be a way to move forward again.

It had begun with that damn dress.

The Molyneux.

The implication sledge-hammered her mind. Why hadn't she thought of it before? The sixty-year-old dress had been her passport to the past. Therefore, it had to be the key to returning to her own time. Nothing else made any sense.

A heady rush of optimism surged through her as she hurried to the closet. The dress hung there, glowing in the half-light like fairy fire in a medieval forest. She stripped off her nightgown with feverish haste and tossed it aside. Then she took the dress and slip from the hanger, pulling first one and then the other over her head, hoping against hope to feel the earth spin out of control.

The delicate silk and chiffon swirled around her naked body and fell into place, tugged down by the weight of the crystal beads. But the earth didn't tilt. Nothing changed. Megan's clothes still surrounded her, giving off a provocative perfume.

Jade sagged under the profound weight of her disappointment. She had been wrong. The Molyneux held no magic. It was simply an expensive couturier gown, nothing more.

Her despair was so acute, she felt it as pain. Years ago, she had borne the loss of her parents and Paul's defection with a stiff-lipped stoicism. She had forced herself to keep a tight rein on her emotions, and her friends had reinforced her behavior by seeming to admire it. But now all the willpower in the world couldn't stay her tears.

She had lost her past—her present—her future. She had lost her entire world.

She had lost herself.

For the first time in years, Jade surrendered to emotion. She crumpled onto her bed, pulling a pillow close and wrapping her arms around it. Rocking back and forth, she wept until her throat felt raw, her eyes puffy and red, her nose as stuffed as if she had a bad head cold. She was utterly without allies, trapped in an alien time, caged in another woman's life, her very existence tied to that woman's husband.

When she'd first woken up, she hadn't taken the time to wonder what had happened to Duncan Carlisle, to ask herself where he was. Now, hearing the door to the suite opening, she realized he must have gone out earlier. She didn't want him to find her like this—didn't want to face him while the knowledge of what had happened throbbed like an open wound. She jumped to her feet, grabbed some lingerie from the dresser and an outfit from the closet, and raced into the bathroom, locking the door.

A long, hot bath helped soothe her ragged nerves. She took her time dressing, frowning as she put on unfamiliar undergarments that included tap pants and a breast-flattening brassiere. The outfit she had grabbed at random proved to be a sporty three-piece jersey suit boasting the Chanel label. It reinforced her assumption that Megan Carlisle had excellent taste in clothes—and Duncan Carlisle had the money to indulge it.

But what did he feel for his wife, other than the disdain that had been so evident last night? Was there still passion between them? Good God! Did he hope to kiss and make up?

And how the hell did she intend to deal with the fact that for the first time in ten years, she had met a man she wanted to make love with? A man who was married to another woman.

Just before leaving her sanctuary she checked the time and realized she was still wearing her battery-powered wristwatch. Thank heaven no one had noticed it at dinner. She took it off and stuffed it in her jacket pocket, then opened the bathroom door.

Duncan was sitting in the parlor, an almost smug expression on his face, smoking a cigarette and reading the morning paper. Damn him, she thought. He looked even more rugged and virile in casual clothes than he had in a tuxedo.

She'd given up smoking five years ago, but now she felt an irresistible urge to start again. After all, she reasoned, she could hardly die of lung cancer when she had yet to be born. "Could I have one of your cigarettes?" she asked.

He looked up, his eyes widening as they roved her face and figure. Had she made a fatal mistake? she wondered. Could it be that Megan didn't smoke the way everyone else seemed to in 1929? Did Duncan realize she was an impostor? What would he do? Visions of a jail cell or worse raced through her mind.

Gathering all her courage, she said, "Why are you looking at me that way? Is my slip showing, or is it something more serious?"

He shrugged and the questioning expression left his eyes. Reaching into his shirt pocket, he produced a pack of Lucky Strikes, lit one, and held it out.

She put it in her mouth, feeling the lingering warmth of his lips on the unfiltered tip as she inhaled deeply. The powerful tobacco hit her lungs and the nicotine instantly made her dizzy. She gasped, coughed, wobbled.

"Are you all right?" he asked, bolting to his feet and steadying her with a supportive arm.

For a moment she permitted herself the comfort of his touch, then she pulled away. "I'm fine."

The disdain had returned to his eyes as he asked, "Are you ready to leave?"

Not trusting herself to speak, she nodded. She would have liked to ask where they were going but she didn't dare. Until she had the chance to learn more about the woman whose place she had taken, she had to be very, very careful.

Five minutes later, after a brisk walk through downtown Santa Fe, Duncan ushered her into the K. C. Waffle House. The decor was Southwestern, the crowd lively. A long counter ran down the left side of the restaurant and a line of booths down the right. Several people called out a greeting when they walked in. Then she saw Malcolm and Hilary in the booth nearest the entrance.

"Here we are, darlings," Hilary called, waving them over.

Both Hilary and Malcolm rose to greet them. While Malcolm and Duncan shook hands, Hilary bussed the air in the vicinity of Jade's cheek. Turning to Duncan, she threw herself at him and kissed him on the lips—hard. Jade couldn't help wondering how the real Megan would react to Hilary's obvious poaching. Something told her Megan would regard it as a declaration of war. To be honest, she didn't like it much herself.

Hilary was wearing a hacking jacket and close-fitting jodphurs that drew attention to her slim hips and legs. Malcolm had on a cable-knit sweater, tweed knickers, and argyle socks. The two of them looked as if they'd escaped from the pages of *The Great Gatsby*.

"I hope you won't be too bored today, Megan," Hilary said as Jade slid into the booth next to Duncan.

"Why would I be?"

"Frankly, I was surprised when you agreed to go. I didn't think my little excursion would be your style."

Jade smiled enigmatically. "A lady should always be prepared to change her style."

"Touché," Malcolm exclaimed gleefully.

Jade was grateful that the arrival of the waitress interrupted the conversation. Until she knew Hilary better, she had no desire to cross verbal swords with her. Hilary's dislike of Megan was obvious. The reason for it was not.

During the meal, Jade listened attentively, squirreling away bits of information the others revealed as they chatted. Apparently Hilary owned a gallery/shop that sold the finest Indian arts and crafts, as well as the work of some local artists who were known as the Santa Fe Five. She boasted of selling their pieces to famous Eastern collectors.

Although Duncan seemed to know all the artists Hilary mentioned, the fact that he didn't belong to the Santa Fe Five, or any other artists' group discussed, reinforced Jade's impression that he was a loner—like her. Perhaps that explained the attraction she felt.

The booth was so narrow that his left shoulder and thigh brushed hers no matter how hard she tried to keep some distance between them. No doubt he and his wife touched casually all the time without either one being aware of it. Jade, however, was acutely conscious of his scent, the bulk of his body, the muscled feel of his leg where it pressed against hers.

She wondered how he would react if she casually dropped her hand onto his thigh. Then, having thought it, she could barely keep herself from doing it. Last night she'd noticed that he had great legs for a man. Noticed? Face it, she had been riveted by the sight of him moving around the bedroom half nude. What in the world was wrong with her, wanting a man she didn't even know— another woman's husband? She was relieved when the check finally came and she could escape his immediate proximity.

She still didn't know where they were going as they strolled back to the hotel. Duncan left them in front of La Fonda, saying he would get his car. A few minutes later he came around the corner driving the longest, most elegantly sculpted car Jade had ever seen —a red-and-black beauty with gleaming chrome, wire-rimmed wheels, and the name *Duesenberg* written in flowing script under the hood ornament.

"Now that's a doozy!" Malcolm said in a voice filled with admiration.

With a writer's love of words, Jade delighted in the realization that the slang word *doozy* could have derived from the car's name.

"How do you like the Duesenberg?" Malcolm asked her.

"I love it," she replied honestly, instantly smitten with the magnificent machine.

"Have you driven it yet?" Hilary asked.

Jade looked from Malcolm to Hilary, wondering how she should answer. Malcolm unwittingly came to her rescue. "Hil, you know how Megan feels about cars. Of course she's driven it. Are you planning to be our chauffeur today?" he asked, giving Jade a broad smile.

No way, she thought. "I'd rather enjoy the scenery," she extemporized as Duncan came around the car.

He took her arm and escorted her to the Duesenberg. "Why don't you sit in back with Malcolm so you two can visit?" Without giving her a chance to reply, he helped her into the rear, behind the driver's seat.

"Splendid idea, old chap." Malcolm was grinning as he joined her. He seemed more youthful and less intellectual when he smiled. She would have loved to talk to him about writing, but that was completely out of the question until she knew more about his relationship with Megan.

Hilary looked as smug and self-satisfied as a cream-fed cat when Duncan handed her into the front seat. Jade sat back and made herself relax while they drove through town, turning north on a concrete road that climbed to a high ridge with a spectacular view.

Prompted by her occasional comment or question, Malcolm kept up a steady stream of conversation. Had Jade given him a list of things she needed to know, he couldn't have done a better job of filling her in on his history. He had been born to a wealthy American woman and her titled English husband, had dual citizenship, and maintained homes in London, the south of France, and Santa Fe, as well as a pied-à-terre in Manhattan. He and Hilary had met in Europe a decade ago and they'd been together ever since. Currently, he planned to stay in town until he finished what he described as "a quintessentially American novel, loosely based on the life of Al Capone."

How strange to think she'd already read it.

She had to probe judiciously to get Malcolm to reveal a little of Duncan's background. The Carlisles were an old and aristocratic banking family from the Main Line in Philadelphia. Duncan had been disowned when he chose art over commerce. He owed his fortune to a small inheritance from a maiden aunt—and his own considerable talent.

Jade was too busy listening to Malcolm to be able to eavesdrop on the conversation taking place in the front seat. But seeing the wet-lipped smiles and the intimate touches Hilary bestowed on Duncan, she suspected the bleached blonde was hell-bent on seduction. It made Jade irritable and tense—a ridiculous reaction since Duncan wasn't really her husband and she intended to return to her

62

own time and her own worries as soon as she could figure out how.

An hour out of Santa Fe they turned west on a dirt road marked New Mexico 4. As Duncan eased the heavy car across a dry wash, he pointed to his right. "That mesa," he said, "is called Tunyo. The Indians believe it's the home of the giant Tsaybiyo. Legend has it that many years ago, Tsaybiyo ate all the children in the pueblo of San Ildefonso. The horrified villagers asked a great *cacique* to help them kill the giant. When Tsaybiyo died, his blood metamorphosed into the lava fields you see all around us."

"What a grim myth," Malcolm said.

Duncan shook his head. "It's no more grim than the story of the Crucifixion."

Malcolm leaned forward. "You sound as if you half believe in Tsaybiyo yourself."

"As Shakespeare put it so eloquently, there are more things in heaven and earth than are dreamt of in our philosophy."

Jade stared at the back of Duncan's head, wondering if he really meant what he said. Did she dare trust him? She wanted to— desperately. Could a man who had never heard of atomic power, let alone spaceships that landed on the moon or tiny computers that held a world of knowledge, be open-minded enough to accept time travel? Or would he think she was crazy and have her committed if he learned the truth?

They came to an intersection with another dirt road, and Duncan turned right. Ahead, snuggled against the banks of the Rio Grande, Jade saw a small village surrounded by green fields.

"That's San Ildefonso," Duncan said.

A few minutes later, he pulled up in front of an unprepossessing adobe house. While he set the parking brake, Malcolm got out of the car, then opened Hilary's door and helped her out. Jade, who was accustomed to getting in and out of cars without assistance, was about to push her own door open when Duncan opened the door himself. Off balance, she spilled out of the Duesenberg's backseat and would have fallen had he not caught her.

The runaway physical attraction she'd experienced during break- fast increased tenfold when she found herself in his arms. She blushed crimson as she became aware of the flat planes of his chest pressing against her breasts. To her dismay, she felt her nipples harden. Praying he was unaware of her sexual response to him, she jerked free.

He didn't even bother to look at her as Hilary led the way to the door. She knocked loudly and called out, "Maria."

A diminutive, dark-haired woman in her late forties or early fifties answered the summons. She seemed to be looking right at them without actually seeing them. "Who's there?" she asked.

She must be blind, Jade thought. Why had Hilary wanted to visit a blind Indian woman? Hilary certainly didn't seem like a charitable do-gooder.

"It's me, Hilary Delano. I brought some people with me."

"I've been expecting you, Miss Delano," the woman said in a lightly accented voice. "Won't you and your friends come in."

Jade followed the others into a small, neat-as-a-pin parlor. The walls were whitewashed, the furniture old and inexpensive. A few magnificent pieces of Indian pottery with distinctive black-on-black designs were the only touches of luxury in the room. Jade had a vague memory of seeing pottery pieces just like them somewhere, but she couldn't recall the time or place.

"Maria Martinez," Hilary said, "I'd like you to meet Malcolm Ashford, Duncan Carlisle, and his wife, Megan."

A smile illuminated the blind woman's face. "I know your work well, Mr. Carlisle. Unfortunately, I no longer have the pleasure of seeing it."

"And I know and admire yours," Duncan replied. "If you don't mind my asking, how have you been able to go on with your work, considering . . . ?" His voice trailed off.

"Considering that I'm almost blind?" Maria said. Her smile deepened. "I don't need eyes to make pottery. I see it with my hands. And my husband, Juan, has always painted the designs."

"Speaking of Juan," Hilary interjected, "is he home?"

Maria shook her head. "He's out digging clay. But I have several pieces for your shop. If you'll wait here, my helper will get them." She called, and a young woman appeared from the back of the house. "Elena, would you please bring in the pots Juan set aside this morning."

A few minutes later Elena returned, her arms laden with the

same magnificent black ware that adorned the tables. Memory sparked in Jade's mind. She had seen Maria's work in a posthumous exhibition at the Southwest Museum in Highland Park a few years ago. Maria Martinez had been a world-renowned and much revered artist when she died.

Filled with the special reverence she reserved for true geniuses, Jade turned to the potter. "It's an honor to meet you, Mrs. Martinez."

"You're very kind to say so, Mrs. Carlisle. But I'm just a humble potter."

"You're famous," Jade said, before she realized that probably few people had heard of Maria Martinez in 1929. She would have loved to tell the dignified woman that the pottery she and her husband created would one day sell for thousands of dollars and grace the finest museums.

Hilary had been examining the pieces Elena had brought in. Now she turned to Maria and asked, "Is this all you have for me today?"

Maria nodded. "It takes time and patience to create something of beauty. Juan and I can't keep up with the demand for our work these days."

"But you did save me your best pieces?" Hilary insisted.

"They are *all* our best pieces," Maria replied. "The clay comes from our mother, the earth. We always treat it with the respect and love it deserves."

Malcolm looked delighted. "Well said, Mrs. Martinez."

After Hilary finished her business, the four of them climbed back into the car and, with Hilary supplying the directions, continued west to the tiny hamlet of Otowi where they lunched at Edith Warner's Tea Room.

Throughout the meal, Jade was aware of Duncan's occasional speculative glance. It made her so uncomfortable she could hardly eat. Was he onto her masquerade? Did he intend to confront her as soon as they were alone?

Duncan was hard pressed to respond to Hilary's conversational gambits on the drive back to Santa Fe. His stomach churned as if he had eaten something disagreeable. Every time he checked in the rearview mirror, Megan and Malcolm had their heads close together, chatting away like magpies. They made a striking couple, he thought with sour displeasure. Malcolm was far too glib to suit Duncan. But women liked that trait in a man—at least Megan seemed to.

The bells of St. Francis were chiming five times as he jockeyed the Duesenberg into a parking place in front of Hilary's shop. He helped her carry the pottery inside, ignoring the obvious invitation in her eyes as she asked him if he would like a drink . . . or anything else.

When he returned to the car, Megan and Malcolm were still talking. He shut the door too loudly and turned to Malcolm. "I have a favor to ask."

"Ask away."

"Megan had her heart set on seeing *Our Dancing Daughters* at the Paris cinema tonight. But I was up before dawn and I'm tired. Would you mind filling in for me?"

Malcolm beamed. "I'd be delighted. I hear the new star, Joan Crawford, is simply smashing."

For a moment Duncan thought, even hoped, that Megan was going to object. Instead, as he pulled up in front of La Fonda, she gave Malcolm a dazzling smile. "Since my husband isn't feeling well, why don't we have dinner together too?"

"Is that all right with you, old chap?" Malcolm asked.

Duncan nodded. His plan was working faster than he'd expected. He kept his smile firmly fixed while Megan and Malcolm got out of the car and walked to the corner, disappearing from sight. But a scowl had taken up permanent residence on his face by the time he left the car in the hotel lot. He couldn't figure Megan out. What kind of performance had she been giving today—and to what end? He'd never known her to wear the same outfit two days in a row—some clothes she only wore once, period—yet she'd worn that Chanel suit both yesterday and today.

Her behavior at Maria's had astonished him too. She had been oblivious to the beauty of Indian arts and crafts from the day he brought her to Santa Fe as a bride. So why had she fallen all over Maria Martinez, spouting that nonsense about Maria being famous, when few people outside of New Mexico had heard of the potter?

And why hadn't Megan mentioned that they owned half a dozen of Maria's pieces themselves?

He'd been so sure he knew his wife through and through. Now he found himself wondering what other surprises she had in store for him. And why the hell did he feel so attracted to her when every ounce of reason he possessed told him it was madness?

With great effort, Jade pushed aside her growing list of concerns and managed to have a thoroughly enjoyable evening with Malcolm. He took her to the Chop Suey Café just down San Francisco from the hotel, then on to the Paris, an ornate art-deco movie palace. The lobby was adorned with fanciful gilt figures, the seats covered in lush mohair, the walls decorated with pillars. Even the ceiling had been embellished. The structure was the complete antithesis of the stark, modern, multiscreened cineplexes of her era.

The film was a gritty black and white, but it was fascinating to watch Joan Crawford strut her youthful charms, dancing and flirting with the camera, oblivious to the price fate would exact for her success. Being at the movies reminded Jade of home, of Malibu Beach, of Beverly Hills and Hollywood. She had left without a second thought, and now she wasn't sure she would ever get back.

After the movie ended, Malcolm walked her back to the hotel, gave her a gentlemanly kiss on the cheek, and left her in the lobby. Duncan was asleep when she tiptoed into their room. She undressed in the bathroom and went to bed, expecting to spend the night wide awake. But her sleep was profound, dreamless, and refreshing.

When she woke up in the morning she found that Duncan had left a note on the nightstand, saying he'd return at eleven to take her back to Rancho Cielo. It seemed the man made a habit of disappearing. She suspected he did it to annoy Megan. She wasn't Megan, though. All she felt was relief.

An hour later, she was eating a solitary breakfast in La Plazuela while glancing through the *Santa Fe New Mexican* that she'd bought in the lobby. The headlines—FARM RELIEF BILL VOTED INTO SENATE CONFERENCE, FLYING HAZARDS WILL BE GREATER, GRADE SCHOOLS CONDEMNED AS BEING UNSAFE—could easily have been lifted from any newspaper in her own time.

To her surprise, she found the advertisements more absorbing than the news. The M System grocery store was featuring butter at 44 cents a pound, Del Monte peaches for 25 cents a can, and roast pork loin at 24 cents a pound. The J. C. Penney's on Saint Francis was selling plain spring coats for $9.90, and fur-trimmed ones for $14.75. A men's store had Hart, Schaffner & Marx suits for $25.

The paper was replete with ads for products such as Hills Bros. coffee, Goodyear tires, Canada Dry Ginger Ale, and Swift's Premium bacon. The very names made her homesick. She found herself growing sentimental over the knowledge that she could still shop at a Skaggs, a Safeway, or a Piggly Wiggly. She saw so many familiar names that she felt almost at ease, until, tucked in Roberts Motor Company's advertisement for Oldsmobiles, Fords, and Chevrolets, she saw a 1927 Marman Sport Roadster for sale.

Those few words filled her with despair and a rising anxiety that nearly sent her running from the restaurant and out into the street. She had known about Duesenbergs, but this new make of car was totally unfamiliar. How the hell could she continue this charade when she knew so little about Megan Carlisle and her world? How long would she be stuck in 1929? How much of herself might she lose? And what would Duncan do to her if he discovered her imposture before she found her way out? Instinct told her to flee as fast and as far as she could. Logic commanded her to stay. If travel through time was linked to place, then in order to return to 1989, she would have to remain as close to La Fonda as possible. The only way she could safely do that was as Duncan Carlisle's wife.

She had to believe there was a way back to her own time, a door, an opening that swung both ways. All she had to do was find it. The dress was part of the key, yet there must be more. She suspected that Megan Carlisle's life, her home with Duncan, could provide some more answers. Yes, despite her instincts, despite the heart-stopping fear she felt every time someone gave her a peculiar look, she had to stay.

At eleven sharp, she was waiting in the lobby surrounded by the Carlisles' luggage. When Duncan appeared he offered no explanation for his absence. He simply escorted her to the car as two bellhops loaded their suitcases.

"It's a nice day for a drive," she said as he turned south on the Santa Fe Trail.

He grunted. "Uhuh."

"You could be more civil."

"No one's around. Why pretend?"

She bit back an angry response. This was Megan's fight, not hers.

Despite her earlier rationalizations for maintaining the masquerade, she couldn't help feeling that every mile they traveled took her farther from her own time and place. Half an hour after leaving the hotel, they turned east onto a narrow two-lane road. A sign identified it as the highway to Las Vegas, New Mexico. To her, it felt like the road to nowhere.

The Duesenberg leaped forward as Duncan's foot settled more firmly on the gas pedal. The speedometer slid past eighty miles an hour. Jade found herself longing for a seat belt. Was the man trying to kill them both?

To mask her fright, she forced herself to concentrate on the landscape, a series of piñon-covered foothills that reached south to a broad plateau. The occasional homestead accented the loneliness of the scenery rather than relieving it.

Duncan finally slowed the car and turned left onto a narrow dirt track. The potholed, washboard path climbed through a fragrant stand of pine and juniper. Squirrels scampered amid the trees, and piñon jays and crows congregated in the branches, announcing the car's passage through the woods with their own raucous cacophony.

The car crested a steep rise, and Rancho Cielo lay revealed in a grassy meadow beneath them. Jade's breath caught in her throat. The green of the trees, the intense blue of the sky, the golden gleam of adobe walls reflecting the spring sunshine would forever be etched in her memory. She had an inexplicable sensation of having come home.

"It's beautiful!" she said softly.

"Yes," Duncan said, turning to look at her. "Rancho Cielo is beautiful. It's too bad it took you ten years to appreciate it."

He had been stealing glances at Megan throughout the drive, trying again to figure out why she seemed so different. Could she really be growing up now that it was too late? Or was he just suffering from some stupid male instinct that made him loath to part with a woman once he thought of her as his?

He had literally thrown Megan at Malcolm last night, then he'd been furious at how well the writer fielded the pass. Visions of the two of them locked in each other's arms, writhing in bed, had kept him awake. To add to his idiocy, he'd pretended to be asleep when Megan returned to their suite. Damn fool, he thought as he eased the Duesenberg down the incline that led to the ranch house compound, honking the horn so Dulce and Jorge would know they were home.

When he pulled up in front of the main house, Blackjack burst from the surrounding forest to greet him. The huge black Newfoundland wagged his tail vigorously as Duncan got out of the car. "Missed me, did you?" Duncan said, giving Blackjack a quick pat.

He was about to help Megan from the car when a primeval growl rumbled in Blackjack's throat.

Jade stared at the enormous snarling dog. Should she refuse to get out of the Duesenberg? She might look and sound enough like Megan Carlisle to fool a human being, but she was damn sure she couldn't fool a dog. And this one was big enough to do her considerable damage. He continued to growl ferociously in response to her alien scent.

"Blackjack, behave yourself," Duncan said, extending his hand to Jade.

Blackjack quieted momentarily. Then, as she got out of the car, he bared an impressive set of teeth and growled even louder.

"Good God," Duncan said. "You'd better get back in the Duesenberg until I can put him in his run."

Jade had always loved animals—dogs, cats, horses, all creatures—and she'd never had a problem winning them over. So she stood her ground.

"That won't be necessary. Blackjack, come," she ordered in her most authoritarian tone.

The animal looked bewildered. His ears drooped and his tail hung between his heavy haunches. To her relief, he finally obeyed. When he was just inches away, she held out her hand, palm up. Blackjack's nose twitched as he took in her unfamiliar scent.

"Good boy, Blackjack," she said as the dog wagged his tail tentatively. After he'd had the opportunity to experience her scent to his satisfaction, she patted him on the head, the traditional sign of human dominance. Blackjack submitted to her gesture, the beat of his tail increasing.

"Well, I'll be damned," Duncan murmured, wonder and admiration mingling in his voice. "I never thought you two would make friends."

Releasing her pent-up breath, Jade knelt so she would be at the animal's eye level and gave him a good ear-scratching. "I don't know why you're so surprised. After all, Blackjack does know me."

"That's just it," Duncan replied. "He's never liked you much."

Her stomach muscles clenching with the now familiar fear, Jade gazed up at Duncan. When would he catch on to her? she wondered. She hadn't been able to fool the dog, and she didn't know how much longer she would be able to deceive the man.

CHAPTER 8

Rancho Cielo
May 19, 1929

"*Muy delicioso*. You make a fine breakfast." Jorge Ortiz sat back and sighed with pleasure. He was a slight man whose enormous appetite seemed out of synch with his diminutive stature. That morning he had consumed four eggs, scrambled with Dulce's homemade chorizo, and half a dozen thick flour tortillas still hot from the *comal*.

Knowing her husband preferred to concentrate on one thing at a time, Dulce had been waiting impatiently for him to finish. Now she rose from her place at the table and carefully banked the fire in the huge wood-burning stove that dominated the ranch house kitchen. Picking up an enameled coffeepot, she refilled her husband's mug, then sat back down across from him.

"We must talk," she said.

"I have work to do in the stable," he protested.

"The horses can wait. This can't. It's the señora."

"What about her?"

Impatience sparked in Dulce's dark eyes. Jorge wasn't slow or stupid, but he pretended to be when it suited his purpose.

"Don't play the *sencillo* with me, *esposo*. I saw you watching her yesterday."

"Of course I watched her. The señora is a beautiful woman—and you sound like a jealous one."

Dulce refused to be put off. "There is something wrong with her."

"She seems well enough to me."

"I'm not talking about her health. I'm talking about the way she's been acting, the things she's been doing since she got back from town yesterday."

Jorge shrugged. "What the señora does or doesn't do is none of our business."

"How can you say that? It's our duty to watch over Rancho Cielo."

"You sound as if you are the mistress instead of Señora Carlisle."

Dulce lowered her voice. "Do you know what I think?" She didn't give Jorge a chance to reply. "The woman who returned from La Fonda is not Señora Carlisle. I am afraid that a *bruja*, a shape-shifter, has taken the mistress's place." As she spoke, Dulce made the sign of the cross.

Jorge's eyes narrowed, and he crossed himself too. "It's dangerous to even think such things."

"You weren't in the parlor looking out the window when the master and mistress came back to Rancho Cielo yesterday. You didn't see the way Blackjack growled and showed his teeth when the señora got out of the car."

"So what? The dog has never liked her. You yourself have said he would bite her one day."

"That's what I'm trying to tell you. I was sure yesterday would be the day." Dulce couldn't help shuddering as the homecoming played again in her mind. "The dog was ready to attack her. But she bent down and did something to take away his hatred. I think she cast a spell on him."

Jorge pushed himself to his feet. "If that's the only proof you have of this *bruja* business, your *sencillo* has work to do. And so do you."

Putting her hand on his arm, Dulce urged him back into his chair. "There's more. I kept my eye on her for the rest of the day.

She was snooping around as if she'd never been in the house before. Every time she saw me she stopped what she was doing and gave me such a look that my blood runs cold just thinking about it. This woman—this *bruja* has the *mal ojo*, the evil eye." Fear spasmed in Dulce's stomach. "I felt those looks in my guts. This morning when I got up and made water, there was blood in it. I tell you, the woman in this house is not Señora Carlisle. She is a *bruja*."

Jorge threw up his arms in a gesture of surrender. "All right. There is something very strange going on. I didn't want to worry you but now I think you should know. Last night I dreamed an owl flew in our bedroom window and perched on the edge of the bed. It looked straight at me and said '*Cuidado*, Jorge—take care.' "

Dulce reached for his work-roughened hand and held it tight. "We must be very cautious until Señor Carlisle realizes what has happened. Promise me that you will do nothing to draw attention to yourself. Stay out of the house as much as possible today."

"What about you?" Concern clouded Jorge's normally sunny expression.

"I will stay in the kitchen all morning. Later this afternoon I will tell the *bruja* we have errands to do in town. We won't return until suppertime. Our only hope is that the señor will notice the difference between the *bruja* and his wife before the day is over."

"And if he doesn't?"

Fear gripped her again, but the need to protect Jorge gave Dulce courage. She reached into her apron pocket for the crucifix she had put there when she got up that morning, and placed it on the table. "There are ways to handle a *bruja*," she said, her voice filled with certainty and menace.

Jade woke to a sun-washed room filled with the cheery sound of bird song. She stretched, luxuriating in the comfort of fresh linens and a firm mattress. Then, with a start, she remembered where she was and panic welled in her throat. She had slept in Megan Carlisle's bed last night—next to Megan Carlisle's husband.

In case he happened to be looking her way, Jade peered at his side of the bed through barely open eyes. The only indication that he had slept next to her was the indentation in his pillow.

After the relative safety of La Fonda's twin beds, she had dreaded sleeping so close to Duncan that she could reach out and touch him —or he her. Yet the painful truth was that last night she had hoped he would. She had been feeling terribly alone, achingly vulnerable, and in desperate need of solace. Perhaps that accounted for her intense reaction to the presence of his large, warm body only a few inches from hers.

Yes. She had wanted him to hold her.

She had fantasized about being in his arms, feeling his lips against her own, tasting his kisses. But she had done so on her own side of the bed, as far away from him as she could get without falling on the floor.

Duncan had seemed oblivious to the emotional storms sweeping through her. As far as she could tell, it had been another business-as-usual, sleep-like-the-proverbial-log night for him. After she'd realized he had no interest in making love, she had tried to relax. She had been too aware of his proximity, though, too nervous every time he changed position, to fall asleep easily. She hadn't drifted off until the small hours of the morning. Now she was grateful to be alone.

He had said something during dinner the night before about getting up early and going to the studio to paint. If she could think of a way to get rid of Dulce for a few hours, she would finally be free to explore the house. With any luck—and God knows she was overdue for some—she might even learn enough about the Carlisles to continue safely masquerading as Megan until she found a way back to her own time.

Cheered by the prospect, she got out of bed and went to the closet. Despite the size and scope of Megan's wardrobe, Jade searched in vain for something casual like the jeans, T-shirts, and Nikes she preferred. She finally settled on a pair of Schiaparelli trousers with a tunic top and crepe-soled sandals. Ten minutes later, she followed the seductive aroma of fresh-brewed coffee to the kitchen.

It was a large, sunny room with a high ceiling, from which dangled strings of chilis and garlic, and a variety of drying herbs. A huge stove bulked against one wall. A refrigerator stood against another, with a cylindrical cooling mechanism perched on its top like a flying saucer. A fireplace that looked big enough to barbecue half a steer took up the third wall, and a double sink set in a long counter filled the fourth. The windows over the sink looked out onto a flower-filled garden.

Dulce was working at a table in the center of the room, stirring something in a large yellow bowl. Blackjack lay near her feet. Sensing Jade's presence, the dog began to wag his tail. The rhythmic thumping alerted Dulce and she looked up. Seeing Jade, her eyes opened so wide, the whites completely surrounded the dark irises.

"What are you doing in the kitchen?" she demanded.

Jade was startled by the housekeeper's abrupt tone. She had seemed so deferential—almost disturbingly so—the day before. "I'm afraid I overslept," she said, quelling the impulse to apologize. "If it isn't too much trouble, I'd like some breakfast."

"If you wanted something, why didn't you use the bellpull by your bed to summon me?"

"I didn't want to inconvenience you." Jade had seen the narrow tapestry ribbon, but she hadn't known its purpose. She pulled out one of the chairs and sat down at the table, giving the housekeeper what she hoped was an ingratiating smile.

Dulce ignored her friendly overture. "Señor Carlisle wouldn't want me to serve you in the kitchen."

Jade didn't believe that for a minute. Duncan didn't strike her as a stickler for the niceties of etiquette. Furthermore, she had hoped to get to know Dulce. "I'm sure he won't mind," she said.

Dulce shook her head. To Jade's dismay, the housekeeper looked frightened. Of her!

"All right," Jade said, getting to her feet. "Have it your way."

"What would you like to eat?" Dulce asked, following Jade into the breakfast room.

"Juice, coffee, and toast," Jade replied, hoping Megan wasn't one of those rare women who ate a stevedore's breakfast. "And I'd like the newspaper too."

"It's by your chair, as usual." Dulce stabbed a finger in the direction of the table where the Santa Fe daily lay by a single place setting.

When she delivered the meal a few minutes later, she seemed to take great pains to avoid Jade's eyes and she left quickly, without a backward glance.

The coffee was fragrant and strong, the toast made from home-baked bread, and the orange juice freshly squeezed. Jade was too confused to enjoy it, though. Something was obviously bothering the housekeeper. Another riddle to be solved, she thought, as if she didn't face enough of them already.

She ate quickly as she scanned the slender newspaper. When she finished, she called Dulce back into the room. "I want you to go into town to run a few errands."

To her surprise, Dulce smiled. It made her look ten years younger. "Sí, señora."

"I'd like to have some fresh flowers in the house." Too late, she remembered the garden she'd seen through the kitchen window, a garden bursting with spring blooms. But Dulce didn't mention them either.

"And I've got a craving for fresh fruits and vegetables," Jade continued. "The Piggly Wiggly is advertising asparagus and spinach, and the M System has peaches and strawberries. And fish—I want fish for dinner tonight."

The housekeeper nodded. "Is there anything else, señora?"

Hoping to prolong the woman's absence, Jade thought about the other ads she'd just read. "If it isn't too much trouble, I'd like you to buy a portable typewriter from the Santa Fe Book and Stationery Store."

"But Señor Carlisle has a typewriter in the den."

Damn. No wonder there was so much suspicion in Dulce's dark eyes. "I know, but I want one of my own. Just ask the clerk to help you. Any brand will do. Since I've given you such a long list, why don't you get Jorge to drive you into town right now?"

"What about lunch?"

"I'll take care of it." She dismissed Dulce with a nod, then rose and headed for the living room where she stationed herself at a window.

Fifteen minutes later she saw an old-fashioned Ford heading down the drive with Jorge at the wheel and Dulce by his side. The Ortizes didn't even glance toward the ranch house as the car crested the rise, then disappeared from view. Jade sighed with relief. At last she was on her own and free to explore without Dulce spying on her.

The living room was lovely, tastefully furnished with an eclectic blend of old-world antiques and New Mexico–style furniture. She flushed with embarrassment when she saw six pots by Maria Martinez decorating a chest. What must Duncan have thought when she failed to mention them to Maria? And how many other errors and omissions had she made without knowing? With every one the danger of discovery increased. She had to find out more about Megan and Duncan and their life together before it was too late.

She slowly turned a full circle, her gaze darting here and there, as she wondered where to begin her search. The painting over the fireplace caught and held her eye. She had noticed it the day before and had been about to examine it more thoroughly when Dulce walked into the room. Now Jade stepped back to take in its full scope before moving close enough to read the signature. Duncan had scrawled his name in the right-hand corner.

The painting was splendid, evocative, masterful. Quite simply, it was the most beautiful canvas she had ever seen. Yet the word *beautiful* didn't do it justice. Duncan had painted an Indian girl on the verge of womanhood, sitting alone by a flickering fire. She gazed into the distance, her expression so yearning that you knew someone, perhaps a lover, was just off the canvas. The light, playing across her features, conveyed a sense of mystery—the eternal mystery of all femininity.

From what Jade had seen of him so far, Duncan Carlisle was thoroughly intimidating and unapproachable. But the man who had painted this canvas was warm, human, filled with emotional depths that touched some deep part of her own psyche. She wanted to get to know that man better, much better, and not because of her masquerade. She wanted to know him for herself. And that, Jade realized, was far more dangerous than any masquerade.

She spent the rest of the morning exploring the parlor, dining room, and sun room. She didn't get through the house as quickly as she had hoped, because she kept stopping to admire yet another of Duncan's paintings.

Duncan glowered at the canvas on the easel in front of him. He had been trying to concentrate on it all morning, but his mind had refused to cooperate. Instead of thinking about his work, he had been thinking about Megan.

He shook his head in disgust and dropped his brush into a turpentine-filled jar. What a perverse, idiotic fool he was. He had asked Megan for a divorce two days ago and had wanted her desperately ever since. Lying next to her last night, pretending to be sound asleep while his body ached with longing, had driven him crazy.

Time and again during the past two days he had found himself studying her when she wasn't looking his way. Suddenly everything about her fascinated him—the way little tendrils of hair curled at the nape of her neck, the perfect and beautifully symmetric arrangement of her features, the new way she had of tilting her head. There was no doubt that she had changed. She looked different, acted different. Hell, she even smelled different.

He shook his head in despair. He obviously wasn't going to do any meaningful work today. He cleaned his palette, put his oils away, and cast a last unforgiving glance at the painting on the easel before leaving the studio and heading for the stables. A ride might help to clear his head.

Jorge always spent the mornings caring for the horses, putting them out to pasture so he could muck out the stalls. But Jorge was nowhere in sight.

"Jorge?" Duncan called. Not getting any response, he headed for the main house.

The kitchen was empty when he walked in. "Jorge—Dulce?" he called again. It wasn't like them to leave Rancho Cielo without telling him where they were going and when they would be back.

To his surprise, Megan answered his summons. "Is something wrong?"

"I was looking for Jorge and Dulce."

"I'm afraid I sent them to town." Her tentative smile made his heart do a flip-flop. "Is there something I can do for you?"

"I was going to ask Dulce for lunch before I went riding."

"I was just going to fix something to eat. Won't you join me. I make a mean omelette."

Duncan couldn't help laughing at the thought of Megan cooking.

He had never heard food described as *mean,* but it was probably an apt characterization for anything she prepared. "I appreciate the offer—but we both know you don't cook."

Jade's brow knit in a frown. Damn. She had made another blunder.

"There's no reason to look so upset," Duncan said. "I'll fix the omelettes and you can set the table. Dulce keeps the dishes and silver in the pantry."

So Megan didn't know where the place settings were kept, let alone how to cook, Jade mused as she hurried to do his bidding. Apparently Megan didn't work in or out of the house. So what did she do to hang onto a man like Duncan Carlisle? Jade didn't think she wanted to know the answer.

When she returned to the kitchen a minute later, Duncan was breaking eggs into a bowl with casual expertise. She watched approvingly as he added chopped green onions and grated cheese to the mixture. Suddenly, she felt tears stinging the back of her eyes. No one had cooked a meal for her since her mother died, and now this hard, rugged man was fixing her lunch. She swallowed and turned away.

His preparations complete, he stoked up the fire in the wood-burning stove and began cooking the eggs. "Why don't you get a bottle of wine to have with lunch?" he said without looking up.

Oh no, she thought, her heart pounding frantically. She didn't have the vaguest idea where he kept the wine.

Seeming to sense her indecision, he glanced at her. "Sorry. I forgot you don't like going down into the basement. Come on over here and stir the eggs and I'll get the wine."

Relieved, she hastened to the stove. She was about to take the spatula from him when his hand closed over hers. "You stir the eggs like this," he said. "Gently."

Although they had shared a bed the night before, Jade had never been this close to Duncan for so long. He stood directly behind her as he guided her hand. The full length of his body pressed against hers, and she had to lock her knees to keep from collapsing. The eggs blurred as her heartbeat and her breathing quickened. What the hell was the matter with her, practically swooning like some lovesick teenager?

Thank heaven he seemed oblivious to his effect on her. He broke the contact as casually as he had initiated it and left the room.

Duncan opened the cellar door, turned on the lights, and hurried down the stairs. The cold of the basement barely cooled his heated skin. He'd been a fool, touching Megan like that, but he hadn't expected to react so strongly. It had been all he could do to keep from spinning her around and kissing her. Kissing her? Hell. If that wasn't the understatement of the year. He wanted to fuck her brains out. And unless he missed his guess, she wanted it as badly as he did.

He strode to the tall wine rack against the far wall and blindly took down a bottle, not bothering to read the label. The way he felt, any wine would do as long as there was lots of it.

The rack, so well stocked before Prohibition, was only half-full. A week ago the thought of running out of the fine French vintages he preferred with his meals and having to depend on bootleggers instead, who were notorious for putting expensive labels on bottles of cheap wine, had seemed like a calamity. Now it was dwarfed by the realization that, after so many years of a disastrous marriage, he was becoming obsessed with his wife.

By the time he returned to the kitchen, she had finished the eggs and divided them between two plates, to which she had added sliced tomatoes. She had also put a loaf of crusty bread, butter, and jam on the table. He was surprisingly touched by her contributions to the meal. The old Megan would never have thought of doing something like that. He uncorked the wine and poured it, then joined her at the table. "You've been unusually quiet lately," he said, trying to engage her glance.

She refused to meet his eyes but the look on her face was one of pure panic.

"Is it because I asked you for a divorce?"

Jade hadn't known what to say to Duncan. Now she latched onto the explanation he had provided. "You're right. I am upset about it. It's such an admission of failure. I just wish . . ." Her voice trailed off. She could hardly tell him what she wished. "Has it been that bad?" she asked.

His grim expression told her that it had. "Lately—yes."

"What about at the beginning?" she asked.

81

He shrugged. "You know about the beginning as well as I do."

No, damn you, I don't know, she thought. "Couldn't we start over? We could pretend we were complete strangers and get to know each other all over again. It might even be fun."

Unexpectedly, anger flashed in his eyes, and his voice took on its familiar biting edge. "You and your games, your little dramas. You never give up, do you?"

"Not when it's this important," she replied, refusing to be cowed.

They had both been picking at their food. Now he pushed away from the table and stood up. "I guess I'm not as hungry as I thought. I think I'll go for that ride. If anyone telephones, I'll be back by supper."

"Will you think about what I said?"

He was halfway to the door and turned to face her. "I'll think about it. But don't expect any miracles."

Jade stayed in her chair for a long time while the eggs grew cold and the wine warm. She had made an effort to save the Carlisles' marriage. But who was she saving it for—herself or Megan?

She finally stood, carried their plates to the sink, and washed up. Then, refusing to surrender to despair, she headed for the den to continue her search.

She found Blackjack sleeping in a pool of sunshine on a well-worn Navajo rug. He looked up when she entered the room. His acceptance of her was so complete, he merely wagged his tail before dozing off again. The dog's presence told her that the den was Duncan's lair. The room was completely masculine in decor and atmosphere, right down to the lingering aroma of pipe smoke. The typewriter Dulce had mentioned sat on a heavily carved credenza next to a massive rolltop desk.

A wall of photographs captured Jade's attention. The pictures showed Duncan and a dark-haired woman with various famous people. So that's Megan, she thought with a swift intake of breath.

Although she recognized President Herbert Hoover, Will Rogers, Charles Lindbergh, Noël Coward, and a still young-looking Pablo Picasso, among others, it was Megan who held her attention. Feature by feature, she and Megan could have been twins. And yet, while she had always considered herself to be unattractive, some

magical alchemy had made Megan Carlisle breathtakingly beautiful.

Were they doppelgängers who had changed places at the behest
of some unknown cosmic force? Jade wondered. And where the hell
was Megan?

The questions reverberated through Jade's mind as she moved on
to a book-lined wall. Choosing at random, she opened F. Scott
Fitzgerald's novel *The Beautiful and Damned* and saw that the author
had inscribed the title page to Duncan. Books by D. H. Lawrence
and Malcolm Ashford were similarly inscribed, as was a folio of
Noël Coward's plays. The books and photographs told her the Carlisles kept exalted company—and little else.

Frustration and the ever-present panic billowed inside her. She
felt as if she were trying to put together a jigsaw puzzle without
knowing what the picture was. Pieces of the border were falling into
place, yet the heart of the puzzle—the secrets of the Carlisles' lives
—remained blank.

She spent the next half hour going through the contents of the
desk. The neatly filed bills, canceled checks, insurance policies, and
stock certificates offered proof of Duncan's success. He had money,
a great deal of it from what she now knew of the value of the 1929
dollar. He was, she realized with admiration, a self-made man.

When she opened a rubber-banded packet of correspondence,
she blinked as she saw the letterhead of the Max Gallery. Good
God! She knew David Max—that is, she had known David Max.
He was Ira's father. She'd met him shortly before his death ten
years ago and had taken an instant liking to him. He'd been a
wonderful man, wise and gentle like his son.

She clutched the packet to her heart while a giddy surge of hope
raced through her. She had to see David Max as soon as possible.
After confessing her true identity, she'd throw herself on his mercy,
beg for his help. Maybe he'd figure a way to get her back to her own
time. Feeling almost euphoric, she began to read his letters, devour-
ing the neat script.

By the time she finished, her elation had disappeared. This David
Max was not the man she knew. This David Max was a virile
thirty-nine-year-old with an infant son. He would have no memory

of meeting a writer named Jade Howard, any more than he would know that his little boy would grow up to be a famous literary agent.

Duncan had been riding for an hour, thinking about his lunch with Megan. He had enjoyed being with her, talking to her, listening to her, looking at her. Had a stranger walked in, he would have been convinced they were a happily married couple. God knows, Megan was trying. Could he believe what she said about wanting to start over?

She had seemed sincere.

After ten years of marriage, he thought he knew every nuance of her voice. He could usually tell when she was lying, and this time he could swear she had been telling the truth. She wanted a second chance to make their marriage work. To be perfectly honest, if she continued to act the way she had the last few days, so did he.

He reined his horse to a stop. "What do you think, Excalibur?" he asked the Arabian stallion. "Should I give Megan another chance?"

Why not? he answered himself. What did he have to lose? He turned Excalibur back toward Rancho Cielo and spurred the horse to a gallop. Half an hour later, he rode into the stable, jumped off the horse's back, unsaddled him, and, although he felt guilty about putting the horse up wet, led the stallion into his stall.

Megan wasn't in the kitchen when he walked in, although she had obviously washed their lunch dishes before leaving. He expected to find her in their bedroom, but she wasn't there either. Walking back toward the living room, he heard sounds coming from the den.

Megan was seated at his desk, going through his papers. Stock certificates, canceled checks, insurance policies, and his personal correspondence lay scattered in front of her. The hopeful feeling that had swelled within him on the ride home dissolved. Anger replaced it.

"What the hell are you doing?" he asked, walking up behind her and pulling her from the chair.

The papers in her hands spilled to the floor as he spun her around to face him.

"I was just . . ."

"Just what? Trying to figure how much money you'd get if I didn't change my mind about the divorce?"

She tried to pull away but he held her fast. She had been so disarmingly sweet an hour ago. Now he realized it had just been a ruse. The bitch. She had betrayed his trust again. Rage surged in his chest as he glared down at her.

Jade wanted to look away from the fire burning in Duncan's eyes, but his fury riveted her. She didn't dare tell him why she had been snooping through his papers, yet her continued silence seemed to heighten his wrath.

Her breath caught in her throat, her pulse pounded in her ears as he gripped her harder. She could feel the heat pouring from his body, the same heat that had been so comforting in bed last night. Now she took no solace from that warmth. She feared it, feared what it was making her feel.

Duncan was magnificent in his anger. Compelling. She knew she ought to struggle, try to free herself. But her body had stopped responding to her mind. She continued to stare into his eyes, seeing pain there—and something else. Desire. God. Her stomach tightened as she realized that he wanted her.

Her arms seemed to rise of their own volition. Her fingers tangled in his hair as she pulled his head down to hers. A wildness burst into life inside her. She heard him groan, a primal sound that sent urgent messages coursing through her blood. Then her lips met his.

Duncan pulled her against him and kissed her so hard, he knew her lips would be bruised. She had used sex as a weapon before. How like her to use it now.

He wanted to punish her, to hurt her the way she had just hurt him. Instead he found himself drowning in the sweet curves that fit his body so perfectly. Her lips parted under the pressure of his kiss, and he explored her mouth with his tongue while his eager hands explored her body with rough urgency. He gripped her buttocks, forcing the swell of her stomach against his cock.

She was so hot. He wanted to bury himself inside her, to devour every inch of her flesh—the ruby-tipped breasts, the deep well of her navel, the generous black bush that hid the honeyed depths of her cunt.

Her tongue found his, flaring his lust so that it burned even brighter than his anger. He felt her nipples harden through the cloth of his shirt and remembered the sweet ache of sucking them. She met his rising passion with a frenzied need of her own that implored, urged, taunted. Megan. Oh God. *Megan.*

Suddenly, without even realizing he was going to do it, he pushed her away. He wanted her, dammit, with a hunger that blasted his bones. But he'd see himself in hell before he made love to her again. An hour of pleasure wasn't worth a lifetime of misery and regret.

Jade was so weak with desire, she wasn't sure she could stand without Duncan's arms around her. She clenched her hands and locked her knees to keep from swaying, then opened her eyes wide to gaze at the man she wanted more than she had ever wanted anything or anyone. She ached to give herself to him, to yield up the secrets of her body and her soul.

Now she saw rejection plainly written on his face. She had seen that look on a man's face before, the day Paul broke their engagement. Seeing it again made her want to weep, to scream out her anguish. She wanted to fly at Duncan and rake her nails across his face, to draw blood to match the hemorrhaging wounds he'd inflicted on her soul.

But she wouldn't give him the satisfaction. Instead, she stiffened her spine and walked out of the den without a backward glance. She would have liked to keep right on walking straight out of the house, up the drive, out of Duncan Carlisle's life. But she didn't have that option.

She had never been more aroused by a man. The realization that he didn't want her, could barely stand to touch her, made her sick. Where were her pride and independence now? Trampled under his feet, that's where. Although she had never been much of a drinker, she would have gladly gotten blind drunk. She didn't have that option either.

It took all her courage, all her considerable willpower to force herself to do what she had to do. She returned to the quiet of the master bedroom and, with a calculation born of desperation, began cataloguing what she'd learned so far.

Duncan Carlisle was successful, wealthy, a gifted artist who would go down in history as the finest painter of his era. In addition he was handsome, and she now knew that, despite the coldness he often displayed with her, he was a passionate lover when he wanted to be. But she would see him in hell before she let him touch her again.

The only thing she knew about Megan was that she had a passion for clothes. It wasn't enough—not by a damn sight. Jade sat down at Megan's dressing table and looked at herself in the mirror, comparing her reflection to the woman in the photographs.

She saw the differences so clearly. Why didn't Duncan? And what had happened to Megan? Had she too passed through the door to time? Was Aurora the key? Was it the dress? Or was it some unforeseen combination of circumstances that might never happen again?

She knew nothing about time-travel theories, except that it was a popular topic in science-fiction novels. Perhaps serious books had been written about the possibility, though. Perhaps in the Santa Fe library . . . No. She rejected the idea. From what she recalled, Einstein had just developed his space-time theory. A local library wasn't going to be any help.

Her shoulders sagged. She sighed heavily. She was stuck here, trapped in another woman's life, sleeping with her husband. And she had to face it. Part of her wanted to stay.

She opened the top drawer of the dressing table. Megan's cosmetics filled it, and she began applying them, as if she could absorb the other woman's personality through her pores. When she finished, she studied herself in the mirror again. That was better. The makeup did make her look more like Megan. But what good would that do unless she could think and act like her as well?

She simply had no choice. She would have to tell Duncan the truth tonight. Grimacing at the possible consequences, she idly opened the bottom drawer where Megan kept her jewels. Dazzled by the array, she picked up the velvet-lined tray and put it on her lap. She was about to shut the drawer when she realized the tray had covered a series of slender leather-bound books. Bending down for a closer look, she saw each one was stamped with a year, beginning with 1919 and ending with 1929. They had to be Megan's diaries.

Bingo, she exulted, and picked up the first volume.

Dulce sat in the dark, watching the lights blink out in the Carlisles' bedroom. She'd been so sure Señor Duncan would realize the *bruja* wasn't his wife. But men were such fools. They saw only what they wanted to see. It was up to her, Dulce Katerina Marino y Ortiz, to protect them all. Thanks be to the Savior and the Blessed Virgin, she felt more than ready.

Her family had a long history of dealing with witchcraft, stretching back to the seventeenth century. It was said that her great-great-great-grandfather, Don José Patricio Marino, had been turned into a woman by the *bruja* Marcelina. He had triumphed, though, turning Marcelina's evil against her. Marcelina had died before her time while Don José lived to a ripe old age, siring many children along the way.

As recently as 1909, her cousins, the Quintanas who lived in El Llano just south of Taos, had been plagued by a supernatural assault on their home. Dulce still had vivid memories of her mother hurrying to their aid after the police and the parish priest had been unable to do anything. Her mother, the most famous *curandera* in northern New Mexico, had finally exorcised the powerful evil spirit.

Now it was Dulce's turn. Sitting in the dark, she began to plan. Before she was done, this *bruja* would regret the day she dared come to Rancho Cielo.

CHAPTER 9

Santa Fe
May 19, 1989

Megan Carlisle felt terrible. She had a crick in her neck, her mouth tasted dreadful from all the cigarettes she'd smoked, and a nagging pain pulsated behind her eyes. Putting a hand to her forehead, she eased into a sitting position. Sunlight seeped through the parlor drapes, and sound still poured from the magic box with the moving pictures. She'd fallen asleep on the sofa at eleven, mesmerized by its ever-changing images. As far as she knew, the thing hadn't shut up all night.

Getting to her feet, she stretched, feeling the unaccustomed pull of a pajama top across her shoulders. She picked up the champagne bottle from the coffee table and, seeing that it still held a couple of inches of liquid, put it to her lips.

The golden fluid cooled her parched throat. Imagine being able to order the best Rothschild from room service! Laughter welled in her throat, the chuckles crescendoing to a series of hysterical guffaws that left her gasping.

What was it Duncan always said about being careful what you wished for, because your wish might come true? Two days and sixty years ago—another peal of laughter broke from her—she'd been longing for a change, for freedom.

Duncan had been right, damn him. She had what she wanted—and it terrified her.

A few days ago she had been able to think of herself as a true sophisticate, a well-traveled woman of the world, at home in half a dozen foreign cities. She and Duncan had sailed to Europe three times. Their last crossing had been on the fabled *Ile de France*, so she could visit the great couture houses in Paris before they went on to Rome, Venice, Nice, Monte Carlo. But she had never been anywhere without a man to smooth the way. She had never even walked into a restaurant alone.

Now she had taken the ultimate trip—a journey beyond imagination or understanding—all by herself.

She didn't know how it had happened or why, and at this moment she didn't care. All she knew was that two nights ago she had been in this very suite, dressing for another evening with Malcolm and Hilary. She had taken the Molyneux from the closet, pulled it over her head, and the next thing she'd known, she was on the floor.

By the time the stomach-upside-down sensations had passed, she'd been genuinely frightened and wanting her husband. "Dammit, Duncan," she had muttered, lurching to her feet, "where the hell are you?"

She vividly recalled reeling into the empty parlor, opening the door, and peering down the hall, expecting to see Duncan heading back to their suite. But she didn't see anything she expected. The hall was empty. And there was something peculiar about it, something about the light fixtures, or the color of the paint . . .

Before she could sort it out, she heard a masculine voice coming from the suite. How in the world had Duncan managed to get past her? she wondered, spinning around to confront him. Only it wasn't Duncan. In fact, the voice didn't come from a living, breathing human being. It came from what she instantly thought of as the "magic box." A man with wavy hair and dimples was looking right at her, talking about something called aids.

"Well, what have we here?" she said, boldly walking up to the box. The man's voice reverberated through the parlor, a parlor that looked even more peculiar than the hall. What in the world was going on? How had the magic box and all the other strange things gotten into the room? And where in the world had they come from?

The box had been just the first of a long series of surprises, however. When she went downstairs to La Plazuela, thinking she'd misunderstood Duncan and they were supposed to meet in the restaurant, she realized that this La Fonda wasn't the one she knew so well. The lobby had changed even more than her suite. She marched up to a hotel employee who was stationed, oddly enough, behind a massive desk in the part of the lobby where the band played four nights a week.

"What's going on here?" she demanded. "Where is everybody?"

"Are you looking for someone in particular?" the desk clerk asked deferentially.

"Duncan Carlisle."

The man stared at her as if she had lost her mind. "You can see his paintings at the Museum of Fine Art tomorrow morning. It opens at ten."

Of course she didn't believe him. Duncan never exhibited in the new museum. He said that letting a museum be run by the artists who showed their work there was akin to letting the lunatics run the asylum.

Duncan. Dear God. Megan sat down on the sofa, sighed, and took another sip of champagne. She still hadn't adjusted to the idea that she would never see him again. She couldn't help wishing . . .

Oh hell. She'd better not do any more wishing! Duncan wasn't going to come to her rescue. She was on her own for the first time in her life.

A shiver ran up her spine as she contemplated the future. She was scared silly and excited at the same time. A whole new world was just outside the window. She couldn't go on hiding in the suite, ordering from room service, pretending nothing had changed. Everything had changed, and the sooner she learned to deal with it, the better.

But how?

She chewed on her lower lip while the glimmerings of a plan took shape in her mind. She stood up abruptly and gazed around the parlor, searching for the purse she'd found that first night, the bag that belonged to a woman named Jade Howard. It was on the desk next to that funny typewriter that didn't use any paper. She retrieved it and upended it onto the coffee table.

A bulging wallet, a small leather book with a matching portfolio, a key chain, some pale pink tissue, half a dozen pens of a type Megan had never seen before, a lipstick, and a compact tumbled out. She fingered the tissue, marveling at its color and softness, then she opened the compact.

It contained what appeared to be some sort of powder, pressed into a hard cake. Surveying herself in the mirror, she dabbed the puff into the powder and patted it on her nose. It spread smoothly, and the shade couldn't have been a better match for her skin.

Megan's beauty had always been a source of comfort for her, but never more so than this morning. She continued to stare at herself, spellbound, congratulating herself on the fact that her nerve-shattering journey hadn't harmed her appearance. Although she knew it was May 19, 1989, she didn't look a day older than she had in 1929.

When she had looked her fill she closed the compact and opened the little portfolio. It was a checkbook with Jade Howard's name and a Malibu Beach, California, address printed on the upper left corner. Was Malibu near Hollywood? she wondered, feeling a frisson of excitement. She flipped the checkbook to the last entry, and her eyes widened as she read it—$25,279. That was a hell of a lot of money—enough to buy several houses! The realization that Jade Howard was rich blunted the sharp edge of Megan's fear. At least she wouldn't have to worry about money.

She picked up the key ring and saw that one of the keys had the word *Yale* printed across the top. It must be a house key, she thought, relieved to find something familiar. Two other keys had the words *Mercedes-Benz* stamped on them. Megan pursed her lips. She had heard of a German automaker named Benz. Malcolm had even mentioned something about buying a Benz.

A burst of pure pleasure brought a smile to her face. Jade must own a Benz. Driving might daunt other women, but Megan adored it. One of her few pleasures at Rancho Cielo had been getting behind the wheel of her Packard convertible and motoring around

the countryside. Mastering a complex machine made her feel confident and worthwhile.

She quickly thumbed through the little leather book. It appeared
to be a daily diary with a section for names, addresses, and phone
numbers at the back. Aside from an appointment on May thirteenth with a Harrison Denby, Jade Howard apparently didn't have
much to fill her time. Megan felt a sudden kinship with the other
woman. Had Jade been unhappy too?

She had saved the wallet for last. Picking it up, she ignored a
twinge of guilt at going through the other woman's possessions.
Unless her intuition was completely wrong, Jade Howard was sure
as hell going through hers.

Megan counted the cash first—$2,032, enough to make whoopee
for a very long time. The wallet also had a special compartment
that held a series of thick cards. They all bore Jade Howard's name,
but one had the words *American Express* on it, another read *Visa,*
and a third, *MasterCard.* Megan slipped them out and turned them
over, trying to figure out their use.

Last she took out the California driver's license with a woman's
picture printed right on it. That must be Jade Howard, she thought.
Her pulse quickened as she stared at the picture. The woman
looked enough like her to be her twin—her homely twin, she
amended. They had the same coloring, the same features. The only
appreciable differences were in age, height, and weight. Jade was
three years older, an inch taller and—considering the fact that she
was a few pounds lighter—obviously less curvaceous. But with the
right hairdo and makeup, it wouldn't be easy to tell them apart.

Was that why their fates seemed twined?

Megan put her hands to her head and massaged her brow. She
had a vicious headache. Perhaps it was from the champagne she'd
consumed last night; perhaps it was due to the strange circumstances. Whatever the reason, trying to explain the unexplainable
made her feel worse.

Duncan was always accusing her of acting without thinking. Trying to think things through wouldn't do her one damn bit of good
in this situation, though. Courage. That's what she needed now.
The daring to seize the moment and live it to the fullest.

She put everything back in the purse, then walked to the window and opened it wide. Three stories below, a steady parade of cars circled the plaza—gorgeous cars, streamlined automobiles with deep-throbbing engines. And Jade Howard owned one.

Megan left the window and walked into the bedroom. Now she knew how to begin her new life. She was going to drive the Benz.

In his youth, Ira Max had been a pleasant-looking man with a thick head of strawberry-blond hair, a freckled face adorned with a pair of twinkling blue eyes, and a guileless smile. His most memorable trait had been an aura of restless energy. Today, at the age of sixty-one, his hair was thin and gray. The color of his eyes had faded like a rose past full bloom, and he rarely smiled. But his aura of energy remained.

Ira had gone through his entire life on fast forward, cramming into each day what other people needed two to accomplish. Widowed and with three grown sons scattered across the country, he could have been—perhaps should have been—a lonely man. He had no time for loneliness, though. He was accessible to his employees and his clients twenty-four hours a day.

That morning he'd awakened at five-thirty, showered, and put on a sweat suit. After a Spartan breakfast, he settled in a deep wing chair in his living room and began reading a manuscript by an author he was considering representing. He finished the book at nine-thirty, made a few notes, and dressed for the business day.

His personal secretary, Elinor Mathews, was at her desk, a phone tucked between her head and shoulder, when he walked into his office, located on the ground floor of his Manhattan townhouse. "Harrison Denby's on the line from California," she said. "Will you take the call?"

Ira nodded. A few seconds later, after settling at his desk, he picked up the telephone. "Ira Max here. What can I do for you, Mr. Denby?"

"Call me Harry," Denby replied with an easy laugh. "As far as I'm concerned, my dad is Mr. Denby."

"All right then—Harry. And you must call me Ira. I presume you're phoning about your meeting with Jade Howard. How did it go?"

"It didn't."

Ira's bushy eyebrows lifted. "I'm surprised. Jade Howard is professional, cooperative, and hardworking. But more to the point, she was thrilled when I told her you were interested in her book."

"It wasn't her fault," Denby said. "In fact, we never met. I had a family emergency and I neglected to tell my secretary to cancel my appointment with Miss Howard. I'm afraid I really blew it. I've left half a dozen messages on her home phone, but she hasn't replied to any of them. I was hoping you'd call her, explain the situation, and ask her to get in touch with me."

"I'd be happy to," Ira said, smiling. If only all the problems he encountered in the course of his business day were so easily solved.

Giving Jade the bad news about *Power Play* had been one of the most painful things he'd had to do in his forty years as a literary agent. In many ways she was the daughter he'd always wanted, bright, gifted, independent, and very determined. She held a special place in his heart. It had been that way from the first time they met. Although they never talked about it, he knew she felt it too, a bond so strong it almost seemed a blood tie. Even his father, who had died shortly after Ira had become Jade's agent, had taken to Jade immediately, telling Ira he'd signed on a real winner this time.

Still smiling, he dialed her number. She didn't answer, though, nor did she answer the half a dozen other times he tried her number throughout the day. As he left his office late that afternoon, Jade was very much on his mind. Worry gnawed at him. She always checked her messages when she was away, and it wasn't like her not to return his call.

On her way to La Fonda's lobby, Megan caught a glimpse of herself in a mirror. Jade Howard had terrible taste, she thought, frowning at her reflection. The ugly denim trousers that dominated Jade's wardrobe might be the dernier cri for a bricklayer, but Megan hated them. She had already dropped the hideous white shoes with the thick soles and the word *Nike* written on them in the trash.

"I feel like such a fool," she said, walking up to the desk clerk and giving him the dazzling smile she used when she wanted to distract a man, "but I had a little too much to drink last night and I don't remember where I parked my car."

The clerk returned her smile. "I understand completely. If you'll tell me what sort of car it is, I'll ring our lot and see if it's there."

"It's a Benz," she replied.

"Do you mean a Mercedes?"

"Uh-huh."

"What model and year?"

When in doubt, Megan thought, flirt. She batted her lashes at him, her mind racing. "I know you'll think I'm a complete idiot, but I don't know. You see, the car is a gift, a brand-new gift."

He shrugged. "I'd like to help, but you haven't given me much to go on." Suddenly, his expression brightened. "Have you checked your purse for your parking stub?"

"I guess I forgot." She gave him another smile and rummaged through Jade's purse. An oblong piece of thick paper with a series of numbers stamped on it was tangled in the tissue. "Is this it?" she asked, holding it out.

The desk clerk nodded. "Just give it to the attendant in the garage and he'll get your car for you."

Not daring to ask him directions to La Fonda's garage, Megan left the hotel by the nearest exit and found herself on Saint Francis. Except for the cars and the heavy pedestrian traffic, Santa Fe hadn't changed much since her day. *Since her day.* The phrase reverberated through her mind as she looked around with avid curiosity.

In 1929, La Fonda had a parking lot at the end of the block, opposite the cathedral. Megan saw a multistoried garage in its place. She headed toward it, praying one of the cars inside was Jade's.

Five minutes later an obliging attendant delivered a dream of a car to the exit and handed her the keys. Megan opened Jade's wallet, fished out a dime, and gave it to him.

"Are you sure you can spare it?" he asked.

She was too busy taking in the car to pay attention to his sarcastic tone. The Benz was small compared to her Packard, and incredibly sleek. She opened the door and climbed in, smelling the rich scent of leather. The attendant had left the engine running. This was some sweet machine, she thought, settling her right foot on the gas pedal. The Benz purred as she fed it more fuel.

Megan gazed down at the dashboard, hunting for the magneto

and spark. The dials and switches she expected to find had been replaced by a different series of instruments, the dash inlaid with high-gloss wood. Looking at the floorboards, she realized this car had no clutch, and the long-shafted gearshift had been replaced by a short rod set knee high, in a rubber skirt. How the hell was she supposed to change gears? When she'd decided to go for a spin, she hadn't given a thought to how much automobiles might have changed.

She reached for the stick protruding from the steering wheel. A quick tug made a light flicker on the dash. Turning a knob caused the windshield wipers to sweep across the windscreen. Twisting the knob even harder produced a sudden squirt of water that the wipers efficiently pushed aside.

Megan laughed with delight. Emboldened, she reached for the stubby rod to the right of her seat and pulled it. The Benz leaped forward like a Thoroughbred out of the starting gate—and Megan's heart jumped with it. The automobile burst from the garage and sped across the sidewalk so quickly, she didn't have time to react. She saw the building across the street looming in her path and spun the wheel hard to avoid imminent catastrophe.

The Benz responded to the touch of her hand as easily as an autumn leaf responds to a sudden breeze. The car swerved 180 degrees, and to her horror, Megan found herself headed back toward the parking garage. Her hand reached for the shift that wasn't there, her left foot for the clutch.

An agile pedestrian leaped out of her way as the Benz mounted the sidewalk. The garage attendant looked up from his place in a glass-enclosed booth, saw the oncoming car, and bolted. In desperation, Megan tramped on the brake pedal. With a screech of protesting tires, the Benz slammed to a halt just inches from the booth, and the motor stalled. Megan trembled from head to toe, paralyzed by the close call.

Suddenly the driver's door jerked open, and the attendant was looking down at her. "What the fuck do you think you're doing, lady? You damn near killed me."

Megan flushed with embarrassment. The one thing she had always prided herself on, the only thing she could do better than most men, was drive. Yet here she was getting screamed at by an infuriated stranger who said a word no gentleman ever employed in front of a lady, and all because she couldn't figure out how to drive the Benz.

Using the one weapon that, in her experience, reduced the most hardened man to utter incompetence, she lowered her head to her hands and began to weep. She didn't have to pretend, because she was genuinely upset.

A few seconds passed, then she heard the attendant's voice, lower this time and husky with concern. "I'm sorry, lady. Are you all right?"

Megan gazed at him through the blur of her tears. He was a young man, in his early twenties, and very cute, with expressive brown eyes and flashing white teeth. "I think so," she said. "I didn't mean to scare you like that, but this is my boyfriend's car and I've never driven it before. He'd skin me alive if he knew what happened."

The attendant's tone became conspiratorial. "To tell you the truth, my boss would have my balls if he knew how I talked to you."

"I'll make you a deal." Megan fished in Jade's purse for one of those wonderfully soft tissues and dabbed her eyes. "I won't say a word to your boss. But I want you to do me a favor in return. I want you to show me how to drive this car."

The young man nodded, his eyes as warm and eager as a puppy's.

Megan sighed with relief. A hell of a lot had changed since 1929. But, thank heaven, men hadn't.

CHAPTER 10

Rancho Cielo
June 12, 1929

Duncan stood outside his studio, looking out across the treetops. Although stars still shone in the west, the light of the rising sun blushed the eastern horizon. He had always enjoyed early morning, when the rest of the day lay ahead like an unopened gift. However, he now had a new and urgent reason for hurrying from the bed he and Megan shared.

Megan. Why did all roads, all thoughts lead him back to her? He shrugged, unconsciously expressing his confusion. He had expected so much more of their marriage; love, sex, friendship, the sharing of a common ground, a profound understanding derived from breathing the same air, eating the same food, sleeping in the same bed. He had dreamed of a sweet symbiosis that would make life apart unendurable.

The first time he saw Megan, he had experienced a sort of déjà vu, a feeling that here at last was the woman he had unconsciously been seeking all his life. He couldn't have been more mistaken. Sex was the only thing he and Megan ever shared.

He had no right to blame her for being true to who and what she was. The fault had been his for completely misreading her character, for wishfully imbuing her with traits she would never possess.

In time he'd realized the magnitude of his mistake. The passion that had swept him off his feet ten years earlier had proven to be as fragile as a butterfly's wings. So why had it returned, with the power of a force 10 gale?

How had Shakespeare described Cleopatra—as a woman of infinite variety? These days, that description seemed tailor-made for Megan. She was metamorphosing in front of his eyes. She had never cared for animals, yet she had turned Blackjack into her devoted slave. And last week she had come across a baby sparrow that had fallen out of the nest. With the blind persistence of a mother bird, she had run all over Rancho Cielo searching for insects to feed the fledgling. By the third day Duncan had been a more-than-willing participant in what seemed a hopeless project, keeping a weather eye out for flies and moths to add to the larder.

He would never forget the look on her face when, just yesterday, she had released the bird and watched it fly away. Nor would he forget the way it had made him feel. Something long dormant in his heart had threatened to break free. Lust had been the common currency of their marriage, never tenderness. Yet that was what he had experienced.

It terrified him.

He fought the emotion, using their unhappy history as a barricade. He could not, must not give in to the feelings she so easily stirred in him these days. Logic told him her behavior was a sham. Yet sometimes when she didn't realize he was watching, he saw the saddest expression in her eyes, something so much deeper than her previous dissatisfaction that it shook him to the core. He found himself wanting to take her in his arms and comfort her the way he would comfort a lost child. And this new bent of hers for writing—sitting at her typewriter for hours at a time—simply added to the deepening mystery.

For ten years, Megan hadn't devoted her energy to anything more serious than adding to her wardrobe. Where had she found the inner fortitude to tackle a new career? Was she doing it to impress Malcolm?

Duncan shook his head. Megan was woman enough to know she

didn't need to go to extreme measures where Malcolm was concerned. Besides, she wouldn't spend hours locked away in a room to impress God himself. No. She was changing, really changing.

The hell of it was he had never wanted her more. Sharing a bed every night, feeling her warmth, hearing the small sounds she made in her sleep, smelling her scent—a lighter, fresher aroma that made him think she must be using a new perfume—kept his passion at the boil. So he rose early and worked late, took long solitary walks and even longer cold showers in a vain attempt to quiet his body's clamoring need.

It hadn't worked. It wasn't working. At night, he longed for her, dreamed of her. During the day, he encouraged her to spend time with Malcolm. Was it masochism, or self-preservation?

Angrily, he turned away from the beauty of the new day. He couldn't go on like this. He needed advice and counsel, needed to be told that what he was doing was inevitable and morally correct. And he knew just the man to confide in. Ralph Braithwaite was more than an old and cherished friend. He was a crackerjack attorney, and he knew how to keep a confidence.

Filled with purpose, Duncan strode into his studio, picked up the phone, and asked the operator to connect him with a Manhattan number. Ralph came on the line a few minutes later.

"You're up early," he said cheerfully. "I just got to the office. It must barely be daybreak in Santa Fe."

"This couldn't wait."

"So this isn't a hello buddy, how-the-hell-are-you social call?"

"I'm afraid not." Duncan wasted no time getting to the point. "I need to talk to you about getting a divorce."

Ralph was instantly all business. "Have you discussed it with Megan?"

"Yes. She won't even consider it."

"That's going to make it very difficult." Ralph's voice had taken on the sonorous timbre he reserved for clients.

"I know. That's why I telephoned. I have an idea that might end the stalemate." Duncan swiftly described his plan.

When he finished, Ralph asked, "Are you sure you know what you're doing?"

"Absolutely."

"Let me get this straight. You're encouraging Megan to spend more time with Malcolm Ashford in the hope they'll have an affair?"

"I wouldn't put it quite that way." Despite the morning chill, sweat beaded on Duncan's forehead.

"Do you plan to name Ashford as the corespondent in your divorce?"

"I don't think Megan will give me a divorce at all unless she has another man waiting in the wings. Once she does, I'm hoping she will be the one to file."

"If you'll forgive the cliché, I'd like to point out that you're playing with fire. Frankly, I've read the man's novels and I wouldn't want him hanging around my wife."

"You've missed the point. We don't have a marriage anymore."

Duncan could almost hear Ralph's mind clicking away. Finally he said, "What the hell . . . it might work. But if you insist on going through with it, for God's sake don't have sex with Megan. In a court of law it's called condonation. In simple English it means you're willing to go on with your marriage no matter what she does with Ashford. Megan could use it to hold up a divorce forever."

Duncan's mouth filled with cotton. He felt as if iron bands were constricting his chest. Three weeks earlier he had come damnably close to making love to Megan. An urgent heat pooled in his groin as he remembered the way she had kissed him, pressed her body against him. Could he really give that up?

His body said no.

But Ralph had given him no choice. He didn't dare touch Megan again.

Hilary Delano was never at her best in the morning. Left to her own devices, she would have slept until ten. But Malcolm insisted on rising early when he was working on a book. Now she sat alone in his dining room, uncomfortably aware that she looked dreadful in last night's dress, her makeup smudged beyond the repair of the powder and rouge in her purse.

She should never have spent the night. But, dammit, she had needed the reassurance of Malcolm's physical presence. He had been drifting away from her emotionally for weeks. She sensed a fundamental shift in their relationship that, although it had yet to be verbalized, was as real as the chair she sat in. Why now? she thought angrily. She had done everything, in and out of bed, to bind Malcolm to her side. What—or who—-was coming between them?

She stared blindly around the lovely room while the question echoed through her mind. Sunshine poured through the windows, sparking prisms of light from the Baccarat chandelier. The table and chairs were Chippendale. A heavy pair of Sheffield candelabras sat on a satinwood Atherton sideboard. The fireplace mantel had come from a château in the Loire Valley. Apricot wallpaper and emerald upholstery repeated the colors of the Savonnerie carpet on the floor.

She had been with Malcolm when he bought the furnishings. What golden days they had shared, playing vagabond across three continents, enjoying an endless variety of sexual romps in half a dozen languages. It couldn't end. She wouldn't let it. She didn't love Malcolm, but she was addicted to him and the lifestyle he made possible.

His arrival brought an abrupt end to her unhappy musing. "Sorry to keep you waiting. I asked cook to prepare eggs Benedict."

He sat down across from her, opened the morning paper, and hid behind it, as if having ordered her favorite breakfast fulfilled all his obligations as her host.

Ten minutes later the aroma of hollandaise sauce and Canadian bacon wafted through the room, as Malcolm's houseman carried in two plates of eggs Benedict. Hilary ignored the food. Worry had spoiled her appetite. Pushing her untouched plate aside, she inserted a cigarette into her long ivory holder.

"I see you're watching your figure," Malcolm said, finally setting the paper down.

"If I don't, no one else will." She didn't bother to curb her waspish tone.

"Are you finished, Miss Delano?" Raoul asked from behind her. There wasn't a hint of past sexual intimacy in the houseman's demeanor or tone as he waited for her response.

"You can take my plate," she said with an uninterested shrug.

"You may go now, Raoul," Malcolm said. "I'll ring for you when we're finished."

As the houseman's footsteps receded, Malcolm concentrated on his own food, eating with obvious relish.

"My, you do have an appetite this morning," Hilary said sourly. There was a bloom on his cheeks, a joie de vivre in his eyes that she hadn't seen for a long time. And she felt damn sure it had nothing to do with her.

"I'm famished," he said. "You gave me quite a workout last night."

She studied him from under her lashes, wondering if he really believed what he said. Since when did he think a single orgasm constituted a "workout"? But she knew better than to tell Malcolm —or any man—that his performance in bed had been less than memorable. Lately his lovemaking lacked the imagination, the originality, the staying power that had made him such an exciting, erotic playmate in the past.

She didn't realize she was staring until he said, "Do I have my tie on crooked—or did I forget to close my fly?"

She shook her head, sending her platinum bob flying.

"Then why are you looking at me like a specimen under a microscope?"

"I was just wondering what's going on in that head of yours."

"You'd be bored if you knew."

"Malcolm, darling, I'm not one of your casual little conquests. Don't toy with me."

He pushed his plate away, sat back, and crossed his arms. "As usual, you're very perceptive."

Here it comes, she thought, the old this-hurts-me-more-than-it-hurts-you dumperoo.

"I did want to discuss something before you go home," he continued.

Her stomach churned. Thank God she hadn't eaten. It wouldn't do to spew eggs Benedict on the table.

"How would you like to have Raoul work for you?"

She almost cried with relief. The feeling evaporated as quickly as dew on a hot summer morning, though. She leaned forward, her emotional antennae on full alert. Was this Malcolm's way of writing finis to their occasional ménage à trois? "But you've always said Raoul was an indispensable part of your household."

"I've been selfish. We found Raoul together, and it isn't fair of me to continue monopolizing his services."

She bit her lip. If Malcolm got rid of Raoul, how soon would she follow?

Forcing herself to smile, she said, "You're in a very generous mood this morning, darling. I can't help wondering why you suddenly want Raoul off your payroll."

"Altruism, dear girl. First, the shop keeps you busy. Second, you've had nothing but problems with your help. Third, Raoul is more than capable of running your house for you."

Although it couldn't be that simple, she decided to play along for the moment. "What can I say except yes—and thank you. Have you talked to him about the new arrangement?"

Malcolm grinned. "Raoul liked the idea. Especially when I said you'd give him a raise."

"You naughty boy." Hilary laughed, pretending delight although she was deeply disturbed. The familiar terrain of her life was eroding, and she didn't like it one bit.

"Would you like me to ring for Raoul so you can conclude the arrangement now?"

She took her time lighting another cigarette. "What's the rush?"

"I don't mean to hurry you," Malcolm said, getting to his feet, "but I've got a busy day."

"Are you doing anything special?" Refusing to follow his lead, she stayed in her chair.

"The usual. Catching up on my correspondence, making a few calls, writing." He paused before adding, as if it were an afterthought, "Oh, and I'm lunching at Rancho Cielo. Megan and I are going riding afterward."

Hilary's hands clenched under the table. "That's the second time in as many weeks, isn't it?"

"I suppose so—but who's counting."

I am, she thought, digging her nails into her palms. In the past, she and Malcolm had visited Rancho Cielo together, and not very damn often at that. "Give Megan my best when you see her—and

Duncan too. I haven't talked to either one since our little jaunt to San Ildefonso. Frankly, I don't think it's very considerate of Megan to monopolize your time when you're in the middle of a book."

Malcolm frowned. "She isn't doing anything of the kind. Don't try and read between the lines on this one. It's just a lunch."

"Of course, darling. It's just a lunch." Hilary put out her cigarette and stretched languidly, pretending indifference. She had no intention of turning a deaf ear and blind eye to the situation, however. She was nobody's fool—certainly not Megan's.

Jade rolled the letter out of the typewriter, checked it one last time for errors, and boldly signed *Jade Howard* at the bottom.

Realizing her mistake, she angrily tore the query letter to shreds and tossed it in the trash can by her desk. Would she ever get used to Megan Carlisle's name—or her life?

Frustration propelled her from her chair. The guest room had generous proportions, but her long-legged stride quickly brought her to the doorway. She stopped in her tracks and rested her forehead on the frame. She had no place to run.

Muttering imprecations under her breath, she returned to the desk, shook a cigarette from a crumpled pack, and began marching across the floor. Back and forth, back and forth she quick-stepped, her mind in turmoil, her emotions ragged.

It was all too much to deal with—the abrupt, incomprehensible journey through time; the need to pose as another woman; the frightening and powerful attraction she felt toward that woman's husband.

She still had no better ideas of how to return to her own time than she'd had a month ago. Nearly every day she stared at the Molyneux, hoping that this time it would reveal its secrets. It never did. She'd asked both Dulce and Malcolm if they knew a clothing shop called Aurora's Borealis, pretending that she'd shopped there once but couldn't remember in what city. Neither had ever heard of it. She had even found a copy of H. G. Wells's *The Time Machine* in Duncan's den one day, and read it avidly. It was only a novel, though, and of course provided no answers.

All she knew for certain was that she had been unhappy in 1989, wishing she were someone else, and Megan had been unhappy in 1929, possibly wishing the same thing. Chance had led them to the same place, sixty years apart. Certainly the Molyneux had played a role, but there had to be more involved, an unknown power that was strong enough to pierce the warp of time.

As for her imposture, no one seemed suspicious of her. Dulce did avoid contact with her as much as possible, and watched her closely whenever they were in the same room. From what she knew of Megan, though, Jade doubted that Megan and the housekeeper had ever gotten along.

As for Duncan . . . Dear God, what was she going to do about him?

Although she had made a conscious effort to forget what had happened in his den three weeks earlier, she couldn't shut it out of her mind. She had never played the aggressor with a man before, but she was the one who had initiated that kiss. She had wanted Duncan then and, despite his rejection, she wanted him now.

In the past she had been able to keep a tight rein on her emotions. What had happened to her self-control? She was helplessly spinning into a new orbit where feelings far outweighed logic.

She had vowed not to let Duncan touch her again and yet that morning she had almost wept for joy when she woke to feel his body cozily spooned against hers. She had reveled in that sweet contact, drawing a universe of previously unknown and unexplored pleasure from his unconscious intimacy. Then, feeling him stir and awaken, she had crept from their bed before he had the opportunity to reject her again. Locking herself in the bathroom, she had turned on the tap to drown out the sound of her tears.

Following her usual pattern, for these past weeks she had sought refuge from the pain in her life in words. Writing was the only thing that kept her sane. And now she had a firm grasp on the quality her books had increasingly lacked.

Emotion. She could pen volumes about emotion. If she ever got home, she would be able to write one hell of a book.

But all the emotion in the world wouldn't help her draft a convincing query letter, she reminded herself. It felt strange to be starting her career all over again. Back in her own time she would have been able to telephone almost any magazine editor in New York and pitch an idea for an article on the phone. But no one in 1929 had ever heard of her.

How she missed her computer, missed being able to correct a mistake with the touch of a key. She had typed the query to *Harper's Magazine* three times that morning before getting it letter perfect. Signing her own name instead of Megan's had been the last straw. She'd never had trouble concentrating on her work before, yet now her mind skittered in a thousand directions. She puffed furiously on her cigarette, struggling to keep her desolation at bay. What did one letter matter when her entire life . . .

She refused to complete the sentence. Instead, she returned to her desk, sat down, and resolutely put a new sheet of paper in the Remington. Face it. She had to launch a new writing career because it looked like she'd never get back to the old one.

She began typing and immediately made another mistake. Frustration bubbled up in her throat and burst from her lips. "Fuuuuck!" she shouted so loudly, the very walls reverberated.

Voicing an expletive didn't begin to drain the reservoir of tension inside her. She looked around the room, then her gaze settled on the typewriter. She loathed the damn thing, hated it for what it represented. Before she knew what she was doing, she picked it up and heaved it across the room.

Duncan was in the kitchen, pouring a cup of coffee, when he heard Megan's voice. No matter how angry she had been in the past, she seldom swore. Now the word *fuck*, a word he had never heard her use before, ululated through the house like the howl of wounded wolf.

Something must be wrong, terribly wrong.

He put his cup down so hastily, coffee spilled from it, and raced up the stairs, taking them two at a time. Before he reached the second floor he heard a loud crash. Good God. What if someone had broken in and found Megan all alone?

He burst into her office. She was standing behind her desk, staring blankly into space. Her new typewriter lay on the floor ten feet away. Apparently the changed woman he had just been agonizing over, had had one of her all-too-familiar tantrums. He was unreasonably angry at finding her safe.

"What the hell is the matter with you now?" he shouted.

She seemed to have been unaware of his arrival and started at the sound of his voice. Suddenly, her shoulders began to heave. "I can't tell you what's wrong," she wailed. Tears poured down her face, but she made no effort to staunch them.

Megan was a past master at false weeping, pretending to cry to get her way. But this was no pretense, Duncan realized. He had never seen or heard her so heartbroken. Ten seconds earlier he would have gladly throttled her. Now he strode across the floor and pulled her into his arms.

His shirt quickly grew damp with her tears. "For God's sake, Megan, can't you talk to me?"

"I can't. I want to . . . but I can't." Her sobs were so harsh, she could barely speak, but she didn't have to. He knew what troubled her. Even as his body responded to the feel of hers, he knew their marriage was over. And she couldn't even talk to him about it.

Jade could have stayed in Duncan's arms all day—all night, too, for that matter. But she didn't dare. The last time he had held her, she had given in to passion. She mustn't let that happen again. Only she couldn't make herself leave the sweet succor of his embrace. The gentle sensation of comfort was every bit as seductive as passion. The constriction in her throat eased as she felt the pounding of her heart match the beat of his. Instead of stepping away, she pressed closer. The last time she'd wept in a man's arms, it had been her father who held her. Now she sobbed for that love which had been lost, as well as the love which could never be. She cried out her hurt, her fear, her loneliness into the solid wall of Duncan's chest, letting him absorb some of her pain. Shared tears, she realized, could be even more intimate than shared kisses. Knowing she had no right to share anything with Duncan, she wept even harder.

When she regained control of her emotions a few minutes later, she didn't have to ask Duncan to leave. He seemed to be in an even greater hurry to get out of her sight than she was to have him gone. She listened to the sound of his retreating footsteps. When she was sure he had left the house, she lowered her head onto her arms. She didn't know how much longer she could go on.

She saw the typewriter out of the corner of her eye. It had landed on its base. Feeling guilty, she walked across the room, picked it up, and returned it to her desk. Thank heaven it didn't seem any the worse for her temper tantrum. With a final sniffle, she inserted another piece of paper and began to retype the query letter. At first the words seemed like a meaningless jumble. Although Duncan had left the room, he lingered in her mind. How could one man seem so cold, so cruel, and yet so tender and caring? And how could she deal with all the feelings he evoked, some of them so new that she, who had always prided herself on her command of language, couldn't even label them?

She stared at the typewriter, forcing herself to concentrate, to seek refuge in her professionalism. Words had been her salvation, her shield in the past. If she gave them half a chance, they would serve her again. She began typing faster, each strike of the keys helping to raise that shield. When she was done she felt infinitely better. One way or another, she told herself as she addressed and stamped the envelope, she was going to find her way through the mine field of her predicament.

An hour later, freshly bathed and dressed for riding, Jade walked into the living room to await Malcolm Ashford's arrival. Settling on one of the sofas, she wiggled her boot-shod toes, trying to make them comfortable. Megan's feet were shorter and broader than hers. Jade was aware of other differences as well, ones too slight for the eye to discern.

The differences she didn't know about were the ones that kept her up at night. Did she smell like Megan, taste like Megan? What about the size and shape of Megan's nipples, the growth pattern of her pubic hair, the depth of her navel?

Duncan had yet to comment on the fact that his wife dressed and undressed in the bathroom with the door firmly shut between them. One of these days, though, he was bound to make some scathing comment about her modesty.

How long would he be content to sleep by her side without touching her? That question sent urgent messages along her nerve paths. Her skin tingled and her nipples hardened as she imagined him holding her, crushing her lips with his own, taking what she so feared and longed to give. Oh God. What was wrong with her? Why couldn't she seem to control her feelings for this intimate stranger?

She bolted to her feet and hurried to the sideboard, where a decanter and half a dozen Waterford goblets sat on a tray. The sherry was the best amontillado, a light dry wine that would soothe her rattled nerves. She had brought it up from the wine cellar that morning, even though she knew Duncan was concerned about the dwindling supply. In fact, she had taken pleasure in the small act of defiance just the way Megan would have.

She was pouring a drink when she heard the now familiar sound of Malcolm's Bugatti. He came bounding into the room a minute later, bringing the fresh scent of the outdoors with him. "What a day for a drive," he exclaimed. "I had the Bugatti up to a hundred miles an hour."

"I wish you'd stop playing Mario Andretti," she said.

"Mario who?"

She had done it again, alluded to something from her own time. "He's an old friend in New York who always drove too fast," she extemporized. "One of these days you're going to kill yourself."

"Can this be my favorite daredevil talking? You've driven the Bugatti faster than that yourself."

"Just promise me you'll be careful," she said, thinking she would be bereft if anything happened to him. If she confided in anyone—and that was a very big *if*—it would be Malcolm. Yet could Malcolm separate his friendship with her from his obvious infatuation with Megan?

"What's this about Megan driving the Bugatti faster than you?" Duncan asked, striding into the room.

She hadn't been certain he would join them for lunch. Now her heart beat faster at the sight of him. His presence seemed to fill the room. He was more alive than any man she had ever known, yet there were times when she read death in his eyes—the death of a marriage, the death of hope.

Malcolm laughed. "I don't need to tell you how fast Megan drives, or how well."

111

"What would you say if I told you Megan hasn't taken the Pack-ard out for a spin for weeks?"

Malcolm's eyes widened. "You must be joking."

Duncan smiled grimly. "Megan's quite a changed woman these days. She hasn't gone for one of her drives since we got back from La Fonda."

Malcolm stared at her, and Jade managed an insouciant shrug. She'd been meaning to drive Megan's car, but she didn't want anyone around the first time she got behind the wheel. "I've been busy with a new project."

"A new project?" Malcolm looked from her to Duncan, and back again.

"I just finished drafting a query letter to *Harper's*," she said, "proposing an article on Maria Martinez." When both men looked dumbfounded, Jade realized she'd seriously miscalculated Megan's abilities.

Malcolm's evident surprise, however, was quickly replaced by ex-citement. "May I dare presume that knowing me has influenced your new venture?"

"What in the world do you know about query letters?" Duncan interrupted.

Her heart pounding, she tried to produce an enigmatic smile. "Darling, you'd be surprised what a girl picks up along the way."

"Really, Megan, I must say I'm impressed." Malcolm gave her an encouraging, thumbs-up sign. "Would you like me to read it?"

"You're very kind to offer but I've already sealed the envelope."

"Don't be disappointed if *Harper's* turns you down. I wrote for three years before I sold my first novel."

How she would have enjoyed telling them both that she was more than capable of writing an impressive query letter. She had sold her first novel before her twenty-second birthday and it had been a best-seller.

"You wouldn't believe how dedicated Megan has been," Duncan said. "She spends half the day at a typewriter in one of the guest rooms." He sounded incredibly patronizing, and she longed to punch him.

"I don't know why you're so amazed," she said instead. "I've been writing secretly for years. My dear Duncan, you don't know the half of it."

Thank heaven Dulce's appearance, announcing lunch, fore-stalled any further comment.

As they sat down to eat, Jade deliberately steered the conversa-tion onto less threatening ground. Since arriving at Rancho Cielo she had read every newspaper and magazine in the house. Now she felt confident of her ability to participate in a discussion of the stock market's amazing climb, the Hoover presidency, the failure of Prohibition and, with it, the rise of organized crime.

The ensuing table talk illustrated the differences between her companions. Malcolm was lively, enthusiastic, and open, while Duncan guarded his thoughts and feelings. What secrets hid behind his measured words and glances? The question tugged at her throughout the meal. She still hadn't come up with an answer when they finished.

"If you two will excuse me," Duncan said as Dulce cleared away their dishes, "I've got to get back to my studio."

"I wouldn't dream of keeping you from your work, old chap," Malcolm replied. "My thanks for the lunch."

"Delighted to have you. Feel free to stop by anytime. I know Megan would appreciate any help you can give with her writing."

"I'll take you up on the offer." Malcolm stood to shake Duncan's hand.

The two of them were talking about her as if she weren't there, Jade thought, watching them. It infuriated her. She resented being treated like a second-class human being, but she had come to real-ize that women of the twenties, even the boldest flappers like Hilary Delano, were little more than indulged children. They were permit-ted to drink, to smoke, to flaunt their sexuality—but only for the pleasure of and at the discretion of the men in their lives. No wonder Megan had been so bored.

After Duncan left, Malcolm sat back down. He had been keeping a watchful eye on Megan throughout the meal. No doubt about it, he thought. She was under a strain. It showed in her eyes, the nervous movements of her hands, the way she often seemed about to say something and then cut herself short. Unless he read the signs wrong, the marriage wouldn't last much longer. She and Duncan treated each other with the distant politesse of mismatched tablemates on an ocean liner.

The man had to be crazy to risk losing Megan. Her sensual beauty had always been a given. But the last few times they'd been together, Malcolm had been fascinated by her growing maturity and intellectual depth.

"So you want to be a writer," he said, gazing at her across the table. "Permit me to offer my services as your editor."

For a moment he savored the fantasy of working with her, growing closer and more intimate every day. He'd be at his desk, editing her copy while she looked over his shoulder, leaning so close that her breasts touched his arm. He would turn and press his lips to her sweet flesh. Her dress would have a deep neckline. He'd push it aside, pulling her closer, tasting her, seeing her nipples harden under the thin fabric . . .

"Malcolm."

He started at the sound of her voice. "What is it, Megan?"

"I've been wanting to talk to you about some of my other ideas for articles."

"Novice writers can't go wrong when they deal with things they know. How about doing something on fashion?"

"I'm really not interested in the traditional things you read about in *Good Housekeeping.*"

"I was thinking more on the lines of *Vogue.*"

"I may own a lot of clothes, but I have no intention of writing about them. I intend to do some human-interest pieces, character studies. God knows, enough famous people come to Santa Fe to supply me with plenty of material. And I have a special interest in looking at how present conditions—Prohibition, the runaway stock market—can affect the future."

Normally he wouldn't have given a plugged nickel for a novice writer's chances of getting into print with her first try. But as Megan continued to talk, he realized she seemed to have a sixth sense for the sort of things magazine editors were likely to buy— providing her ambition didn't overreach her capabilities.

In time, she might be able to write a readable character study, but he had serious doubts about her ability to analyze how present conditions might affect the future. Hell. He wouldn't want to tackle such a project himself. Still, he didn't want to discourage her, not when her writing was bound to bring them closer together. He had gotten enough rejection letters in his day to know the difficulties she faced. He intended to be around to comfort her when they started arriving.

When she got to her feet, signaling the end of their discussion, he realized he had been too busy listening to his own thoughts to pay attention to her words. "We'd better get over to the stable," she was saying. "Jorge is probably wondering what happened to us."

Although he would have been content to spend the afternoon listening to her, flirting a bit—playing the tantalizing game of advance and retreat that was the first step in getting a woman in bed —Malcolm dutifully followed her from the room.

The sun had passed its zenith as they walked the hundred yards to the stable. It was a perfect summer day, not too hot yet, with a few fleecy white clouds floating in the pure blue sky. Blackjack gamboled across the lawn toward them. Funny, Malcolm mused, the way the dog had taken to Megan after all these years.

"Good afternoon, señor, señora," Jorge said when they reached the corral.

Two horses were saddled and waiting, their reins wrapped around a post. One of them was Megan's mare, Dancer. Malcolm began to perspire when he saw that the other was Duncan's purebred Arabian stallion, Excalibur. Excalibur was fighting the bit, curvetting, stomping his hooves, whinnying. In the past, Jorge always saddled a fifteen-year-old Tennessee walker on those rare occasions when Malcolm was invited to ride.

He looked askance at Jorge. "Where's the walker?"

"He threw a shoe this morning, señor."

"I hope you don't expect me to get on that thing." Malcolm jerked his head toward the stallion.

"The señora will ride Excalibur," Jorge said.

Malcolm released his pent-up breath as Jorge handed him Dancer's reins. "Are you sure you want to go?" he asked Megan. "I don't know much about horses, but that stallion doesn't look right to me."

CHAPTER 11

Jade eyed the stallion warily as Jorge handed her the reins. The horse was snorting through flared nostrils and jerking his powerful head and neck from side to side. She'd heard Duncan describe Excalibur as high-strung, but this afternoon he looked demented. She nearly told Jorge she didn't want to ride the Arabian, but she stopped herself.

Jade Howard would not get on Excalibur in his present state. Megan Carlisle wouldn't hesitate. She was an expert horsewoman who had ridden to the hounds at the age of twelve and competed in dressage at fourteen. Jade had already done so many unMeganlike things in the last four weeks, she didn't dare do any more. Gritting her teeth, she put her left foot in Jorge's waiting hands and leaped upward.

The instant she hit the saddle she knew she'd made a mistake. Excalibur grunted with pain as she landed on his back. She felt his muscles bunch, then he reared. Out of the corner of her eye, she saw Jorge and Excalibur collide. The man flew into the air and landed flat on his back ten feet away.

Instinctively, she kept a death grip on the reins as her right foot searched for the stirrup. "Whoa, boy!" she shouted, trying to control Excalibur with the force of her voice. "Settle down."

She heard someone shouting but couldn't make out the words as Excalibur moved into high gear. He leaped forward like a high-performance car at Le Mans, reaching for top speed in a few strides. The next thing she knew, they were racing toward the trees.

Jade had always prided herself on being a better-than-average rider. During her teens she'd loved animals so much, she'd considered becoming a veterinarian. She'd nursed baby birds that fell out of trees, dog-sat for neighbors, and worked at a stable on weekends. In return for mucking out stalls, she'd been allowed to ride before the paying customers showed up.

A harsh cry of panic escaped her throat as she realized how little those pleasant canters on stable nags had prepared her to ride a runaway Thoroughbred. Although she sawed on the reins with all her strength, she felt Excalibur's stride lengthen. The horse was beyond reason or control, lost in his own equine nightmare. All she could do was hang on until he was too winded to run another step. She leaned into his speed, flattening her body against his neck, tightening the grip of her thighs on his sides as they broke into the trees.

The dense forest didn't slow the horse. Heedless of danger, he plunged straight ahead. Branches whipped past, snagging her clothes. A bright smear of blood painted Excalibur's shoulder, but he charged straight ahead. Sweat lathered his neck and foam flecked his mouth as he fought the bit. Her hands ached from trying to rein him in, her breath came in short gasps. It couldn't end like this.

Duncan didn't even know her true identity. Oh God, she didn't want to die as Megan Carlisle.

Although her hands burned, she tugged on the reins even harder, shouting "Whoa" into the wind. Ahead, a massive fallen tree trunk barred their way. She had never taken a horse over a jump, and this obstacle would have tested the finest rider. Pulling the reins to the right until her muscles screamed with the effort, she tried to turn the stallion. He kept straight on. She heard a hoarse cry as they neared the barrier and realized the sound came from her. Fifty feet, then thirty, then ten—and then none.

Using her body, hands, and knees, she urged Excalibur to leap the obstacle. At the last moment he balked and crashed into the tree trunk. She had been rising in the stirrups in preparation for the jump. Now she felt herself leave the saddle and fly through the air. She could see the ground coming up fast and tried to curl into a protective ball.

A dense layer of oak leaves and pine needles covered the forest floor. Their pungent aroma filled her nostrils as she landed, shoulder first. For a fraction of a second she thought she was going to be all right. Then her head hit something solid. An agonizing pain jolted through her and the world went black.

Duncan couldn't concentrate. He kept on looking up from his easel every few minutes and gazing out the studio windows, expecting to see Megan and Malcolm on their way to the stable. He checked his watch, wondering what was going on in the house. Were they talking about writing? Somehow he doubted it, although he still couldn't get over the fact that Megan was determined to get published.

Suddenly, his collar felt too tight. He unfastened the top buttons of his shirt, then removed his tie and dropped it on a chair. Shaking his head in disgust, he returned to work. The new painting was crap. Unmitigated garbage. He hadn't painted anything worth keeping for weeks. He'd had dry spells before when every canvas was a disaster, but they'd never lasted this long. What the hell was wrong with him?

Nothing suited—nothing satisfied—nothing served.

He pulled a pack of cigarettes from his shirt pocket and lit one, taking a few quick, angry puffs before he walked over to the window to watch and wait. Malcolm and Megan finally emerged from the house at three. Malcolm must have said something that amused Megan, because she looked up at him, smiling in a way she never smiled at Duncan.

When Malcolm took her hand as they strolled toward the stable, Megan made no effort to pull away. The two of them had grown noticeably closer in the last few weeks. He ought to be pleased. So why was his gut in knots?

Malcolm and Megan didn't even glance at the studio as they passed it. After they'd gone by, Duncan stepped out onto the *portal*. The wind blew Megan's voice in his direction. Although he couldn't make out her words, he heard the happy lilt in her tone. He continued watching—spying if he were honest—as the two reached the corral.

Malcolm began talking to Jorge and shaking his head. From Malcolm's gestures, the conversation must have something to do with the waiting mounts. Duncan felt a certain satisfaction that while Malcolm cut a fine figure in a drawing room, he didn't amount to much on top of a horse, especially when the animal was as spirited as Excalibur.

The big white stallion was fighting the reins, jerking his head up and down, raising miniature clouds of dust with his pounding hooves. Something was wrong with him—very wrong.

"Don't get on that horse!" he shouted as he sprinted for the corral.

A freshening breeze caught his voice and blew it back in his face. Neither Megan, Malcolm, nor Jorge heard him. From that moment on, everything seemed to happen in slow motion. Megan stepped forward and took Excalibur's reins. Jorge cupped his hands and helped her to mount. She seemed to float upward, as lithe and graceful as a ballerina *en l'air*.

When she hit the saddle, Excalibur exploded into motion. One second the horse was standing there and the next he reared up, knocking Jorge aside as if the man were a tenpin. Then the stallion surged forward, racing for the forest a hundred yards away. Even as terror washed through him, Duncan felt a thrill of pride as he saw Megan settle in the saddle. Any other woman would be screaming bloody murder, but she kept her wits and tried to get the horse under control.

Of course it was hopeless. Duncan had seen other runaway horses in his lifetime, animals that were snake-bit or bee-stung or crazed on loco weed. He knew Excalibur would race the wind until his great heart burst—or someone far stronger than Megan stopped him.

Even as Duncan's brain processed what was happening, he never broke his stride. When he reached the corral, Jorge was sitting up, rubbing his head. Malcolm stood there, slack jawed and utterly useless.

Duncan grabbed Dancer's reins from Malcolm's hands and vaulted onto the mare's back. He'd deal with the writer later, he promised himself as he kicked Dancer to a gallop. If anything happened to Megan . . .

He had wanted to be free of her, but not like this. Never like this.

Dancer was no match for the stallion when it came to speed or strength. She would never have been able to force her way into the forest at a gallop. But Excalibur had already broken the trail—and he had done so at top speed. Duncan shuddered, thinking what that must have cost both horse and rider.

Lashing the reins across Dancer's neck, he urged her onward. He could hear thudding hooves ahead and Megan's wind-borne voice. Her inarticulate cry tore through him. She must be scared to death —with good reason. Megan knew enough about horses to be fully aware of the danger she faced. Duncan ignored his own pain as oak and piñon branches lashed his arms and legs. All he could think about was Megan, fighting for her life.

He dug his heels into Dancer's heaving sides, cruelly forcing the mare to greater speed. He had to catch Excalibur before it was too late.

Suddenly, he glimpsed the stallion through the trees. He had come to a halt by a fallen tree. But there was no sign of Megan. Duncan reined Dancer to a skidding halt beside the stallion, dropped her reins, and jumped to the ground in one fluid motion. "Megan!" he called. "Where are you?"

The only response was the sound of the horses' labored breathing.

"Megan," he called again, searching the forest for any sign of her presence. Then he realized what must have happened. The stallion had been running full tilt when he came to the log fall. He must have balked in midstride. The best rider in the world wouldn't keep his seat under those circumstances.

Duncan scrambled over the obstacle. An anguished cry burst from his throat when he saw Megan. He hurried to her side and knelt. She was alive but her pulse felt thready, her flesh clammy. She was going into shock. "Megan, can you hear me?" he said, running his hands down her arms and legs to check for broken bones.

It might be dangerous to move her but he didn't have any choice. She needed medical attention. As he gathered her against his chest, he saw a small pool of blood where her head had lain. Brushing the leaves aside, he touched bedrock. She didn't make a sound as he carried her to the waiting mare. With a strength born of desperation, he managed to get the two of them onto Dancer's back. The mare whickered her dislike of the double weight, but Duncan steadied her with a couple of soothing words. Keeping the mare at a careful walk, he turned her toward the ranch house.

Looking down, he saw Megan's blood staining his shirt. She lolled in his arms like a rag doll, and he tightened his hold on her, trying to will his strength into her body. If he hadn't felt her heart beating, he would have been sure she was dead.

When they reached the clearing, Malcolm and Jorge ran toward them. Malcolm's eyes grew enormous when he saw Megan. "Is she alive?"

Duncan nodded. "No thanks to you."

"I shouldn't have let the señora ride Excalibur," Jorge exclaimed in a woeful voice as he helped Duncan dismount.

"We can talk about blame later." Duncan cradled Megan in his arms and headed for the house.

"What can I do to help?" Malcolm asked, hurrying to catch up.

"Telephone Dr. Adelman. Tell him Megan hit her head when the horse threw her. She's in shock. Then ask Dulce to bring my first-aid kit to the bedroom."

Malcolm took off at a run.

"What can I do, señor?" Jorge asked in an unsteady voice.

"Go get Excalibur. I don't know what got into that horse but I sure as hell intend to find out."

Jade was floating in a gray, dimensionless world, drifting toward a dark horizon. She wanted to let go and fall into the seamless void, but a man's voice kept calling her back.

"Megan, Megan, wake up."

She felt something cool and soothing on her forehead—heard other voices, other sounds. Footsteps. Murmured words. A door being closed.

It took so much effort to concentrate, and now she became aware of pain, a white-hot poker stabbing at her brain. She prayed for the darkness to take her, but the voice called again.

"Megan, can you hear me?"

She tried to answer and only produced a groan.

"Megan, don't be afraid. You're going to be all right. I'm here with you."

"Not Megan," she rasped, struggling to pry her eyelids apart. She squinted. The light lanced into her pupils. God, it hurt. A man loomed over her, filling her field of vision. "Who are you?"

"It's me, Duncan. Do you remember what happened?" He took her hand between both of his and held it tight. He felt warm, strong, alive.

The comforting gesture brought tears to her eyes. She clung to him.

"Do you need anything?"

She licked her lips.

"You're thirsty?"

She blinked yes.

He held a glass to her mouth, lifting her gently while she drank. His touch was so tender, so caring. She wanted him to hold her forever. But then she remembered exactly who he was. "How long have I been out?"

"About an hour. Dr. Adelman says you have a bad concussion. He'll look in on you again tomorrow. Are you in much pain?"

To hell with being brave. "Yes," she said, her voice quavering.

He released her hand long enough to change the cloth on her forehead. "Is that better?"

She tried to nod yes, but the slightest motion sent lightning through her head.

"The doctor said you mustn't even try to move for a few days. He's sending a nurse to take care of you. In the meantime, you'll have to put up with me."

"Where's Dulce? Why can't she look after me?"

"You know how superstitious she is. She muttered something about evil spirits." He squeezed her hand reassuringly.

"Don't leave me."

"I won't. Try to sleep."

"Is Excalibur . . . ?" She couldn't bring herself to ask if the horse had survived.

"He's fine."

She wanted to stay awake, to luxuriate in his soothing touch, but she didn't have the strength. She closed her eyes and drifted back into the gray haze.

Duncan continued to hold Megan's hand even though she was asleep. She looked so pale, almost as white as the bandage circling her forehead. No matter their differences, he couldn't bear seeing her like this. Regret and remorse were poor company, he thought. God. If only they could begin all over again, as she had suggested weeks ago, he would find a way to make her happy. But it was too late for new beginnings. He had seen to that himself. One of these days she would make a new beginning with Malcolm. All he could do now was watch over her while she slept.

He was still sitting by her side in a silent vigil two hours later when the nurse arrived, sailing into the bedroom with the confidence of the Spanish Armada. "I'm Miss Binghampton," she said, "and you must be Duncan Carlisle."

She was a starched, no-nonsense angel of mercy with a well-corseted body, a tight marcel, and a steely gleam in her eyes.

"Guilty," Duncan replied.

"Has Mrs. Carlisle regained consciousness?" Miss Binghampton demanded, sotto voce.

"Briefly. I gave her some water."

"You're lucky she didn't throw up. You should have just dampened her lips." The nurse's tone and her forbidding expression let Duncan know that she regarded all men as untrustworthy hooligans.

"Now, if you'll get out of the way, I'll see to my patient," she said, elbowing Duncan aside.

Megan slept on while her pulse was taken, her covers smoothed, and the cloth on her forehead changed.

"Is there anything more I can do for my wife?" Duncan asked, feeling like an intruder in his own bedroom.

The nurse nodded. "You can pack your clothes. You'll be sleeping someplace else until your wife is fully recovered. She needs complete quiet and rest."

He'd been trying to think of a good reason to absent himself from Megan's bed. Now that he had one, he hated the thought of leaving her.

"Well?" Miss Binghampton prompted, a disapproving gleam in her eyes.

"I'll send the housekeeper to fetch my things," he replied, feeling like a chastened schoolboy.

He cast a last reluctant look at Megan and tiptoed out of the room, shutting the door with infinite care.

To his surprise, Malcolm was waiting in the hall. "I hope you don't mind, but I couldn't leave until we talked."

"I do mind!" At that moment he would have taken great pleasure in throttling the writer.

Malcolm ignored Duncan's anger. "I know you're upset and I don't blame you. It was hell, seeing Megan like that. Before I go I'd like your permission to visit her regularly while she's recovering. The doctor told me she won't be able to do anything for a couple of weeks, and you know how she is. She'll be bored to death."

"Whatever you like. Just do me one favor."

"Of course."

"Get the hell out of here now."

Malcolm gave him a startled glance.

"*Now.*"

Malcolm turned to go, glanced back to murmur, "I really do understand how you're feeling," and tiptoed away.

A few minutes later Duncan heard the Bugatti leaving Rancho Cielo. He looked at the closed bedroom door one last time and headed for his den. Blackjack was snoozing on his favorite Navajo rug. Seeming to sense his master's distress, the big dog got up, walked to his side, and licked his hand.

Duncan dropped to his knees and buried his face in the animal's fur. A harsh groan escaped him. He stayed on his knees, staring into nothingness while the accident played over and over in his mind. Something must have been wrong with Excalibur. But what?

Dulce was sitting at the table running her rosary beads through her fingers, her lips moving soundlessly, when he walked into the kitchen. She seemed lost in prayer and started at the sound of his voice.

"Where's Jorge?"

"In the stable, Señor Carlisle. He feels very bad about what happened."

"He damn well should."

"I've been praying for the señora. Will she be all right?"

Duncan forced himself to speak in a reasonable tone. Dulce had nothing to do with Megan's accident. It wouldn't be fair to vent his rage on her. "The doctor assures me your prayers will be answered. Mrs. Carlisle will be fine in a couple of weeks."

Dulce put her rosary aside. "Please tell Jorge."

Duncan nodded, then opened the kitchen door and stepped outside. He'd been unaware of the passage of time and was surprised to see how late it had grown. The sun had already set and the first stars could be seen in the eastern sky.

He found Jorge in Excalibur's stall. "How is he?" he asked, jerking his head at the stallion.

"Dulce gave me a salve for his cuts. They have stopped bleeding. How is Señora Carlisle?"

"She has a concussion. What the hell happened, Jorge?"

Jorge's head drooped. He stared at the floor, his fingers nervously plucking at his pant legs. "I don't know, señor. I thought the horse was a little *nervioso*, but I was sure the señora would be able to handle him."

"Was there any warning of trouble earlier? Has Excalibur been off his feed?"

Jorge finally looked Duncan in the eye. "If anything was wrong with him, I would have told you. I love that animal, señor."

"A horse doesn't just bolt. There has to be a reason."

"I know. Excalibur was still *loco* when I brought him back from the forest. He didn't calm down until I took his saddle off, but he's been fine ever since."

125

"Did you check my wife's tack?"

"No. I didn't think of it."

"Let me see it now."

"*Sí, señor,*" Jorge replied, letting himself out of the stallion's enclosure. A few minutes later he piled Megan's bridle, saddle, and saddle blanket at Duncan's feet.

Duncan picked up the bridle first. The leather was soft and supple, the metal bit smooth. No problem there. Next he bent down to examine the custom-made English saddle. He could find no problem with the pommel, cantle, pad, or girth either. Megan's one concession to Western riding tradition was the Navajo blanket she used under the saddle. Duncan picked it up and examined first one side and then the other. His eyes widened as he saw several dagger-like thorns protruding from the wool. No wonder Excalibur had taken off the minute Megan mounted him. The horse must have felt as if he'd been bee-stung.

Duncan thrust the blanket under Jorge's nose and pointed at the thorns. "How did these get here?"

Jorge began to tremble. "*No se, señor.* I don't know."

"The hell you say!"

"I swear it on the Blessed Virgin of Guadalupe."

"Did you check the blanket before you saddled Excalibur?"

"No, señor." All the blood had drained from Jorge's face. "It was fine the last time the señora rode, and no one has touched it since."

Duncan could see that Jorge was close to tears. "These thorns didn't get in the blanket by themselves."

"I swear on my mother's grave, I know nothing about them."

Duncan stared at Jorge, trying to read guilt in his face. It wasn't like the man to be negligent. But Duncan couldn't imagine Jorge putting the thorns in the blanket on purpose. The Ortizes had been with him for twenty-some years and they'd never given him any reason to doubt their loyalty. "All right, Jorge. I believe you. Accidents happen. In the future, though, I want you to double-check the tack before you saddle any of the horses. *Comprende?* I won't be so forgiving if anything like this happens again."

"*Sí, señor.*" Jorge's head bobbed up and down. It was still bobbing when Duncan turned and left the stable.

Dulce stood at the kitchen window, gazing out at the stable, wondering what was happening inside. The señor had looked angry enough to kill. But she knew he wouldn't harm Jorge, even if he found the thorns. Jorge would protest his innocence, and the señor would have to believe him because Jorge knew nothing. It was best that way.

¡Dios mío! When she saw Excalibur run away, she'd been sure her plan to rid them of the *bruja* was going to work. But she hadn't counted on the *bruja*'s power.

Dulce plucked her rosary from her apron pocket and began running the beads through her fingers. How easy it had been to convince the señor she was praying for the señora's recovery. Nothing could have been further from the truth. She had been praying for the Blessed Virgin's help in ridding them all of the *bruja*.

She had failed this time, but she would try again. What was it the priest was always saying? God helps those who help themselves.

CHAPTER 12

Malibu Beach
June 15, 1989

Megan Carlisle sat at Jade's desk and stared into space, oblivious to the beauty of the white sand beach and the bubbling surf beyond the windows. A pile of bills sat to her right, a checkbook to her left. She stubbed a cigarette out in the already overflowing ashtray and immediately lit another. A frown seemed to have taken up permanent residence on her forehead. The last thing she needed was wrinkles on top of her other problems, she thought as she rubbed the scowl away.

She had driven to Malibu almost a month ago, so thrilled by the prospect of having a more exciting life than the one she was leaving behind that she could hardly wait to get to California. She had imagined herself going to parties, mingling with movie stars, attending premieres.

Now, after spending a month in Jade's beachfront house and realizing what it cost to live there, Megan wished she had never left La Fonda. The dollar sure didn't buy much these days. She shuffled through the bills despondently, wondering how long she would be able to pay them—and what she would do when she ran out of money.

She hated Jade's life almost as much as she had hated her own. How could the woman have spent every damn day writing and have so little to show for it? How could she have such dreadful taste in clothes? How could she do her own housecleaning, for God's sake? Megan's anger exploded. She picked up the ashtray and threw it against the wall. The heavy glass shattered and ashes and butts sprayed across the floor.

"Dulce," she called automatically.

Her voice echoed through the silent house. Tears began to ooze down her cheeks. For a moment she had forgotten that Dulce wasn't around to clean up the mess. She lowered her head to the desk and sobbed her heart out.

She was still sniffling twenty minutes later when the telephone rang.

"Hello," she quavered.

"Is Jade Howard there?"

"I wish to hell she was!"

"Can you take a message for her?"

"Sure. But I can't guarantee she'll get it."

"This is Harrison Denby's secretary calling. He asked me to remind Miss Howard about their lunch at the Polo Lounge today."

Megan frowned. She had forgotten the meeting. It had something to do with an option—whatever that was. She was about to tell the secretary that Jade couldn't make it when she realized it would do her good to get out of the house.

"She'll be there."

She hung up, got to her feet, and headed for the kitchen, skirting the mess on the floor. She took a cucumber from the refrigerator, cut two thick slices, and carried them into the bedroom. Setting the alarm to go off in an hour, she lay down and put the cucumber slices on her eyes.

Harrison Denby gazed around the Polo Lounge from the vantage of his booth opposite the entrance. It was the best table in the house and his whenever he dined there. Although he acknowledged the greeting smiles that came his way, his mind was on Jade Howard.

He opened his dog-eared, annotated copy of *Better Than Sex* and began flipping through the pages, wondering about the woman who had written it. From what he had heard, she was a workaholic and a cold fish. He knew the type. Dictatorial, didactic, temperamental. In short, a pain in the ass. Before he finalized the option he wanted to be sure she understood the ground rules. He believed in putting all his cards on the table up front. It always simplified things later on.

He snapped the book shut and turned to her picture on the back cover. The author smiled serenely at him. She was quite attractive. But, if she turned out to be the standard Hollywood issue, she would have an adding machine for a brain and a pile of press clippings for a heart.

He looked up to see a handsome young waiter approaching the table with the worshipful attitude of a pilgrim approaching Mecca.

"Can I get you something to drink, Mr. Denby?" The waiter flashed a too-perfect smile.

"Just Perrier for now. I'm expecting a guest." He could smell the I-wanna-be-a-star-and-all-I-need-is-a-break nervous perspiration coming off the man. Why did everyone in Hollywood have to be on the make?

"I know you must hear this all the time," the waiter gushed, "but I just love your work."

Harrison shifted uncomfortably, disliking what he was going to do but knowing he had no choice if he wanted to be left alone during the meeting with the Howard woman. "How you feel about my work isn't important. How you feel about yours is. I suggest you get back to it."

The waiter's expression changed instantly from worship to loathing. So much for getting good service, Harrison thought. He checked his watch. Jade Howard was five minutes late and unless he missed his guess, she'd keep him cooling his heels a great deal longer than that.

She had already made him wait a month. Considering what he had learned, she should have been falling all over herself for the chance to sell her book. Either his sources were all wrong about the sorry state of her career, or she had the balls of a riverboat gambler.

Megan's heart was doing her favorite dance, the black bottom, as she drove up to the Beverly Hills Hotel. The possibility of making a complete fool of herself sent a shiver up her spine. Would Harrison Denby realize she wasn't Jade Howard?

She stepped out of the Mercedes, handed the valet her keys, and swayed up the red-carpeted walk and through the entrance. Pausing near the registration desk, she looked around to get her bearings. The lobby had an aura of glamour, although the people inhabiting it were informally dressed by 1929 standards. She missed hats and gloves and stockings with seams up the back. She missed her own couturier wardrobe and felt terribly underdressed in the little black frock that had been the best thing Jade's closet offered.

"Can I help you, madam?" the bell captain asked.

"I'm meeting someone in the Polo Lounge."

"The restaurant is to your right."

She thanked him and slowly made her way across the lobby, wondering if her nervousness showed. A tanned, bosomy blonde in a divine dress walked by, did a double take, and caught her by the arm.

"Jade, darling, is that you?"

Megan's mouth went instantly dry. "Who else would it be?"

"You look absolutely ravishing. I love your hair straight. Love that dress too. It's so simple—so you!" The woman moved closer. "I saw Harrison Denby in the restaurant and he said you were lunching with him. How did you manage it after playing hermit for a couple of years?"

"Manage what?"

"Latching onto one of the most eligible bachelors in town."

"It's a business meeting," Megan replied, her pulse racing. She hadn't known Harrison Denby was single. To think she'd almost stayed home!

The woman winked. "Sure it is, darling. Monkey business. It's good to see you out and about again. Do give Harrison my love." She kissed the air near Megan's cheek and strolled away before

Megan could ask her name. Although, come to think of it, that wouldn't have been too smart.

Megan paused before the entrance to the Polo Lounge and took a deep breath. As she surveyed the crowded room, she wondered which of the well-dressed diners was Harrison Denby. A gray-haired man sitting alone at a corner table seemed the most likely candidate. She wet her lips and smiled in case he looked her way.

"Ah, Miss Howard, I'm delighted to see you again," a man said, materializing at her side. From his obsequious manner, Megan assumed he was the maitre d'.

"It's lovely to be back," she said.

"If you'll follow me, Mr. Denby is waiting."

As she walked behind the maitre d' she tried to look around him to see where they were going, but the man's head and shoulders blocked her view. "Here we are, Miss Howard," he said, coming to a halt in front of a booth and pulling out the table.

The man sitting there jumped to his feet and reached out to shake her hand. His grip was warm and firm. "I'm delighted to meet you at last."

At first glance, Harrison Denby looked about twenty-five. Seeing the laugh lines engraved around his blue eyes, Megan realized he must be somewhere in his thirties. He had a square masculine jaw, strong cheekbones, and a powerful brow softened by the unruly blond hair tumbling over it. Where Duncan was tall, lithe, and lean, this man had the powerful, broad-shouldered build of a football player. Attractive, she thought. Damn attractive.

"I hope I didn't keep you waiting long," she said, settling herself on the banquette by his side. "I got lost on the way here."

"Lost?" He looked puzzled.

"Did I say that? I meant stuck in traffic." She took a pack of cigarettes from her purse, hoping her hand wouldn't shake. "Do you mind?"

He grinned, displaying strong ivory teeth. "Not a bit. In fact I'll join you. I've given up liquor, red meat, and unprotected sex—but a man has to draw the line somewhere."

Thoroughly confused, Megan searched for an appropriate response. "Does it have something to do with your religion?"

To her surprise, Harrison Denby burst out laughing. "I guess you could say that. Lots of Californians have made a religion of keeping fit, as if they didn't breathe that awful shit day in and day out. I hope you're not one of those calorie counters who worships the great god Pritikin."

Breathing shit? Worshiping Pritikin? What in the world was he talking about? "I was raised Episcopalian," she said.

Harrison laughed again. "Miss Howard, you have a delightful sense of humor."

She basked in his praise. So far, so good. More than good! "I wish you'd call me Megan," she said, turning her gaze on him at full voltage. Seeing his startled expression she added, "Jade's my pen name."

"Then you must call me Harrison."

She shook her head. "I have a funny thing about names. I hope you won't be insulted, but you're not the Harrison type."

"My father would regard that as heresy, but I agree with you."

"You look more like an all-American Harry to me."

"I'll take that as a compliment. Dad picked Harrison over my mother's objections. His name was Schlomo Dershowitz before he changed it to Samuel Denby. Of course that was right after he went into the movie business. When I came along, he named me Harrison because he thought it sounded aristocratic."

Harry had a rapid-fire delivery that left Megan breathless. The best she could manage by way of reply was an interested "Really?"

His chuckle was self-deprecating. "I didn't ask you here to bore you with stories about my family."

"But I'm not bored. I'd like to know more about you."

She seemed sincere, but he had heard that line before. "We have business to discuss, but I prefer doing it on a full stomach." Snapping his fingers, he summoned the waiter.

Harrison was accustomed to dining with women who kept up a nonstop stream of chatter while they ate, as if even a moment's silence made them ill at ease. He liked the way Jade—Megan, he corrected himself—concentrated on her food, leaving him free to enjoy his. He watched approvingly as she finished the last of her Cobb salad.

"Do you know who invented that dish?" he asked.

"No," she replied, dabbing her mouth with her napkin.

133

"Back in the thirties when John Wayne and his buddies—guys like Ward Bond and Yakima Canutt—were under contract at Republic, they used to stop at the old Brown Derby at the end of the day's shooting. Half the time the kitchen was closed, but the chef, a man named Cobb, used to take a little bit of this and a little of that and make them something to eat. Voilà, Cobb salad. Of course the old Derby's long gone, and so is the Duke. According to my dad, those were the good old days."

"As far as I'm concerned, these are the *good days*," she said emphatically.

"I like your attitude." He gazed at her, thinking what a surprise she was turning out to be. The first time he met most women, they did their best to impress him, reciting all their accomplishments with practiced ease. But Megan had yet to mention her books.

"About a month ago, I adopted a new philosophy," she said, pulling a cigarette from the pack she'd left on the table. "What's past is past. You can't go back. You can't change it. You can't do a damn thing about it. The present and the future are the only things that count as far as I'm concerned."

He pulled a lighter from his pocket and held it to her cigarette, feeling an unexpected jolt of pleasure when their fingertips touched. "Let's discuss the future then. Do you have any questions about the option?"

"I trust Jade's agent—I mean, my agent—and now that we've met, I feel the same way about you."

He sat back, too stunned to reply. This was a first and he wanted to savor the moment. Every writer he'd ever worked with, given the opening he'd just given Jade Howard, would have had a long list of things they wanted to renegotiate, including but not limited to price and terms of the option.

"Are you saying you'll sign a contract based on my initial offer?"

"Absolutely."

He blinked, then blinked again. There had to be a hitch. "I want to be completely up front with you, Jade—I mean, Megan. I liked the book, but we both know it didn't sell well. I won't pay a penny more than the figure I discussed with Ira Max."

"And how much would that be?"

What was her game? He couldn't believe she didn't know. "Seventy-five thousand."

"Is that dollars or pesos?"

If she intended to disarm him, she was succeeding. "Dollars, of course. You'll get one third on signing, one third when the project goes into development, and the last third when we start filming."

She was looking at him with such wide-eyed gratitude that although he hadn't planned to, he said, "I know it's not much, but I will talk to Ira about giving you a small percentage of the gross. If the film does well, you'll do well too." The minute the words were out of his mouth, he felt like kicking himself. A percentage wasn't part of the deal he'd discussed with Ira Max.

He reached for one of his own cigarettes and lit up, using the business to give himself time to consider the situation. Either Megan was one in a million, or she was the shrewdest negotiator he'd ever met. "That's my best offer."

"It's wonderful!" She was beaming. Damn! The woman had a killer smile.

"You can forget all about script approval," he added more harshly than he intended. "I plan to change the ending."

She nodded enthusiastically. "I just read—I mean reread *Better Than Sex,* and if I had it to do all over again, I'd have both couples kiss and make up."

"All right," he said. "I give up. What the hell do you want?"

"I would like dessert."

He found himself grinning. He'd never met a more refreshing woman. But a nagging voice told him there had to be a catch. Megan, alias Jade Howard, was too good to be true.

On his way back to his Century City offices, Harrison Denby was still trying to figure out what made Megan tick. She could have put him over the jumps for missing their first appointment, but she hadn't even mentioned it. Her agent had described her as a consummate professional when it came to her work, yet she hadn't made a single demand or asked him to change his original offer in any way.

She was bright, funny, and very sexy. An appealing naïveté kept shining through her surface sophistication. Although she had lived in Hollywood for years, she seemed to take an almost childlike pleasure in dining at the Polo Lounge, as if she were seeing it for the first time. She ate as if she enjoyed food, smoked and drank with unself-conscious pleasure, and was the best damn listener he'd ever encountered.

He pulled into his private parking space and sat there for a moment, still thinking about the woman he'd just met.

The Denby offices were on the top floor of a building that sat in the middle of what had once been the Twentieth Century lot. The twelve rooms had a sensational view of Los Angeles to the east, the Hollywood Hills to the north, and the Pacific to the west. The interior decorator had been told to spare no expense in creating a serene working atmosphere. Still, the soothing gray-and-silver color scheme and the ankle-deep carpeting couldn't conceal the muted hum of computer printers, the urgent sound of telephones, or the harried comings and goings of his busy staff.

After spending a few hours away, he usually stopped to talk to anyone who needed him. But today he hurried through the outer rooms to his office and firmly shut the door behind him. Sitting at his desk, he gazed out the window. After a painful love affair with an actress who proved to be more interested in what he could do for her career than in him, he made a practice of dating women who had nothing to do with the entertainment industry. If he had any sense, he'd forget all about Megan.

He picked up some papers and tried to concentrate on work, but the memory of her face and the husky sound of her laughter kept getting in the way. The least he could do was check her out. He reached for the phone and dialed a Manhattan number. To his surprise, Ira Max answered on the first ring.

"This is Harrison Denby. I hope I'm not calling too late."

"Not at all."

"I just left Jade Howard and we have a deal."

"That's good news."

"I've offered to give her a small percentage of the gross in addition to the price you and I agreed on."

"That's even better news."

"You'll have the contracts in a couple of weeks."

"Good." Ira paused. "Is there anything else I can do for you, Harrison?"

"How well do you know Megan?"

"Who?"

"Miss Howard."

"Is your interest personal or professional?"

He cleared his throat. "The former."

Ira didn't even hesitate. "I never discuss my clients' private lives, Mr. Denby. All I can tell you is what I've said before. Miss Howard is a consummate professional. She is devoted to her career and her work."

Harrison tuned out the rest of the agent's comments. He had his answer. The woman was a pro—devoted to her career. He wasn't about to start a relationship with someone who was devoted to her career, not when he was looking for a woman who would be devoted to him.

Megan basked in the afterglow of Harry's admiration all the way home. She just knew he would call and want to see her again. For the first time since being thrust into Jade's life, she felt as if she had some connection to it.

She parked the car in the garage and closed the door with the remote control—a nifty gadget that still seemed quite miraculous—and entered the house through the kitchen. The room smelled stale, and dirty dishes were stacked in the sink. Suddenly she had a vision of Harry showing up unexpectedly and seeing the house in its present condition. That would never do.

Although she hated what washing dishes did to her hands and nails, she ran hot water into the sink, added liquid detergent, and left the contents to soak. Then she hurried into Jade's bedroom and put on a pair of shorts and a T-shirt. On her way out she automatically paused in front of the mirrored wall.

She still couldn't get used to wearing pants that barely covered her buttocks while displaying every inch of her legs. Four weeks ago they had been pale as milk, but a month of beach living had turned them a toasty tan. Not bad, she thought, giving herself an admiring glance.

It took half an hour to wash all the dishes. The skin on her hands had pruned and her nail polish was chipped by the time she finished, but the kitchen smelled better. Next she opened the cupboard under the sink, hoping Jade kept her cleaning things there the way Dulce did.

What appeared to be window cleaner, furniture polish, floor wax, and a variety of other cleaners were neatly set in a wire rack. She read the labels, figured out the usage, then gathered up a pile of dust cloths and headed for the back of the house. It was far smaller than Rancho Cielo, with two large bedrooms and three baths, a living room, formal dining room, and den in addition to the kitchen. Still, dust coated every surface and she had tracked sand all over.

Megan grimaced as she surveyed what one month of living had done to the once pristine house. She had never cleaned before, but now she set to work with a will, determined that the place would make a good impression on Harry the first time he came calling. Which had better be damn soon, considering the energy she was expending on his behalf.

It was dark by the time she finished. She wandered from room to room, enjoying the gleam of waxed surfaces and the potpourri of scents that came from the cleaning materials. As she surveyed what she had accomplished, she felt a swelling pride. It hadn't been easy. Just figuring out how to use the vacuum had taken fifteen frustrating minutes. And she was sore all over. Her body ached in places it never had before. But she found herself beaming, taking real pleasure in what she had done. Although she knew she didn't smell half as good as the house, she felt clean and shiny inside.

She poured herself a glass of wine and lit a cigarette, then carried them out to the deck to contemplate her day. She had enjoyed Harry's company and his obvious admiration, but even more, she enjoyed the way she felt about herself at this moment. Gazing out to sea, she sipped her wine and thought about what that meant. She had never been introspective or analytical, yet she believed she was on the brink of something momentous, something that could change her outlook on life.

What was it about the last few hours that made her feel so good? In the past she had only been happy when some man was at her feet, pledging his devotion. Now she had the glimmering of a whole new way to feel good about herself. But how could she apply it to her future?

CHAPTER 13

Rancho Cielo
June 28, 1929

Jade moved with the stealth of a jewel thief as she got out of bed and tiptoed to the bathroom. Nurse Binghampton slept in one of the guest rooms down the hall, and Jade didn't want to wake her. Two weeks had passed since the accident, but Binghampton still treated her like an invalid, threatening her with dire consequences if she so much as flexed a muscle unaided. Now that she felt better, she couldn't stand being told what she could and couldn't do by the Torquemada of the bedpan.

Ignoring the whisper of pain behind her eyes, she brushed her teeth and then her hair, carefully avoiding the ridge of scar tissue at the back of her head. Then she ran a hot bath, splashed in some of Megan's bath oil, and climbed into the huge claw-foot tub. Sitting back, she luxuriated in the perfumed warmth. The sun, pouring through a skylight, dappled the tiled floor with gold. Through an open window she heard the rustle of leaves, the chatter of birds.

Rancho Cielo had proven to be a peaceful haven. The first few days after the accident, she'd needed that peace. She had drifted in and out of consciousness, floating on a sea of pain. Binghampton had cared for her with starched efficiency during the day. In the small hours of the night, when her body and spirit were at their lowest ebb, she often woke to find Duncan sitting by her bed.

He had gotten into the habit of arriving with a small gift, a sketch of flowers newly blooming in the garden, or a treat from the kitchen to tempt her appetite. When she couldn't sleep, he whiled away the hours by telling her about his student days in Paris. How she wished she had known him in the sweetness of his youth, before his marriage to Megan.

Jade trembled despite the water's warmth, remembering the gentle strength of his hands as he plumped her pillows, smoothed her covers, or helped her into a more comfortable position. He seemed like the white knight every little girl dreams about. He always kissed her on the forehead before he left. Even now her skin tingled there as she remembered the gentle caress of his mouth.

Before the accident she had been confident she knew every aspect of his personality. She had never seen his tenderness, though. Thinking back on those nights when he kept his vigil, she knew she liked that side of him best of all. How sad that she would probably never see it after she had fully recovered.

Sitting up abruptly, she lathered a washcloth and began soaping herself with swift, jerky motions. She had to stop succumbing to romantic daydreams about him. His concern had not been for Jade Howard. He had been doing his duty toward the woman he thought was his wife. He belonged to that woman—a woman who might reappear at any moment.

Thank heaven the concussion hadn't interfered with her ability to think clearly, Jade grimly concluded. Duncan Carlisle was out-of-bounds. Nothing, not even her foolish heart, could change that.

She got out of the tub and toweled herself dry, catching a glimpse of herself in the mirror over the sink. Two weeks of enforced rest had softened the athletic lines of her body. She looked more womanly. It was an unwelcome reminder of the needs she had so long ignored.

How many bed-bound hours had she spent with nothing to do but think about Duncan—and remember. The boyish warmth of his rare smiles. The way his eyes seemed to darken when he was angry. The rich baritone of his voice. The generous spread of his shoulders. The thatch of hair trailing from his chest to his groin. The feel of his body, hard and hungry against her that day in the den.

Everything.

She ran her hands up her sides and over her breasts, feeling her nipples harden. A deep tug of longing throbbed between her legs. "Duncan," she moaned.

The needy sound of her own voice shocked and dismayed her. She had to stop it. She returned to the bedroom, pulled on one of Megan's nightgowns, and climbed back into bed. There were more urgent things to consider than her runaway emotions. In a few short months the world was going to come crashing down. If she didn't find a way to return to her own time she would be caught in the disaster along with everyone around her—Duncan, Malcolm, Hilary, even the Ortizes.

Did she dare warn anyone?

Who would believe her?

Who could she trust?

A peremptory knock on the door brought her back to the present. Nurse Binghampton bustled into the room carrying a breakfast tray.

"How are we feeling this morning, Mrs. Carlisle?"

"Fine, thank you."

Binghampton deposited the tray on the dresser with an audible clink of cutlery. Giving Jade her full attention, she frowned as she took in Jade's freshly brushed hair and clean nightgown. "Have we been a bad girl again this morning?"

Jade bit her lip, wondering why she let Binghampton make her feel like a recalcitrant five-year-old.

"You don't need to answer. I have eyes. I'd better see if we've hurt ourselves." Frowning fiercely, the nurse reached for Jade's wrist and took her pulse. "Hmmph," she snorted. "Our heart rate is definitely elevated. Doctor said we're not supposed to get up for a few more days. What would we do if we got dizzy and no one was here to help us?"

"Please stop saying *we*. I'm the one with the concussion and I'm feeling much better. In fact, if you try to give me one more sponge bath or make me use a bedpan again, you'll need to consult Dr. Adelman yourself."

"Now, now." Binghampton fussed with the covers, tucking them so tight that Jade felt like a butterfly in a cocoon. "We mustn't get worked up."

Jade closed her eyes, trying to shut out the sound of the nurse's voice. She couldn't take much more of this megalomaniac angel of mercy.

"Is our tummy bothering us? Have we had a bowel movement today?"

"I give up," Jade muttered.

"What's this about giving up?" Duncan asked, strolling into the room. Dressed in a V-neck sweater and a pair of jeans, he carried a cup of coffee in one hand and a vase of fresh cut flowers in the other.

"It's just a misunderstanding," Jade said, ignoring the tumult his presence always stirred in her. "I'm fine."

"Have you had breakfast yet?" He came and sat on the edge of the bed.

"I was just about to feed Mrs. Carlisle," Binghampton replied.

"I don't need feeding!"

Ignoring Jade's protest, Duncan gave Miss Binghampton a beatific smile. "Dulce just took a peach coffee cake out of the oven. I'd be happy to feed my wife if you want to go get a piece."

"That's very kind of you, Mr. Carlisle."

"I don't know how to thank you," Jade said after Binghampton had gone. "I know she means well but she's driving me crazy. She won't let me sit up, she won't let me read, she won't even allow me to use the bathroom by myself."

"Are you hungry?" Duncan asked, retrieving the breakfast tray and setting it on her lap. A wicked grin tugged at his lips. "As I said, I'll be happy to feed you."

Before she could answer, he picked up her napkin and tucked it in the top of her gown. She repressed a gasp when his hand grazed her breast. Although he seemed unaware of the casual contact, Jade felt herself flush. It hadn't been an intimate caress and yet her skin burned where he had touched her.

She suddenly realized that Duncan was staring at her. "Well," he said lightly, "shall I feed you?"

"That won't be necessary."

She had been hungry when Binghampton arrived with her break-fast, but with Duncan watching with a curious expression in his eyes, she couldn't eat. She nibbled her toast, trying to ignore her fluttering stomach.

"Seriously, how are you feeling?" he asked.

"I really am much better. Well enough to have cabin fever. I'd give anything to get out of this room for a while."

"If you like I'll come back after you finish breakfast and help you to the living room. At least you'll have a different view from the sofa."

"That would be nice, although there's something I'd like even more."

"And what might that be?"

"If it's an imposition, just say so . . . but I'd love to watch you paint." There—it was out. She lowered her eyes, feeling as diffident as a teenage girl asking the local high school football hero for a date.

He was silent for a minute. "It's not an imposition, Megan—just one hell of a surprise. If you recall, the last time you watched me work, you were bored to death."

"If it's a bother, forget I asked." Disappointment felt leaden in her stomach.

"You're not eating."

She glanced at the eggs congealing on her plate. "I'm not hungry."

Duncan stood and headed for the door. She thought he was going to leave without even saying good-bye, but he turned to face her at the last moment. "The studio can be chilly in the morning. You might want to put on something warmer. I'll send Miss Bing-hampton to help you."

The words were no sooner out of Duncan's mouth than he re-gretted them. He knew painters who turned their studios into sa-lons where they held court while they worked. He wasn't one of them. He found the creative process so intimate, he'd always be-lieved having an audience would be tantamount to letting a stranger watch while he made love.

He considered telling Megan he'd changed his mind. Seeing the pleasure in her green eyes, the soft smile that curved her lips in a sweet ellipse, he knew he couldn't disappoint her.

On his way to the kitchen, he took a blanket from the linen closet and tucked it under his arm. Miss Binghampton and Dulce were sitting together when he walked in. Dulce, who had been talking, shut her mouth as soon as she saw him. For a moment he had the feeling she didn't want him to hear what she'd been saying. He dismissed the idea immediately as unfair to a loyal servant.

"Do you want that washed?" Dulce asked, nodding at the blanket.

"Megan will be spending some time in the studio today. I'm taking this over with me in case she gets cold."

Miss Binghampton jumped to her feet. "Did Dr. Adelman give Mrs. Carlisle permission to leave her bed?"

"I didn't think that was necessary."

"But the señora has been so sick," Dulce chimed in.

Duncan had expected the nurse to object, but the worried look on Dulce's face took him by surprise. He hadn't realized how much she cared about Megan.

"Ladies, although I appreciate your concern, I'm perfectly capable of caring for my wife for an hour or two." He gave Dulce a reassuring pat before he left the kitchen.

His studio, in a separate building fifty feet from the main house, echoed the main house's Santa Fe style of architecture. He spent a few minutes tidying up, picking discarded sketches off the floor, opening windows, plumping the cushions on the sofa, laying a fire in the kiva fireplace. Then he returned to his own room to freshen up.

Although he'd put on a clean shirt a couple of hours earlier, he stripped it off and tossed it on the bed. He walked into the bathroom and washed his hands and face. Feeling a tiny stubble on his cheeks, he decided to shave for the second time that morning. Finishing his toilette with a splash of cologne, he inspected himself in the mirror over the sink.

He was behaving like a man getting ready for a rendezvous with a new and exciting woman. Damn fool. Nothing had changed. Yet a tiny voice in the dark recesses of his mind insisted that everything had changed because his feelings for Megan had changed.

Executing an almost military about-face, he strode out of the bathroom. He had to stop fooling himself. The weeks since the accident had been a sweet entr'acte, but the play would go on. His decision had been made. His plan was working. Malcolm had made the drive to Rancho Cielo half a dozen times since the accident, and Megan obviously looked forward to his visits. It was only a matter of time before their friendship evolved into something else.

Megan was sitting on the edge of the bed when he returned to her room. She was wearing the blue satin lounging pajamas with the Raoul Dufy print jacket that she'd bought on their last trip to Paris. Duncan recalled how annoyed he'd been at the time because the famous painter had lent his art to something as plebeian as a pajama coat.

Megan had been unable to understand, let alone empathize with his anger. She couldn't get it through her head that there was a qualitative difference between fine art and haute couture. Recalling the incident now helped to remind him of all their other differences, and he was grateful for it.

"Mr. Carlisle," Miss Binghampton said, "I must protest. No matter how well your wife feels, she is very weak and she still has a headache. She's in no condition to walk all the way to the studio."

"She won't have to. I'm going to carry her. Are you ready?" he asked, heading for the bed.

For an instant, Megan seemed to shrink from him as if she had changed her mind about the outing. Then she reached up and put her arms around his neck. Miss Binghampton was still sputtering predictions of disaster as they left the room.

Duncan hadn't held Megan in his arms for weeks, although he'd fantasized about it more than he cared to admit. She'd lost weight, he realized. But her womanly curves were still an infinite distraction. Despite his resolve he found himself reveling in them.

Jade's heart was beating so hard, she was certain Duncan could hear it. No matter how she willed herself to be calm, she couldn't slow the racing of her pulse. The last time he had held her like this, she had been unconscious and unable to enjoy it. Now she took a deep sensual pleasure in smelling his after-shave and the soap he used, and underlying both—a musky male scent that she remembered from the nights when they shared a bed.

He carried her easily, not even breathing heavily. She felt foolish, being toted around like an invalid, yet she couldn't help surrendering to the seductive strength of his arms.

He didn't put her down until he reached the sofa in the studio. "Are you comfortable?" he asked, arranging the pillows behind her back.

"Yes. It's wonderful to be out of the house. I can't thank you enough."

"There's no need to thank me." The warmth in his eyes belied his gruff tone. He stood in the middle of the room, looking around as if he didn't know what to do next. Silence stretched between them, as taut as piano wire.

Finally, he cleared his throat. "I feel funny about letting you watch me paint after all these years."

Not so very long ago literary critics had praised her clever dialogue. Now all she could come up with to ease the awkwardness between them was, "Please—just ignore me."

He nodded and began moving around the room, positioning his easel in the best light, setting up his palette, choosing brushes. Whenever she sensed him glancing her way, she looked out the window. A profound quiet settled over the room.

Half an hour later, after he grew too absorbed in his work to be aware of her presence, she was able to gaze at him openly. The canvas had been blank when he started. She watched spellbound as he filled it with a freehand sketch. There was something magical about the way he worked. It seemed as if the charcoal in his hand was synergistically connected to his mind, heart, and soul, so that thought, action, and reaction were seamlessly intertwined. One moment the canvas had a pristine surface and the next the figure of an Indian warrior began to appear out of the void. The warrior sat before a fire, the sorrows of his race clearly delineated on his aged face.

Watching Duncan reminded Jade of those perfect days when she worked at her computer and the words flowed with the sweet inevitability of honey dripping from the comb.

After completing the preliminary sketch, Duncan filled his palette with myriad squibs of color and began underpainting, working from the darkest tones to the lightest. As he laid in the areas of color he made small adjustments to his preliminary sketch, redefining the tilt of the head, the line of the body, until the painting evoked a powerful mood that spoke as clearly as the written page.

He worked with an intensity that was, at times, directed toward the canvas. At others he seemed to be gazing inward at a vision only he could see. Her intensity equaled his as she watched him moving in front of the canvas with an athlete's grace. She hadn't realized how physical painting could be. Now she saw it as an adagio, where every move had meaning and purpose. Was it his talent that stirred her—or was it the man? Could she ever separate the two?

She was unaware of the passage of time until she heard a knock at the door. "It's me, señor," came Dulce's voice. "Where would you like your lunch?"

Duncan put down his palette and glanced at Jade, seeming surprised to find he wasn't alone. "Are you ready to go back to your room?"

"Please, not yet."

"What would you like to eat?"

"Anything."

He walked to the door and opened it. "Mrs. Carlisle and I will be eating here. Bring us a couple of sandwiches and a bottle of pouilly-fuissé."

"But señor—"

Jade was surprised when she caught a glimpse of Dulce's face. The housekeeper looked far more concerned than the situation merited.

Duncan ate methodically, not tasting his food. He kept on glancing toward Megan, wondering for what had to be the hundredth time if he could put any credence in the woman she seemed to have become. A couple of months ago she wouldn't have dreamed of watching him paint. She would have fidgeted constantly, complained of the smell of turpentine and oil, and given every evidence of terminal boredom while incessantly chattering about all the things she missed, the Broadway openings, the supper clubs, the speakeasies, the shopping, the social life she had enjoyed before they married.

148

This new Megan had been so still while he worked, he'd all but forgotten her presence. Yet now he was uncomfortably aware of it. "Would you like some more wine?" he asked.

"Binghampton would have a fit if she knew I'd had any."

"What Binghampton doesn't know won't hurt her."

"Then I would like a little more," Megan replied, holding out her glass.

He poured for both of them. This was the way it should have been all these years, he thought wistfully. How many hours had they wasted in argument? How many days had been spent in recrimination? How many weeks lost to anger? But he had to face the truth. This morning wasn't likely to be repeated. Megan and Malcolm were growing ever closer.

Jade studied Duncan's face as she sipped her wine. He looked so serious, she wondered what he was thinking. Her own head was spinning with all the things she wanted to say. Watching Duncan paint has been a revelation. While he worked his face was free of its habitually dour, guarded expression. He had been completely in touch with his emotions, smiling with satisfaction or frowning when he wasn't pleased. How she wished he could be that open with her.

He had so much passion for his art. She loved that in him. If only she could tell him she felt the same way about writing. Years ago, before she closeted herself away from her emotions, she might laugh out loud as she wrote, or even shed tears when her stories took a tragic turn.

It would be wonderful to talk about the creative experience with Duncan, to share those deep emotions with him, but she didn't dare. First, she would have to tell him who she was, and she wasn't strong enough yet to face the consequences of that. She could, though, try to get him to talk about painting.

"Do you mind if I ask some questions about your work?"

He shrugged. "What do you want to know?"

"You didn't work from a sketch or a photograph, and you didn't use a live model. How did you know what you were going to do?"

"I start with an idea firmly fixed in my mind. Sometimes I sketch it on paper in advance. But I usually draw directly on the canvas because I want to be free to let the unexpected happen. I guess it would be fair to say I depend on serendipity."

"That's just the way I write. I usually type up a pretty extensive outline, but I don't always stick to it."

Seeing Duncan's puzzled look, Jade could have kicked herself. She'd been so pleased to hear him echo her own thoughts on the creative process, she'd forgotten that Megan couldn't know that much about writing.

"I don't see how you can compare your writing to my painting," he said.

"Why not?" Oh God. She was only making it worse. Again she'd spoken like an author who had more than paid her dues rather than as Megan.

"It's a matter of longevity. I don't see how you can make a comparison between your one query letter and the lifetime I have devoted to—" He stopped in midsentence. Standing abruptly, he put their dishes and glasses back on the tray and carried it outside.

The stiff set of his shoulders told her how upset he was. He set the tray down with a clatter while she waited with indrawn breath, wondering what he would do next. To her relief, he walked back in.

"I'm sorry," she said. "I know how presumptuous I must sound. My only excuse is that I am serious about my writing."

He nodded curtly but the chill in his eyes told her he wasn't as interested in an apology as he was in nursing his anger. And why was he so angry? It had to be more than her ill-considered comparison. Was it that Duncan Carlisle would prefer to have a wife who continually waited on his pleasure, rather than one who had interests of her own? At that moment, Jade thought it would be much easier to hate Duncan than to love him.

Hilary checked her watch. Malcolm wouldn't be picking her up for an hour. She had more than enough time for a leisurely bath—and a little amusement. She stripped off the suit she'd worn to the gallery that morning, a copy of a Chanel made by a local seamstress. It would take an expert to tell it from the real thing. Unfortunately, Megan Carlisle was an expert, damn her.

Hilary massaged away the ugly lines grooving her forehead. It wouldn't do to get wrinkles at this stage of the game, with her situation growing more precarious with every passing day. Her looks were the only thing she had ever been able to count on—until Malcolm. And now she couldn't even count on him. Double damn Megan!

Life was so unfair. Megan hadn't done a thing to deserve her good fortune, but she had everything Hilary had ever wanted. A gorgeous husband, a gorgeous house, and a gorgeous bank account. And all because she had been born into the right family. Hilary's scowl returned as she recalled her own family.

Family? What a laugh. Having a whore for a mother and being born in a New Orleans brothel wasn't exactly having a family, even if the other whores fussed over her when she was little. No, she hadn't had much of a start in life. But she had made up for it. She was as attractive as Megan, a damn sight smarter, and certainly as deserving of all the good things. And she had worked hard for everything she owned. Her house, her shop, may have been paid for by Malcolm, but by God she had earned them. On her back. With her cunt. Now, unless she did something to prevent it, Megan was going to take Malcolm away from her.

Hilary walked to the bellpull next to her bed and gave it a sharp yank. A minute later Raoul appeared at her bedroom door. In the two weeks he'd spent in her employ, he'd reorganized her household, fired all her old help, and hired new people who were more suited to her special requirements.

"You rang?"

"Where's the new maid?" she asked.

"In the kitchen having lunch."

"Does she understand her duties?"

"Perfectly. I trained her myself."

"Good. She can finish eating later." Hilary chuckled at the double entendre. "I want her to draw my bath. And have her bring some champagne. The Roederer will do nicely."

"As you wish, madame."

Hilary was naked when the new maid entered the bedroom. The girl's brown eyes widened as she saw her mistress's nudity, and a blush stained her skin from her hairline to the high neck of her black muslin uniform. She was a pretty thing, Hilary thought, barely out of her teens. Raoul had chosen well. The girl's youth, inexperience, and poverty would make her malleable—as malleable as Hilary had been years ago when she was seduced by one of her mother's johns.

"Do you understand your duties, Enid? It is Enid, isn't it?"

"Yes, ma'am." The girl kept her gaze downcast.

"Look at me when I talk to you." Hilary studied Enid, enjoying the apprehension she saw in her eyes. She could remember a time when she had been just like Enid—frightened, defenseless, someone to be used and discarded at a whim. Now she relished her hard-won status. When it came to the Santa Fe art scene, she was a mover and shaker. Power—the ability to make people do what you wanted no matter what they wanted. Power—the ultimate aphrodisiac. Today, before she saw Megan, Hilary needed a power fix, a vivid reminder of how far she had come.

"I'm only going to explain this once," she said, taking Enid's hand and leading her into the bathroom. "I like my bathwater hot, my towels warm, and my champagne cold."

After Enid had filled the tub, Hilary climbed in and handed the girl a washcloth. "What are you waiting for?" she asked.

"Nothing, ma'am."

Hilary laughed softly. "I'm a woman just like you, Enid, with breasts and a vagina. You've washed yourself, haven't you?"

Enid blushed furiously. "Yes, ma'am."

"Then you shouldn't have any problem bathing me." She shut her eyes and leaned back, her breasts half-floating on the water.

She waited for Enid to do as she had been bidden. When the girl hesitated, Hilary reached for her hand and placed it on her own breast. She could feel the girl trembling. Although Enid would become more skillful, nothing would ever be as exciting as this first time. Still holding the girl's hand, Hilary moved it over her breast.

She felt her nipple harden at the touch of the washcloth. "That's not so difficult, is it?" she asked, smiling up at the maid.

Enid tried to return the smile. "No, ma'am."

"Can you manage by yourself now?"

"Yes, ma'am."

"Mind you, I want you to bathe every inch of me. Is that clear?"

"Yes, ma'am."

Hilary took a deep breath and leaned back again. At first Enid's touch was feather light. Then the girl relaxed, and the stroke of the washcloth became more confident. The maid's hands were farm-girl strong as they moved over Hilary's body, massaging while they washed. Hilary's skin began tingling, and she purred with pleasure as the maid laved her shoulders, her breasts, her belly, legs, and feet.

"I want to be clean inside and out," she murmured when the girl stopped. "Did Raoul explain everything to you?"

She opened her eyes to see the girl nod yes.

Enid leaned over the tub.

Hilary spread her legs in anticipation.

The girl plunged her hand into the water and Hilary felt the cautious parting of her labia. Raoul had done his job well, she thought, realizing that the girl was using two fingers. The first strokes were slow and cautious, but as Enid grew more sure, the speed increased. Hilary sat up a little, the better to watch what was happening between her legs.

She could feel the premonitory tension deep within her, the precursor of orgasm. "Faster," she commanded.

Enid obeyed.

A harsh growl of pleasure rose up Hilary's throat. She felt herself tightening around the girl's fingers as spasm after spasm shook her body. And then it was over.

"You can get the towel now," she said. God, she felt glorious, completely in control. Power. She just couldn't get enough.

CHAPTER 14

Dulce Ortiz didn't understand Anglos, except for Señor Carlisle whom she had known for two decades. Anglos were changeable as chameleons and as unreliable as the Rio Grande's shifting banks. One minute Anglos acted friendly, like a stray dog looking for its next meal. The next they were cold as the Sangre de Cristos in a blizzard.

This nurse Binghampton was no exception, Dulce thought, studying the woman who sat across the kitchen table from her. Spending the morning with her had tested Dulce's patience.

"If men had hot flashes," the nurse was saying, "medical science would soon find a cure for them. Don't you agree?"

"Sí." Dulce nodded her head vigorously even though she was shocked by the nurse's comment. A well-bred Hispanic woman wouldn't dream of discussing such personal matters. To hide her discomfort, Dulce walked over to the stove and refilled their cups from a fresh pot of coffee. Then she returned to her seat. The time had come to turn the nurse's unwelcome presence to her own advantage.

"It must be wonderful to know so much about medicine. I feel much safer with you here."

"Oh. Why is that?" the nurse asked, helping herself to another slice of coffee cake.

"The ranch can be a dangerous place. Just this morning, I killed a large scorpion in one of the kitchen cupboards." Dulce paused for dramatic effect. "Aiee, I've always wondered what would happen if a scorpion found me before I found it."

"I can see why you might be worried. But there's no need. The scorpion's sting isn't fatal to adults."

"Never?"

"An elderly person with a weak heart, someone who already has a medical problem, or a small child might die from such a sting. But a healthy woman like you . . ." The nurse shrugged away Dulce's concern.

"What about tarantulas and black widow spiders?"

"Like scorpions, their venom isn't fatal to healthy adults."

"But I've heard stories," Dulce said.

"Old wives' tales," Nurse Binghampton declared authoritatively. "I assure you, you have nothing to fear."

"You make it sound very simple."

"I'm not saying you wouldn't get sick. But you won't die."

Dulce forced herself to smile although she was deeply disappointed. Getting rid of the *bruja* wouldn't be as easy as she had hoped. She put her hand in her dress pocket, seeking the familiar comfort of her rosary.

Nurse Binghampton leaned closer. "There's only one poisonous creature you need fear, and I've never heard of anyone being bitten by one around Santa Fe."

"Ah, you must mean the rattlesnake."

The nurse gave Dulce a condescending smile. "You're wrong, Mrs. Ortiz. Rattlesnake venom will make you very sick, but most victims survive." The nurse's large breasts touched the table as she leaned even closer, lowering her voice to an almost conspiratorial whisper. "When I worked at the county hospital in Phoenix, someone brought in a man who had been bitten by a coral snake. He was D.O.A."

"What is this—what do you call it—D.O.A.?"

"Dead on arrival, Mrs. Ortiz. The victim passed away before he reached the hospital. And a horrible death it was too. You should have seen his face. Poor soul." Although a shudder ran through the nurse's body, she took another bite of coffee cake.

"Have you ever heard of these coral snakes around here?"

"No. And I hope I never do."

Dulce sighed. Another dead end. "It isn't just snakes or insects that worry me. Sometimes my grandchildren come to visit and I'm afraid they'll get into the poison Jorge keeps."

The nurse's thick eyebrows shot up. "What in the world can your husband be thinking, keeping poison on the premises?"

"He has arsenic in the shed in case gophers get into my vegetable garden."

Nurse Binghampton took a moment to consider the information. "I don't think you need to concern yourself. It takes a great deal of arsenic to kill someone. I doubt a child would consume that much, even by accident. Just to be sure you'd better tell Mr. Ortiz to keep it out of reach. In fact, he should keep it under lock and key. You wouldn't want him to be charged with manslaughter."

Dulce's brow furrowed. What was this talk of slaughter? It worried her. "I don't understand."

"Any time someone dies under questionable circumstances, the coroner does an autopsy to determine the cause of death. If someone at Rancho Cielo died of arsenic poisoning, Jorge might be blamed."

"But that's ridiculous!"

"Is it? I would certainly testify to the fact that he kept arsenic on the premises—and that you questioned me about its lethal properties." Nurse Binghampton smiled archly. "You're not planning to kill someone, are you?"

Dulce shifted in her chair. Things weren't going the way she intended. Could the *bruja*'s power have touched the nurse too?

"Because if you are," the nurse continued, "you have other means at hand." She pointed out the window. "Take that hedge."

Dulce's gaze tracked the nurse's index finger. "Surely you don't mean the oleander."

"I do indeed. It's a toxin. And that's just the beginning. I noticed a patch of jimsonweed—datura—growing at the end of the drive by the highway. It's a powerful hallucinogen, deadly in a strong dose. Certain other plants—mushrooms, foxglove, hemlock, even poppies like the ones in the garden can be fatal if ingested in large amounts. But being an Indian, you must know more about these things than I do."

Dulce felt herself redden. An Indian indeed! She set her cup down so hard, some of the aromatic coffee slopped over the top. "My ancestors came here from Spain in the sixteenth century. They were conquistadores—noblemen promoting the one true faith." She crossed herself reflexively.

"There's no need to take on so," Nurse Binghampton said. "I didn't mean any offense. It's just that Mexicans and Indians . . . Well, to tell the truth, I can't tell them apart. But I assure you, I have nothing against them."

Dulce rose, straightening to her full five feet with all the dignity she could muster. "If you will excuse me, *señorita*"—she emphasized the word, thinking it wasn't at all surprising that no man had married this woman—"I must get the lunch tray from the studio."

The nurse checked the watch pinned to her uniform. "Goodness gracious. It's one-thirty. I'm going to have to call the doctor and tell him how long Mrs. Carlisle has been up." She too got to her feet. "I wonder what those two have been doing all this time?"

And well you might wonder, Dulce thought as she left the kitchen without another word. She couldn't remember the last time Señor Carlisle had spent so much time with his wife.

Hilary studied Malcolm's profile as they drove toward the Carlisles' home. He sat hunched over the wheel of the Bugatti, urging the car forward with unconscious intensity as if he couldn't get to Rancho Cielo and Megan fast enough. He'd always lusted for Megan's body, but now he seemed to want more than a sexual escapade. Could he have fallen in love?

She would have found the whole thing—a brilliant man like Malcolm going gaga over a scatterbrained twit like Megan—profoundly amusing if she didn't have so much at stake. She had come a long way from those days in New Orleans, and she intended to go even further. Someday she hoped to open a gallery in New York that would cater to the carriage trade. But she needed two things to reach her goal. Money and social cachet. Malcolm had both. She wouldn't give him up without a fight.

He was, she thought, even more attractive now than when they'd met in Rome all those years ago. Success became him. He looked confident, utterly sure of himself in a way that only those whose dreams have come true can be. Although Malcolm lacked Duncan Carlisle's powerful aura of sensuality, he had compensating charms.

"I hope Megan doesn't mind my tagging along," she said, resting her hand on his thigh.

"If I thought she wasn't up to it, I wouldn't have agreed to let you join me."

"Believe it or not, darling, I've missed Megan. How is she— really?"

"Much better now. But those first few days"—his voice roughened—"were hell. She was in a lot of pain."

"If I know our Megan, she didn't suffer in silence."

Malcolm continued to look straight ahead, but she could tell from the way his eyes narrowed that something was bothering him. "I'm not sure any of us knows Megan. Her brush with death . . ." He paused. "Well, she's changed."

"How?"

"I can't quite pin it down."

What fools men are, she thought. Maybe he didn't know how Megan had changed, but Hilary sure as hell did. The big change was that Megan wanted Malcolm. "What in the world have you found to discuss with her these last few weeks? She isn't exactly in your league intellectually."

He ignored the jibe. "Books. Literature. As it turns out, Megan is quite well read."

Hilary emitted a startled guffaw. "As far as I know, the only thing she reads is the labels on couturier gowns."

"You misjudge her. She got quite an education at finishing school."

If you consider majoring in clothes and men getting an education, Hilary added silently.

"I've been reading my new manuscript to Megan. Her comments have been quite astute."

"Since when do you read a work in progress to anyone?"

He turned to face her, his eyes flashing a danger signal. "You don't get it, do you? I should have been on that damn horse, not

Megan. I'll do anything in my power to make her convalescence as pleasant as possible. Duncan understands perfectly. I don't see why you can't."

Hilary decided to try another tactic. She sidled closer to Malcolm and squeezed his thigh, feeling the muscles in his leg working as he downshifted on a curve. Sliding her hand higher, she fondled him through his trousers.

He pushed her hand away. "For God's sake, do you want to kill us both. Or hadn't you noticed that I'm driving?"

She managed a sexy pout although her chest felt tight. "You could pull over. I've missed you, darling. How many days has it been?"

Malcolm didn't even blink at the implicit invitation. "It's getting late. Duncan told me to drop in anytime, but I'm certain he didn't mean the dinner hour."

Hilary bit her lip. Damn. Things were worse than she feared. Reaching inside her purse, she removed a cigarette from a case that had been custom-made for her by a Navajo silversmith. A graphic depiction of Kokopelli, an ancient Anasazi fertility figure, had been inscribed on the cover. The exaggerated phallus usually made her smile. Today, however, she gnawed her lip anxiously before lighting up.

"You're right as usual," she said. "It wouldn't do to be too late. But you owe me. Besides, I have a surprise for you. I've been teaching that new maid of mine a few tricks. I know you'd enjoy seeing her at work."

They rode the rest of the way to Rancho Cielo in silence, Malcolm concentrating on the road while Hilary puffed on her cigarette, her hands moving in nervous, jerky bursts. The feeling of power induced by the maid's timid compliance earlier in the day had faded by the time they reached the turnoff.

"Oh look," she said, gesturing toward the Carlisles' mailbox. "The flag's up. Why don't we save them a trip and take their mail up to the house?"

Malcolm braked the Bugatti to a stop and got out. He retrieved a rubber-banded packet and handed it to Hilary before restarting the car. She sorted through the mail with idle curiosity, noting a number of letters from art galleries in other parts of the country. What a fool Duncan was, refusing to show anywhere except with his old friend David Max.

If he weren't so damn loyal, if he let someone like her mastermind his career, he could double or even triple his prices before the year was out. Everyone seemed to have money these days, thanks to the stock market. People were in the mood to spend—to splurge.

She continued sorting through the mail until she came across an envelope from *Harper's Magazine*. "What's this?" she murmured.

"What's what?"

"Megan has a letter from *Harper's*."

Malcolm slowed the car as they crested the final rise before the ranch and glanced sidelong at the envelope. "God, I hope it's not a rejection. That's the last thing she needs after what she's been through."

"I don't understand."

"I guess I forgot to tell you. Megan had an idea for an article. She sent a query letter to *Harper's* the day of the accident."

"Megan? Writing?"

"She told me she's kept a journal for years. She's quite serious about becoming a writer."

Hilary bit her lip so hard, she tasted blood. The fact that Megan was pretending an interest in writing could only mean one thing. Unless Hilary missed her guess, Megan wanted a permanent alliance with Malcolm. Any way Hilary looked at it, that spelled marriage.

If Megan wound up with Malcolm, Hilary would be damned if she'd leave the game empty handed. Duncan Carlisle would be a more than acceptable consolation prize.

Jade watched as Duncan lifted the new canvas from the easel. "I love that painting," she said. "Aren't you going to finish it?"

"Not now," he said, carrying it to the rack at the far end of the studio. He set it on the already crowded shelf. "The imprimatura has to dry."

"Imprimatura?"

"Underpainting," he answered succinctly, as if he felt compelled to hoard words.

He took another half-finished canvas from the rack and carried it to the easel. After scraping his palette clean, he stood back, studied the new work, then chose half a dozen different colors from the tubes of paint on the table by his side. Jade watched silently as the adagio began again, the courtship dance between the artist and his creation.

She leaned back against the pillows, suddenly aware of a numbing weariness, a physical and mental malaise. Duncan had been so open and warm, so communicative until she'd made the mistake of talking about her writing. Now, for reasons she couldn't quite fathom, the wall between them seemed higher than ever.

If he wasn't so absorbed in his work, she'd ask him to help her back to the house. But that would undoubtedly make him even angrier. She closed her eyes and tried to ignore the stab of pain behind them.

The distinctive sound of the Bugatti's engine roused her just before she dozed off. She had forgotten that Malcolm had said something about dropping by today. Duncan seemed oblivious to the impending visit. He didn't even look up until he heard a knock at the studio door, and even then he took his time answering the summons.

"I hope you don't mind us barging in, old chap," Malcolm said. "We stopped at the house first, and Dulce told us Megan was out here. Hilary couldn't wait to see her."

"I most certainly do mind. You know my studio is off limits." Duncan's mouth was set in an angry line.

Although Hilary was looking around with avid curiosity, she said, "I understand completely, Duncan. Your studio is your sanctum sanctorum and we shouldn't have barged in."

She tugged Malcolm back toward the door, but her gaze continued its ferretlike darting. "It's just that I was so anxious to see Megan, and when Dulce told us she was here, well . . ." She had succeeded in maneuvering Malcolm to the entrance. "We'll wait for the two of you in the house."

Duncan's expression softened slightly. "I don't mean to be rude, but I do have a rule about no visitors in the studio. I'll join you at the house in a moment. In the meantime, would you help Megan back to her room?"

Nurse Binghampton barged into the studio at that moment, looking as formidable as a man-of-war under full sail. She wasted no time firing her first salvo. "I just telephoned Dr. Adelman. He was furious when I told him what's been going on."

Jade couldn't help smiling. Binghampton made it sound as if they'd been having an orgy.

"I just asked our guests to escort my wife back to her room," Duncan replied.

"Surely you don't expect her to walk!" Binghampton looked as if Duncan had assaulted her virtue rather than her authority.

Jade had endured enough of the brouhaha. She got to her feet, pulling her pajama coat tight around her. "I suggest we all get out of my husband's hair. Malcolm, if you'll just give me your arm, I'll be fine." Although the pain in her head made her quite dizzy, she remained resolutely upright while Malcolm hurried to her side. But she didn't object when Binghampton took her other arm.

Jade didn't realize that Hilary had stayed behind until the little procession reached the house.

"I hope you don't mind my staying a moment," Hilary said. "We need to talk."

Duncan scowled. He didn't want Hilary's company, or anyone else's for that matter. "If you'll go up to the house with the others, I'll join you soon."

She ignored his suggestion. "We need to talk," she repeated. "In private."

"Can't it wait?"

"No, Duncan, it can't." She walked over to the sofa so recently vacated by Megan and sat down, then began nervously playing with the hem of her skirt. The sun, pouring in through one of the skylights, turned her platinum hair into a golden nimbus as she leaned into the cushions with sinuous grace.

Despite himself, Duncan thought about how he'd paint her. A Byzantine setting would suit her well. Or . . . He had a vision of her reclining on a chaise, her otherwise nude body glowing through gauze. He'd portray her as an odalisque, a sultan's concubine. For a moment the tantalizing mental picture was more concrete than the

162

reality of her sitting there. "Hilary, why don't you just tell me what's on your mind?"

Hilary smiled to herself. Duncan had looked so angry when she and Malcolm barged in, she'd half expected him to eject her forcibly after the others left. Now she paused, preparing to put on the performance of her life. "I wish it was that easy," she said, allowing her voice to quaver a little. "I don't want to hurt you the way I've been hurt. If I were the only one involved, I wouldn't hesitate to tell you."

"Involved in what?"

"Oh God, I wish I didn't have to do this." She sniffled loudly, thanking her lucky stars that she'd always been able to weep on cue. "It's Megan . . . Megan and Malcolm."

"What about them?"

"You mean you haven't noticed?" She reached in her purse for a monogramed handkerchief and dabbed at her tears, being careful not to smear her mascara. "I'm afraid they're falling in love," she sobbed.

Duncan reacted right on cue. He sat down beside her and put an arm around her hunched shoulders.

"I never told you this," she went on, "because I don't like people to feel sorry for me. You see, I'm an orphan. My parents died when I was in my teens. I was desperately lonely when I met Malcolm and he— Well, he's all I have. He's been promising to marry me for years, but now . . ."

Duncan felt he had no choice but to comfort Hilary. He held her, letting her cry it out. She felt frail, her bones as delicate as a fawn's. He'd always thought of Hilary as tough, a bit of a doxy and more than capable of taking care of herself in any situation. Now he realized her brash exterior must be a cover, a defense against being hurt. The woman was vulnerable and in real pain.

He felt like a heel. When he began throwing Megan and Malcolm together, it hadn't occurred to him to consider how Hilary might be affected. "I'm so sorry, Hilary," he murmured into her halo of golden hair.

"It's just that I don't know what to do. I don't know where else to turn. Please forgive me." Her voice was husky with misery. "I shouldn't have said anything. This can't be easy on you either."

"It's different for me," he replied, giving Hilary his own handkerchief when he saw that hers was sodden. "Megan and I—we aren't exactly Romeo and Juliet."

Hilary gave a sad little laugh. "Neither are Malcolm and I. But that doesn't mean I don't love him."

She pulled away and straightened, looking at Duncan through lashes dewy with tears. He found himself admiring her courage, her honesty. He'd gotten her into this mess and he silently vowed to see she wasn't hurt too badly, no matter the outcome. "Feeling better?" he asked.

"I'm terribly embarrassed." She took her compact from her purse and began repairing the damage. "I usually fight my own fights."

He couldn't help but appreciate her independence, her spunk. "I hate to see you like this."

She managed a brave smile. "I know I don't always put my best foot forward, but I've always considered you a friend and I hope you feel the same way about me. I know it's asking a lot, but could you talk to Megan, ask her to stop spending so much time with Malcolm?"

"You must know I can't. But even if I could, I don't think it would change things. Megan doesn't listen to me. She hasn't for years."

She dropped her head. "I shouldn't have said anything to you. I'm so ashamed. I just needed to talk to someone. If you won't help . . ." Her voice broke.

She was trembling so hard that he pulled her closer. The poor kid. He'd had no idea she was so alone in the world. "I can't do what you want," he said, "but that doesn't mean I won't help you. If you ever need anything, anything at all—someone you can confide in, a little financial help—just let me know."

Binghampton had been fussing and fuming ever since Malcolm had helped Jade back to her bed. Despite his presence, the nurse had insisted on taking Jade's pulse and temperature. Next, Jade thought, she'll probably try to put me on a bedpan.

"Would you get Mr. Ashford some sherry?" she asked, hoping Binghampton would take the hint and leave the room.

"I think we've had quite enough excitement for one day," the nurse replied.

"We have not," Jade said firmly.

Malcolm turned to the nurse and smiled his most reassuring smile. "I promise, I'll only stay a few minutes. And I really would like a glass of sherry."

"Oh, very well," Binghampton said. She returned Malcolm's smile before she bustled out of the room.

"You handled that quite well," Jade said. "But then you handle most things well."

Malcolm beamed. "You bring out the best in me."

"I wonder what's keeping Duncan and Hilary?"

"You know Hilary. She's probably trying to convince Duncan to show his work in her gallery."

"You're wrong," Hilary said, suddenly walking through the bedroom door with Duncan at her heels. "I was just asking Duncan's advice."

"About what?" Jade asked, unable to keep the suspicion out of her voice.

Hilary gave her a guileless smile. "Why don't you ask Duncan?"

Before Jade could, Binghampton walked in and glared disapprovingly at everyone.

Duncan relieved Binghampton of the tray she was carrying and told her he'd call her when she was needed. After hustling her out of the room, he busied himself pouring drinks, being very careful, Jade noted, to avoid her eyes.

Half an hour later she was too exhausted to care about Duncan or Hilary or anything. She was on the brink of saying she needed to get some rest when Malcolm suddenly interrupted the conversation. "I forgot to tell you we picked up your mail. I left the rest of it with Dulce, but this letter is addressed to you, Megan." He reached into his pocket and produced an envelope as he approached the bed. "It's from *Harper's*."

Jade's head hurt so much, she had trouble focusing on the print. She opened the envelope, then handed it back to Malcolm. "Would you read it to me?"

He gazed at her intently. "Are you sure you want me to? It may be bad news."

She appreciated his sensitivity. Why was Malcolm so in tune with her feelings and Duncan so oblivious to them? If *Harper's* rejected her idea for an article about Maria, Malcolm didn't want her to have to deal with it in front of the others. She wished she could tell him she'd long since learned to handle the rejection that writers—even the best—must face. "It's all right. Go ahead."

As Malcolm slipped the letter from the envelope, Duncan studied his wife's face. She looked exhausted, and he knew he should have told Malcolm and Hilary to leave. But now they'd all have to wait to hear what *Harper's* said. He hoped it wasn't a rejection. He'd hate to see her hurt in that way. Yet if they accepted her idea, would Malcolm then offer to be her personal editor, giving them even more opportunities to be together?

Malcolm cleared his throat. " 'Dear Mrs. Carlisle,' " he read, " 'we were delighted to receive your proposal for an article about Maria Martinez. The subject matter is one we think our readers will find interesting . . .' " He stopped reading and tossed the letter in the air, letting out a jubilant whoop. "You did it, Megan, you did it!" he exclaimed, sitting on the edge of the bed and giving her an impulsive hug.

"Congratulations," Duncan said. He took a step forward, surprised to realize that he was truly pleased, that he was proud of her success. He wished they were alone so they could share this moment together. But he stopped in midstride when he saw her face. From the look in her eyes as she gazed at Malcolm, she had no desire to share her success with anyone else.

Bitterness welled in Duncan's throat as he admitted he had brought this moment on himself. Earlier in the day, he had gotten angry when Megan talked about her writing because it reminded him of Malcolm's growing importance in her life. But he had failed Megan as a husband long ago. He had no right to begrudge her the all-too-obvious happiness she had found with another man.

He didn't realize that his mouth had narrowed to a thin line as he considered the strange twists and turns of fate that had brought him to this denouement. The first time he'd seen Megan at the Max Gallery, he'd felt that eerie shock of recognition, as if he had known her all his life. But the passing years had made it clear that they had been and always would be strangers. Yet now, when it was too late, there were times when he looked at her and experienced that uncanny feeling all over again.

Jade gazed over Malcolm's shoulder and saw a flurry of emotions —surprise, confusion, and finally sadness—chase each other across Duncan's face. He wasn't alone in his displeasure, though. If looks could kill, she would have died on the spot from the one Hilary sent her way.

Malcolm alone seemed oblivious to the emotional currents in the room. "If you're up to it," he said, "I can come over tomorrow and help you get started on an outline. I rather fancy myself as your amanuensis. Oh, Megan," he said gleefully, "this can be the start of a whole new life for you."

After they were gone, Jade remembered his words. A whole new life. No one knew she already had one.

CHAPTER 15

Rancho Cielo
August 5, 1929

Duncan sat at the breakfast table drinking coffee and watching Megan pore over the *Santa Fe New Mexican* from front page to back. Two or three months ago she thought the local paper a terminal bore and confined her reading to the society pages of *The New York Times*, *Vogue*, *The New Yorker*, and *Harper's*.

Her conversation used to be dominated by two subjects—the latest fashion trends and her own unhappiness. Now there were times when her blossoming intellect managed to bridge the widening gap between them, when she engaged him in lively debate about such diverse topics, he almost forgot their marital problems.

He still couldn't deal with the fact that she had actually written an article for *Harper's*, or that she had embarked on a novel. If she had matured earlier, their marriage might have been saved. That she had changed at all was directly due to Malcolm Ashford's influence. Megan had reinvented herself to please the writer. Clearly he meant more to her than Duncan ever had.

Suddenly she looked up and caught him staring. She blushed

from neck to hairline, another example of her metamorphosis. The old Megan never blushed.

"Why are you looking at me like that?" she asked.

"I was just wondering what you have planned for the day."

"I'm driving into Santa Fe to lunch with Malcolm. He insists on going over the article about Maria Martinez one last time before I mail it. Can I get you anything while I'm in town?"

"You might stop at the travel agent and double-check on our train tickets."

She stared blankly at him. She had been doing that a lot the last few months. They would be in the middle of a conversation and, without warning, the light in her eyes would blink out and he'd have the feeling he was talking to a stranger who didn't understand English.

"Surely you remember our trip?" he said.

"Of course." Her voice was firm but she didn't meet his gaze. "I just have a lot on my mind this morning. What were you saying about tickets?"

"Never mind. I'll get them myself the next time I go to town." He knew too well what distracted Megan. Half the time she seemed so far away, she might as well have been on another planet. He knew, however, that her thoughts weren't on an astral plane. They were with Malcolm. The knowledge was a cancer in his soul, a fatal disease he had brought on himself.

He stood, turning away before the look in his eyes could betray him. "If you need me for anything I'll be in the studio the rest of the day, crating paintings for the show."

"Show?" She had blinked out again.

"For God's sake, Megan, you know I do a show at the Max Gallery every year. Remember? That's where we met." To his eternal regret.

She had the good grace to look embarrassed. "I'm so sorry, Duncan. I know how important the show is to you."

"Sometimes I think the accident left you with a mild case of amnesia. Dr. Adelman said it might happen."

She cut him a quizzical glance. "I wish you had told me before.

I've been worrying because I do seem to have forgotten a number of things."

"What kind of things?"

"All sorts. The date of the show for instance." She reached up and touched the scar hidden beneath her hair, a seemingly unconscious gesture.

For a moment Duncan returned to the afternoon when he had found her injured on the forest floor. He had been so afraid for her then. Now he feared for his own well-being. He had fallen desperately in love with his wife all over again . . . and it was too damn late. Admitting that hurt like no pain he had ever experienced. "I'm sorry," he said, aware that she was gazing at him with puzzlement. "What were we talking about?"

"The date of the show."

"It's scheduled to open on October 16."

"Thanks for reminding me. I won't forget this time. I can't wait to see Ira Max." She sounded so enthusiastic, he almost believed her. Autumn in New York used to hold a special charm for both of them—but he doubted their marriage would last until the fall. When Megan left Santa Fe, it wouldn't be with him.

What was it he used to tell her? Beware of what you wish for because you may get it. He had wished Megan out of his life. Despair swept over him as he grappled with the knowledge that his wish would soon come true.

"I'd better be going," he said abruptly, and fled the room without looking back. He had to get away from Megan, because if he didn't, he would make a fool of himself by telling her how he felt.

After he left, Jade poured herself another cup of coffee, lit a cigarette, and waited for her pulse to slow. Why hadn't Duncan told her about the possibility of amnesia before? With injury-related memory loss for an excuse, she could stop worrying about all the things she didn't know and concentrate on the ones she did. Such as the coming stock market crash and all the tragic things that would follow on its heels. Soon the Four Horsemen of the Apocalypse would be loose in the world.

She picked up the paper and reread the headlines. The *Graf Zeppelin* had crossed the Atlantic. Chinese tongs were at war with each other in Chicago. Drug addicts had escaped from a state institution in Los Angeles. And the stock market continued to climb. She let go her breath. There was no sign of trouble on Wall Street yet.

Before tumbling through time, she had read very little about the twenties. She did know that the stock market crashed at the end of October 1929. In two and a half months the bubble would burst, the good times would come to a screeching halt. Millionaires would become paupers overnight, stock brokers would leap to their deaths from office windows, middle-class investors would lose their life's savings, and the new poor would wander the streets panhandling for dimes. A decade of darkness was going to shroud the world—and Hitler would emerge from the shadows.

She shuddered at the thought of what lay ahead.

She couldn't change the inevitable. But she could try to protect the people she knew. Whom should she confide in? Malcolm or Duncan?

Dulce was washing the breakfast dishes when she saw the señora running up the drive. She was wearing tennis shoes and a pair of shocking, abbreviated pants she had made herself. Shorts she called them, and short they were!

"She's doing it again," Dulce said, gesturing out the window.

Jorge rose from his place at the table and joined her. "Why in the world would a woman want to run like that?"

"I don't know. It's unnatural!" Dulce rubbed her forehead as if doing so would dispel the doubt and confusion that troubled her. "There are so many things I don't understand about that woman."

Jorge put his arm around her waist and gave her a comforting squeeze. "It might help if we talked."

She nodded as she dried her hands, then she walked to the table with leaden feet. Suddenly she felt old and weary. "I can't get Señora Carlisle off my mind."

"With you, it's always the señora," Jorge replied, pulling out a chair and sitting down. "First you swear to get rid of her. Then you almost do and I get blamed for it. Now what?"

She hesitated. "I may have . . . made a mistake about her."

"*Madre de Dios.* What are you saying?" Impatience harshened his voice.

171

Although she occasionally made fun of him and called him *sencillo*, deep down Dulce knew Jorge was a better person than she could ever hope to be. She wanted him to think well of her. How would he react when she admitted she had misjudged the woman who lived in this house as Señora Carlisle? He sat back, waiting for her to speak.

"I have watched the señora very carefully," she said, "looking for signs of her sorcery . . . but I haven't found any. She doesn't act like the old señora, but I no longer think this new woman is a *bruja*."

Jorge didn't speak, but he leaned forward, nodding his encouragement.

"Remember how the old señora used to let me plan all the meals and do all the shopping, and then got furious if I didn't do things exactly the way she wanted?"

Jorge nodded again.

"This new señora has made every effort to be my friend. And believe me, I have done my best to discourage her. At first I was terrified in her presence. But she is never angry or impatient the way she used to be—just a little sad sometimes. She insists on planning the menus and we make the shopping lists together. She has even asked me to teach her how to cook the señor's favorite dishes. And she is trying to learn Spanish."

Jorge frowned so fiercely, his bushy eyebrows met over the bridge of his nose. "And this is the woman you almost killed?"

Dulce squeezed her hands together tightly, until she felt a twinge of pain. *Mea culpa, mea maxima culpa*, she thought. Thank heaven she had never told Jorge about her talk with the Binghampton woman. He would be even more upset if he knew she had planned to poison the señora. "My only excuse is that I truly thought she was a *bruja*."

"And now what do you think?"

"The señora isn't a *bruja* . . . but she isn't the señora either."

"You speak in riddles."

"I know it doesn't make sense. But neither do the señor and señora. Sometimes I look at them and I would swear on my family's honor that they are in love again."

He nodded. "I have seen it too."

172

"Then answer me this. Why don't they sleep together anymore? Why do they seem so happy sometimes and so miserable at others? And why does the señora run around the countryside on foot like a mad woman?"

"It's as you have always said. Who can understand the ways of Anglos? But I know you. You always have a plan. What are you going to do?"

She took a steadying breath. "I am going to tell Señor Carlisle the truth—what I did, what I think, the whole thing. And then I am going to tell him that you and I are leaving Rancho Cielo. We are too old to deal with this mystery."

Malcolm arrived for breakfast at La Plazuela early. He wanted some time to compose himself before Hilary showed up. He had chosen a public place to tell her of his decision, counting on her being too mindful of her standing in the community to make a spectacle of herself—and him.

He had just finished his first cup of coffee when he saw her standing at La Plazuela's entrance. She paused and looked around, posing like a mannequin, giving the other diners the opportunity to take in her superb appearance. This morning she wore an ice-blue marocain cape over a matching one-piece dress. Artfully arranged wisps of her platinum hair peeked out from a turban in the same shade of blue. With her delicate ivory skin, she looked like a delectable confection. The outfit, he realized, had been carefully chosen to remind him of her considerable charms.

Although he waved to catch her attention, she continued to hold her pose until she was the cynosure of all eyes. Then she gaily called, "There you are, darling," and headed toward his table with a lubricious glide that reminded him of the tango.

"Having breakfast with you is a lovely way to start the day," she said as he helped her into a chair. "I've missed you, darling. But I know how single-minded you can be when you're working on a book. How is it going?"

"Quite well."

Her affable demeanor was a pleasant surprise. Hilary wasn't the sort of woman who tolerated being left alone for very long. And she was far too intuitive and clever not to realize he had been avoiding her. He expected, even hoped, she would be angry at his recent lack of attention. He could say good-bye to an angry Hilary without a qualm. Saying good-bye to a smiling one would be a lot harder.

"I've been really busy at the shop the last few weeks," she said. "The rest of the world seems to have discovered Santa Fe. You have no idea how hard it is to keep things in stock with so many tourists in town."

Her chitchat was interrupted by the arrival of a waiter. She ordered ham and eggs but Malcolm, who dreaded the next hour, just asked for juice and more coffee.

"You're not very hungry this morning," she said after the waiter left. "I hope it's not the company."

"You know better than that."

"Do I? Lately, I've wondered. I really have missed you."

He looked at her, wondering how to begin. She gazed back, giving him a wide-eyed innocent stare. But Hilary was not the naïf she pretended to be. If he knew her, she already suspected what he was going to say.

"I have been busy writing," he said, "but that's not the reason I've been out of touch."

"You don't need to tell me anything. We always agreed we were both entitled to a private life."

"I'm glad you remembered. That's part of why I wanted to see you today—to talk about my private life." Damn, she was making it hard on him. When Hilary wanted to, she could charm the devil himself.

She gave him a dewy-eyed smile. "Confession may be good for the soul, but you don't need to bother. You've strayed before and I've always ignored it. Forgive and forget—that's my motto."

"This isn't about a casual fling. It's much more than that."

"I assume you're talking about our mutual friend Megan. For all I care, you can screw her on the plaza during Indian Market. But you'll get tired of her the way you tired of all the others. And when you do, I'll be here waiting."

He reached across the table and grasped Hilary's wrist hard enough to make her flinch. "Don't you dare talk about Megan that way."

"Let me go," Hilary whispered fiercely, jerking her wrist free.

Realizing that fury wouldn't help her in this encounter, she kept her tone more reasonable as she said, "Look, I know you have a crush on Megan. If you've been sleeping with her, that's your business. I certainly have no objections. But if I were you I wouldn't want to be around when Duncan finds out. I don't think he'll take kindly to being a cuckold."

"Why is sex the first thing, the only thing you ever think about?"

"Because it's the only thing you or any other man really cares about."

"That's the problem, Hilary. You're convinced everyone else is just like you." Malcolm shut his mouth abruptly as the waiter arrived with their food.

Hilary ignored his jibe and attacked her ham and eggs as if she hadn't eaten for days. "This is delicious. Do you want a taste?" she asked.

He shook his head. "We can fence all morning but it won't change things. I've made a decision and I think it's only fair to tell you about it."

"You know what they say, darling. A stiff prick has no conscience. So don't talk to me about being fair. You've got the hots for Megan. So what?"

He had an almost uncontrollable urge to get up and leave. But he didn't want unfinished business to tarnish the rosy future he contemplated. "I don't, as you so succinctly put it, 'have the hots for Megan.' The details of our relationship are none of your business. In all *fairness*, and I ask your pardon for using the word, I do have something to tell you. I intend to ask Megan to marry me."

Hilary's carefully penciled eyebrows elevated. "Did I hear you right?"

He nodded.

Her laughter rang through the restaurant, causing heads to turn in their direction. "But Malcolm, you're not the marrying kind. Besides, Megan has a husband."

"It's a marriage in name only," he replied. Then, realizing he'd broken his resolve not to discuss the situation, he clamped his mouth shut.

She put down her fork and leaned toward him, a look of utter

175

disbelief in her eyes. "I don't understand. What makes this woman so special? What can she do in bed that I can't?"

"We haven't gone to bed. I told you, I want to marry her."

"Why her and not me?" Hilary's voice actually trembled.

"That should be obvious."

For a second, he thought Hilary was going to pick up her plate and throw it at him. She didn't, and when she spoke, her voice was steady again. "I assume you mean I'm good enough to sleep with but not good enough to marry. You cold, unfeeling bastard."

"A cold, unfeeling bastard would tell you to get lost. Surely you must have known this day would come sooner or later?"

"Why? We've been happy. I've never denied you anything, in or out of bed. Have I?"

"Don't make this any harder than it has to be. We had an arrangement, a business deal, a rapprochement—not a love affair. I'm prepared to live up to my side of the bargain." He reached into his jacket and pulled out an envelope, dropping it on the table. "This is for you, with my thanks. I hope we can still be friends."

Hilary seemed mesmerized by the envelope. She stared at it with the concentration of a snake charmer confronting a cobra. Then she snatched it from the table. Her lips pursed as she tore it open. One by one, she removed the contents—the deed to the house he had bought for her when they arrived in Santa Fe, the deed to her gallery, and a check for twenty-five thousand dollars. She read the documents, licked her lips, put them down, then picked them back up and read them all over again.

Malcolm sipped his coffee and waited for her to say something. He had been, he thought, more than generous. The deeds represented a hundred-thousand-dollar investment on his part, and the check would give her a very comfortable financial cushion.

She finally seemed to remember he was there. "Am I supposed to thank you for dumping me?" she asked.

"Of course not. But you could thank me for giving you a house and a gallery, to say nothing of the money."

"I earned all of it." She opened her purse and quickly put the documents inside as if she thought he might take them back. "Now, since you want to part as friends, why don't you tell me when you plan to pop the big question."

"Today. I'm having lunch with Megan." No sooner were the words out of his mouth than he knew he should have kept silent.

To his relief, though, the fire in her eyes seemed to burn out. "I think you're riding for a fall, darling. If it doesn't work out, if she turns you down, if you need consolation, I'll be at the gallery all afternoon." She pushed her chair back and got to her feet. To his surprise, she reached down and captured his chin in her hand. "I know you don't want to admit it, but you and I were made for each other. You'll be back. Just don't make me wait too long."

Before he could tell her how wrong she was or even say good-bye, she spun on her heel and walked away, her pace increasing with every step. She was in full flight by the time she left La Plazuela.

A sense of freedom washed over him as he watched her departure. She couldn't have been more wrong, he thought as he dropped a couple of dollars on the table to cover their bill. He would never go back to her.

Hilary ignored Raoul's surprised good morning when she returned home several hours before she was expected. "Get me a drink," she snapped.

"Coffee?"

"No. Whisky, straight up."

At first she roamed from room to room, glass in hand, taking no pleasure in the fact that she now owned the place. The thought of letting Malcolm walk out of her life without a backward glance sent bursts of acid through her stomach. Who the hell did he think he was? There had to be a way to stop him—or failing that, to put a monkey wrench in his plans. She would be damned if she'd sit idly by while he and Megan lived happily ever after.

At half past twelve, freshly bathed and dressed in a new outfit, she climbed into her Chevrolet. The car heightened her fury. Malcolm had bought it for her in 1926 and she had never liked it. She had been planning to wheedle him into buying her a Packard convertible like the one Megan drove. But now, unless she quickly found a new sugar daddy, she would have to buy the automobile herself. She cursed under her breath as she backed out of her drive. Damn all men for what they had done to her. Someday, somehow, she would find a way to take her revenge.

She gave her anger free rein until she turned onto the rutted drive that led to Rancho Cielo. Then, knowing she needed to think with perfect clarity when she confronted Duncan, she closeted her rage in the darkest corner of her mind.

She checked her watch one last time as she parked near the studio. It was one in the afternoon. Malcolm and Megan would just be finishing their lunch. If she knew Malcolm, he wouldn't want a waiter to interrupt their romantic tête-à-tête. He would wait until the table had been cleared before he spoke his mind. Megan couldn't possibly get back to the ranch for a couple of hours.

Hilary checked her appearance in the rearview mirror, powdered her nose, reapplied her lipstick, and fluffed her hair. The sun disappeared behind a cloud as she exited the car, and she glanced up. It seemed a storm was coming.

"Duncan," she called out, knocking on the studio door, "it's Hilary."

Her heart sank as she waited for an answer—and waited. So much depended on his being there. She knocked again and called his name even louder. Putting her ear to the door, she heard the rhythmic sound of hammering. She opened the door and stepped inside.

Duncan had his back to her. He was bending over a large wooden crate, driving nails into the lid with powerful strokes. She delayed announcing her presence long enough to observe him, enjoying the interplay of muscles in his shoulders and arms. He had a raw power, a virility she had always wanted to explore. Today was as good a time as any to start. But she would have to lure him to the hook with infinite care.

She assembled her features into an appropriately grief-stricken mien, then walked up behind him and tapped his shoulder. He whirled to face her, his hammer slightly raised as if to ward off an intruder. For a second she felt a delicious thrill of fear. Dangerous men excited her.

"What are you doing here?" he demanded.

Not exactly an auspicious beginning, she thought. "You said to let you know if I ever needed help—and I need it today." She let her shoulders slump.

His forbidding expression softened. "I'm sorry. You took me by

178

surprise. I wasn't expecting anyone. Can I get you some coffee, or would you like a drink?" While he talked, he unbuckled his tool-laden carpenter's belt and put it on a shelf.

"I'd like a brandy, and you'd better pour one for yourself while you're at it. What I have to say involves you too."

The only indication that her remark aroused his curiosity was a lift of his eyebrows as he walked to a cupboard. He took out a bottle and a couple of glasses and set them on the table in front of the sofa. After beckoning for her to join him, he busied himself pouring drinks.

"What's on your mind?" he asked, handing her a glass.

She brought it to her lips and swallowed a burning draft that brought tears to her eyes and left her gasping. "I needed that," she said.

"I can see you're upset. I don't have to be a mind reader to figure out it has something to do with Megan and Malcolm. Why don't you tell me what's happened now."

"Did you know they're having lunch today?"

He nodded. "Megan said something about Malcolm wanting to go over her *Harper's* article."

"That was just an excuse. Malcolm has far more important things on his mind. He plans to ask Megan to marry him."

Duncan didn't flinch. He continued to look at her steadfastly, but his eyes seemed to darken as if an angry storm had swept through them. "How long have you known?"

"I had breakfast with Malcolm this morning. That's when he told me."

"Why are you here? What do you want from me?"

Hilary took her time lighting a cigarette. She hadn't expected his question. Any other man would have reacted to her news with anger. She had hoped to fan his emotions until they reached a fever pitch. After he was out of control and vulnerable, she would seduce him. "Doesn't it make you angry, thinking of the two of them together? God knows how long they've been carrying on behind our backs. They're probably laughing at us this very minute."

"I know this must be painful for you, but if Megan asks me for a divorce for whatever reason, I intend to agree."

Hilary was so startled, her mouth gaped open. "Don't you have any pride?"

Now it was his turn to drink deeply. "I won't fight a divorce. There's no point. You can't make someone love you or want to stay with you."

Hilary couldn't repress her rage any longer. "Damn you!" she screamed as she leaped to her feet. "You promised to help me."

"I will if I can." His voice was eerily calm. "But I won't ruin three lives to do it."

She stormed across the studio, then whirled back. "You men are all alike. You talk a good game but when the time comes, you refuse to play by the rules. I told you I'm alone in the world. Your wife has stolen the only man I ever cared about and you just sit there and tell me how you won't ruin their lives. What about mine?" Her voice had risen until it reverberated through the studio.

She could see the muscles in Duncan's jaw clenching. "I'm truly sorry, Hilary. I said I would do what I could for you, and I will. I assume Malcolm has been giving you financial help. Has he done anything to provide for your future?"

"Not a damn thing. The bastard just walked out on me." Immediately she saw the way to turn the situation to her advantage, to grasp a sizable profit from the wreckage of her life. She moderated her tone and lowered her hate-filled eyes. "I don't mean to take it out on you. The problem is that I've depended on Malcolm for operating capital. I have a huge mortgage on the gallery as well as one on the house, and the business isn't making a profit yet. But I believe in its future. I know I can turn the situation around with a little help."

"How much?"

She sighed heavily and sank back down on the sofa beside him. "Oh, Duncan, I wish it didn't have to come down to money. I wish we could just be friends and support each other emotionally through the months ahead."

"I know. It's hard to deal with the knowledge that you've made the mistake of a lifetime." He seemed to be talking to himself.

"I had plans to renovate the gallery," she continued, "plans that would help make Santa Fe a mecca for art collectors. And now . . ." She shrugged in defeat as her voice trailed off.

"There's no reason for you to change your plans." He got up and walked over to a battered desk, then returned to the sofa carrying a blank check. While she watched, he entered the date and made the check out to her. "I'd feel a lot better if one of us profited from this whole mess. How much do you need?"

"Ten thousand dollars to start."

He didn't blink as he filled in the amount.

She took the check from his hand and tucked it inside her purse. "Is there anything I can do for you? I know you must be hurt and lonely. I could comfort you. We could comfort each other." She reached over and traced the line of his mouth with her fingertip.

He pulled away from her and got up. "I appreciate the offer, but I don't think that would solve anything. And now, if you don't mind, I'd like to be alone."

She got to her feet as well, then stood on tiptoe and kissed him, running the tip of her tongue over his closed mouth. When he didn't respond she turned to leave, fluttering her hand in farewell as she opened the studio door. Once outside, she could hardly contain her jubilation. Duncan Carlisle was a pigeon—a golden goose!—ripe for the plucking. All she had to do was play on his guilt and there would be lots more where the ten thousand came from.

She scurried to her car, started the engine, and turned up the drive. She could hardly wait to put the day's earnings, all thirty-five thousand dollars, in her stockbroker's hands. The way the market was climbing, she wouldn't need Malcolm or Duncan or any other man much longer.

"I love you," Malcolm was saying, "and I want you to be my wife."

Jade had just taken a gulp of water and now she was choking on it. She could feel herself turning red as she fought for breath. Malcolm leaned across the table and pounded her on the back. "I'm sorry. I guess I shouldn't have blurted it out . . . but I thought you knew."

He looked so abashed, her heart went out to him. "I'm touched, truly I am, but I never thought of you that way."

"Not once in all these weeks? I can't believe that. You and I, well, I've never felt closer to another woman. When we're together and talking about writing, you come alive. I've never seen you so happy, so excited. Don't you see how right we are for each other?"

Jade felt sickened by his sincerity. What a mess she had made of Megan's life. She'd known Malcolm had a crush on her, or rather on Megan. The trouble was, she had been too preoccupied with her own problems to realize it had gone far beyond a crush. Now she was going to have to hurt Malcolm and there wasn't a damn thing she could do about it. "I like you more than you can possibly know, and I respect your talent. But I'm not in love with you."

As she said the words, the truth she had been hiding from for so many weeks burst free. No, she wasn't in love with Malcolm. As well suited as they seemed, as much as she admired his talent, enjoyed sharing the joys of writing with him, she did not love him. She would always be grateful to him for so many things, his friendship most of all. But it wasn't friendship she wanted. It wasn't friendship that kept her awake in the small hours of the night, when she burned for, ached for, hungered for another man. It was Duncan. As much as he irritated and frustrated her, as much as she longed to batter against him until he dropped his cold shield and let her see the warm, joyous, and loving man he kept hidden from her, she loved him. Completely, irreversibly, wildly. All her doubts and fears fled before that admission. She felt like a blind woman whose sight had been restored, an amputee who suddenly had legs.

Malcolm was searching her face as if he couldn't bring himself to believe what she had said. "I guess I should have waited a little longer before I told you how I feel."

She shook her head. "Waiting wouldn't have changed anything. Love has its own rules, its own time." She was so eager to return to Rancho Cielo and tell Duncan the truth, she had to force herself to stay in her chair. For the moment, Malcolm deserved her complete attention.

"Please hear me out," he said, seeming to sense her anxiety. "It's been obvious to your friends that you and Duncan haven't been happy for years. I've watched you wither at Rancho Cielo. Then a couple of months ago, you began to blossom, emotionally, intellectually. The change seemed to go hand in hand with our spending more time together. Don't you see what that means?"

"You're misinterpreting the situation." If only she could tell him the truth, she thought. It might make this less painful. "If I seemed to change, it's because I decided to write. You helped me and I will always be grateful—but gratitude isn't love. Besides, Hilary loves you."

"No she doesn't. She needs me. I should say she needs my money."

He sounded so bitter, tears gathered in Jade's eyes. They had both experienced an epiphany, but hers held out hope for the future while his led to a dead end. "I'm not the person you think I am," she said as she stood. "I wish I could be." She turned away from the bleak landscape of his eyes and left.

Tomorrow or the day after, she would try to help him deal with his disappointment. Right now, though, the only thing on her mind was returning to Rancho Cielo and the man she loved. She had already wasted too much time.

CHAPTER 16

Jade put the key in the Packard's ignition, set the choke, advanced the spark, and pushed the starter button. To her relief the engine snarled into life, rocking the car with its power. She threw in the clutch, shifted into first gear, released the brake, and tentatively fed the car gas. Muscles in her arms and shoulders strained as she pulled away from the curb in front of La Fonda.

She had disliked the car the first time she sat behind the wheel, and her feelings hadn't altered since. The Packard had bucked and juddered every time she shifted gears that first day. She'd spent two frustrating hours practicing her driving, and by the time she parked the car, she had been arm-weary. For the life of her, she couldn't see why Malcolm and Hilary raved about the Packard.

That afternoon, though, she didn't curse the complicated ignition sequence, the stiff gearing, or the absence of power steering. The Packard was the magical coach and four that would carry her to the Prince's castle. She could hardly wait to get there. *Home.* She could finally admit that Rancho Cielo had become her home in a way the Malibu house had never been. The Malibu house held her possessions while Rancho Cielo held her heart.

Nothing could dull her shining happiness, not even the thought of Malcolm and Megan. Malcolm was a grown man who would handle his disappointment with his customary élan. And Megan had disappeared into the void of time.

Jade had spent the last three months paying homage to Megan's memory, existing in her shadow, acting as a caretaker for her life, thinking of Megan's yesterdays when her own todays should have been the only thing that mattered. Today might be all she had. At any moment the unknown force that had pulled her back through time might propel her forward again.

Soon she would face Duncan as Jade Howard. She knew the risk her revelation entailed, but she couldn't let fear stop her the way it had so many times before. Wasn't the truth supposed to set you free?

She was oblivious to the darkening sky until the first drops of rain splattered the windshield. She turned on the wipers and kept the car moving at a steady forty miles an hour. Duncan was the magnet that drew her onward. A simple rain shower wouldn't stop her, or even slow her down.

By the time she reached the Rancho Cielo turnoff the day had grown unnaturally dark. The road appeared suddenly out of the gloom, and she braked hard. The Packard slewed out of control when it made contact with the already muddy surface, snapping branches as it careened up the tree-lined drive. She hadn't come this far to fail now, she thought, gripping the wheel with desperate determination. The tires finally found some traction, and she was able to guide the car down the rutted path.

Lights glowed in the studio and the Ortizs' cottage, but the main house was dark. Blackjack sat in the shelter of the front *portal,* his sodden fur making him seem small and forlorn. Why was he still out in the storm? It wasn't like Dulce not to let him in.

Jade got out of the car and ran to the front door. She let the dog in and called Dulce's name. No one responded, and she turned on the lights in the entry. Blackjack shook vigorously, spraying everything in the vicinity. Then he padded off in the direction of the den, looking over his shoulder as if to say he hoped Jade would join him.

"I'll be back," she promised.

Heedless of the pelting rain, she plunged back outside and raced for the studio. She knocked on the door and, not waiting for a response, let herself in. Duncan was sitting on the sofa, an open brandy bottle, two glasses, and an overflowing ashtray on the table in front of him. He didn't look up, although he had to have heard her arrival. The only sign of life in the preternaturally quiet room was the curl of smoke that drifted from his cigarette.

The fears she had been repressing resurfaced. What-ifs rose in her throat like bile. What if Duncan thought she was crazy? What if he blamed her for Megan's absence? What if he wanted Megan back?

"I'm home," she said past lips that didn't want to work.

Still he didn't look up. "I've been expecting you."

She ignored his glacial tone, comforting herself with the thought that something must have happened to upset him during her absence. She gestured at the two glasses. "Did you have company this afternoon?"

He nodded.

She knew how he hated being interrupted when he was working. Perhaps that explained his mood.

"How was your lunch?" he asked, finally turning to look at her. His face was an ice sculpture.

She shrank from his gaze. Good God, what had happened to make him look like that? Never mind, she commanded herself. It didn't matter. The only thing that mattered was telling him the truth—now, before she lost her nerve.

"Lunch was fine," she said.

"I'll bet," he muttered.

She wanted to sit down beside him, to touch him just once before they talked, but she didn't dare. She stood stock still, rooted by her own diffidence. "I have something to tell you," she said haltingly, "something you may have a hard time believing."

He turned away from her, leaning forward to fill one of the empty glasses with brandy. He drank it down as if it were lemonade.

"Please," she said, "won't you look at me? I can't talk to the back of your head. This is too important to both of us."

He put the empty tumbler down with a thump that threatened to shatter the glass. "There's no need to have this conversation. I already know what you have to say."

"But you couldn't possibly—"

"Shut up! For once in your life, just shut up." He thrust himself to his feet so suddenly, he knocked the table over. The glasses tumbled onto the floor.

She could feel her resolve withering under his glare. "For both our sakes, you've got to hear me out."

He began to advance on her. "If you have any decency, any thought for anyone but yourself, you'll get the hell out of here before I do something we'll both regret."

Her worst nightmare was coming true. Somehow he'd found out she wasn't Megan, and he hated her for it.

"Get out," he repeated.

Jade felt as if her legs were trapped in primordial muck. She forced herself to take one step and then another, moving toward the door in what seemed to be slow motion. She wasn't aware of opening the door or shutting it behind her, or of standing in the heavy rain that quickly drenched her to the skin. The next thing she knew she was in the Packard, shivering and weeping, heading back up the drive.

Duncan poured another brandy, filling a fresh glass to the brim. He brought the heavy tumbler to his lips but he didn't taste the liquor. Getting drunk wasn't the answer, he told himself. Although he would have welcomed the oblivion, he raised his arm and threw the glass against the wall, releasing a self-hatred that left him shaking.

How could he have treated Megan so badly? He liked to think he was a better man than that. She had had the courage to face him when she could have let a lawyer, or even Malcolm, handle everything. Instead she had come to him, seeking his understanding, needing to talk, and he had responded by throwing her out.

She had no idea his feelings for her had changed. Like a stubborn fool, he hadn't permitted himself to show it. The last time they had discussed their marriage, he had asked her for a divorce. He had even refused to return to their bed after she recovered from the concussion. Now he had tossed aside what was probably his last chance to tell her how he felt.

What was it she had said—something about wanting to tell him the truth, and that he might have a hard time believing it? He shook his head, trying to clear away the miasma that fogged his mind. What if she had turned Malcolm down and his own behavior had driven her straight back into the writer's arms? Duncan groaned at the thought. He had to find her, talk to her, tell her his own truth.

Two strides took him to the door and he pulled it open. He started in surprise when he saw Dulce standing there. She was sodden despite the heavy wool rebozo that covered her head and shoulders.

"I have something to tell you, señor," she said.

"Can't it wait? I'm in a hurry."

She shook her head and brushed past him into the studio.

"All right, Dulce. Make it quick."

She stopped in the middle of the floor and turned to face him. Her lips moved, but no words came out. He finally realized that she looked dreadful, as if she had barely survived a disaster.

"Is something wrong with Jorge?" he asked, thinking no other calamity could render her speechless.

She shook her head, yet remained mute.

"I don't have time for guessing games. What is it?"

Dulce astonished him by beginning to weep. She didn't sob out loud and her face remained set in its habitual stoic mold, but tears glistened on her cheeks. "Jorge and I have decided to leave Rancho Cielo," she said.

He reeled back. "Why? You've been with me for twenty years. You're like family. If you need more money, all you have to do is ask."

"It has nothing to do with money. Jorge and I have more than enough to live out our lives in comfort. We're tired, señor. We want to go home to Truchas. We want to live in peace."

"There must be more to it than that."

Her lips worked again. She seemed to be fighting an internal battle. She took a threadbare handkerchief from her dress pocket and blew her nose, then she cleared her throat. "You're right. There is more. It's your wife."

"My wife? What about her? Where is she?"

Dulce blinked owlishly, as if she hadn't expected his question.

"Where is the señora?" he demanded.

"I saw her driving away in the Packard about half an hour ago."
A clap of thunder punctuated Dulce's answer.

"She drove away in this storm?" Anxiety formed a hard lump in Duncan's chest.

"*Sí, señor.* But that's not why I wanted to talk to you."

Duncan had never laid a hand on Dulce before, but he found himself pushing her out of his way none too gently. Dear God, Megan was out in the storm. Although it couldn't be more than late afternoon, the sky was a menacing charcoal color.

"We'll talk later," he said as he pulled open the door. "Right now, I have to find the señora."

Dulce followed close behind. "Shall I ask Jorge to get the Duesenberg?"

Wind buffeted them as they stepped outside. The oak trees and piñon pines swayed like aspen, and large puddles dotted the lawn.

He turned back to Dulce, raising his voice to be heard. "I'll never get a car up the drive in this mess. Have Jorge saddle Excalibur."

Duncan left Dulce where she stood and ran for the house to prepare for what he knew might be the most dangerous ride of his life. He grabbed some clothes, a flask filled with whisky, and a flashlight. A few minutes later he emerged to find Jorge waiting, holding Excalibur's reins, with Dulce by his side. The two of them seemed oblivious to the rain that had already soaked their clothes.

He barely heard their parting, "*Vaya con Dios,*" as he vaulted into the saddle and spurred Excalibur up the drive.

The concrete paving was slick with rain as Jade drove toward Santa Fe. Water filled the guttered embankments on both sides of the road, threatening to overflow onto the highway. Daggers of lightning splintered the sky, and the roar of thunder sounded like timpani.

She had been too upset when she left Rancho Cielo to think about anything but getting away from Duncan. Now she realized how dangerous her precipitous flight had been. The windshield wipers couldn't keep up with the deluge, and she couldn't see more than a few feet ahead. She couldn't even tell how far she had come. Nothing looked familiar. The very ground seemed to be in motion as water ran across its surface.

She knuckled away her tears, then gripped the wheel harder, trying to concentrate on driving. But her mind kept on replaying the scene in the studio. Why had Duncan been so angry?

There's no need to have this conversation, he had said. *I already know what you have to tell me.*

She struggled to bring order to the chaos of her thoughts. She had seen anguish in his eyes—and something else she couldn't identify. Could he have found out about Malcolm's proposal?

No. That wasn't possible.

No one knew.

No one would even care, other than Hilary.

Hilary!

Malcolm had said something about having breakfast with her. He must have told her he planned to propose. Knowing Hilary, she would have wasted no time getting to Duncan with the news.

No wonder he had been so sure he knew what she wanted to tell him. The fact that it upset him was proof that he cared. The only question was, who did he care about? Could he still be in love with Megan?

He had asked Megan for a divorce months ago, Jade reminded herself. The Duncan who had ordered her from his sight today had looked like a wounded lion brought to bay. And that something else she had seen in his eyes—could it have been love?

The bonds that constricted her heart loosened, and the enormous lump in her throat began to dissolve. She slowed the car and carefully braked to a stop. Was she right? Did Duncan care for her? There was only one way to find out.

Turning the car was no easy task on the narrow two-lane road. She didn't dare let the wheels leave the paving for fear of getting mired in the muddy soft shoulder. She was panting with the effort when she finally succeeded in heading the Packard back toward Rancho Cielo.

The black heart of the storm was directly overhead. Thorny clumps of tumbleweed skittered across the road like half-seen phantoms. Lightning struck a tree not fifty feet away, and it flared fire for an instant before the deluge drowned the flames.

She hadn't seen any cars this entire time. Everyone else must have had the good sense to seek shelter. She imagined them sitting by cozy fires, enjoying the special comfort that comes from having a safe haven in a storm. If only she hadn't run away.

She fought her fear, commanding her hands not to shake, her teeth not to chatter, her knees not to knock. Peering ahead, she saw water flowing through a dip in the road. Praying the brakes wouldn't get soaked, she eased the Packard through it.

A few miles later another dip blocked the way. This one was so full of water, it looked more like a river. She tromped on the brake and skidded to a stop. As she was wondering if she should get out to see how deep it was, a nearby lightning-strike changed her mind. She had seen other storms get hung up on the Sangre de Cristo's jagged peaks, but never one as malevolent as this. She had to reach the safety of the ranch before it was too late.

She eased the car down the wash and into the water. Her heart flailed as muddy brown water immediately seeped through the floorboards. The car vibrated from the force of the current.

Between the pounding rain and the steady rumble of thunder, she couldn't hear the engine. She wasn't aware it had stalled until the car stopped moving. She shoved the shift into neutral, advanced the spark, and pushed the starter with frantic haste, but the motor didn't respond. Then she felt something thud into the Packard. Another blow like that and the heavy car would be shoved into the depths of the wash.

By the time Duncan reached the highway, he hoped that his was a fool's errand. Megan had enough of a head start to have made it to Santa Fe before the worst of the storm hit, and she knew enough about the dangers of the weather to stay put once she got there.

The thought comforted him until he realized that she had been too upset when she left to be thinking logically. He had driven her from Rancho Cielo. He would never be able to forgive himself if she came to harm.

Although he'd only been out a few minutes, rain had already trickled under the collar of his slicker and cold rivulets were running down his chest and back. He ignored the soaking and spurred Excalibur into an easy canter. The city lay miles away, a hard ride at any time and a daunting one under these conditions.

The stallion seemed to relish the challenge. He plowed into the rain like a ship battling a heaving sea, never deviating from his course. Duncan leaned over the Arabian's neck, encouraging him with a few words. Rain punished the two of them with an icy sting. It sluiced the highway, painting it red with mud.

The steady clop of Excalibur's iron-shod hooves assured him that they hadn't strayed off the paving, even though he could no longer distinguish the concrete surface from the rest of the landscape. Duncan had no fear of encountering traffic. No one in their right mind would be out on a day like this. He grimaced into the teeth of the storm. He certainly wasn't in his right mind, not after everything that had happened.

Dammit, he had fallen in love with Megan again. It didn't make sense. He hated himself for letting it happen, but he couldn't go on denying it. He wanted her back and if it meant riding through a killer of a storm, so be it.

Water filled every dip and depression, creating miniature lakes or runaway streams. A little farther ahead, the highway ran through a deep wash that was impassable in bad weather. There had been talk of bridging it, but somehow the state was never able to come up with the money.

He could feel the horse tiring. He knew Excalibur would give the last vestige of his strength to do what was asked of him, and he would have to be careful not to ask too much.

Suddenly, he saw a faint glow up ahead. He spurred the horse to a gallop, raising a hand to shield his eyes from the downpour. He was finally able to make out the outline of an automobile, or at least the upper half of one. The bottom half was hidden by muddy water flowing through the wash.

As he drew closer, he saw that it was Megan's Packard. And she was huddled on the hood. He almost laughed with relief and joy as he realized the car faced east, toward Rancho Cielo. She must have been trying to return when the Packard stalled in the rising waters.

Jade had stayed in the car until the rising water reached the seat. Then, shaking with cold and fear, she had opened the convertible top, climbed over the windscreen, and crawled onto the slippery hood. She didn't know how long she crouched there, praying to see another car.

She was racked by the worst terror she had ever known as she felt the Packard shimmying under the onslaught of the flood. Death by drowning was supposed to be peaceful, but she knew there wouldn't be anything peaceful about drowning in the wash. She quickly became so cold that staying upright required an act of will. Her teeth chattered uncontrollably, yet she clung to the hope of rescue with gritty determination.

When she saw a thin beam of light piercing the gloom in the distance, she thought she was hallucinating. She kept her gaze fixed on it, and soon glimpsed an apparition moving toward her, a massive white shape that seemed to materialize from the storm itself. As the ghostly shape closed the distance between them, she realized it was a horse and rider. Although the man wore a yellow slicker and a broad-brimmed hat that concealed his face, there was something familiar about the easy way he sat his mount.

She sobbed with released tension. Thank God. It was Duncan. He urged Excalibur down into the wash, then reined him to a stop in the sheltered lee of the car.

With the last of her strength, she held out her hand, met his gaze, and said, "My name is Jade Howard."

CHAPTER 17

Duncan gaped at the woman as her words ricocheted through his mind. He felt as if he had been hit by one of the bolts of lightning that was arcing through the sky. He was shocked, confused, angry, but in some strange way, he was also profoundly relieved. He had cursed himself a hundred times for falling in love with his wife again, had thought himself the world's biggest fool. And all the while he had been a different sort of idiot, a blind one.

"You're not Megan?" he asked, just to be sure he'd heard right.

"No, I'm not," the woman said.

"Then who the hell are you and what are you doing here?"

"My name is Jade Howard," she repeated. "The rest takes a lot of explaining."

He looked at her, stared hard. Dear God, why hadn't he seen it earlier? Of course she wasn't Megan. The storm had washed away every trace of her makeup, and her hair was plastered to her skull. Damn and double damn. She looked enough like Megan to fool any but the most discerning eye. He was an artist, though, and supposedly skilled at seeing the bone underlying the flesh. This woman had a more delicate bone structure than his wife, and in his eyes, she was infinitely more beautiful.

Then it hit him. He *had* seen the differences that long-ago evening at La Fonda, but he had rationalized them away.

The woman's voice interrupted his addlepated musings. "Can you get me out of here?"

There was nothing funny about the situation. God knew they were in considerable peril, yet he couldn't help grinning. Suddenly, he felt wonderful. "This is a hell of a place to park," he said.

"I didn't have much choice." She tried to smile past her chattering teeth.

Good, he thought, she had spunk. She was going to need it before they were out of danger. Although the Packard protected Excalibur from the full force of the current, the water reached the stallion's belly. He whickered anxiously as he fought to keep his footing. The three of them had to get out of there fast, but a second look at Jade told Duncan she wasn't in shape to be much help.

"I want you to do exactly what I say," he told her. "I brought some dry things for you but I've got to get you out of here first. Are you strong enough to get in the saddle by yourself?"

"I—I don't think so."

"Can you slide a little closer?"

She nodded and began inching across the rain-slick hood.

He wrapped the reins around the saddle horn, controlling the nervous stallion with his knees and thighs as he leaned sideways and reached for her. He caught her by the waist and lifted her free of the car, then lowered her in front of him.

"Hang on," he said.

Her arms had no strength so he held the reins only in his right hand and pulled her closer with his left. Although the rain was diminishing, the water in the wash was still rising. As they moved away from the shelter of the car, the stallion lost his footing and the current began pushing them downstream. Duncan put the reins between his teeth, gave the horse his head, and locked both arms around Jade's waist.

The horse struggled beneath them, pitting his great strength against the current. It seemed an eternity before his churning hooves made contact with the ground. He pushed forward step by agonizing step, then with a final heave pulled free of the water.

Duncan had been holding Jade so tightly, it took him a moment to unlock his frozen fingers. "Are you all right?" he asked.

"I am now that I'm with you." Her voice was strong despite the chill that continued to shake her body.

Just then he heard a deep rumble coupled with the screech of tortured metal. He looked over his shoulder to see the Packard being swept away. A few more minutes and he would have been too late. The thought of almost losing her . . .

He had so many questions, but they could wait. Everything could wait until he got her safely back to Rancho Cielo. He guided the stallion back onto the highway and reined him to a stop.

"Time for those dry things." He reached down and unbuckled one of the saddlebags, then pulled out a heavy sweater and an oilskin poncho. After helping her into them, he produced the whisky-filled flask from his pocket.

"Drink this. It will warm you," he said, putting the flask in her hand.

The wind had been blowing in his face while he rode toward Santa Fe. As they headed home it gusted at their backs. Despite the dry clothes and the liquor, he could still feel Jade shaking with cold. Still, he ignored the instinct to spur Excalibur to a gallop. Neither woman nor animal had the stamina for such a ride. Instead he put the horse to a quick walk that would get them back to the ranch in half an hour.

Jade's body pressed against his as she huddled closer for warmth. Despite their recent peril and the fact that they were both cold and wet, sparks of desire shot through him. And all he really knew about her was her name. Jade Howard. A fine name—a glorious name. He wanted to shout it to the storm. What sweet, sweet madness, he thought, grinning into the rain.

"Jade Howard, Jade Howard," he murmured, trying out the sound.

He felt her stir. "Did you say something?"

"Just your name." He had to stop himself from adding, "It's beautiful, like you." It was too soon for that.

She snuggled even closer, resting her cheek in the hollow of his neck and shoulder. He liked it, liked it a lot. There were so many things he wanted to know about her, to say to her, that it would take a lifetime to know and say them all. He was worried about Megan, too, but she must have left Santa Fe months ago. After all that time he could certainly manage to wait a little longer to find out the why and how.

Jade's trembling had eased by the time they reached the Rancho Cielo turnoff. Excalibur quickened his pace as he sensed his warm stall near at hand. The driveway was littered with branches and leaves, and the wheel ruts flowed like diminutive streams, but the worst of the storm had fled to the east. Overhead an occasional star peeked through the scudding thunderheads. As they crested the rise, Duncan saw the welcoming lights of Rancho Cielo.

He reined the weary stallion to a halt in front of the house, jumped from the saddle, and held his arms out to Jade. She slid into his embrace and he pulled her close. She smelled of wind, rain, damp clothes, and femininity. She smelled delicious.

"I wasn't sure I would see this place again," she said. "How can I thank you?"

"There's no need." He stepped back and looked down at her. In the light from the windows, he could see a little color had returned to her cheeks, but it only emphasized her pallor. She looked as fragile as a porcelain figurine. How could he have ever mistaken her for Megan? he mused with quiet wonder. Megan had an earthy sensuality, while Jade had a quiet, almost otherworldly loveliness that he knew would haunt him to the day he died.

"I must look like a drowned rat," she said, fidgeting under his scrutiny.

"Only if you think drowned rats are beautiful," he replied. Keeping a supporting arm around her waist, he led her to the front door.

Blackjack waited in the entry to greet them, his tail beating a wild tattoo. Duncan chuckled softly, thinking the Newfoundland was a hell of a lot wiser than his master. The dog had known Jade was a stranger the day Duncan had brought her to the ranch. Blackjack had fallen in love with her, too, and he hadn't wasted weeks and weeks before letting her know how he felt. He had followed her around the house during the day and slept by her bed at night.

Smart dog! Lucky dog!

Jade reached down to pat the Newfoundland. "I told you I'd be back," she said. Duncan could see the astonishment in her eyes, as if she couldn't believe she was home. And this was her home, he thought, if she would have it—and him.

"I think you'd better have a hot bath and change into something warm before we talk," he said.

She straightened up and met his gaze. "You must have so many questions. Are you sure you don't mind waiting?"

"You're soaking wet and so am I. Excalibur needs attention, too, so take your time."

She nodded and headed for the bedroom, leaving a wet trail on the tile floor. He continued watching until she disappeared from sight. Opening the front door, he looked out and saw Jorge leading Excalibur toward the stable. He and Dulce must have been waiting and watching for their return.

He hurried to the room where he'd been sleeping since Jade's accident and changed into dry clothes before going to the kitchen. It was empty except for a savory aroma that made his mouth water. Dulce had left a note on the kitchen table saying he would find arroz con pollo and fresh flour tortillas in the oven. Suddenly he felt ravenous.

He opened cupboards and drawers, gathering place settings, napkins, and plates, all the while imagining himself sitting at the table with a fire burning in the hearth, sharing a meal with Jade Howard like any ordinary long-married couple. They would go to bed afterward—but their lovemaking would have nothing to do with being ordinary or long married.

He shook his head to dispel the fantasy. He would make love with Jade soon, that he promised himself. But he wouldn't rush her. He wanted her to come to him eagerly, with a passion that matched his own.

He had set the table, built a fire, and made a jug of hot buttered rum by the time Jade joined him. He looked up to see her standing in the kitchen doorway. Her face was scrubbed clean and she was wearing a blue velvet robe belted tight at the waist. Blackjack ambled along behind her. The dog dropped down in front of the fire, groaning with pleasure as he stretched out on the sheepskin rug.

"Feeling better?" Duncan asked, filling two mugs with the aromatic rum.

"Much, thank you," she said. She gazed into his eyes, and he felt as if something electric had passed between them. "I'm terribly sorry about the car. I should have known better than to try to cross that wash."

"Forget the car. It can be replaced. You can't."

"I wouldn't be too sure of that." Her smile was ironical, even rueful. "Wait until you hear my story."

"We can eat first if you're hungry."

"I'd like that. I'm starved. Can I help cook?"

"Dulce left our supper in the oven."

"Sit down and let me wait on you then. It's the least I can do after you saved my life."

He settled into a chair and leaned back. He knew so little about Jade, yet his questions could wait. He was content to watch her quiet efficiency as she brought their food to the table. He felt as if his entire life had been a prelude to this night.

They did indeed eat in companionable silence like a long-married couple. The first part of his fantasy was coming true.

Jade thought she knew all of Duncan's moods. She had seen him angry, worried, inspired, disdainful, challenged, tender, and impatient. But she had never seen him at peace. He seemed utterly relaxed, as if discovering that he had been living with a counterfeit wife was an everyday occurrence. Any other man would have insisted on questioning her the minute they got back to the house, but he concentrated on his food with obvious appreciation. How good he was, how kind to give her a chance to bathe and eat.

She owed him her life, yet she wanted to give him her love. Would he accept it, and how would she find the courage to go on if he didn't? She certainly couldn't stay at Rancho Cielo. Where would she go? A thousand questions teemed through her mind just as she knew they did through his.

He didn't broach the subject of her identity until she finished clearing the table. Then he lit two cigarettes, handed her one, and said, "I like your name. Is it English?"

It was the last thing she'd expected him to say. "I think so. I don't know very much about my family history, though. My parents died before I was interested in such things."

Sympathy warmed his eyes. "That must have been hard on you."

"It was. However, I don't think how I spent my childhood is first on the list of things you want to know about me."

"You're wrong. I want to know everything. Where you grew up, the name of your favorite teacher, what you like to eat, what you like to do, if you look like your mother or your father, the name of the first boy you kissed. I want to know all about you from the day you were born until the day we met."

"That could take all night. Don't you want to know what I'm doing here?"

"That too." He grinned, then got up to put another log on the fire. "Take your time," he said as he returned to his seat.

Nothing in his manner suggested even a hint of impatience, yet she felt as nervous as a student taking a final exam. She wanted him to like her. No, she wanted him to love her. But how could he when every day they'd spent together had been a lie?

"I don't quite know where to begin," she said. "As you may have guessed, I'm a writer. That's how I make my living."

"So you're a working woman?"

"Yes."

"Married?"

"No."

"That's the best news I've heard in a long time."

So he did care—at least a little. She felt as shy, as awkward, as a girl on her first date. She had never known how to flirt, to seduce with looks and gestures, so she decided to woo him with words. "When I begin a book I often start at the end of the story. But this story doesn't have an end. Not yet. It's about shattered dreams, about running away and getting lost."

"It sounds like a sad story." He rocked on the back legs of his chair and crossed his long legs. "But you make a stunning Scheherazade."

She felt herself redden. Compliments always flustered her.

"You're even prettier when you blush." He smiled, yet his eyes were suddenly remote. "My wife never blushed."

"Perhaps we ought to talk about Megan first."

"No. Megan can wait. I want to hear about you."

"All right." She cleared her throat and wet her lips. "When I was very little I loved stories that began 'Once upon a time.' So that's how I'll begin my story. Once upon a time, sixty years from now—"

"I thought you were going to tell me about you," he interrupted.

"I will. Be patient."

She couldn't tell him that she'd traveled back through time without some preparation, so she began by telling him about the future and her life in it, omitting her name and referring to herself only as "the writer." She had always believed in the power of words, in their unique magic. Now she wove a spell, letting Duncan experience the triumphs and tragedies she had known, holding nothing back, paying homage to honesty rather than pride in the telling. She ended by describing Ira's reaction to her book and her precipitous journey to Santa Fe.

He had been listening intently. When she finished, he leaned forward anxiously. His eyes looked troubled. "You paint a very believable picture of the future. Jules Verne would envy your imagination. But I don't understand why you're telling me about this woman, this writer, when I want to know about you."

Jade swallowed the cotton in her throat. "Because I am that woman."

Duncan couldn't believe he had heard her right. "Would you mind repeating that?"

"I am that woman. You wanted to know where I come from. The answer is from the future—from 1989."

Good God, he had fallen in love with a lunatic. A desirable, imaginative lunatic with an angel's face and a woman's body that could arouse him to the point of reckless passion. "Don't do this to me—to us. Please don't be afraid to tell me the truth, no matter how bad you may think it is."

"But I am telling you the truth."

He didn't know whether to laugh or cry. Weren't the most incurable lunatics supposed to be the ones who firmly believed their own ravings? There had to be a way to reach Jade, to put her in touch with reality. "Back in the wash, when I realized you weren't Megan, I assumed you must have known her. Perhaps the two of you met by accident somewhere. Isn't everyone supposed to have a double?" Without waiting for her answer, he plunged on. "So you're Megan's double. I can deal with that. How much did she pay you to take her place?"

"She didn't pay me anything. I've never met—"

"Then how do you know so much about her? About us?"

"I read her diaries from cover to cover. Why would I lie? I know it's incredible, but I do come from the future. I was born in Davenport, Iowa, in 1957. My parents died when I was in my teens. I sold my first book when I was twenty-two."

"For the love of God—"

"How do you think I know so much about the future?"

"You said you're a writer. Imagination is a writer's stock in trade."

"I'm not making anything up. All I can do is ask you to trust me."

He stared at her, letting silence fill the room. She met his gaze and held it. "All right," he said finally. "You believe you come from the future and that's good enough for me."

"But it's not good enough for me. You must believe me. I'm not crazy. I swear I'm telling the truth." She jumped to her feet. "If you'll give me a minute, I just remembered that I do have proof of what I say." She dashed out before he could say another word.

He sat waiting for her return, hoping against hope that she really did have tangible evidence to validate her claim. Because he wanted, needed, to believe what she said.

When Jade returned to the kitchen a few minutes later she was carrying the items she had worn that first night at La Fonda, the sheer underwire bra, the pantyhose, and her sports watch. She put them on the table and perched on the edge of her chair, not even daring to breathe while Duncan examined them.

He picked up the undergarments first. A bemused smile played across his lips as he handled them.

"They're just what you think," she said.

"I'm no expert on ladies lingerie, but I've never seen anything like these. The material looks like silk but silk doesn't stretch like this."

"It's a synthetic fabric called Lycra. Synthetic fabrics were invented during World War II when silk became unavailable."

"World War II?"

"It will begin in 1939. The United States, England, France, and Russia will be allied against Japan, Germany, and Italy."

"But we just beat the hell out of Germany a few years ago. It was supposed to be the war to end all wars."

"There have been a lot of wars since then."

He sighed heavily, then put down her undergarments and picked up the watch. It hadn't gained or lost a second despite its trip through time. His eyes widened as he saw the digital readout that gave the day and date as well as the time. "Amazing!" he exclaimed.

"Not in my time."

He examined it, front and back, then held it to his ear. "Why can't I hear it ticking?"

"It's battery powered." She took it from his hand, removed the back of the case, and exposed the innards. Then she put it back together and showed him how to work the light and the alarm.

"Where did you get this?" he asked.

"I bought it in 1987 in the Beverly Center in Los Angeles. It's a mall," she explained. Seeing incomprehension in his eyes, she continued, "Malls are huge places with dozens of stores under the same roof. I bought the watch at Bullocks. That's a department store."

He laughed. "The only thing you've said that I understand is 'department store.' Megan loves to shop. But there aren't any department stores in Santa Fe."

"There will be. I passed a mall on Cerillos Road the evening I drove into town."

"When—when did you get here?"

"The night of May 16, 1989."

He picked up the watch again. She could hear the amiable crackle of the fire, the sigh of the diminishing wind, the sounds Blackjack made in his sleep. She could hear everything except the words she prayed for. Time stretched taut as Duncan continued to study the digital watch. When she thought she could not endure the tension a second longer, he put the watch back on the table and looked at her.

"I believe you." His voice was low and hoarse. "Megan and I drove into Santa Fe on May seventeenth to spend the weekend at La Fonda and nothing has been the same for me since."

She released her breath in one long sigh. The worst was over. "I know. That's when we met."

"I still don't understand how you could have traveled through time."

"Follow me and I'll tell you what I know," she said, getting to her feet. She led the way to the bedroom, hoping he wouldn't misinterpret her reason for wanting him there. Opening the closet, she took out the Molyneux. "Do you remember this dress?"

He sat on the edge of the bed, watching intently. "Of course. Megan bought it at Molyneux's in Paris last year. It cost a fortune but she never was one to worry about money. As I recall, she planned to wear it to dinner that night at La Plazuela."

Jade spread the dress out on the bed. The crystals winked seductively in the room's soft light. "Megan isn't the only one who planned to wear this dress to dinner. So did I."

"I don't understand."

"I bought the Molyneux in Santa Fe on May 17, 1989, at a store that specializes in antique clothing."

He looked down at the Molyneux, then back at her. "If you wore it that night and the dress came with you when you traveled through time, it would be sixty years old." He fingered the fabric. "But it looks just the way it did the day Megan bought it."

"I'm as baffled as you are. All I can do is tell you what happened." She began by recounting how she'd found the Molyneux, describing the strange shop and its even stranger owner.

"How did this Aurora get the dress?" Duncan asked when she had finished.

"She said something about Megan bringing it in a few days earlier." Jade closed her eyes, searching her memory for Aurora's exact words. "As I recall, Aurora said, 'Megan's been selling me clothes for years.' Then she said something about Megan not wanting to sell the dress because it had changed her life. I'm afraid I wasn't paying that much attention at the time. Now I wish I had."

Duncan got up and walked to the window, standing there with his back to her. "So Megan was alive in 1989. You wouldn't happen to know if I was too?"

Jade was glad he couldn't see her face. She remembered Aurora's words all too well. *Poor thing*, she'd said about Megan. *She's had a hard life since her husband passed away in the fire.* Jade shivered. She couldn't bring herself to repeat those words to Duncan. "Aurora said something about Megan being a widow."

He turned from the window to look at her. "I'm not surprised. Let me see. If I'd lived that long I'd have been one hundred and five." He grimaced. "But it is a little like hearing my own obituary. What happened after you bought the dress?"

"I went back to the hotel and took a nap. The last thing Aurora said before I left the shop was that I ought to wear the dress that night. When I woke up I saw it in the closet and I just couldn't resist putting it on. The minute I did, the bottom seemed to drop out of the universe. The sensation was sickening, horrifying. When it stopped I went into the sitting room. You walked in a minute later. And you know what happened next."

He touched her shoulder, as if to reassure himself that she was a flesh-and-blood woman. "Megan had asked me to get some ice. I was coming back to our suite when I felt something—something I couldn't identify. It scared the hell out of me at the time. The second I laid eyes on you . . ." He paused.

"It's such a relief to be able to confide in you," she said. "I've felt so alone. Scared too." She didn't realize she was crying until he handed her a handkerchief.

"I haven't been much help."

"It's not your fault. You didn't know." She wanted him to hold her but she didn't know how to tell him.

"I should have. Deep down, I think I did know." His expression sobered. "Do you have any idea what happened to Megan?"

"I've thought about it and thought about it. I can't be sure but I've come to the conclusion that we changed places. I've read her diaries and I know she wasn't very happy. God knows, I had made a mess of my life. There we were in the same suite, both wishing we were somewhere else—and we both had the Molyneux."

"So you think the dress is some sort of key to time."

She dabbed her eyes and nodded. "I know how incredible it must seem. I had a hard time accepting it myself. I've had three months to come up with a better explanation, though, and I haven't been able to."

He was silent, thoughtful. His very being seemed concentrated in his eyes as he grappled with her incredible supposition. "The pieces do seem to fit," he said after a moment. "Still, I can't help thinking there has to be more to it. I can't believe a series of coincidences could unlock some sort of door through time." He repressed a shudder, not wanting her to see how the idea disturbed him. "So that brings us to today. When you came home this afternoon you said you wanted to tell me something, and that I would have a hard time believing it. Were you planning to tell me who you are?"

"Yes." Apprehension shook her. She still had so much to confess.

"Why today?"

"I realized I had made a total mess of Megan's life and I couldn't let it continue. I had to tell you the truth."

Duncan gazed at her. His features were rigid, his self-control awesome, considering the emotional strain they both were under. "Malcolm asked you to marry him today, didn't he?"

So he had known. She nodded.

"Does he realize you're not Megan?"

"I'm sure he doesn't."

"What did you say when he proposed?" Duncan kept his voice firm. Only the thinning of his lips betrayed his concern. He wasn't sure he could live with the wrong answer, yet his heart pounded wildly at the thought of hearing the right one. He ached for, coveted, pined after, desired, needed this woman who had traveled all the way from another time to the center of his heart. He would joyfully abandon all he possessed to hear she felt the same way.

"I told him that I liked him and respected his talent, but that I wasn't in love with him and never would be." She shrugged helplessly, oppressed by the burden of her knowledge. "I've read books he hasn't even thought about writing yet, books that were required reading in one of my college classes. Malcolm Ashford and F. Scott Fitzgerald will emerge from the twenties as literary giants."

"My God," Duncan blurted out. "You really do know what's ahead."

"I thought you believed me." She tried to get to her feet, but he reached for her shoulders and pulled her back down. The warmth of his touch reeled through her senses with the bubbling intoxication of May wine. There were a thousand reasons why they shouldn't, couldn't be together. But love listened only to its own imperative.

206

"I do believe you," he said. "But I'm just beginning to realize what that means." He looked into her eyes so deeply, she felt as if he were seeking her soul. "I have a confession to make too. Before you and Megan changed places—and for the moment I think we can assume that's what happened—I asked her for a divorce. When she refused, I decided to encourage her to see more of Malcolm in the hope that they would fall in love."

Now it was Jade's turn to be surprised. "Why?"

Concern furrowed his brow. He had to make Jade understand. Yet how could she, when he had barely sorted out his motives, let alone his feelings? "You would have to know Megan to understand my reasons. We didn't have a happy marriage. She was bored, dissatisfied, but she wasn't strong enough to stand on her own two feet. I knew she wouldn't give me a divorce unless she wanted to marry someone else. It sounds pretty callous now, but my motives weren't entirely selfish. I wanted her to be happy, and God knows, she wasn't with me."

So he still cared about Megan. The realization pummeled Jade's heart. "I ruined everything, didn't I? For you. For Malcolm. For Megan. You must be worried sick about her."

"I am worried about Megan. But I can't do anything except wish her the best and hope she's found what she wanted."

"So where does that leave us? I can go back to Santa Fe in the morning if that's what you want." Jade bit her lip. She'd had to ask, but she wasn't sure she had the courage to live up to her offer.

"No. I don't want you to leave." He reached for her hand.

She gave it gladly, grateful for the reassurance of his touch. Dear God, how she needed it.

His grip tightened. "I haven't finished my confession. While I was throwing you and Malcolm together, something was happening to me. Do you know the expression, *coup de foudre?*"

Her mouth was so dry, she barely managed to whisper, "It means 'love at first sight,' if I remember my French."

"The night you took Megan's place, that's what happened to me. I couldn't deal with it for a long time. The thought of falling in love with Megan again made me sick. That day in my studio when you watched me paint . . . Hell. This isn't easy. I never was very good with words. I usually say what I want with a canvas and a brush." He turned her palm up to his lips and kissed the sensitive flesh. "I love you, Jade Howard, more than I know how to tell you."

She felt breathless, lighter than air, as if a tiny gust of wind could send her floating to the ceiling. She was smiling, crying, laughing, reaching for him. "I love you too, Duncan. That's why I tried to get back to the ranch in the middle of the storm."

He reached out and pulled her into his arms.

Alone in bed night after night, she had imagined this moment, played out the scene a dozen different ways. But the reality, the solid feel of his chest, the strength of his arms, was so much better than any fantasy.

"Before we met," she said, staring up at him, "I'm not sure I believed in love. Then, after coming here, there were times when I thought I would die of it."

She trembled and he held her tight. "Don't be afraid," he murmured into her hair. "I won't let anything hurt or frighten you again."

At last, he kissed her. She strained closer, opening her mouth to his, savoring the sweet tang of his tongue, the bruising softness of his lips. A melting urgency hardened her nipples and dampened the tender tissue between her thighs. She wanted him as she had never wanted anything or anyone in her life.

"I love you so much," she said in a voice so husky with desire, she barely recognized it as her own.

He released her to sweep the Molyneux and the spread from the bed. Turning back to her, he untied the belt around her waist and stripped the velvet robe from her body. She was naked underneath. She felt a shiver of worry as he gazed at her. She knew her breasts were smaller than Megan's, her body leaner and more athletic. Would she be diminished by the comparison? He stared so long and hard, her skin prickled in the cool air.

"You're so beautiful," he finally said. "So very, very beautiful."

His eyes continued their urgent caress as he too undressed. She watched him hungrily, her natural shyness forgotten in the enchantment of being with the man she loved.

Duncan embraced her, holding her tight against his naked body. Once again he felt that shock of recognition, as if his skin had known hers before. He had made love to many women before he married and had reveled in his ability to pleasure them. But he knew making love to Jade would be a life-altering experience, far beyond mere physical pleasure.

Her body seemed made for his, as the stars are made for the night. His need to take her quickly—to fill her and bind her forever to him—warred with the desire to prolong his rapturous exploration.

He lingered at her mouth, feasting on the velvet-soft inner surface of her lips before plunging his tongue deeper. While they kissed, his hands explored her back, delighting in the delicate interplay of muscle and flesh as he pulled her closer still, making their kiss both promise and sacrament. He could have spent forever just knowing her mouth, but his need drove him hard.

He laid her on the bed and trailed kisses down her throat, moving lower until he found the rosy tip of one breast. He tongued the sensitive nubbin, feeling it harden, then he took it in his mouth, sucking, nipping, and sucking again while she groaned with pleasure. Then he turned to the other breast, exploring the delicate crease where rib and swelling globe met before seeking the nipple. He took the twin mounds in his hands, memorizing the warm, smooth texture of her flesh.

Her own hands and mouth were not idle. Her kisses and caresses trailed fire across his body as she met his passion with her own. When she cupped his buttocks and her fingers explored the crease between, it took all his will not to ravish her then and there.

He left the sweet fruit of her breasts and slid lower, feathering her body with his breath and lips, teasing her navel with his darting tongue. He pulled away to gaze at the swelling mound of Venus cradled between her slender thighs. His fingers followed his gaze, and he parted her cleft to touch the petaled flower of her womanhood. And then he drank from its depths.

The lift of her hips, her harsh gasp, signaled her readiness. He parted her legs and poised above her, holding off one last moment. She gazed up at him, love and trust shining from her eyes. Instinctively he knew she was offering him more than she'd given any other man, more than any other woman had given him. He could do no less than return her gift in equal measure.

Murmuring her name, he plunged deep and hard into the wet

well of her womanhood. Then he lay still. With their bodies at last joined as one, time ceased. No world existed beyond the confines of their bed. No future, no past, no regret and no fear.

Duncan surrendered to her with a totality he had never known before. He feasted his senses and his soul, pouring his love and then his seed into her while she cried out in rapture. She clung to him as her body pulsated around him, and the joy he felt at her pleasure filled all of the emptiness inside him that he'd ever known.

He held her close until their breathing slowed, the pounding of their hearts eased. Then he raised up on one elbow and gazed down at her, trying to imprint every line of her face and body on his brain. The thought of how close he'd come to losing her was so painful, he felt as if splinters of glass had found their way to his heart.

Her eyes opened and she smiled up at him. "For the first time in my life," she whispered, "I don't trust words to express what I feel. I love you. I think I've always loved you."

"We don't need words. Not tonight," he said as his mouth found hers again.

CHAPTER 18

Rancho Cielo
August 10, 1929

Duncan yawned and rubbed his tired eyes as the first golden light of morning chased away the dark. Another night's vigil was over. He glanced down at Jade sleeping beside him, as if to reassure himself that she wasn't a chimera, an impossible dream that would fade with the sun. He loved her more than he had imagined loving anyone, more even than his art. He hadn't known the human heart could encompass so much feeling.

The fear of losing her was never far away, though. The last few days should have been the happiest in his life. He had found love, understanding, intelligence, talent, and passion in one miraculous feminine package. He longed to revel in the discovery, to let his spirit take wing. But he couldn't shake the sense of foreboding that lurked in his brain like an uninvited guest at a feast.

He couldn't cope with the thought that Jade might disappear as suddenly as she had appeared. And so he slept fitfully, coming awake often to watch her while she slept, his heart lurching every time she turned over or murmured in her sleep.

Careful not to wake her now, he slipped from between the sheets and walked to the closet. The Molyneux hung where Jade had put it five days ago. He stared at the dress for a long time while dread thickened in his throat. If the Molyneux held the key to time, it was more dangerous to his new-found happiness than any human or natural threat could be.

It gleamed in the dark like banked embers that could burst into flame without any provocation. His instinct was to destroy it, cut it to ribbons, slash it into a thousand pieces so it could never take Jade away. But destroying the dress would be a selfish act, and he had never been a selfish man.

Although Jade said she wanted to stay with him, she didn't belong in the twenties. No matter how much they tried to forget it, she had a life and a career sixty years in the future. She belonged to her own time. She was used to shaping her life, choosing her own path, being independent in ways that threatened his sense of how things should be between men and women. Sooner or later they would clash. He would want more than she could give, or she would need more freedom than he could grant. Would she hate him then and curse the day she'd decided to stay in his time?

He couldn't completely forget Megan either. From what Jade had told him of the future, Megan would be as lost in it as an abandoned puppy. He didn't want her back, but he couldn't willfully leave her imprisoned in an alien era either. So no matter how much he might want to destroy the dress, his conscience stayed his hand. If Jade ever decided to leave, she would need the damn thing.

He shut the closet door and returned to the bed to kiss her awake.

"Mmmn, delicious," she murmured. "You sure know how to start my day right."

"It gets better." He kissed her again while his hands explored her body. Her tantalizing curves sent a heated message to his groin. They had made long, lingering love the night before, but now he wanted her again.

"Do you know what I'd like for breakfast?" she asked as she squirmed free of his embrace.

He shook his head. He hadn't been thinking about food.

"You!" she declared, kicking the covers aside and throwing herself at him.

212

An hour later, freshly bathed and dressed for the day, Jade studied herself in the mirror over the bathroom sink. She had never looked better, she decided. She had Duncan to thank for that. He filled her heart the way he had filled her body a few minutes ago. She glowed with the force of his love. It made her strong and unafraid. If only he could share her certainty that all was right with their world, that her being with him was as inevitable as the pull of the moon on the tides.

Something was bothering him. She saw it in his face when he thought she wasn't looking, and she heard it in his voice all the time. Please God, don't let it be me, she thought.

He was in the kitchen, starting a fire in the stove when she walked in. Although they had been alone only a few days, they had sorted out the chores without having to talk about them. Now that he knew she could cook—and loved cooking for him—he left that job to her.

"Do you miss Dulce and Jorge?" she asked, taking a bowl of eggs from the refrigerator.

"A little." He looked across the room at her, and she saw so much love in his eyes, her womb tightened in response.

"I feel guilty about them leaving," she said. "But it is a relief, not having to pretend to be Megan anymore. You couldn't call me Jade while they were here, and I love hearing my name on your lips."

"Are you sure taking care of the house isn't too much of a burden?"

"I think you could call it a labor of love." The sight of him doing something as banal as setting the table made her grin like a fool. She divided the eggs she had scrambled between two plates, giving him the larger share, and carried the plates to the table. "Breakfast is served."

"I thought I was breakfast."

"You were. The eggs are dessert." She gave him a gay smile, hoping to lighten his mood.

He ate quietly, so lost in thought that they didn't exchange another word until she got up to clear the table. "Can I help with the dishes?" he asked.

"No. But you can sit there and talk to me. You're obviously worried about something. I wish you'd tell me what it is."

He abruptly pushed away from the table and stood. "I could use some fresh air. Let's take a walk."

She nodded her instant agreement, hoping that away from the house and all its memories, he'd be able to share his concerns. "The dishes can wait. But I warn you, we're going to talk while we walk."

She followed him into the sunshine. Blackjack hurried to join them as they headed up the drive.

"There's a hint of fall in the air," Duncan said. "It reminds me of how quickly time is passing."

She took his hand firmly in her own. "You promised to tell me what's bothering you. Is it your work?"

"No."

"Is it me?"

"No," he said so emphatically, it left no room for doubt.

She stopped in midstride, pulling him to a halt and turning to face him. "I know you weren't in the habit of discussing your problems with Megan, but I can't live that way. I want to share everything with you, the good and the bad. So give. What's been keeping you awake nights—aside from yours truly?"

He looked down at the ground, then back up at her. "I guess I'm not used to being happy. You're the best thing that ever happened to me, but I'm scared to death you'll disappear in a puff of smoke."

Relief flooded through her. She knew she ought to be as confident of his love as she was of her own, but trust came hard. "I think you're worrying needlessly."

"Am I? Think about it. What if Megan is still in Santa Fe sixty years from this very moment. What if she just happens to pay a visit to Rancho Cielo for old times' sake and she's wearing that damn dress. How do I know you won't wind up back in your own time?"

"I don't think it's that simple. My first morning in this time, I tried the dress on again and nothing happened."

His gray eyes probed hers. "Megan and the dress aren't the only things on my mind. I know how you got here. Now I want to know why. I won't have peace of mind until I'm certain you can stay if you choose."

"There's no if about it." Still holding his hand, she resumed

214

walking up the drive. It was a glorious day. The air smelled of sunshine and pine pitch and newly mown grass. Still, she felt as if a dark cloud had come between them and the sun. Duncan was right. The thought of being whisked, willy-nilly, back to her own time made her legs weak.

"I want answers just as much as you do," she said. "But I think the questions would tax even Einstein's genius."

"Isn't he the physicist who won the Nobel Prize a few years back?"

"Yes, and if I remember my history, he's doing research at Princeton. But I don't think he'd see us."

For the first time since they got out of bed, a genuine smile illuminated Duncan's face. "I don't think we need to consult Einstein, although I'm sure he'd be fascinated by our story. The man we need to see is a lot closer to home."

"And who might that be?"

"Gabriel Natseway."

"Gabriel who?"

"Knot-say-way. He's the *cacique* of Acoma—the 'Sky City.' "

"Is he a shaman, a sort of wise man?"

"Not unless you think a graduate degree from Yale qualifies him for the title. I met him there when I was an art student. Gabe was finishing his doctorate in philosophy and teaching a few undergraduate classes to make ends meet."

"So you want to see a doctor of philosophy who lives someplace in the sky to ask him why I traveled through time. Makes sense to me." Jade giggled. "At least, considering his résumé, I won't have to worry about him thinking we're strange."

Duncan laughed, too, a hearty sound that lifted her spirits the instant she heard it.

"Gabe doesn't live in the sky, sweetheart. He lives in the Sky City. It's another name for Acoma. Wait until you see it. It will take your breath away."

They're coming!

Gabriel Natseway was eating a bowl of Kellogg's cornflakes and looking out over the edge of his world when the thought came into his mind with the clarity of the spoken word. Duncan was coming and bringing a new woman with him. A smile gentled Gabriel's hawk-fierce features. He and Duncan had spent far too little time together lately. How quickly the years went by these days, crowding into one another like children eager for a treat, with never enough time for an old and cherished friend.

He looked around his simple house, trying to see it the way it would appear to the woman. The two rooms were built of mortar-washed stone. The hard-packed dirt floor and the smoke-stained pine vigas that supported the low ceiling had seen four centuries or more of use. The front room, which served as parlor, kitchen, and dining room, was no more than twelve feet square. The back room where he slept was even smaller. Not exactly the Ritz, he thought.

Megan Carlisle had visited only once, a time of embarrassment for both him and Duncan. She had hated the place on sight and refused to have even a cup of coffee, let alone spend the night. She had been blind to the beauty of Acoma. But then most Anglos were blind to beauty, unless it came in crisp green bills.

Gabriel rose, went to the room's single window, and gazed down three hundred and fifty feet to the Cebolleta mesa country. He could see Mount Taylor holding up the sky in the distance. His eyes watered at the splendid sight. No matter how many times he looked, the view still filled him with a sense of wonder.

He knew it would be different this time. This woman would see the beauty and ask to spend the night. She might even want to stay longer.

Like the other dwellings atop the windswept mesa, his had neither electricity nor running water. A single well served the entire pueblo. Oil lamps lit the rooms at night, and kiva fireplaces warmed them. Gabriel's worldly goods, his clothes, blankets, and his much-prized silver-and-turquoise jewelry, hung from the walls. Strings of red chilies and dried muskmelons, bags of dried peaches, strips of jerked mutton and venison were suspended from the ceiling. *Colchónes*—rolled-up mattresses covered with blankets—lined the walls.

The only signs of the modern world were a scarred table and mismatched chairs, a couple of cupboards he had built himself, and the books and magazines stacked in the corners; the only luxury, a telescope. He loved to contemplate the stars, to watch the majestic passage of the years in the march of constellations and planets across the sky. He also loved to follow the season of corn from the first tip of hopeful green breaking through the soil, to the last dried stalk rattling in the autumn wind. What different time scales each represented, and yet each had its place in the great scheme of things.

His own place, he reminded himself, was below the mesa where fields of squash, corn, and beans ripened in the late summer sun. Every pair of hands was needed to harvest the bounteous blessing the Great Spirit had given the people of Acoma this year. The women of his mother's lineage, the Antelope Clan, would not take it kindly if he failed to do his share.

He rinsed his dishes in the cast-iron basin by the window, then went outside to pour the dishwater on a wind-seeded bush that had set itself the unlikely task of growing on the sandstone mesa. His chores done, he tied a red cotton sweatband around his forehead, closed the door, and set off for the fields far below.

Jade checked the contents of the picnic basket, her mouth watering at the aroma of the fried chicken she'd just made, before handing the basket to Duncan. He put it in the Duesenberg's trunk along with the backpacks, sleeping bags, and duffels that contained their clothes, toilet tissue, candles, and the other necessities he had told her to pack.

Getting ready to leave for Acoma had taken most of the morning. In view of what they were taking, the trip had the makings of a safari.

"Are you sure we haven't forgotten anything?" she asked.

He looked into the trunk, cataloguing its contents. "Nope. It's all there." He shut the trunk firmly, then walked to her side of the car and opened the back door. "Get in," he told Blackjack.

The huge dog had been dashing around the drive chasing a butterfly, but he hopped in the Duesenberg and instantly curled up on the backseat like a seasoned traveler.

Duncan opened the front door for Jade and handed her in. She didn't think she'd ever get used to having doors opened for her, cigarettes lit, her elbow firmly held when they went for a walk—all the niceties of manners that women's lib had swept aside.

In the hurry to leave, there hadn't been much time to talk. Her curiosity was at a boil as they drove away from Rancho Cielo. "I want you to tell me all about this friend of yours," she said.

"There's not much to tell." Duncan smiled easily. He seemed more relaxed now that they were on their way. "I told you we met at Yale. Gabe taught my introductory philosophy class. He was just ten years older than I chronologically, but he seemed a couple of lifetimes more mature. He was—I mean he is a brilliant man. I don't know what he saw in me when he took me under his wing, but I was very grateful. Still am. I was pretty much of a loner even then. It's hard to be on the outside looking in when you're young."

"I know what you mean. I didn't exactly fit in at the University of Iowa either." She grimaced, remembering the inchoate angst of being young.

Duncan glanced at her, sympathy in his eyes. "I wish I had known you then."

"I'm glad you didn't. I was pretty much of a geek."

"Geek?"

"You know. A nerd. An egghead."

He frowned.

"A bookworm."

"At last," he said, grinning, "you've used an expression I understand. I was a bookworm in college too. An art geek. Gabe introduced me to the larger world of ideas. If he had stayed at Yale, I think he would have headed the department one day. After his wife died, we grew even closer."

"His wife?"

"He married an Anglo. She was an anthropologist, a very special woman. She died of influenza in 1904. Gabe never got over it. A year before I graduated, he went back to Acoma permanently. I visited the following summer. That's when I fell in love with New Mexico. A number of outstanding painters, men like Ernest Blumenschein, Oscar Beringhaus, and Irving Couse, had already settled in Taos. They invited me to join them, but I preferred the artistic isolation of Santa Fe. I didn't want anyone to influence my work."

Jade had been listening with fascination. Duncan was so intensely private that he rarely talked about his life—particularly the years he spent with Megan—and when he did, he scowled. She knew that he came from an upper-class family, that his father, a banker, had disowned him because he didn't think art was a manly career. Duncan had told her of working his way through college. She knew that he had stayed in contact with his two roommates, David Max and Ralph Braithwaite. But this was the first time he had mentioned Gabriel Natseway.

"After Gabe's wife died," Duncan continued, "he decided to devote his life to his people."

"That seems a waste, considering his education."

Duncan shook his head. "I suggest you reserve judgment until you meet him."

"Is he a chief?"

"Most tribes don't have chiefs—or Indian princesses either. Those are Anglo misconceptions. The Acomans choose someone they respect, typically an elder, as a sort of spiritual guide and arbitrator. By virtue of his intelligence, his fairness, Gabriel was a natural for the job. The only requirement is that the *cacique* belong to the Antelope Clan. Gabe did. He's a unique man, very wise in the truest meaning of the word."

"And that's why you want to talk to him."

"That and the fact that, aside from David and Ralph, I consider him my best friend." Duncan reached for her hand. "I hope you like him—and Acoma. They both have a special place in my life."

They drove south, retracing the route Jade had taken on her way to Santa Fe. The countryside was even less populated than it had been in 1989, and the sky seemed larger. At Albuquerque they turned west onto Route 66. Duncan proved to be a well-informed guide, pointing out everything of interest in the sparsely settled landscape.

The sun was hanging low in the western sky when they turned off the highway onto an unmarked dirt road. Half an hour later, he slowed the car and gestured at two golden mesas looming on the horizon.

"The one on the left is Enchanted Mesa," he said. "Gabe took me up there once. It was a hell of a climb, straight up most of the way. There's a ruined pueblo on the top. The Acomans believe their ancestors lived there until the only path to the top was destroyed during a storm. It was a tragedy of epic proportions. The people tending the fields couldn't get back up. They had to stand by helplessly while the families they had left behind starved to death. Their spirits are said to haunt Enchanted Mesa to this day."

She cut a glance at him. "Do you believe in ghosts?"

"Sweetheart, considering the fact that you're here, I'm willing to believe anything is possible. There are lots of legends about this corner of the earth. When Coronado's army came here in 1540 in search of the Seven Cities of Gold, Acoma was already ancient. It's been continuously occupied for nine hundred years or more." He gestured at the second monolithic mesa. "That's where we're going. That's Acoma—the Sky City."

Jade's gaze tracked his pointing finger. A few miles away a mesa, gleaming white in the late afternoon sun, rose in splendid isolation from the plain, a geologic fist defying the sky, magnificent in its solitariness. Her heart bumped at the sight. "Why would anyone build a village up there?"

"To defend their granaries from marauding tribes."

"Like the Apaches?"

"No one knows for sure. Acoma was here long before the Apaches arrived on the scene. If you look hard, you can just see crops growing in the fields around the mesa."

Jade searched the area, expecting to see the sort of geometrically precise rows of crops that farmers in Iowa planted. But the Acoman fields appeared more tan than green. She saw sparse clusters of cultivated growth that blended into the surrounding *chamisa.*

"The name Acoma," Duncan continued, "comes from the Keresan word *akome.* It means 'people of the white rock.' "

"I see the white rock," Jade said, "but where are the people?"

"I imagine most of them are in the pueblo fixing supper by now."

"What pueblo?" She stared at the looming mesa, trying to see anything man-made. At first, the buildings were indistinguishable from the rock. Then, as they drew closer, she could see structures rising from the stone. It seemed inconceivable that anyone, let alone a tribe of primitive Indians, would have been able to build a village on the top of the cliff-girt ramparts.

"How in the world are we going to get up there?" She didn't like heights, and that included anything higher than a stepladder.

220

"There's a path."

"In case you haven't noticed, I'm not part mountain goat."

His answering grin made him look boyish and carefree. "Oh, I noticed, all right. Just this morning, as I recall."

Jade was still worrying about how they would get up to Acoma when they parked ten minutes later. Blackjack jumped out of the car as soon as Duncan opened the door and bounded around, barking with excitement.

"Has he been here before?" Jade asked.

Duncan, who had opened the trunk and was parceling their belongings between the two backpacks, looked up. "I didn't like leaving him home with Megan, so I always brought him with me. Sometimes I think Gabriel likes Blackjack more than he likes me." He finished stuffing their belongings into the packs and helped Jade shoulder hers.

"What about the picnic basket?" she asked.

"I'll carry it."

She made a disappointed moue. "Too bad. I was hoping you'd volunteer to carry me."

As they approached the base of the mesa, Duncan pointed out a precipitous path that made Jade's knees quiver. "That's the Ladder Trail," he said. "It's a combination of toe- and handholds cut into the rock. There are a few ladders in places where it really gets steep. It was the only way up the mesa in 1629 when the missionary Fray Juan Ramírez came here, and can you imagine making the climb in armor the way Coronado and his men did?"

"I can't imagine making the climb in this backpack. I'm eager to meet your friend, but this is 1929, not 1629. Don't they have an elevator, or a skyhook?"

He took her elbow and tugged her forward. "There is an easier way up these days. Just follow me."

Ten minutes later, after scrambling over a wind-deposited sand rampart that climbed partway up the mesa, they reached a steep stone stairway. Jade looked up to see a man waiting for them at its top.

"I was expecting you," he called, waving a greeting.

She tugged at Duncan's shirt. "Is that Gabriel?"

"Yes."

"How did he know we were coming? Did you telephone him?"

"There are no telephones in Acoma."

"Then how did he know?"

Duncan gave her an enigmatic smile. "All I can tell you is that every time I've come, Gabriel has been waiting for me at the top of the stairs."

CHAPTER 19

Jade was surprised to feel a twinge of jealousy as she watched Duncan and Gabriel embrace at the top of the stairs. The two men bear-hugged, pounding each other on the back and beaming like a reunited father and son.

"It's been too long," Gabriel said as he held Duncan at arm's length. Then he turned to Jade, a welcoming smile on his face. "And I see you brought me company—and beautiful company at that. Why don't you introduce us?"

Duncan grinned wickedly at Gabe. "Don't you remember Megan?"

Gabriel turned his dark-eyed gaze back to Jade. He looked confused for a second, then he smiled. "My friend here"—a nod of his head indicated Duncan—"seems to be in a playful mood. Perhaps you had better introduce yourself."

She extended her hand. "I'm Jade Howard. But how did you know I wasn't Megan?"

He continued to study her intently, smiling like a man who liked what he saw. "Duncan should know that only fools judge a book by its cover—or a woman by her appearance."

To Jade's surprise, Duncan responded to the gentle rebuke with a hearty laugh. "I told Jade you were wise. I should have told her you were a wiseass."

Gabe's answering guffaw echoed across the mesa. "You must be weary from your journey. Permit me to offer you the hospitality of my home," he said, reaching for Jade's backpack.

He wasn't what she had expected. She had pictured a professorial type, someone who looked as if he had never done a day's physical labor. But Gabe's heavily seamed skin and work-gnarled hands spoke of a lifetime spent outdoors. Bluntly trimmed bangs and red-flannel-wrapped braids framed his wide forehead. He had a wrestler's thick neck and broad shoulders, a trim waist and slim hips, and the slightly bowed legs of a man who had spent a great deal of time in the saddle. Had she judged him by appearances, she would have concluded that he had never set foot inside a classroom, let alone taught at Yale.

Blackjack, who seemed to know his way around, raced ahead as Gabriel led the way through the quiet pueblo. Jade looked around avidly, trying to take in every last detail of the Sky City.

Gabe followed her gaze. "I'll give you the two-bit tour after you've had a chance to freshen up."

They walked down a narrow street lined with what Jade would describe as row houses. Soft lights, wonderfully different from the harsh glare of electricity, glowed in the windows.

"Are you familiar with New York brownstones, Miss Howard?"

"Please call me Jade, and yes, I am."

"These are our brownstones. My people were building in stone while Europeans were living in straw-thatched huts."

She couldn't blame him for the pride she heard in his voice. The white stone buildings, so carefully crafted by long-gone generations, were truly remarkable.

"Here we are," he said, stopping in front of the last door in the row. He lifted the latch and ushered them inside.

A single window let light into the room, but the view from it was spectacular. The furnishings were humble, yet the overall effect was one of serenity and peace. She turned to Gabe. "You have a lovely home. And Acoma is breathtaking. I apologize for showing up on your doorstep without a word of warning."

"You couldn't have come at a better time. We finished the har-

224

vest today. Tomorrow we celebrate. Have you ever seen a corn dance?"

"No. But I'd love to stay—if it's all right with Duncan."

"Of course we'll stay." Enthusiasm suffused Duncan's voice. "We came to talk to Gabe, though, and the sooner the better."

Gabe nodded. "First I want to show Jade the Sky City, and then we must eat. There will be time to talk after dinner. I've prepared the back room for your stay. Please join me outside after you've unpacked." He opened the door and slipped out so quietly that had Jade not been watching, she wouldn't have realized he had gone.

"What do you think of him?" Duncan asked, carrying their things into the back room.

It was smaller than the front room, and the decor more Spartan. Two thin mattresses had been spread out on the floor. A water-filled pitcher and washbowl sat on a hand-hewn table beside them. The only touch of color came from a Navajo blanket hanging on one wall. A tiny window, no more than a foot square, created a sort of permanent twilight.

Jade waited for her eyes to become accustomed to the gloom. "I know you and Gabe are old friends, but there's something eerie about him."

"What do you mean?" Duncan asked as he spread their sleeping bags out on the mattresses.

"Eerie is probably the wrong word. I expected him to ask what we were doing here, but I have the feeling he already knows."

Duncan handed her backpack to her and began unloading his, spreading the contents on the sleeping bags. "You may be right."

"Aren't you the least bit curious about how he knows?"

"Of course I am—just as I'm sure Gabe is curious about you. But Indians don't interrogate their friends. It's considered bad form. Acoma has always been a place of mystery. Gabe will reveal his when and if he can."

"And you want me to keep my mouth shut in the meantime."

Duncan nodded. "When in Rome, Jade. When in Rome." He continued unpacking with swift, economical movements.

"I hate to ask about something so mundane, but are there any bathrooms up here?"

He chuckled. "I hope you don't mind outhouses."

225

She smiled down at him. "I don't mind anything as long as we're together."

Gabe was sitting on a stone bench by the front door with Blackjack curled contentedly at his feet, when they left the house. "It will be dark soon," he said, "but we have time for a quick tour if you like."

"I'd love it," Jade replied.

They had driven past several of the Rio Grande pueblos on the way to San Ildefonso back in May, but Jade had never seen anything remotely like the Sky City. The village consisted of several contiguous structures, each about a thousand feet long and three stories high, lining the three streets. A foreboding-looking mission church sat some distance from the other buildings.

For the next thirty minutes she and Duncan followed Gabe while he pointed out the well, the communal grinding stones where the women made cornmeal, the beehive ovens where they baked, and the seven kivas where the clans worshiped.

"Our society is quite different from yours," he explained as they walked. "Women here are regarded as equal to men. In fact, they own all the property." He gestured at the quiet homes they were passing. "We're a matrilineal, matrilocal people. Property is passed on through the mother's line."

The tour ended at the church. "This is the San Esteban Rey mission church. It was built in 1629 by the people of Acoma."

Jade gazed at the building looming against the brilliant sunset. "It's hard to believe it's been here that long."

Gabe led the way inside the building and pointed at the huge vigas that supported the roof. "Those beams are forty feet long. They were cut in the Cebolleta Mountains thirty miles away and carried here by the men of Acoma. The rest of the construction materials, including acres of dirt for a cemetery, were carried to the top of the mesa by the women. It was a backbreaking job for both sexes.

"After the church was done, the priests were afraid the men would run away and take their families with them. The soldiers were ordered to cripple the men."

"How?" Jade asked. "How did they do it?"

"Each male villager had one foot amputated. Some of them bled to death." Anger rasped in Gabriel's voice. "But the priests got what they wanted. The survivors couldn't run away."

Jade shuddered. She never stopped being amazed at man's inhumanity to his fellow man. "That's horrible. But it happened three hundred years ago, yet it obviously still upsets you."

"My people don't have the same understanding of time as you Anglos. To us, three hundred years is yesterday."

Half an hour later the three of them sat around Gabe's table, finishing a meal of the fried chicken and potato salad Jade had made at Rancho Cielo, and guayave, a paper-thin bread made from blue cornmeal, which Gabe had cooked on a polished stone set over the fireplace.

"You must be wondering why we're here," Duncan said at last, pushing his plate aside.

"I knew you would tell me in your own time."

"Time. That's what it's all about." Duncan hooked his heels in the rungs of his chair, rested his elbows on the table, and looked from Gabe to Jade. "That's why we're here."

Gabe had never seen two people so in love. It reminded him of his youth—his beloved Sarah. He closed his eyes, picturing her dear face. Her spirit seemed so close that he felt he could reach out and . . .

"Gabe, are you all right?" The sound of Duncan's voice pulled Gabe from his reverie.

He sighed heavily. He would dream of Sarah later. Right now his friends needed his help. "I'm fine. What's this you want to tell me about time?"

He watched while Duncan and Jade exchanged another deep and meaningful glance. "It's really Jade's story," Duncan said, and gave her the floor with a slight nod of his head.

She looked directly into Gabe's eyes. "Have you ever read any books or articles that dealt with time travel?"

Her question took him by surprise. "Yes. I'm familiar with Mark Twain's and H. G. Wells's time-travel novels, among others. You see, the subject has a certain fascination for me."

She seemed equally startled by his answer. "Do you think time travel is possible?"

He nodded, wondering where she was heading.

"That's going to make things a lot easier." She leaned toward him and began recounting a story that fascinated and excited him, and filled him with awe.

Duncan chimed in occasionally, but she carried the burden of the tale. Gabe sat back and closed his eyes while she talked, allowing himself to sink into her story, to experience it with his heart as well as his ears. She had a gift for words, a talent for painting a verbal picture that matched Duncan's skill with oils and canvas. When she finished, silence settled over the small room, the deep silence of an Acoma evening.

Gabe opened his eyes to see her gazing anxiously at him. "What do you think? Isn't that the wildest story you ever heard?"

Duncan didn't give Gabe a chance to reply. "Do you believe Jade's being here is just a coincidence, that the dress was the key that accidentally unlocked time?"

"That's a bit like asking which came first, the chicken or the egg?" Gabe stared off into nothingness, probing his own knowledge in search of the answer Duncan sought. "We philosophers spend our lives trying to define reality, only to discover that there is no absolute definition. Reality is based on culture. Because my culture is different from yours, my reality is different. My answer will be based on who I am."

"That's good enough for me," Duncan said.

"For me too," Jade added.

"As I said, reality differs for every culture. My culture is rooted in our desire to exist in harmony with nature. Everything we do, the way we built Acoma from local stone, the way we plant crops in keeping with the natural contours of the land, even our decorative arts stem from that desire.

"We perceive time as an integral part of nature. The seasons change, our children grow, we feel the aches and pains of age. We live from solstice to solstice, celebrating the sun's passage through the sky." He paused and licked his dry lips. He hadn't put so many words together in a long time. "Your people have a different view of the world. You see nature as something to use at your discretion. It follows that you seek to control time. You're surprised because time did something that was completely out of your control. But you can no more control time than you can control the workings of your heart."

While he had been speaking, he noted that Jade and Duncan shared a lover's glance. How he envied them the precious moments they would share. But he didn't envy them the pain of parting. And all lovers parted sooner or later, by choice or by chance. "You asked me if I believed in time travel and I said I did, but I didn't tell you why." He paused to sip his coffee. It had grown cold while he spoke.

"Please, don't keep us in suspense." Jade's features had a pinched and troubled look.

"I'm sorry, my dear. I didn't mean to do that. I believe my people traveled through time many centuries ago."

Jade sat bolt upright, completely stunned by Gabe's revelation.

"Give me a minute to explain how I reached that conclusion," he went on. "The people of this pueblo, as well as the peoples of Cochiti, Taos, Santo Domingo, Zia, San Felipe, Jemez, and Santa Ana, all speak Keres.

"Linguists who have studied Keres tell us it is unique. We are surrounded by tribes who speak Uto-Aztecan or Aztectan-Tanoan tongues, but our language has no relation to theirs. Do you realize what that implies?"

Jade nodded. "I think so. It means that Keres-speaking people are unrelated to any of the other tribes in the Southwest. I don't know that much about linguistics, but I know that's pretty unusual."

"You're on the right track," Gabe said. "The linguistic experts tell us that Keres speakers have been in the Southwest from time immemorial. Our legends tell of our lives in another world, a world that was a great deal like this one. The legends say we came into this world at the *shipop*."

"Is that a real place?"

"I'm sure it is, but I can't give you it's geographical location. *Shipop* means 'the hole of emergence.' I have spent a great part of my adult life trying to interpret the legend, and I have come to the conclusion that the *shipop* was a door through time, much like the one you came through at La Fonda."

Gabe stopped speaking, but his words reverberated through Jade's mind. A *shipop*—a door through time. She looked around the room, noting the way the flickering light from the oil lamp cast distorted shadows on the ancient stone walls. She could feel the past all around. The very air seemed heavy with its musty fragrance.

Duncan turned to Gabe. "You told me the emergence legend years ago but you never mentioned your time-travel theory. Why not?"

"I had no reason to until tonight."

Duncan shifted in his chair. The room had grown cooler. "Do you have any idea why the Keresans came through the *shipop?*"

"Only guesses."

"Then you can't tell me why Jade did either?"

Gabe got up to put another log on the dwindling fire. "I didn't say that. I do have an idea, one I would like to explore, with your permission." He finished stoking the fire and returned to the table. "Do you know anything about datura?"

"Only that it's poisonous." The fine hair at the back of Duncan's neck began to elevate. He didn't like the direction this conversation was taking.

"Datura belongs to a group of plants called *Solanaceae*. My people have used *Solanaceae*, plants like henbane, thorn apple, and belladonna, for medicinal purposes for centuries. That cigarette in your hand contains tobacco, another of the *Solanaceae* family. Although datura can be deadly, it has some very interesting properties. Taken in small doses, it's a hallucinogen. I have used a datura tea many times to seek the truth, to journey where my body cannot go."

"Are you suggesting that Jade take datura?" Duncan asked, shocked.

"I'm suggesting all three of us drink a tea made from the plant. I used the tea when I was trying to find out what lay on the other side of the *shipop.*"

"And did you?" Excitement burned bright in Jade's eyes.

"No . . . but I think you might. And if you do, Duncan and I may be able to go with you."

"When do you want to do it?" Duncan asked.

"What's wrong with right now?"

Hilary closed her shop at five, stuffed the day's take into a bank bag, and put it into her oversize purse. First thing in the morning, she would deposit the proceeds in the bank. Second thing, she would go on to her broker's office to buy more stock. Hot damn. She was going to be rich. Buying on margin had to be the best idea since sliced bread.

She shimmied with glee as she walked to her car. A couple of male pedestrians gave her startled but approving glances, which she ignored. If the market kept on rolling upward at its present pace, she wouldn't ever have to depend on a man again, let alone worry about pleasing one.

Every dollar Malcolm and Duncan had given her, every cent she could pull out of the shop, had gone into her margin account. She smiled ruefully, thinking that right now she didn't have enough money to meet next month's salaries. That didn't matter, though, because tomorrow the market would climb a few more points and she'd be richer than she was today. She was on a glorious financial skyrocket to the moon.

She pulled up in front of her house, kicked off her shoes, and ran in her stocking feet to the front door.

"You seem to be in a very good mood today, madame," Raoul said, letting her in.

"You don't know the half of it. I feel like celebrating with some champagne."

Raoul shrugged. "We're out of champagne."

"What the hell are you talking about? I told you to order another case last week." Shit. She could feel her good mood evaporating. She had really wanted some bubbly.

"Indeed you did, madame. But you failed to leave me enough money to cover the cost. And your bootlegger says he won't allow you to add to your tab until you pay some of it off."

"Stupid bastard." She pulled her cigarette case from her purse and lit up, inhaling deeply. "He knows I'm good for it."

"That's what I tried to tell him."

"So?"

"He said the word is out that you're overextended all over town."

"So?" she repeated.

"It's not my place to interfere in your business, but the grocer, the dry cleaner, even Enid—they've all been complaining that you haven't paid them."

"What about you, Raoul? Is this your way of putting the arm on me too?"

"Of course not. I know how much I owe you." His brown eyes glistened with emotion.

"Forget those people. They all have small minds, small ambitions. You and I, Raoul, we're dreamers, gamblers, risk takers. I know I've shorted the household accounts, but I'm on a roll. One of these days I'm going to have enough money to open a gallery in New York, and when I do, you're going with me."

Hilary could tell from the glazed look in his eyes that he hadn't understood a word she'd said, but she didn't care. All the other men she'd ever known had walked away from her sooner or later. At least she could always count on Raoul. "We still have some Scotch, don't we?"

He nodded.

"Good. How about bringing a bottle to my bedroom and joining me for a drink?"

"Are you certain it's safe to drink?" Duncan asked.

"The datura tea won't cause us any harm." Gabe had been moving around the room, gathering ingredients, putting a kettle on the fire. Now he paused and looked from Duncan to Jade. "But once you drink it there will be no turning back, even though you may learn things that upset or frighten you. Are you sure you want to take the risk?"

"I'd do anything to put Duncan's mind at ease," Jade said with the solemnity of a bride taking her vows. "I'm supposed to be a competent writer and yet I can't find the words to tell you how much he means to me."

"Surely you must have been in love before?"

"I thought I was. In fact I almost got married several years ago. My fiancé broke our engagement a few days before the wedding."

"Does it still trouble you?"

"Duncan has more than filled that hole in my heart. I feel as if I've spent my whole life waiting for him."

"Did this young man look like Duncan?"

Her eyes widened with surprise. "Now that you mention it, he did."

232

"Do you think it's a coincidence that you look so much like Megan?"

"What else could it be?" she and Duncan asked simultaneously.

Gabe smiled. They didn't understand yet. But they would before the night ended. "It's ready," he said, and carried the kettle and three cups to the table.

He motioned for them to take seats, took one himself, then positioned the oil lamp in the center of the table and dimmed the light. After filling the cups with a dark liquid, he handed them around.

A slightly unpleasant aroma filled Jade's nostrils as she sniffed the brew. "I hope it tastes better than it smells."

"It does. It will take a few minutes to get into your bloodstream after you drink it. I want both of you to finish it as quickly as possible. Afterward, the three of us must hold hands. No matter what happens, no matter what either of you thinks you're seeing, don't let go. Do you understand?"

Jade nodded and Duncan murmured a low "Yes."

"I believe," Gabe continued, "that Jade will lead the way through the *shipop*. But I think she will need our help to return again." He looked from Duncan to Jade one last time. "Ready?"

Jade nodded. "Here's to the *shipop*," she said, and drained her cup. The tea did taste better than it smelled. Gabe must have added honey to sweeten it, she thought. She quickly reached for Gabe's and Duncan's hands.

"It will hurry things along if you stare at the lamp," Gabe said, and his voice seemed to come from far away.

He had said the datura wouldn't take effect for a while, but already she felt herself slipping away, spiraling down a long, dark tunnel. She sensed Gabe and Duncan making the fearful journey with her. The sensations were similar to the ones she had experienced months ago in the hotel. But that time she had been intensely aware of her physical reactions. This time, she had left her body behind.

Down, down, they spun, ever further, until Jade feared they would be lost forever in the endless tunnel.

Suddenly, they hit bottom.

They were in a cave, or rather their spirits floated above one. It was snowing outside, but several fires lit the interior. People dressed

233

in fur huddled around a central blaze where a woman with black hair and eyes the color of emeralds seemed to be telling a story in a guttural language Jade didn't comprehend. That's me, she thought with amazement, or another doppelgänger.

A man sat near her. When she finished the story, he took her hand and guided her to a smaller fire at the farthest corner of the cave. The man, who could have been Duncan's twin, helped her onto a fur-strewn pallet and stretched out beside her. They lay in each other's arms and quietly made love as if they were the only two people there. Later, while the rest of the people slept, they retreated to the deepest recess of the cave. By the light of tallow lamps, the man began to paint on the walls.

The scene dimmed and Jade felt herself caught in a wind that sent her tumbling, spinning through a seamless void. Blessedly, a part of her remained aware of Duncan's and Gabe's firm grasp.

When the wind stopped she saw another couple who looked like her and Duncan. They were inside some sort of temple. He was painting on the walls while she inscribed what looked like hieroglyphs beneath his frescos. Egypt, she thought, we're in Egypt, before the wind sent her tumbling away once more.

No matter how swiftly she spiraled through the centuries, she was aware of Duncan's and Gabe's spirits by her side. Time and time again, the swift journey stopped long enough to let her glimpse herself and Duncan in yet another setting, leading yet another life.

Then they were riding over a high plain in a Conestoga wagon. From the style of their clothes and their mode of transportation, she assumed it was some time shortly after the Civil War. She was sitting in the wagon just behind the driver's bench, writing in a journal, while Duncan drove the team of horses.

At first she thought they might be farmers, settlers moving West. But then, seeing the wagon was full of landscapes, she realized Duncan must be an early painter of Western scenes like Albert Bierstadt. Her spirit hovered above the wagon while she thought how strange it felt to be both participant and spectator, to watch over her body and to feel everything it felt.

As she looked to the northwest, she saw the familiar silhouette of the Sangre de Cristo mountains. The couple had to be nearing

Santa Fe—a good thing, because she felt uneasy as she saw how exposed the lone wagon looked under the blue anvil of the sky.

And then she saw four riders coming up hard from the direction of the Pecos Trail, the outlaw's road to Texas. The man must have seen them, too, for he urged his team to a faster pace. Still, the distance between the wagon and the riders shrank. Now Jade could see that the horsemen were heavily armed. The man whipped the horses into a frantic gallop in an effort to outdistance the pursuers, but it was useless. Jade screamed as the outlaws caught the Conestoga.

A gun cracked and a bright red splotch blossomed on the man's chest . . .

Gabe's hand shook as he poured his first coffee of the day. Considering what had happened the night before, the tremor didn't surprise him. If Jade hadn't fainted when she witnessed Duncan's death, if she had been awake long enough to witness her own, Gabe wasn't sure that any of them would have been able to find their way back through the *shipop* to their own time. They had been lucky. Very, very lucky.

He moved around the front room quietly so as not to wake his friends, feeding Blackjack and setting the table for breakfast. Then he unlatched the front door and preceded the dog through it so that both of them could answer nature's call.

When he returned five minutes later, Duncan and Jade were sitting at the table, clutching each other's hands like the survivors of a shipwreck. He knew how they must be feeling—awed, a little frightened—because he felt the same way himself. He poured coffee for them both and waited patiently for the potent brew to revive them.

Duncan was the first to speak. "What the hell happened last night, Gabe?"

"Don't you know?"

"I have my own ideas, but I want to hear what you think."

"We went through the *shipop,* didn't we?" Jade said.

Gabe nodded.

"Yesterday," she went on, "when you were talking about me leading you through the *shipop*, I half expected to find out where your people came from. Instead we saw our own past lives."

"Past lives?" Duncan repeated with patent skepticism.

"One third of the people in the world believe in reincarnation," Gabe said. "You must open your mind, Duncan, expand your horizons."

From the excitement on her face, Gabe guessed Jade didn't share Duncan's dubiousness. "I'm willing to accept the idea that Duncan and I knew each other in previous lives," she said. "But that still doesn't explain why I'm here in 1929 instead of in my own time."

Gabe had hoped they would find their way to the truth without his help. They were obviously too shaken by their spirit journey through the *shipop* to draw the same conclusions he had. He would have to lead the way. "Tell me what you experienced last night, Duncan."

"I kept seeing a man who looked like me and a woman who looked like Jade. Most of the time he was an artist and she was a storyteller or a writer. It was one hell of an hallucination, especially that last part where the man died." He looked down and touched his chest diffidently, as if he half expected his fingers to come away stained with blood. "To tell the truth, it was so real, I felt as if someone had shot me."

Jade had paled while Duncan talked. "I saw the same thing, but I don't remember what happened afterward."

Gabe turned toward her. "You fainted. Duncan and I were able to bring you back through the *shipop* and into this room. Duncan put you to bed."

Her eyes glittered like green stones against her white skin. Gabe relaxed as he saw understanding dawn in them. "Did I find my way to Santa Fe because it was the last place Duncan and I were together?"

He nodded. "Duncan may not admit it yet, but he came to Santa Fe years ago for the same reason. He was subconsciously looking for you. I think he married Megan—just as you almost married your college sweetheart—because of a superficial resemblance."

A hint of pink tinged Jade's cheeks. "Duncan and I have been in love for a very long time, haven't we?"

"I believe you have shared many centuries, many lives. Then, through some cosmic accident, you were reborn in different generations. It could have been the shock for you, Jade, of witnessing Duncan's murder. But you found your way back to each other anyway, against all the odds."

He cleared his throat. "I have spent my life trying to understand our place in the cosmos and I have come to believe that love is the most powerful force in nature. Love means rebirth and regeneration. The earth changes, cultures appear only to fade away. Love alone endures through it all. It is the one constant. Anglo religions teach that God is love. I prefer to believe that love is God."

"Assuming you're right," Duncan said, "how do I know Jade won't just disappear one of these days?"

"Your love pulled her through the *shipop*. As long as your love holds her fast, I don't think you need to worry."

"So love is the answer?" Jade asked, aware of a sublime relief within her soul.

"My dear Jade," Gabe said, "it has been—and will be—for time without end."

CHAPTER 20

Beverly Hills
August 11, 1989

Smog was one of the few unpleasant surprises the late twentieth century had held for Megan. This afternoon, though, a Santa Ana had blown Los Angeles's habitual summer cloak of mustard-yellow air out to sea. The brilliant blue sky mirrored her ebullient mood. She had done it, found a niche where she was accepted without condition, a place where no one made her feel inferior because of her likes and dislikes. And they even paid her for being there, although she would have showed up every day for free because she enjoyed it so much.

High spirits gave her complexion a rosy glow. For the first time in years, she liked herself. She stood in the strong sunshine that bathed Rodeo Drive, gazing spellbound at the envelope that contained her first paycheck and ignoring the stream of pedestrians who brushed past her, until a masculine voice intruded on her self-congratulatory reverie.

"Is that you, Megan?"

She looked up to see Harry Denby a few feet away. Her first instinct was to ignore him the way he had ignored her the last two months. But she was in too good a mood to be unkind. Besides, in a peculiar way she owed him. After word got out that he had optioned one of Jade's novels, Jade's telephone had started ringing with invitations to lunches and dinners.

Megan had accepted them all and learned a lot from the people she met. Without their realizing it, they taught her to handle the accouterments of the modern world, things everyone else took for granted, like credit cards and automatic tellers. They had led her here to Rodeo Drive and ultimately to her job at Attitude, a delightfully eclectic boutique whose clothes ran the gamut from trendy to classic.

"Have you been spending some of your option check?" Harry asked, breaking the awkward silence. A nod of his head took in the upscale stores that lined the famous street.

"No," she replied tersely. "I'm working at Attitude."

His brows elevated and his tone became conspiratorial, as if she had just confessed to a socially unacceptable pastime. "Doing a little research for your next book?"

She bridled. Damn him for thinking she had to have an ulterior motive, something that suited his own lofty status. Since arriving in Hollywood she had learned all about the caste system that put those who were part of the Business—that's what everyone called making movies, as if there were no other industry worthy of the name—people such as producers, directors, agents, and actors at the top of the Hollywood heap and everyday working stiffs like her at the bottom.

Obviously Harry couldn't believe she had willingly given up writing for a job in the nine-to-five world. But she didn't give a damn what he or any of Jade's other acquaintances thought about her employment at Attitude. She loved clothes and she was damn good at selling them. With a little luck and some careful planning, she intended to open a place of her own someday. So she ignored both Harry and his question, turned on her stiletto heel, and walked away.

She hadn't taken more than a few steps when he caught her by the elbow. "I didn't mean to offend you," he said.

She pulled her arm free and turned to face him. He was, she quickly realized, even more attractive than she recalled. And he certainly knew how to dress. When they'd met at the Polo Lounge his loosely draped jacket and trousers had seemed outlandish. Now she knew they were the height of fashion for men, expensive Armani originals that he wore with casual disregard for their cost. She had always been a sucker for a well-turned-out man—but not this time, she commanded herself.

Despite, or because of, his potent appeal, her voice had an angry edge as she said, "I'm not researching anything. I'm just trying to make a living the best way I know how."

Unexpectedly, he fell to one knee and held his hands up in a prayerful attitude. "I didn't mean to put you down. Can you, will you, forgive me?"

She laughed out loud, enjoying his outrageous behavior. Duncan was so dour, she had forgotten how a grown man's eyes could twinkle with boyish mischief. "I will if you'll get up."

He seemed oblivious to the stares of passing strangers as he rose, brushed his trousers, and took her arm again.

This time she didn't pull away.

"Do you have plans for the evening?" he asked. A smile curved his generous mouth, softening the determined line of his jaw.

In another lifetime she would have played hard to get. But her icy determination to hold him at arm's length melted in the warmth of his presence. Besides, she was tired of eating alone. "Not unless you count getting Chinese takeout on my way home as having plans."

"Will you have dinner with me?"

She hesitated, thinking how hurt she had been all those weeks when she hadn't heard from him. A man with his charm, his charisma, could be big trouble for a lonely lady like her. She was just getting her new life under control. Finding a job, learning her way around town, figuring out what people were talking about when they discussed AIDS or the end of the Cold War—just plain fitting in had been hard enough. There had been times when she'd wanted to stay in the house and pull the covers up over her head.

She had made a lot of progress, but it hadn't come easy. A complication in the form of a virile and desirable man might be more than she could or should try to handle. She avoided looking at him and shook her head, no.

240

"Please," he said. "I really would like to get to know you better, Megan."

His grin could have melted an iceberg—and she was no iceberg. "All right," she said grudgingly.

He pointed toward a side street. "My car is just around the corner."

She stopped in her tracks, feeling like a prisoner who has just been paroled. "This isn't going to work. My car is parked a couple blocks away in the other direction. I have a long drive back to Malibu and I don't want to stay out late. I'm due back at Attitude at nine-thirty in the morning."

Harry, who had been heading toward his car, executed a perfect military about-face and gave her a jaunty salute. "No problem. Your wish is my command. We'll take your car and I'll grab a cab back here after we eat." He took her arm again. "Have you ever been to Nick Blair's?"

Harrison tightened his seat belt as Megan threaded her Mercedes through the heavy going-home-from-work traffic. His gut tightened despite the casual panache with which she drove, braking and accelerating with confidence as if she were on the track at Le Mans instead of speeding along Sunset Boulevard. Thank God she didn't try to keep up a conversation. The thought of her doing anything other than concentrating on the road made his mouth go dry.

Her profile, haloed by the lights of oncoming cars, finally took his mind off her driving. She had the sort of bold features that the camera loved, a broad forehead, slightly retroussé nose, strong cheekbones, full lips, and a sweetly curved jaw. He found himself framing her face the way a camera would, thinking how easy she would be to light. It might be fun to give her a screen test, just to see if she could act.

He frowned and cut the thought short. The fact that Megan no longer had anything to do with any branch of the entertainment business removed the off-limits sign he had arbitrarily put on her in June. Now here he was, wondering how she would photograph. Damn fool.

She seemed unaware of the emotional seesaw her presence engendered. The woman was an enigma wrapped in a mystery, a gifted writer and, according to everything he had heard, a real pro. Yet she had abandoned her career to sell dresses. Sure, a couple of her books had failed to live up to her publisher's expectations. Her own expectations as well, he imagined. But her quitting writing surprised him as much as if someone had told him that Steven Spielberg had abandoned making movies because his last film wasn't a blockbuster at the box office.

What Megan had done baffled him, and he was determined to get to know her well enough to make sense of it. He couldn't remember the last time he had been so intrigued by a woman. "Nick Blair's is just ahead on your left," he said, indicating where to turn.

She took advantage of an infinitesimal break in the traffic and pulled into the steeply sloping drive with a screech of rubber that had the car valet's mouth gaping open.

The restaurant, housed on the ground floor of a modern high rise, was a celebrity hangout—the sort of place you took a woman when you wanted to impress her without looking as if that's what you had in mind.

Nicky Blair, a former actor, looked darkly handsome in a well-cut suit as he strode forward to greet them. "It's good to see you, paisan," he said, pumping Harrison's hand in both of his. When he caught sight of Megan, the restaurateur's dark eyes lit up with instant appreciation.

"This is my friend, Jade—Megan Howard, the writer," Harrison said. "We'd like a quiet booth."

Blair nodded, grabbed a couple of menus from the maitre d's post, and escorted them through the bar to the back of the restaurant. "Here you are," he said, gesturing at a secluded table. He suggested an assortment of hors d'oeuvres, courtesy of the house, promised to send a waiter to take their drink order, and left them after cutting one last approving glance at Megan.

The moment they were alone she turned on Harrison, her eyes flashing green fury. "Why did you introduce me as a writer?"

"Because that's what you are."

"We better get this straight here and now. If you asked me out because I'm a writer and you optioned one of my books, we might as well say good-bye this minute. I don't expect to write again."

"Have you told Ira Max?"

"Of course."

"And what did he say?"

"He wasn't happy. But he was smart enough to know he couldn't change my mind."

She looked and sounded deeply upset. He found himself wanting, needing to soothe the disquiet he saw in her eyes. "All writers get blocked from time to time, Megan. You'll get over it."

She shook her head. "I don't even want to write again. I like selling clothes, helping other women to look their best, to feel good about themselves. You men don't understand how important that is to—"

Her impassioned speech was interrupted by the arrival of the waiter bearing hors d'oeuvres and asking what they would like to drink. Megan ordered Scotch on the rocks, an honest drink, Harrison thought. He was accustomed to women who drank Perrier or white wine in public and the stronger stuff at home. He ordered a draft beer for himself. After the waiter left, he wasted no time reclaiming Megan's attention.

"You're wrong," he said. "I do understand. I grew up in a house full of women."

"You did?"

He reached for her hand as if to emphasize what he said next. "I have four sisters, two older, two younger, so I think I have some idea about what's important to a woman." He noted with pleasure that she didn't shrink from his touch.

"Then you don't think less of me for working at Attitude?"

"On the contrary, I admire your courage. Too many people go through life doing things because they think it's expected of them. It's a lousy way to live."

The tension in her face eased. "I guess you do understand."

"Don't you want to know how things are going with your book?" he asked, thinking it was time to change the subject. "I've already seen a first draft of the script."

"To tell you the truth, I haven't given it a thought since I deposited the option check. I feel as if my books were written by another person. The last time we met I told you I didn't care about the past, that I intended to live in the present, looking only toward the future. Nothing has happened to change that. And my future doesn't include writing."

He sipped his beer thoughtfully. The more he learned about her, the more impressed he was by her total honesty, a rare commodity in this or any other town. "Most writers act as if their words are sacrosanct. Knowing that someone is tampering with their creation drives them crazy."

She looked at him from under the longest black lashes he had ever seen. "Does that mean you don't approve of my behavior?"

"Not at all. I find it refreshing. I've never met anyone quite like you. It's almost as if you and Jade Howard are two different women."

She shifted in her seat, her gaze dropping. "In a way we are." She seemed to be talking to herself, but when she looked back at him, the intimacy of her glance sent a shock wave through him. "You seemed stunned by the fact that I'm not writing anymore. But I don't think I'm the only person in the world to change careers. I'll bet you aren't doing what you thought you would when you were growing up."

"You're right. I didn't want to go into movies because that was my father's bailiwick and we didn't have the best relationship when I was a kid. I was a premed student my first two years at UCLA. But then I had a sort of epiphany."

"A what?"

"A moment of truth. One day in chemistry class I realized that I hated test tubes and Bunsen burners. The thought of cutting someone open made me feel sick. The only thing I cared about was making movies. After that I wasn't about to let my feelings for my father deprive me of what I really wanted."

Megan's eyes brimmed with empathy.

"I've never told that to anyone before," he admitted. Something about her made intimacy easy. If he didn't watch his step he'd be telling her his life's story—although come to think of it, he wasn't interested in watching his step with her.

"I'm glad you told me," she said. "I had my own moment of truth before we met. I was in Santa Fe when I woke up one morning knowing that Jade Howard didn't exist anymore. Megan couldn't write her books, so Megan had to do something else with her life. I've always loved clothes and one thing just led to another."

"What exactly do you do at Attitude?"

"A little modeling, a little selling, some personal shopping for male clients who don't have the time or the taste to choose something special for a wife or girlfriend."

"I can see you like it. It shows on your face." She seemed more sure of herself, centered in a way she hadn't been that day in the Polo Lounge.

They talked easily from then on. As Harrison had realized the first time they met, she was one hell of a good listener. Most of the women he knew were too busy talking about themselves or thinking about what they planned to say next to concentrate on anyone else. But Megan had a way of fixing her gaze on him as if the two of them were alone in the room, and that was more flattering than anything she could have said. She made him feel brilliant, charming, and incredibly witty.

Asking her to join him for dinner had been little more than a knee-jerk macho reaction to running into an attractive woman. He had a full calendar the next day and had intended to make it an early evening. But he found himself saying a reluctant good night at ten-thirty.

"Can you join me for lunch tomorrow?" he asked as the valet delivered her car.

"I have to work until six," she replied. She slid into the Mercedes, revealing a silky flash of thigh that made him want to see more. A whole lot more.

"Dinner then—are you free for dinner?" He hadn't been so eager to see a woman in a long time.

"Gee, Harry, I don't know. It's been swell, but . . ."

The way her voice trailed off didn't bode well for the future of their relationship. "Are you trying to tell me you're seeing someone else?" he asked, holding her car door ajar so she couldn't drive away.

She hesitated. "I was. We broke up—sort of—in May. I don't think I'll ever see him again."

"Did he move away?"

"I guess you could say that."

"But you wish he hadn't?"

"No. It's nothing like that. I just feel a little awkward. I haven't gone on a real date in ten years. Look, you can call me," she finally said. Then, spying a break in traffic, she pulled the Mercedes's door shut and accelerated away before he could stop her.

He stood and watched her car recede down Sunset, feeling as smitten as he had twenty years ago when he dated his high school's Homecoming Queen.

Megan Howard. Megan Howard. The name echoed through his mind like a catchy tune.

When Megan walked into her living room forty minutes later, the answering machine indicated there had been several calls during the day. The first two were from her Fred Sands real estate agent.

"The good news," the agent's recorded voice said, "is that I rented your house today. The bad news is the renters want to move in as soon as possible. I'll be up late, so you can call me to settle the details."

The last message was from Harry. "I really want to see you again," he said. "Please call me before you go to bed."

Megan kicked off her shoes and flopped onto the sofa. She wanted to see him, too, but she couldn't forget that she was a married woman. It was one thing to run into a man unexpectedly and join him for dinner, and quite another to accept a real date. She would have to find a way to square that with her conscience.

Why did he have to show up again just when she thought she had her life on track? The job at Attitude was a dream come true. It gave her a chance to do something she loved, something she had a talent for, just as Jade had a talent for writing. And now with the house rented, her money worries were over for the time being. If she could be sure she wouldn't wake up one morning back in her own time, she would sell the house and use the profit to buy her own boutique. She stared into space, wishing . . . Oh hell, there she went wishing again.

When would she learn to be content?

She sat up, rolled her shoulders to release the tension in them, then called her real estate agent and told him she'd move in two weeks. Going into the kitchen, she put on a pot of coffee and set the timer on automatic so it would brew at seven-thirty. As she walked slowly back through the house, she knew she would be glad to leave. Her new place would undoubtedly be smaller and less luxurious, but it would be hers in a way this house and Rancho Cielo never had been.

She had just finished undressing when the phone rang. As she picked it up, she found herself hoping Harry would be on the other end of the line. Conscience be damned, she thought when she heard his voice. Duncan was a thousand miles and sixty years away.

"I know it's late and you have to go to work in the morning," he said before she could even get out a hello, "but I want to see you. Say you'll have dinner with me tomorrow night."

"I can't," she replied with genuine regret. "I've got to start looking for an apartment."

"An apartment? I thought you owned a house in Malibu."

"My real estate agent rented it today."

"Megan, you are probably the only woman in town who would willingly leave a beachfront house," he declared, his voice filled with a curious mixture of confusion and awe.

"I was getting tired of driving to work, but that's not the reason I'm moving. The truth is I can't afford to live here."

"If you're having a cash-flow problem, I'd be happy to give you a loan against the next payment on the option."

She sighed. It would be so easy to go along with him and say she had a "cash-flow problem," but she had left half-truths and white lies sixty years in the past. She didn't want to encumber her new life with her old habits. "I appreciate the offer, only my problem isn't temporary. I'm renting the place while I make up my mind about selling it."

"Did I happen to mention that looking for apartments is a hobby of mine?"

She smiled into the phone. "Do you ever take no for an answer?"

"Not if I can help it."

And so it happened that he picked her up in front of Attitude the next day at six and handed her a neatly typed list of available

247

apartments. Although she knew his secretary had undoubtedly compiled the list, she couldn't help appreciating his thoughtfulness.

She rented the third apartment they visited that evening, a charming two-bedroom, two-bath suite in a mission-style building on a tree-lined street in West Hollywood, just a fifteen-minute drive from Attitude. Since she had rented Jade's house fully furnished, right down to the linens and pots and pans, she spent several evenings shopping for her new home.

Harry was her constant companion, introducing her to the delights of the Melrose Avenue stores. He knew Hollywood as only a native can, knew where to get the best possible price whether she was looking for a bedroom set or a picnic basket for the outings they planned after she got settled.

Before she knew it, they were inseparable. There were breakfasts at Musso & Frank's, lunches at the Bistro Garden, intimate dinners at The Ivy or Campanile, and evenings at the movies which were both Harry's business and his passion. Megan was happiest when he surrendered the wheel of his Maserati and the two of them raced up the coast to out-of-the-way places that were new to both of them.

She didn't know exactly when it happened, and the Lord knew she didn't plan it, but one morning she woke up in her new apartment realizing that she loved him. She loved Harry Denby.

She would never go back to her old life.

Never!

CHAPTER 21

Rancho Cielo
August 20, 1929

Jade hurried to the front door as soon as she heard the Duesenberg coming down the drive. She waited in the shelter of the front *portal* while Duncan parked the car and then, unable to wait another moment, ran across the lawn to greet him. She had spent too many years keeping her emotions in check. Now she threw herself into his arms, kissing him with wild abandon as if they had been apart for weeks instead of hours.

He held her tight, seeming to sense how much she needed to be close to him. When he leaned away, he grinned playfully. "If you promise to greet me like that every time I go away, I'll never get anything accomplished. I'll just spend my days disappearing up the drive and coming right back again."

She laughed. "How did it go? How was your meeting with Dick Davis?" She slipped her arm into the crook of his elbow as they walked toward the house.

"He thinks I've lost my mind."

"He didn't believe what you had to say about the stock market?"

"I'm afraid not."

"I just made a fresh pot of coffee. You can tell me all about it while we have a cup."

In the kitchen, she poured coffee for both of them, then carried a plate of fresh-baked cookies to the table.

Duncan picked up his cup and blew on the steaming brew. "Dick did his level best to talk me out of selling my stocks. Not that I blame him. He's a good broker and he's reacting to the strongest bull market in Wall Street history. Sometimes I have trouble accepting the fact that it's going to crash so soon."

"You do believe me?"

"That goes without saying. I told Dick a topflight analyst was predicting a serious depression in the fall. He wanted to know all the particulars—who, what, where, and when."

"What did you say?"

"That I wasn't at liberty to reveal my source's name, but I hinted that it might be one of my old Yale classmates who has an important position in Washington. Before he would agree to put in my sell order, Dick insisted on sitting me down and lecturing me on the principles of sound investment. He actually tried to talk me into buying more stock."

"Then he didn't believe you at all?"

"Sweetheart, Dick Davis is an optimist. Most brokers are. They couldn't live with themselves otherwise. You can hardly expect him to pull out of the market because some artist walks in with a harebrained story."

"But he did agree to sell your stock?"

"I should have the check in about ten days. I'm not comfortable knowing I'll be rich when everyone is going to be in financial trouble."

"I feel the same way." She shifted in her chair, her earlier happiness evaporating. What good was it to know the future when she couldn't use that knowledge to help anyone? "Is there any chance Dick will warn anyone else?"

"I'm afraid not."

"Then we'll have to do it ourselves," she said resolutely.

He nodded and got to his feet. "I don't relish interfering in my friends' affairs, but this time I don't seem to have a choice. I guess I'll be spending the rest of the day on the phone. What about you?"

"I want to go to town and talk to Malcolm in person. It's the least I can do considering . . ." She was still uncomfortable talking about Malcolm with Duncan. In their own ways, for very different reasons, they had both used the writer. "Do you mind?"

His eyes darkened the way they did when something bothered him. "Yes. I mind. But I know you won't be happy unless you have the chance to make amends."

"I had better see Hilary too."

His eyes grew darker still. "Are you sure that's a good idea?"

"No. There's something a little scary about Hilary, something I can't quite put my finger on. But I have a gut feeling that we'll all be better off if I can make my peace with her."

She got to her feet and carried their cups to the sink. The thought of seeing Malcolm and Hilary, especially Hilary, made her uneasy. What was it about that woman?

Duncan came up behind her, put his arms around her waist, and kissed her neck. She leaned into his embrace, drawing comfort from his touch. "I love you," she said huskily. She wished the day were already over so they could go to bed and lose themselves in each other.

Malcolm sat at the desk in his book-lined library and re-read the page he had just completed. Smiling his approval, he typed *finis* at the bottom, pulled the sheet from the Remington, and added it to the thick manuscript next to the typewriter.

It had been his custom after completing the first draft of a new book to invite a few friends over for champagne. Today, however, he was in no mood for celebration. He took a cigarette from his case and lit it, then walked to the window and looked out.

Summer was almost over and with it, his stay in Santa Fe. Change was in the air. He could smell it, taste it. The long, self-indulgent spending spree that had followed the war was coming to an end. Good times, he thought with a twinge of regret. He'd had good times, indulged every whim.

He had written three books since his army days, giving D. H. Lawrence a run for the money when it came to the sexual content of his novels. Only now he wanted more. He wanted to be known as a serious writer rather than one whose novels sold for their shock value. And he owed it to Megan. She had shown him that it was possible to change, to become a better person and in the doing, a better writer.

His cigarette had burned down, untouched, and he lit another from the smoldering stub. Perhaps he ought to have that champagne after all, he mused. In addition to a completed manuscript, he had his freedom to celebrate. He owed that to Megan too.

As if by thinking about her he had managed to conjure her presence, he saw the Carlisles' Duesenberg pull up to the curb. While he watched, Megan climbed from the car, looking even more beautiful than he recalled. His heart knotted with longing, but he ignored the pain and hurried to greet her.

She was reaching for the bell when he opened the door. "I was just thinking about you," he said as if they had seen each other the day before instead of weeks ago.

"Only good thoughts, I hope."

"When it comes to you," he replied, leading her into the drawing room, "I have only good thoughts."

"I'm so glad you feel that way." She settled on the sofa and he took a chair across from her.

"I heard about the flood and what happened to the Packard. I know how much you loved that car. Are condolences in order?" he asked, hoping to brighten the sober expression he saw on her face.

Her answering laughter seemed a bit uncertain. He missed their former easiness with each other, but his foolhardy marriage proposal had shattered that.

"We weren't able to give the poor thing a proper funeral," she replied. "In fact, we never found the car. It's probably rusting away in some desert wash."

"Can I offer you some tea—or perhaps a glass of champagne? I have one last bottle of pre-Prohibition Veuve Clicquot tucked away for a special occasion. I just finished the first draft of my new book and I was going to celebrate."

"That would be lovely."

Her voice was firm and cheerful, but he noted an anxious look on her face before he left to fetch the wine. When he returned a few minutes later, she had taken one of his books from a shelf and was thumbing through it.

"Have you read it?" he asked, uncorking the bottle and decanting the golden fluid into a couple of Baccarat flutes.

"Years ago, in college."

He handed her a glass. "I didn't realize you had gone to college."

She blushed as she sat back down on the sofa. "Did I say college? I meant finishing school."

"My dear Megan, it's a good twelve years since you were in finishing school and that particular book was published six years ago. You don't need to pretend with me. There is no law that says you have to have read every one of my books."

She looked dreadfully uncomfortable, and that was the last thing he wanted.

"You haven't tasted your champagne," he said, quickly changing the subject.

She clinked her glass against his. "Here's to your new book. I know it's going to be wonderful."

"A consummation devoutly to be wished, dear heart." He laughed easily. "Your dropping in today was particularly fortuitous because I plan to polish the manuscript in England. I'll be leaving in a few days."

She lowered her gaze. "Does your going have anything to do with me?"

He reached out and gently took her chin in his hand, forcing her to look at him. "Not at all. I'm not one of those poor fools who believes the world is well lost for love. I haven't been home for a long time and, although I tend to forget it, England is my home."

"Is Hilary going with you?"

"We've come to a parting of the ways." He downed the contents of his glass and refilled it, then sat in the chair across from her again. "I won't have you blame yourself for that either. Relationships like Hilary's and mine are, by their very nature, not destined for longevity."

"She's going to be lost without you."

"I doubt that. Women like Hilary have no difficulty finding company. Besides, I took very good care of her financially. Before you waste any more sympathy on her, you should know that I paid off the mortgages on her house and the gallery, and gave her twenty-five thousand dollars to boot. Now, why don't you tell me what

253

brings you here today, aside from the undeniable pleasure of my company."

She hesitated.

"I can see something is on your mind. Out with it."

He felt a faint glimmering of hope that all might not be well between her and Duncan, but recalling how radiant she'd looked before she knocked on his door, he quickly squelched it. Besides, hadn't he just been congratulating himself on his freedom?

"Duncan just got a tip about the stock market," she said at last, "and I wanted to pass it on to you."

Her statement took him by surprise. He and Megan had never discussed money before, let alone the stock market. "It must be one hell of a tip to bring you all the way from Rancho Cielo."

"Duncan has a friend, someone with inside information, who is quite certain the market is going to collapse very soon. Duncan is so positive the information is reliable, he had Dick Davis sell all his stock this morning."

Malcolm had been listening intently. People in his circle were forever exchanging information about the market. He had bought shares in Yellow Cab at the instigation of Joe Kennedy, and invested in U.S. Steel after a call from Charles Schwab. He had made a handsome profit in both cases. The thought of Duncan dumping his investments with the market setting new records every day made him doubt Duncan's sanity.

"I'm sure you mean well," he said, "but I hardly think this is the time to get out of the market. In fact, I was planning to make a few more margin buys before I left Santa Fe."

"That would be a terrible mistake," she said, conviction ringing in every word. "You must believe me. The market is going to crash at the end of October."

"Who have you and Duncan been talking to? A stock-market analyst, or a gypsy with a crystal ball?"

"Neither. The person who told us was in a position to know, without doubt or equivocation."

"Where did he come from? The future?"

He had been joking, but seeing the way she paled, he knew he had hit a very raw nerve. What the hell was going on? He sat on the edge of his chair while the flickerings of a most peculiar thought

254

teased at the fringe of his mind. For months, he'd been aware that Megan wasn't the woman she used to be, but he had never thought it in the literal sense. He stared at her now, cataloguing her curly hair—poodle's hair Hilary had called it—her delicate features, her slender body. Good God, he thought, why hadn't he realized it before?

Unable to contain his agitation, he jumped to his feet and stared down at her. "Who are you?"

She froze.

"I repeat, who are you?" Bloody hell! He wanted a cigarette and a stiff drink, but he couldn't tear his gaze from her. He felt himself pulled into the deep green sea of her eyes while the moment spun out to eternity.

"I am a friend," she said softly, surely, "who cares about your well-being. I want you to be free to write the wonderful books that lie in your future."

Her words seemed to hang in the air long after she stopped speaking. Beyond what she had actually said, he sensed a truth she didn't dare voice. He was more than a little frightened by the possibilities that occurred to him. If only he could get her to tell him more, but the firm set of her lips told him she was determined to keep her own counsel.

"May I pass your warning on?" he asked.

She nodded.

"May I tell people its true source?"

"No. You must give me your word that you won't."

Her refusal confirmed what he suspected. He could just about pinpoint the time when she ceased to be Megan Carlisle and became someone else. Someone—dare he even think it—from the future? He longed to probe her knowledge. Above all he yearned to know his own fate. "Can you tell me anything more?"

She got to her feet and he realized she was going to leave. The knowledge that he would never see her again, that she wouldn't permit it, ached through him. "Please," he said. "Don't go yet."

"We both know I have to." She opened her purse and took out her car keys as she headed for the front door.

Before she left she turned and gave him a smile he would remember for the rest of his life. "I can't tell you everything you want to know, but I can tell you this. All your dreams, *all of them*, are going to come true."

All but one, he thought as he watched her walk out of his life.

Hilary was arranging a pottery display at the back of her shop when Megan walked in. How dare she show her face around here? she thought angrily. If she expects to rub salt in my wounds, she had better think again.

"I'm back here, Megan," she called out. "I'll be with you shortly."

As far as she was concerned, Megan could wait until hell froze. Hilary ignored her presence for fifteen minutes, hoping she would take the hint and leave. But Megan was still there, looking around as if the Indian arts and crafts on display were the most fascinating things she had ever seen, when Hilary finally joined her.

"What can I do for you?" Hilary asked, biting off each word.

"I just happened to be in town. I hope you don't mind my coming by without telephoning."

"Oh come on, you can do better than that. You came to gloat, didn't you?" Hilary had to give the devil her due. Megan actually appeared concerned.

"You're talking about Malcolm, aren't you? I just found out he's leaving. I'm so sorry, Hilary."

"No you're not," Hilary said so vehemently, the salesgirls looked in her direction. Six months ago, she wouldn't have given a second thought to staging a knock-down-drag-out public fight with the unpopular Megan Carlisle. Six months ago, she had Malcolm to protect her reputation.

"We can't talk here," she said in a choked whisper. She stalked through the shop to her tiny office, not bothering to look over her shoulder to see if Megan followed. But she could hear the rat-a-tat of her heels.

Hilary sat down behind her desk. "What the hell do you want?"

"Just to talk."

"So talk."

"This won't take much of your time. Duncan had a tip that the stock market is about to collapse and he asked me to pass it on to you."

256

"Why didn't he come himself? Your husband and I get along *really* well—if you get my drift." She was pleased to see that particular arrow hit home.

Megan shifted from one foot to the other as some of her poise deserted her. "He's busy calling other friends to pass on the information."

"So you volunteered to make a special trip to see me." Her voice was poisonous. "How sweet."

"It wasn't a special trip. I stopped by Malcolm's first."

At the mention of Malcolm's name, Hilary felt her self-control slipping. She wanted to leap from her seat and claw out Megan's eyes. The nonsense about the market was just a feeble excuse. The bitch had come to gloat. "I imagine you two had a loving reunion. He's a good fuck, isn't he?"

"Malcolm and I are friends. Nothing more."

"Don't make me laugh. If you were just friends, he wouldn't be leaving without me."

"Have you ever thought you might be to blame?"

Hilary jumped to her feet so abruptly, she hit her shins on the desk. The unexpected jolt of pain fueled her fury. "We were happy together until you set your cap for him. I can't figure it out. You don't look that great, so how the hell do you manage to get men panting after you like dogs slobbering over a bitch in heat?"

She didn't wait for Megan's response. "You must be hot in bed. One of these days you'll have to give me a lesson in sucking cock. I'm pretty good at it myself, but something tells me you're even better."

Megan turned white and then red, backing away until the door stopped her. "I shouldn't have come."

"Damn right. Especially with a stupid excuse like the one you just tried to sell me. I'm not getting out of the market. In fact, I may ask that husband of yours to lend me some more money so I can buy more stock."

"Lend you money?"

Megan didn't sound so confident now, Hilary noted gleefully. "Didn't he mention the ten-thousand-dollar check he gave me in June?" She paused, enjoying the disquiet she saw in Megan's eyes.

"I don't understand."

257

"Duncan said you wouldn't, but what the hell. Just between us girls, it was for services rendered—if you know what I mean. I put every penny in the market and I've already turned a handsome profit."

Hilary relished the flicker of anxiety that passed over Megan's face. But the score wasn't even yet, not by half. Hilary wouldn't be satisfied until she had taken an eye for an eye, a tooth for a tooth— a man for a man.

One word pounded relentlessly through Jade's mind all the way back to Rancho Cielo. *Mistake. Mistake.* Seeing Hilary had been a colossal mistake.

She hadn't expected Hilary to receive her with open arms, yet there had been something irrational about the woman's fury. Jade couldn't help feeling sorry for her, though. Hilary had loved Malcolm in her own way, and she had lost him. Jade couldn't begin to imagine how she would feel if she lost Duncan.

He had just opened the door to let Blackjack out when she drove up. For the first time since leaving Rancho Cielo a few hours earlier, she felt her heart steady in her chest. It was so good to be home again that she dreaded the thought of leaving, but leave they must.

"You look tired," he said, helping her from the car and putting a supporting arm around her waist. "How did it go?"

"Just about the way you'd expect. Malcolm didn't believe me at first but—"

"You managed to convince him."

"Yes, I did," she said, thinking how close she had come to telling Malcolm the truth before he guessed it himself. "How did you manage with your calls?"

"Pretty well. The artists I talked to are a pretty nervous lot when it comes to money. I think they were happy to have an excuse to pull out of the market."

"How about David Max and Ralph Braithwaite?"

"They're both shrewd men. Apparently Ralph has been thinking about getting out of the market for weeks, and he had already talked to David. What I said just speeded up the process." He paused. "That brings us to Hilary. Was seeing her awful for you?"

"Worse than awful. Malcolm is leaving for England in a few days and he isn't taking her. She blames me. I think she would do anything to hurt me. She taunted me with the fact that you had given her ten thousand dollars—for services rendered, she said."

"I did give her money but it was strictly charity. I felt sorry for her. It was the day Malcolm asked you to marry him. I told you how she came here to warn me, to cry on my shoulder. She said Malcolm had left her high and dry financially. I felt more than a little guilty about it, so I offered to help."

"You know Malcolm better than that. He paid off the mortgages on her house and shop, and gave her twenty-five thousand too."

Duncan grimaced. "So she played me for a fool."

"I'm afraid she did. You should have seen her this afternoon. You know what they say about hell having no fury like a woman scorned. Right now I'm afraid Hilary is capable of almost anything."

"She'll get over it." Duncan took her hands in his, soothing her with his touch.

"I may sound paranoid, but that woman scares me. I'd feel safer if we left town for a while."

"I won't be driven out of my home by anyone, certainly not Hilary."

Ice rolled down Jade's spine as she remembered the half-mad look in Hilary's eyes. "I really am frightened. Please, do it for me."

"How can I resist when you put it that way? We were supposed to leave for New York on October sixth, but there's nothing sacred about the date. We can leave earlier if you like."

"I'd love it," Jade replied fervently. Perhaps they would be running away, but right now, she wanted to run as far from Hilary as the two of them could get.

CHAPTER 22

New York City
September 10, 1929

"Well, what do you think?" Duncan asked, coming up behind Jade so silently, she hadn't even realized he had gotten out of bed. "Has Manhattan changed much?"

She gazed with wonder at the part of the city she could see from their Plaza Hotel bedroom and nodded.

"In what way?" he asked, putting his arms around her waist.

"The buildings aren't anywhere near as tall or as sterile-looking as they will be in the eighties. And there aren't as many pedestrians or cars. In fact, there seems to be less of everything except blue sky and trees. I think I'm going to like this New York."

"I'll make sure you do." He nuzzled her neck. "I want these next few weeks to be perfect."

"They will be, as long as we're together." She turned her back on the view and looked him over, liking the way his sleep-tousled hair gave him a sensual, just-out-of-bed look. She couldn't help grinning as she thought how that one word, bed, had taken on a whole new meaning for her in the past month.

"What's so funny?" he asked.

"Nothing's funny. Everything's wonderful. You. Us. Being here. What have you planned for our first day in Manhattan?"

"I want to stop at the gallery first thing. I've missed David."

"I can't wait to see him myself. He's such a sweet old man."

"Sweetheart, you're going to have to be very careful when you're with David. He isn't an old man. In fact, he and his wife, Pauline, had a baby boy less than a year ago."

Jade smiled. "You're talking about Ira, aren't you?"

He lifted an eyebrow. "I still have a little trouble dealing with the fact that David's baby is, or rather will be, your literary agent, when right now all he can say is goo."

"How soon can I see him?"

"The Maxes expect us for dinner tonight. But you have to remember not to make a big fuss over Ira. Megan barely looked at him when we came to New York for his *bris*."

She laughed giddily at the thought of bouncing Ira Max on her knee. "I'm afraid I won't be able to help myself."

"You have to try. Megan wasn't very fond of other people's babies after she found out she couldn't have any of her own."

"Can't we make an exception and tell David the truth about me —about us?"

"That wouldn't be a very good idea."

"I thought you trusted David."

"I do. And so can you. But he would certainly want to tell Pauline, and she might tell her best friend, and the next thing we knew—"

"You're right," she interrupted. No matter where they went or what they did, they could never escape the burden of who and what she was. At times like this, she felt guilty for imposing that burden on him.

Seeing her downcast expression, he quickly added, "We're going to have a wonderful time in New York. After seeing David, I thought you might like to lunch at the Algonquin. A group of writers has a regular table there, and I want to show you off. Perhaps you've heard of James Thurber and Robert Benchley? They're both on the staff of *The New Yorker*."

"They're famous—or they will be."

Duncan laughed. "You had better not tell them. They already think rather well of themselves."

Jade suspected he had deliberately introduced a new subject so she would drop the last one. Still, the thought of lunching with the famous Algonquin writer's group was bait she couldn't ignore.

An hour and a half later a taxi deposited them in front of the Max Gallery. Jade's knees felt rubbery as she looked up at the elegant brownstone, a building that was almost as familiar to her as her own house in Malibu.

"Are you all right?" Duncan asked, sensing her unease. "You look as if you've seen a ghost."

"In a way I have," she said haltingly. "I didn't realize . . ."

His arm circled her waist protectively. "Realize what?"

"Ira's offices used to be in this brownstone. He had an apartment on the top floor." She knew she was confusing tenses, but she was too shaken to untangle the past, present, and future.

"Look, we don't need to go in now. We can come back later."

She tried to smile. "That's very sweet. But I know you're anxious to see David."

"Are you sure you'll be all right?"

She nodded, and this time smiling was less of a strain. "I'll be fine."

She stood on the granite stoop for a moment, swept by an almost painful nostalgia as she remembered all the other times she had walked into this building. Then Duncan opened the door and ushered her inside.

She gazed around. Everything looked different from her memories. Ira's offices had been as homey as a pair of well-worn slippers. The gallery was far more elegant and imposing. In the spacious vestibule, a flower-filled vase and a leather-bound guest book adorned an antique table. An ornate staircase loomed ahead at the end of a carpeted hall. To the left, a wide arch opened into the exhibition space.

"The gallery takes up the first two floors," Duncan explained. "David and his staff have offices on the third. Framing, crating, and shipping are done in the basement. Would you like to go upstairs and see David now?"

"Can we go through the gallery first?" she asked, needing to postpone the moment when she confronted David Max. The last time she had seen him he had been old and frail. She had painful memories of consoling Ira after his funeral.

"Of course," Duncan said.

The gallery had only been open to the public for half an hour, but potential customers were already strolling through its rooms. Jade quickly realized that David Max represented the best American artists of the era. There were wonderful heartland paintings by John Steuart Curry, Thomas Hart Benton, and James Chapin, and more modern oeuvres by Charles Demuth and John Sloan.

She felt a thrill of pride, seeing that Duncan's work was not diminished by comparison with his peers'. She had grown accustomed to watching him paint. Viewing the end product, framed and beautifully presented, made her aware of his talent—his genius—all over again.

She was so absorbed that she didn't notice a short, powerfully built man, his face wreathed in a smile, heading their way. When she finally became aware of his presence she almost cried out. *Ira!* she thought at once. The resemblance was uncanny.

"Duncan, Megan," David Max boomed in his hearty baritone. "I wasn't expecting you this early. I thought you would want to sleep late after your trip."

"I couldn't wait to see you again," Jade blurted out.

"I'm very flattered." He turned the full power of his sky-blue gaze on her. "I know how you value your beauty sleep. But I must say you don't need it. You've never looked better."

She smiled back at him, flushing the way she always did when someone complimented her on her appearance.

David was conservatively dressed in a navy pin-striped suit and pale blue shirt with a high white collar. The sober garb seemed at odds with his youthful features. He had Ira's cherubically round face and red hair, and the same dusting of freckles across his cheeks and pug nose.

"You're a sight for sore eyes," he said to Duncan, clapping him on

263

the shoulder. "I was delighted when you called to say you would be arriving in town a few weeks early. Wait until you see little Ira. You won't believe how much he's grown."

Suddenly, David clamped his mouth shut and cut a worried glance at Jade. He must have realized that boasting about a son wasn't very politic in the presence of a barren woman. She wished she could reassure him, tell him she was as eager to see his son as he was to show him off.

"We're both looking forward to dinner tonight," she said, striving to sound polite rather than excited.

"Pauline has planned a little celebration in your honor." David's smile had returned. "There will be twelve of us for dinner including the Braithwaites. Noël Coward will be joining us too. He's looking forward to seeing both of you again."

"That sounds wonderful," Jade said, but her pleasure at the thought of seeing Ira and meeting Noël Coward was quickly erased by self-doubt. Tonight would be the litmus test of her ability to masquerade as Megan. She had pulled it off in Santa Fe, but Santa Fe had never been Megan's turf. Manhattan was another matter.

Although Megan's wardrobe was replete with evening clothes, Jade had spent part of the day shopping for an outfit to wear to the Maxes' party. She couldn't attend as herself, Jade Howard, but she'd be damned if she would dress up in Megan's things. The decision to wear something new was a way of asserting her own persona. She had chosen a black velour suit by Mainbocher with a matching cloche that dipped seductively over one eye.

Now she secured the hat in place, draped an opera-length rope of pearls around her neck, and clipped to her ears the diamond-and-pearl earrings Duncan had insisted on buying for her at Tiffany's that afternoon.

"Do I look all right?" she asked, joining him in the parlor of their suite.

"You look ravishing," he said, his gaze hungrily roving her face and figure. "So ravishing that I'm tempted to call the Maxes and tell them we've both been smitten with a sudden illness."

"You don't look half bad yourself." She had grown accustomed to seeing Duncan in the casual clothes he wore at home. His tuxedo, however, wonderfully emphasized his superb masculinity, making her weak-kneed with love. A year ago she hadn't known such overwhelming longing was possible.

He was grinning wryly at her. "If you keep on looking at me that way, we'll never get out of here."

"I can't be held responsible for the way I look at you."

Suddenly the smile left his eyes, leaving them as bleak as a lunar landscape. "You're going to have to be very careful tonight. The Maxes and the Braithwaites have known Megan for years. Ralph and David were very surprised when I told them we had reconciled. Frankly, their wives were disappointed."

"Megan, Megan. I'm so sick of being Megan! I wonder if she is as tired of being me."

"I wish I could be sure she was all right," he said, his brow furrowing as he stared off into space.

Jade subdued an irrational stab of jealousy. She felt certain she had gotten the better of the deal when she and Megan changed places. "Are you ready?"

He patted his pockets to make sure they contained keys, wallet, cigarettes, and lighter. "All set."

Twenty minutes later a taxi delivered them to an imposing apartment building on Central Park West. Duncan had told her that the Maxes lived in the penthouse, and had described the floor plan in detail so she wouldn't have trouble finding her way to the powder room.

They rode the elevator to the top floor where a uniformed maid greeted them in a foyer done in a pale mauve.

"It's a pleasure to see you again, Mr. and Mrs. Carlisle," she said, taking their coats and leading them to a spacious living room.

It was, Jade thought as she looked around, a serene and elegant space. The walls were covered with ivory silk moire and hung with the Maxes' personal art collection. The floor was plushly carpeted in the same shade of mauve as in the foyer, and the art-deco furniture was upholstered in lavender and orchid. Beyond a set of French doors, she could see the city lights.

"Ah, here are the guests of honor," said a tall, slender brunette.

As the woman crossed the room to greet them, Jade recognized her as Pauline Max from the photographs she had seen back in Rancho Cielo.

David Max, who had been sitting on the sofa talking to their other guests, rose to greet them too. "How was the Algonquin?" he asked.

"Incredibly exciting," Jade replied. "I never thought I'd be lucky enough to meet James Thurber, Dorothy Parker, and Robert Benchley. Theodore Dreiser stopped by the table before we left."

"Spoken like a true bibliophile," a slim, thirtyish man with a cultured English accent said as he joined them.

Jade studied the new arrival from under the fringe of her lashes. Like Pauline Max, he looked familiar. Noël Coward! she thought suddenly. Good heavens, it's Noël Coward in all his youthful glory.

As if he had read her mind, David confirmed her identification. "Noël," he said in the booming voice that seemed so incongruous with his rotund body, "you remember the Carlisles."

"Indeed I do. Beauty and talent are an unforgettable combination."

Jade repressed a shiver as he bent over her hand and brought it to his lips. This was, she thought, the most incredible day of her life. She had already met so many literary icons that one more shouldn't matter. But this one did. The playwright's genius showed in his eyes, although he masked its intensity with an easy grace.

Like all good times, the cocktail hour passed far too quickly. Just before dinner the Maxes' nurse appeared carrying Ira. The baby was a perfect miniature of his father, with a round body and a round face surmounted by a thick thatch of coppery curls. He beamed at everyone as if he thought they were there just to entertain him.

Jade couldn't resist asking to hold him, even though she knew it was out of character for Megan. He gazed at her solemnly for a moment, then grasped her rope of pearls and put them in his mouth, sucking contentedly.

Jade was unaware of the startled glances her host and hostess exchanged as she looked down at their son with utter delight. Dear, dear Ira, she thought, you're as sweet a baby as you will be a man.

"Naughty boy," the nurse said, reaching for her charge. "You mustn't break Mrs. Carlisle's pearls."

266

Jade reluctantly handed him back. Her gaze never left Ira as he was carried from the room.

Pauline hurried to her side and wiped the pearls with a cocktail napkin. "I must apologize. Ira's at the age where everything winds up in his mouth."

"How I envy you," Jade said. "I've always wanted children."

Pauline's fine dark eyes brimmed with sympathy. "Perhaps you'll be lucky and have a baby when you least expect it. That's what happened to us. Although considering our age, I do worry that David and I won't live to see Ira grow up, let alone have children of his own."

Unexpected tears gathered in Jade's eyes. How she would have loved to reveal the future to her hostess, to tell her she would live to see Ira grown and happily married. She had experienced the same desire the last time she saw Malcolm. She could have told him about the Pulitzer he would win after the Second World War, just as she could tell Noël Coward he would one day be knighted for his work.

She knew so many destinies . . . but not her own or Duncan's. That lack had never bothered her as much as it did at that moment.

Cocktails were followed by a superbly cooked and served dinner. Jade couldn't remember the last time she had been so well entertained. It was, she thought, a minor tragedy of her own time that people who lived with television had forgotten the lively art of conversation.

When they returned to the living room, Noël Coward sat down at the Maxes' concert grand and began to play songs from the musicals he had written. The ballads evoked a sweet sadness, a commonality of mood and experience that all who have ever loved could share. One by one, the guests left their comfortable seats to stand around the piano and join their voices with his.

At last Noël played one of Jade's all-time favorites, and she sang along with him.

Suddenly she realized the others, even Noël, had grown silent. Her soprano floated alone above Noël's accompaniment. Seeing approval in his eyes, she continued.

Noël bridged back to the melody, and this time his own voice joined hers. When the last achingly sweet notes faded, the gathering broke into spontaneous applause.

"You have a lovely voice," Noël said, looking directly at her. She thought she saw something strange in his eyes, but his next question was ordinary enough to make her think she had misread his glance. "Have you ever studied?"

"No, but my mother played the piano and she encouraged me to sing at every opportunity."

"That last song," Pauline said, "I don't think I've ever heard it before. What's it from?"

"It's the love theme from my new operetta, *Bitter Sweet*. It opened in London recently." He turned to Jade. "Is that where you heard it?"

She was tempted to answer yes, but the Maxes and the Braithwaites knew she and Duncan hadn't been to London recently. "I'm afraid I haven't had the privilege. I must have heard it on the radio."

"That's quite impossible, my dear. It hasn't been recorded, and the sheet music has yet to be published in America."

Panic welled in Jade's throat as ten pairs of eyes seemed to impale her on the sword of their curiosity. How could she possibly account for knowing the lyrics to a song the others hadn't heard? Her mouth opened and closed again as she searched for a plausible answer.

To her surprise, Noël came to her rescue. "I should be astounded that you know the song, but to be honest, I'm even more astounded at how I came to write it. Sometimes I spend days at the piano in a fruitless effort to produce one acceptable tune, let alone the lyrics to go with it."

His features took on a reflective mien. "This song came to me full-blown during a taxi ride. I could hardly jot it down fast enough. When I finally returned home and had a chance to play it, I must confess I was moved to tears. It's never happened to me before and I fear it will never happen again.

"So my dear," he continued, looking directly at Jade again, "please don't come up with a rational explanation for how you happen to know it. I much prefer to believe that the same unknown force that gave it to me, taught it to you in your dreams."

CHAPTER 23

Rancho Cielo
May 10, 1930

Jade woke up smiling. She reached down and pressed the slight swell of her stomach to reassure herself that nothing had changed during the night. Rolling onto her side, she looked at Duncan, her smile deepening as she studied his face while he slept. He looked youthful, his lips slightly parted, his features completely relaxed.

How she loved him. Though they had spent nearly every minute together since their return from New York, his constant presence hadn't quenched her thirst for his company. Instead it made her want more, a whole lifetime more.

She felt almost guilty for being so content, so utterly secure in her love for him and his for her, while the rest of the world was in turmoil. Six months ago the crash of the stock market had cannonaded through the economy with the destructive power of an artillery barrage. Businesses had closed, jobs had disappeared, banks had failed. Worst of all, hope had died. People had stopped believing in the government—and in themselves.

How strange it seemed to recall how little attention the Santa Fe newspaper had paid to what was happening in New York last October. She had expected banner headlines on the twenty-ninth, a day that would go down in history as Black Tuesday. Instead, the big print at the top of the *Santa Fe New Mexican* had read, WESTERN AIRPLANE LOST, as if the world would stop turning because one plane had gone down in a blizzard. A much smaller article was headed, BROKERS DUMP WEAK MARGINS, and below that, STOCKS CRASH—BANKERS BELIEVE INVESTMENT BUYING WILL SAVE DEMORALIZED MARKET. Jade had been astonished at the newspaper's sangfroid.

The next day's headlines were no more enlightening. In two-inch bold type at the top of the page the newspaper happily declared, EXPRESS PLANE TURNS UP. ALL HAPPY. Below it in far smaller print an article began, "Official Washington clung steadfastly today to its opinion that American business need expect no adverse results from the collapse of stock exchange prices. . . ."

Weeks earlier Duncan had converted most of his cash to gold and diamonds, which they had cached in a newly installed safe in the study. The knowledge that so many friends had heeded their warning about the coming crash helped assuage the guilt Jade experienced every time she thought about that twinkling hoard.

What was it Gabriel Natseway had said all those months ago? *It's about love. It always has been.* At the time she hadn't realized the full import of his words. She had only related them to Duncan and herself. But it seemed as if loving Duncan had expanded her heart so that she was capable of caring for people who had been strangers just a few months ago.

She and Duncan were deeply committed to helping those who had been financially devastated by the crash. Spurred on by their example, the artists of Santa Fe were pulling together, the haves helping the have-nots. Despite the shadow of economic depression that darkened the world, she had never felt more hopeful, more certain of the good in humankind, more sure that life was truly beautiful. It's about love, she thought. It always has been.

She touched her abdomen again. Today. She would know today.

Duncan stirred and opened his eyes. "You have no right to look so beautiful this early in the morning," he murmured.

He reached for her and pulled her close. She felt his manhood stir against her thighs. How sweet nature was to make a man ready for love the moment he woke up. She couldn't think of a better way to start the day.

The morning sun slid above the eastern horizon, illuminating Hilary Delano's face as she pulled into her driveway. Had she looked in her car's rearview mirror, she would not have liked what she saw. Hatred distorted her piquant features.

Her skin gleamed white against the unrelieved black of her sweater and slacks. A black knit cap obscured her platinum hair. She had chosen the outfit with care, hoping it would make her as hard to see as the other creatures of the night. How laughably easy it had been to approach Rancho Cielo unseen and leave her deadly gift near the back door.

She got out of her car, looked up one side of the empty street and down the other to make certain none of her neighbors was in sight, then hurried to the front door. Inside the house, silence reigned. She had let all the servants go months before when she could no longer afford a staff. Only Raoul, loyal to the end, had stayed long past the time when she could pay him. Eventually he, too, had departed in search of greener pastures.

The newborn sun glistened on motes of dust disturbed by her passage down the hall. As she made her way to the dining room, her lip curled in disgust at the heavy layer of dust coating every surface. Stains from hastily opened bottles and carelessly poured drinks dappled the sideboard. Not that she cared. The furniture no longer belonged to her. In a few days the bank would reclaim the house and all its contents. A gust of anger pulsed through her as she imagined the ladies of Santa Fe pawing through her belongings before the sheriff's auction.

A few inches of brandy remained in the Waterford decanter. She poured the brandy into a glass, then threw the decanter against a wall. It shattered into a dozen sparkling pieces that sent prisms of light dancing around the room.

A harsh sob caught in her throat. Total destruction was preferable to permanent residence in some dreadful barrio. She had spared the decanter such a fate. But how could she spare herself? She took a full measure of the fiery liquid in her mouth and swallowed it down, relishing the long slow burn as it cascaded past her gullet and into her stomach.

Revenge and brandy were well suited, she thought. A marriage made in hell.

Brandy this morning.

Revenge tonight.

She carried the glass into the living room and collapsed into a chair. She and Malcolm had made love in this very chair a year ago, laughing at the need to accommodate their acrobatics to its awkward confines. She had thrust her legs over his shoulders while he held on to her waist and plunged inside her so forcefully, she had been convinced the chair would crumble beneath them.

Well, the damn chair was still here—and so was she. As for dear departed Malcolm, he could go to hell.

It was all Megan butter-wouldn't-melt-in-her-fucking-mouth Carlisle's fault. If she hadn't made a play for Malcolm, pretending to want to be a writer, hanging on his every word as if he were an oracle instead of a man with a prick like every other man, Malcolm would never have left. With her simpering admiration, her worshipful manner, Megan had made him feel like a paragon, a genius, a literary god. Then when she tired of the game, she had dropped him faster than a whore spreads her legs.

Hilary's mouth twisted in a bitter smile. She knew all about whoring; she'd been schooled to it early. She had always taken a certain pleasure in watching some strange man sweat and groan and lose all control when she admitted him into her body. She could do it again. For money. She just needed a little money, enough to get back on her feet.

Damn Duncan. He had promised to help her, to see to it that she wasn't left high and dry by Malcolm's defection. But when the market dropped and she was desperate to save the stocks she had bought on margin, the bastard had turned her down.

She sipped her brandy, staring into the amber liquid, remembering the last time she'd gone to Duncan for help. It had been the first week of November. The Carlisles had just come back from New York. She had knocked at the ranch-house door and when no one answered, had walked across the lawn to the studio and knocked again.

To her astonishment, Megan answered her summons. The minute Hilary laid eyes on her, she knew something had happened. Megan's skin glowed as if an inner fire warmed her. She was wearing one of Duncan's shirts and a pair of jeans, an outfit so incongruous considering her usual taste, Hilary couldn't have been more surprised if Megan had been stark naked.

Dumbfounded, Hilary asked, "Is that a Halloween costume?"

"I wasn't expecting company," Megan replied with chilly equanimity. "What can I do for you?"

Hilary tried to look inside the studio, but the bitch blocked her view. "I have to talk to Duncan. It's an emergency."

Megan opened the door grudgingly. "Please make it brief. We're working."

When Hilary walked inside the studio, she was immediately aware of a new portrait of Megan, wearing something white and ethereal, hanging in place of the old one. If anything, Duncan had made her look even lovelier in the new work. A table laden with a typewriter and a stack of books sat across the room from Duncan's easel. It looked as if Megan was spending her days in the studio, playing at writing.

Duncan had obviously been painting. He looked up from the canvas, but he didn't cross the room to greet her. His "Hello" held no warmth.

"Hello yourself," she said lightly, pretending not to be put off by her chilly reception. "I love your new portrait of Megan. I don't know how you do it, darling, but your work keeps getting better."

Duncan's glacial demeanor defrosted a bit. "I had the perfect model," he said, gazing fondly at his wife.

Hilary almost choked. What the hell was going on? she wondered with growing concern. The Carlisles were looking and acting more like newlyweds than a couple who were irrevocably estranged.

She wet her lips and sent Duncan what she hoped was an imploring little-girl-lost look. "I know it's an imposition, but could we talk alone?"

"I have no secrets from Megan."

Hilary took a handkerchief from her purse and dabbed at her eyes. The last time she had been there, Duncan's natural reserve had been overcome by her tears. She hoped they would serve her equally well today.

"Surely you haven't forgotten the promise you made the last time we talked." She let her voice quiver. "If Malcolm were still here I wouldn't have to come crawling on my hands and knees, but I don't have anywhere else to turn."

"What do you want?" Megan asked, taking up a defensive position in front of her husband.

Hilary's heart jolted. She hadn't expected such a formidable opponent. "As I said, I would like a few minutes with Duncan. It's a personal matter that has nothing to do with you."

"Everything I do involves my wife," Duncan said firmly. "Why don't you just tell us what's on your mind."

Hilary swallowed. Her tongue felt thick and dry. She had no choice. She would have to humble herself in front of Megan. "I need some money to cover the stocks I bought on margin. But I'll pay you back the minute the market gets back to normal. I'd be happy to sign a promissory note."

Duncan closed his eyes, took a deep breath, then let it out. When he looked at her again, it was with a curious mixture of sympathy and impatience. "So you didn't take Megan's warning to heart?"

Hilary fought to suppress her flaring temper. "Why should I? She's not exactly a financial expert. And everyone knows the drop in the market is just temporary."

"How much do you need?"

Hope surged through her. He wouldn't ask if he didn't intend to help. "One hundred thousand dollars."

"That much? My God, what have you done?"

"The same thing everyone else did. I put everything I had into the market and I bought on margin. Your buddy Dick Davis has been calling those margins all day. There's no need to look at me as if I've lost my mind. The market will turn around in a day or two. The newspaper said so this morning."

"That's a hell of a lot of money, more than I can afford to throw away. I'm sorry, Hilary. I can't help you this time. Have you talked to your banker? Perhaps you can get a loan against your house and gallery."

"I mortgaged them to the hilt to buy stock. For the love of God, if you don't help me, I'll lose everything."

But Duncan had been adamant, she recalled. Thanks to him and his bitch of a wife, she had lost everything—Malcolm, the house, the shop. Everything.

And now they were going to pay.

Jade had been ravenous when she woke up, but the smell of food nauseated her. She barely touched the breakfast she prepared. After Duncan cleaned his plate, she carried their dishes to the sink, scraped her poached eggs and toast into Blackjack's bowl, and opened the kitchen door. Duncan always let him out first thing in the morning, but the Newfoundland never went out of earshot before breakfast. She looked out over the meadow, expecting him to see him gamboling in the sun.

She was about to call him when she heard a funny mewling sound. "Blackjack?" she said hesitantly.

"What is it?" Duncan asked, leaving the table to join her.

"I just heard the strangest noise. There. Do you hear it?"

"It seems to be coming from the side of the house."

"What do you think it is?"

"I don't know. But I'm going to find out."

He stepped out into the brilliant spring day. It was such a lovely morning, she thought, following him. Surely nothing could be seriously wrong on a day like this.

As Duncan rounded the side of the house, he stopped in his tracks. "Stay where you are!" he commanded in a strangled voice.

Jade heard the sound again, a pitiful moan that made her throat constrict. She turned the corner and saw Duncan kneeling on the ground, his arms around something big and black. Dear God—it was Blackjack. Foam covered his muzzle and his huge body was convulsing. Still he managed to wag his tail feebly as she bent down by his side.

"We've got to get him to the vet. I'll get the car," she said, breaking into a panicked run.

The trip to town was a nightmare. She drove while Duncan cradled the dog in the backseat. They rocketed down the highway, making the trip in under half an hour. "I'll get someone to help you carry him," Jade said, jumping out of the car in front of the vet's.

"There isn't time." Duncan got out of the backseat with equal speed and gathered Blackjack in his arms.

The muscles in his neck and arms corded with strain as he carried the huge animal into the doctor's waiting room. Jade's nose twitched at the smell of carbolic, and for a moment, she thought she was going to vomit. She forcibly choked down the bile that rose in her throat.

Dr. Gonzalez was a no-frills country veterinarian with a kind, weather-seamed face and an almost magical way with animals. He wasted no time coming forward to help Duncan carry Blackjack into the examining room.

The doctor checked the dog's eyes and gums and listened to his heart and lungs with swift efficiency. Jade ignored the meaningful glance he and Duncan exchanged when he was done. "Blackjack's going to be all right, isn't he?" she asked.

"I'm afraid not, Mrs. Carlisle," the doctor replied.

She ignored the finality she heard in the doctor's voice. He didn't know Blackjack the way she did. The dog was so strong.

"I'm so sorry, Mrs. Carlisle," Dr. Gonzalez said.

Jade bit her lip so hard, she tasted blood. This couldn't be happening. She put her arms around Blackjack, scratching him behind his ear the way he liked, then bending to kiss his massive head. "You're going to be just fine, baby. I know it."

Her heart broke as she saw the light fade in his eyes. One moment he was aware, warm and alive, and the next—he was gone. She kept on hugging and kissing him as if her love had the power to bring him back to life, until Duncan gently pulled her away. She shivered in his arms, locked in the grip of a grief that was very close to rage.

"Why did he die?" she demanded through her tears. "He was always so healthy."

The sympathy on the veterinarian's face made it hard not to break down completely.

"I'd have to do an autopsy to be absolutely sure," Dr. Gonzalez replied. "But, considering the convulsions and the color of his gums, I don't think he died of natural causes. I think he was poisoned."

If Duncan hadn't been supporting her, Jade would have fallen. She could barely speak past the obstruction in her throat. "Who in the world would be that cruel? He was such a sweet, loving animal."

Duncan's arm tightened around her waist. "The sheep ranchers in the area often leave poisoned bait out for the coyotes. I'm afraid it was just Blackjack's misfortune to find some. You know how he was about food. If it wasn't nailed down, he'd eat it."

Although what Duncan said seemed perfectly logical, the raw suffering in his voice made it a mockery of reason.

"Do you want me to take care of him?" the doctor asked Duncan.

"No," Duncan replied, blinking fiercely. "I'll come back for him tomorrow. I want to bury him at Rancho Cielo."

Thank heaven there wasn't any traffic, Duncan thought as he and Jade headed back home. He drove automatically, his mind on Blackjack's death and Jade's reaction to it. She huddled at the opposite end of the front seat, so withdrawn that she seemed unaware of anything but her own pain. She had been looking pale lately and she often couldn't eat. And now this.

Losing Blackjack was hard on him, but he had buried other much-loved dogs. The Newfoundland was her first pet, and from the sorrow etched on her face, he doubted she would ever have the courage to have another.

"It hurts like hell, doesn't it?" he said.

"Oh God, it doesn't seem fair. Blackjack may have looked fierce but he was all bluff. Why would anyone want to poison him?"

"Don't do this to yourself. It was an accident."

"I want to believe you. But . . ."

"But what?"

"A coyote weighs what? Forty pounds or less. And Blackjack weighed almost two hundred. If he ate poisoned bait meant for a coyote, he might get very sick. I just can't believe he'd die."

Duncan's concern for Jade deepened. It was always hard to accept death as a random accident, something without purpose or meaning, but dammit all, that was the way it happened most of the time—a moment of inattention, a misplaced hand or foot—a quirk of fate opened the door and death marched in.

"You've got to face it," he said. "Blackjack's gone and trying to blame someone won't bring him back. He isn't the first dog to die from poison meant for coyotes and he won't be the last."

"How can you be so unfeeling? Don't you care?" She turned her tear-stained face toward him, and for the first time in months he saw despair in her eyes. And something worse. Fear.

"Did losing Blackjack remind you of what happened to your parents?"

"After they died I made up my mind not to care deeply about anyone or anything again. And I didn't . . . until you."

"You also told me you were only half alive—that it affected everything you did, including your writing." He reached for her hand. "You're completely alive now, my love, and that means being vulnerable. But the sorrow will pass. I promise you that. You'll be able to remember what a good life Blackjack had, how much he loved you."

To his immense relief, Jade slid across the seat and curled up against him. They drove the rest of the way home in silence, communicating their love through touch. When they reached Rancho Cielo, Duncan masked his own pain at not seeing the dog come bounding up to the car, barking his welcome.

Jade's footsteps dragged as they headed for the house. When Duncan heard the telephone he hurried to answer it, thinking she might benefit from a few minutes alone.

Dr. Adelman's "Hello" sounded almost offensively cheerful. "Is your wife there?" he asked. "I have the results of her test."

"Her test? She didn't mention having any tests. I thought you wanted to see her to make sure she had no lingering aftereffects from the concussion."

"I'm sure she'll tell you all about it after I talk to her."

"Then she's all right?"

"Never better!" came the hearty reply.

Jade came through the front door just then, looking pale and wan, her shoulders sagging as if she carried the sorrows of the world on them. Despite what Adelman had said, she looked ill.

"Who is it?" she asked listlessly.

"Dr. Adelman—for you."

Her face brightened as she took the phone. "I'm so glad you called, Doctor. I hope it's good news. I could use some."

She listened. Nodded. Began to smile. "Are you absolutely sure?"

Duncan couldn't hear what the doctor was saying, but from the expression on Jade's face, it had to be good news. "Thank you so much," she said. "I'll call later and make an appointment, but right now, I want to tell Duncan."

She put the telephone down and turned to face him, her expression and posture so changed, he suddenly knew what she must have looked like in her teens. "Hello, Daddy," she said.

Daddy? The single word hit him like a thunderbolt. She had called him Daddy. "Does that mean . . . ? Are you . . . ? Are we . . . ?"

"Yes to all three," she said, walking into his arms.

Jade was too tired to write and too excited to sleep. She watched Duncan at his easel, marveling at his ability to work. In the early days of their love for each other, he had told her that he had trouble verbalizing his emotions and expressed them best on canvas. It must be true, she thought. His new painting was an expression of unadulterated joy.

They had spent the afternoon talking about the baby, making a thousand plans for his or her arrival, discussing their hopes and dreams. Sometimes in the middle of it all, they stopped and stared at each other with such wonder and awe, you would have thought they were the only two people in the world ever to have a child.

He had suggested dinner in town to celebrate, but had readily acquiesced when she said she would rather stay home. They lingered at the table long after they finished eating, then tidied the kitchen together. Realizing sleep was impossible, he had suggested they go to the studio and work for a while.

Now Jade looked down at the list she had been typing. Ashley Carlisle. Dianna Carlisle. Melanie Carlisle. Nita, Elizabeth, Carolyn, Linda. The names marched across the page in orderly rows. Reading them, she couldn't help chuckling. Not a boy's name in the bunch. Talk about chauvinism.

"What's so funny?" Duncan asked.

"Come and see."

He put his palette down and walked up behind her, reading over her shoulder. "I don't think you'll be able to sell that to *The New Yorker*. But as far as I'm concerned, it's your best prose ever. Have I told you how much I love you?"

"About fifteen minutes ago. But I wouldn't mind hearing it again."

He kissed her cheek. "You've made me the happiest of men. Every time I look in your eyes, I see all my dreams come true. I'll remember this day for the rest of my life."

"It would be perfect if Blackjack were here." She had avoided thinking about the Newfoundland all day. Now tears stung the back of her eyes.

"He would have been wonderful with a baby."

"Yes, he would." Jade leaned back, resting her head against Duncan. "I don't want to talk about Blackjack, because it will make me cry and I've cried enough for one day. We can mourn him tomorrow. Tonight I want to concentrate on the three of us."

He pressed his lips against her hair. "The three of us. That has a wonderful ring. I used to envy other men their children. But you've given me my own posterity. I may not live to see the future you were born in, but our baby will."

"Please, darling, don't talk that way. Not tonight." She rubbed the back of her neck to ease its stiffness.

"Are you tired?"

"A little. It's been a long day."

"Why don't you go to bed? I'll join you in a little while."

"I'd rather stay with you. If you want to paint some more, I'll just rest here." She stood and kissed him long and deep, then she walked to the sofa and curled up on it while he returned to his work.

How peaceful the night was, she mused. The only sound in the studio was the crackle of the fire Duncan had built in the kiva fireplace. It serenaded her to sleep.

CHAPTER 24

Hollywood
May 10, 1990

Megan stared at her reflection in the three-way makeup mirror, wondering if Duncan would have approved of her transformation. He would probably have found the visible changes—a more natural use of cosmetics, fuller brows, and shoulder-length hair—very becoming. But the inner differences—her maturity, her self-confidence—would have astonished him.

She had adapted to the future with an ease that still surprised her; had learned to make her own decisions, celebrating the good ones while uncomplainingly enduring the consequences of the bad. She truly belonged here, she thought, looking around her bedroom. She had made this time and place her own.

Somewhere along the way she had crossed a mental Rubicon. She had left the past behind—and the ghosts who dwelt there. She no longer woke in the middle of the night with Harry sleeping by her side, expecting Duncan to suddenly materialize in her room. She had even sold the Malibu house, cutting forever the Gordian knot that bound her to Jade's life.

She had a career, friends, a man—or at least the part of himself that Harry could comfortably give. So what if he couldn't make a permanent commitment? She wasn't sure she wanted to either. There was something deliciously sinful about sleeping with a man when you weren't married.

Besides, Harry didn't tell her how to live her life. He didn't question her choices either. They understood each other, which was a damn sight more than she and Duncan ever had.

Duncan. She hadn't given him a thought for weeks. Tonight, she had no choice. Foreboding iced her skin as she contemplated the evening ahead.

It had all begun so innocently. "How would you like to go to an opening at the Los Angeles County Museum of Art tonight?" Harry had asked when he'd called her at Attitude that morning.

"I'm kind of beat. This is the last day of our spring sale and it's been hectic." She had been looking forward to a quiet Friday evening at home, ordering dinner in, watching a movie on the VCR. Harry would, of course, spend the night since neither of them had to work the next day.

"Whatever you say." He sounded disappointed.

"Is it a dress affair?" she asked, thinking about the new Lacroix hanging in her closet. It had cost a bundle, even after her employee's discount. She had been wondering when she would get a chance to show it off.

"It's black tie. I hear the artist's work is spectacular." Enthusiasm suffused Harry's voice as he tried to sell her on the idea of attending the opening. "Does the name Duncan Carlisle ring any bells?"

Megan was so stunned, she dropped the phone. She could hear Harry's voice coming from the dangling receiver. "What the hell happened? Are you still there?"

She bent over and picked up the receiver with fingers that seemed to have lost all feeling. "I'm here."

"How about it? The exhibit opens at seven. We could have dinner at L'Orangerie afterward."

"Will the artist be there?"

He laughed. "Not unless the museum has moved from Wilshire Boulevard to the Twilight Zone. Duncan Carlisle is dead, baby. It's a retrospective."

"Oh no," she said softly. Logic had told her Duncan couldn't be alive. Still, hearing it confirmed . . .

"Does that mean you won't go?"

"I . . . I don't know."

"Come on. Say yes."

Harry could be a bulldog when he didn't get his way, and she didn't want their weekend to start on a sour note. "All right," she reluctantly agreed.

Now as she finished enhancing her lashes with a third and final coat of mascara, she wondered if going to the retrospective would prove to be a mistake. Hell, it might be a disaster. One incautious word, one slip, and she could be in deep trouble. Still, she couldn't help being curious. She had a lot of questions about what had happened at La Fonda almost a year ago. Perhaps the exhibit would supply her with a few of the answers.

She shook her head to give her hair the sought-after just-out-of-bed look, then stood and smoothed her skirt. Her legs felt a bit wobbly, but that, she supposed, was to be expected. She had attended all of Duncan's openings while they were married. How ironic that she would attend this one as well.

She would have to guard against being overly emotional when she saw the paintings. Harry raved about performers who could convey their feelings without saying a word. "Body language," he explained. "It's all in their body language."

She would have to be especially careful of hers tonight.

She picked up her beaded clutch bag and walked to the living room to await his arrival. She could have used a little more time to prepare for what lay ahead, but he was prompt as usual.

"You look dazzling," he said, taking in the miniskirted Lacroix that showed her long legs to their best advantage. He kissed her carefully so as not to mess her makeup. "I'm glad you decided to go tonight. I could use your advice."

"About what?"

"I'm thinking about starting an art collection."

"I didn't realize you liked art."

"It's a damn good investment. The art consultant I've hired tells me Carlisle's prices are about to go through the roof. Two of his paintings are going to be auctioned at Christie's next week and I'm planning to bid on them."

Duncan would have hated to hear the outpourings of his soul reduced to dollars and cents, Megan thought, yet she couldn't deny a thrill of pride that Harry found merit in Duncan's work. It was almost as if the two men knew and approved of each other.

Harry kept up a steady stream of chatter as they drove down La Cienega. The rushes of his latest film looked terrific. He had put a third screenwriter to work on the *Better Than Sex* script and hoped this one got it right. He thought it might be fun to drive up to Carmel tomorrow, have dinner at Clint's restaurant, and spend the night at a cozy bed-and-breakfast he knew.

Harry's monologues required no reply. He used them to unwind after a busy day. All he needed from his listener was an occasional nod.

Megan bobbed her head dutifully every time he paused for breath, but she was barely aware of what he said. She couldn't stop thinking about the exhibit. Her palms felt icy and her underarms were unpleasantly damp by the time they arrived at their destination.

Like many a Beverly Hills matron, the Los Angeles County Museum of Art had recently undergone a face-lift. It showed an impassive, perfectly groomed façade to the casual pedestrian, saving its treasures for those who entered its portals.

Megan recognized several Attitude clients in the crowd surrounding the doors to the Frances and Armand Hammer Building. While she stopped to visit and chat up a little business, Harry bought an exhibit catalogue. When he returned to her, they made their way through the expensively dressed and coiffed throng and into the building.

When Megan saw the first of Duncan's paintings, she almost cried out. It was the portrait of the *penitente* that he had been working on the last time she had been in his studio on that fateful day in mid May. At the time, she had been too anxious to leave for La Fonda to look at it closely. Why hadn't she recognized how unhappy Duncan had been when he painted it? Because she had been too preoccupied with her own discontent, she silently answered herself. What a self-absorbed bitch she had been. If she had to do it over . . .

She moved toward the painting like a sleepwalker, mesmerized by the brooding, evocative work. Reaching out to touch the textured surface, she was unaware of anyone or anything until a powerful hand grabbed her wrist.

A uniformed museum guard moved into her field of vision. "You can look," he said, shaking a stubby finger in her face, "but you can't touch."

"It won't happen again." Harry's voice seemed to come from far away, although he stood just behind her.

The guard nodded and moved on.

Harry took her elbow and guided her away from the painting. "For a minute there I thought the guard was going to ask you to leave. What the hell made you do a dumb thing like that?"

She searched her mind for a reasonable excuse, but the well of her imagination had run dry. Unable to say anything in her own defense, she simply walked on to the next painting, giving Harry no choice but to follow.

The retrospective had been hung in a series of rooms that flowed into one another. Each painting commanded its own space, giving viewers ample opportunity to absorb and enjoy one before being confronted with the next. It was, Megan realized from the superb presentation, an important exhibit—the sort major museums reserved for the most important artists.

She had grown so accustomed to Duncan's work and so jealous of the hours he devoted to it, she had been immune to his talent. Now, confronting his genius in all its splendor, her own achievements seemed childish, her pursuits vain, when compared to his accomplishments.

As she moved from canvas to canvas the paintings enveloped her so completely, the crowd, even the museum walls, seemed to recede into the distance. She could almost see the golden New Mexico light streaming into Duncan's studio and smell the turpentine in the air. Thank heaven the steady murmur of Harry's voice as he read from the catalogue kept her centered in the present.

She recognized most of the paintings, even those that had been completed before she and Duncan married, having seen them in David's gallery or at a collector's home. All but a couple of the canvases had been completed prior to May 1929. Why was that? she wondered. Had Duncan stopped working after she disappeared?

Not likely. He had lived to paint and painted to live. He wouldn't let a little thing like her mysterious absence keep him out of his studio.

By the time they reached the end of the exhibit, she thought she had become reconciled to the bizarre experience of seeing Duncan's work in this place and time. But nothing on earth could have prepared her for what she saw next. Two paintings flanked the exit. On the left was her own portrait, the one Duncan had done at Rancho Cielo after they returned from their honeymoon.

The other portrait could have been her ten years later, but she saw subtle differences that had nothing to do with the subject's age. The clear-eyed gaze, the refined bone structure, belonged to Jade Howard. Megan didn't need to wonder anymore.

They *had* changed places after all.

Harry could feel himself doing the sort of classic double take that comedians from Buster Keaton to Bill Murray employed when they wanted to get a sure laugh. He blinked, his jaw dropped open, and his head swiveled from the paintings to Megan and back again.

"What the hell!" he exclaimed so loudly that he earned a few disapproving glances. "What the hell is going on?"

"I'm sure I don't know," Megan said unsteadily.

He moved back a few feet to better view the twin portraits. Then he consulted his catalogue—and broke out in a cold sweat. "It says the paintings are untitled portraits of the artist's wife. Can you guess her name?"

"I have no idea."

"Megan. Her name is Megan. Quite a coincidence, isn't it?" He felt angry, unsettled, unsure of himself. And he didn't like it one bit.

"What are you implying?"

"I think you're lying."

"About what?"

Her arms were crossed protectively over her chest and she

286

avoided looking at him. If he read her body language correctly, she sure as hell was hiding something.

"You knew all about these paintings, didn't you?"

"Don't be ridiculous. Coming here was your idea. I'm the one who wanted to stay home."

He glared at her. "Then how do you explain the resemblance? And the name—Megan? You must have known Carlisle—" He was talking too loud again, but he didn't seem able to control his voice.

He looked at the portraits once more. Two versions of Megan, one younger, one close in age to the woman he knew, stared serenely down at him, making a mockery of his agitation. The first painting was dated 1919 and the second, 1930.

The significance of the dates finally penetrated his befuddled mind. Sixty, seventy years had passed since Carlisle created the paintings. The artist's wife was either very old or very dead. Any minute now, he thought, Shirley Maclaine was going to walk in and explain the whole thing with one of her New Age theories. He tried to laugh and failed.

"Are you ready to leave?" Megan's voice had a tentative quality. She had moved a few feet away from him.

"I've seen enough," he said, feeling an unpleasant tightness in his chest. "More than enough." Bid on a Carlisle? Not a fucking chance.

He wanted to question Megan. No, he wanted to grill her, cross-examine her. She must have known Carlisle—and yet she couldn't have. What was it he had said about the exhibit being held in the Twilight Zone? He could almost hear the familiar musical theme of the Rod Serling show.

An unaccustomed silence settled over them as they made their way back to his Maserati. He couldn't help cutting sidelong glances at Megan. No doubt about it. She looked just like the woman in the two portraits. Either it was the most bizarre coincidence imaginable, or . . .

Or what?

"I know those paintings bothered you," she said just when he thought he couldn't stand the quiet another minute. "They bothered me too. But I can't explain them. Believe me, I would if I could."

He heard such sorrow in her voice that despite his own disquiet, he put his arm around her waist and pulled her close.

She sighed heavily. "I'm not in the mood to go to a restaurant. Would you mind if we simply went home?"

"What's wrong, Megan?"

"I'm just tired. I could use a good night's sleep before we drive up to Carmel."

"Sounds good to me. We can order a pizza on the way to your place." He glanced at her. Those damn paintings had spooked him so badly, he hadn't given a thought to what they must have done to her.

She looked half sick.

Megan was still shaky when they got to her apartment. She knew she would never manage to insert the key in the lock, so she handed it to Harry. When he opened the door she walked in, kicked off her heels, and dropped her purse on the étagère in the entry.

"I could use a drink," she said, turning to him. "How about you?"

"I'll have a beer when the pizza gets here. In the meantime I think I'll take a long, hot shower. I need something to help me relax after . . ." He didn't complete the thought. "Would you care to join me?"

"I'd better wait for the pizza. You go ahead."

As Harry walked down the hall, she went to the kitchen and poured the double Scotch she had been wanting all evening. Returning to the living room, she sat on the sofa, curling her legs under her. The retrospective had been an unmitigated disaster. She knew Harry still had questions about those damn portraits, questions she didn't dare answer.

She glanced at the catalogue he had tossed on one of the end tables, thinking she ought to throw it out before he finished his shower. Out of sight, out of mind—wasn't that how it was supposed to work? The sooner he forgot what he had seen, the better. But he would probably ask what she had done with the catalogue. Damn. Why did things have to be so complicated?

She could hear the shower running. Harry liked to stand under

288

the water until it ran cold. He wouldn't be out for another fifteen minutes.

She sipped her Scotch, then picked up the catalogue, flipping past the photographs to the short biography at the back. The writer made Duncan's life sound more exciting than it had been—and mentioned her several times. Seeing her name in print like that was weird.

Her gaze came to the final paragraph, stopped, and held there. "Duncan Carlisle died tragically in a fire at his Rancho Cielo studio on May 17, 1930."

That can't be right, she thought. It can't be right! She simply couldn't, wouldn't accept it. Duncan was always so careful to make sure his cigarettes were out before he emptied an ashtray. And he was a fanatic about storing turpentine and oils in the shed rather than the studio.

She looked at the last sentence again, seeing it through a blur of tears. She had imagined Duncan dying in bed at a ripe old age. She began to tremble. There had been little love lost between them at the end. But no one deserved to burn to death. It was too horrible.

May 17, 1930. Sixty years ago. She rubbed her forehead as if she could scrub away the idea coalescing in her brain.

No, dammit, no. She wasn't that brave—that noble.

She didn't owe Duncan a thing. And yet . . .

Forget it, she ordered the nagging voice inside her head. She couldn't go back to 1930, didn't even want to try. She looked around her living room, trying to fix her thoughts firmly in the present. In the distance, she could hear Harry singing off key. Her life was here, with him.

She squeezed her eyes shut in a vain attempt to shut out the image that flashed on her retinas. Rancho Cielo. Nighttime. The studio on fire. Duncan trapped in the building. Everything burning.

Go back. You can save him, the voice said.

No, she couldn't, she answered silently. She was too frightened. Yet she couldn't live with herself unless she tried. She couldn't build her future happiness on the ashes of that deadly studio fire. Not if there was a chance in a thousand that she could change the past. Perhaps the old Megan could, but not her.

Besides, it probably wouldn't work. In a week she would be back in Hollywood. And she would be able to look at herself in the mirror and like what she saw. She groaned and shook her head. She had to be crazy, but it was a good kind of crazy. Who would ever have figured her for a heroine?

She had so much to do and so little time to do it. Little things like emptying the refrigerator and packing her bags, and more important ones like getting a plane ticket to Santa Fe and reserving the same suite at La Fonda. She would have to say good-bye to everyone at Attitude. And then she would have to say good-bye to Harry.

She was unaware of the tears running down her cheeks, unaware that he had walked back into the room, until she heard his voice.

"I didn't mean to lose my temper tonight. I really upset you, didn't I?" A towel draped his hips. Droplets of water clung to his hair. He must have heard her bawling and not taken time to dress.

"It's not you," she said, swallowing her tears.

"Then why are you crying?"

"I have to leave town." The words leaped from her lips as if they had a will of their own.

"What is it? A death in the family?" He sat beside her and pulled her into his arms. She sagged against him, loving the feel of his bare chest, the clean scent of his freshly bathed skin—loving him more, now that she had to go, than she thought possible. Don't be a damn fool, she told herself. She didn't have to go.

"You know I don't have any family," she said, pulling free of the seduction of his embrace. If she stayed in his arms another second, she might not have the courage to leave.

"Then what is it?" Suspicion dawned in his eyes. "You've been planning this all along, haven't you? That's why you sold the house."

"How could you think that, let alone say it? You know that I sold the house because I wanted to buy a part ownership in Attitude."

His shoulders sagged. "For some reason I keep on jumping to all the wrong conclusions tonight. How long will you be gone?"

"I don't know. It could be a long time." She hated what she was doing to him.

"You're not making any sense."

"I know."

He picked up her half-full glass and drank the Scotch down. "Now you're probably going to say this is hurting you more than it's hurting me. For God's sake, I thought we were happy together."

"This doesn't have anything to do with us." She would have given her soul to be able to turn the clock back one day, to tell Harry she wouldn't go to the exhibit. Instead, she was going to try to turn the clock back sixty years.

"Is this your way of punishing me because I wasn't ready for a commitment?" he asked. "Because if it is, I swear I'll change."

"I know you will, darling . . . The next time— If I come back, we'll see what happens. I don't want to leave, but I have to."

"When?"

"As soon as I can. Tomorrow or the day after."

"And you can't tell me why?"

"Maybe someday, but not now."

"Would it make a difference if I asked you to marry me?" He put his arms around her again, holding on tight. "I love you. I should have told you that long ago."

"I love you too. But I think you better leave now, because if you stay much longer, I might change my mind. And I wouldn't be able to live with myself if I did. Please, do this last thing for me. Don't ask me any more questions. Just go."

To her relief, he didn't linger. His face was white with shock, his eyes bleak as he returned to the bedroom to dress. When he walked back into the living room, he wore his impeccable tux. She had always been a sucker for a well-dressed man, she thought with ineffable sadness.

God, how she wanted to change her mind and tell him she would stay. But the thought of Duncan dying horribly, needlessly, stilled the words on her lips.

"Can you tell me where you're going?" Harry barely managed to keep his voice steady.

"To Santa Fe."

"What the hell is it with that place?"

She tried to smile. "Perhaps someday I'll be free to tell you."

He reached blindly for the doorknob. "If you need anything . . ."

"You've already given me more than you could possibly know."

"And what's that?"

"You gave me myself."

A sad little smile tugged at the corners of his mouth. "My mistake. I should have given you me." And then he was gone.

She collapsed on the sofa and gave in to tears. With any luck, she wouldn't be able to find her way back through time. But she had the feeling she had used up all her luck this last year.

CHAPTER 25

Rancho Cielo
May 10, 1930

Duncan had been painting like a man possessed. By the time he finally paused long enough to look at his watch, it was almost midnight. At nine he had promised Jade he would stop soon. Good Lord, what must she be thinking? He glanced over at her. While he worked, oblivious to everything but his hard-driving creativity, she had covered herself with the afghan that draped the back of the sofa. Now she slept, looking even more beautiful in repose.

How fortunate he was, how blessed to have her in his life, and the child she carried beneath her heart. His child, a gift in his middle years and all the more welcome for it. His heart had never been as full, his life as complete as it was this moment. He felt transformed, recreated by love.

When he and Megan had learned she would never become pregnant and she refused to consider adoption, a part of him had died. During their ill-fated marriage, he had forgotten how to share himself and his feelings with another person. Then Jade had journeyed through the *shipop* and his life had had a new beginning.

As he cleaned his brushes, he vowed never again to ignore Jade the way he had tonight. And yet he hadn't been able to stop painting this evening. He had been possessed by joy and the need to express it. The new canvas revealed his feelings more than any words he could ever utter.

He looked at it now, seeing something different in his work, something he had been trying to get down on canvas all his life. Tonight he had come close. The knowledge that he hadn't quite succeeded made him long to attack the painting anew. It took a deliberate act of will to put away his oils and scrape his palette. He had the rest of his life to find what he had sought with his skill this evening.

When he finished his chores, he walked over to the sofa and gazed down at Jade. A sweet smile curved her generous mouth. Did she dream of their child and the life they would share? It would be a pity to wake her when she slept so soundly.

As he bent to kiss her, a tide of love pulsed through him. She was his miracle, the living symbol of the regeneration of his soul. Without her he would have withered, become a bitter aging man locked away in his studio, creating dour visions of a world without light. She was the burning sun at the center of his existence. The radiance filled him now, blazing through his heart with the incandescence of a newborn star.

"Jade," he said softly, "my beloved."

Every day they spent together had been an adventure, every night an infinite journey through the landscape of love. Now a new life had been born of their passion. He stared down at her, so enraptured that he lost track of time until his weary body reminded him that it had been a very long day.

He lowered himself onto the floor and leaned back against the sofa, gazing into the dying embers in the kiva fireplace as he thought about the future. If only he and Jade could marry, if only their child could have his name without question or equivocation, life would be perfect. But, he mused as he closed his eyes, he didn't dare anger fate by asking for more.

He would be content to live with Jade and love her to the end of time and beyond.

Jade smelled smoke. It filled her nostrils with an acrid, choking aroma. She heard the predatory growl of fire feeding on wood. The dream. She was having the dream again.

Wake up. She had to wake up. Everything would be all right once she did. She was sure she would find herself safely in bed with Duncan. His embrace would chase away her terror. She turned and reached for him.

Her hand groped, touching only air. Where was he? Where was she?

Then she remembered falling asleep on the studio couch. He must have built the fire back up, she thought groggily. She rolled her shoulders and stretched her legs, trying to rouse her sleep-sodden muscles. It must be very late.

She pried her eyes open and saw the shadow of flames dancing on the wall across from her resting place. Too bad Duncan had built the fire so high. He was so careful about fire, had warned her about the dangers of living out in the country where the nearest help was so far away, that she knew he wouldn't want to leave the studio until the fire was safely out.

She had been sleeping on her back and now, wanting to put off the moment when she had to get up, she rolled onto her side. To her surprise, she saw the top of Duncan's head just inches away. He had fallen asleep sitting up beside her. She was about to kiss him awake when an ugly sound, like the roar of a hungry beast, made her sit up straight.

The fireplace came into her line of sight. The fire that had been burning there when she fell asleep had gone out. Yet she still saw the shadow of flames on the wall and smelled the acrid aroma of burning wood.

She jumped to her feet and turned around. Fire! The studio was on fire! This time it wasn't a dream. Her heart spasmed in panic. They had to get out of the building.

"Duncan!" she shouted, grabbing his shoulder and shaking him. "Get up!"

He blinked owlishly, slow to come awake despite the desperate urgency of her voice. "What's the matter?"

She tugged him to his feet so that he faced the burning wall. "The studio's on fire."

Sleep fled from his eyes as danger jolted him into complete awareness. He seemed to assess the situation in a single moment. "I want you to go outside, get the garden hose, and turn it on that wall."

Fear stabbed at her innards. Terror shrilled her voice. "You've got to come with me."

"I'm going to save as many of my paintings as I can," he said calmly.

"For God's sake, you can paint other paintings."

"Just do as I say. I'll be all right."

She saw the steel of determination in his eyes. He grabbed her shoulders and spun her around, propelling her toward the door.

"No!" she cried. "You have to get out of here too."

"Don't fight me. You're wasting time. Get some water on the fire," he commanded.

She wanted to do his bidding, but her legs refused to obey her brain. He continued pushing her toward the door while she fought to stay with him. Despite her efforts she suddenly found herself alone outside the studio. She felt grass under her feet. The cool breath of the night air revived her.

Save Duncan. She had to save Duncan.

She glanced back at the studio, hope welling inside her as she saw that the fire seemed to be restricted to one wall. She might even be able to put it out if she got water on it right away.

Working in the dark, it seemed to take forever to carry the garden hose from the back of the house to the studio and then even longer to hook it up. While she struggled, she caught a glimpse of Duncan as he carried her portrait from the building.

"Don't go back in," she screamed. He didn't hear her.

She turned on the water full force, cursing the low pressure supplied by their well. The conflagration had grown in strength and fury during her brief absence. She turned the thin spray on it, attacking first one hot spot and then another, moving so close that her skin became painfully hot. Despite all her efforts the fire continued to grow.

She shouted for Duncan until her throat ached. When she saw flames climbing onto the roof, she left the hose and ran around the studio to the door. From her previous vantage point, she had thought the fire was confined to a single wall. Now to her horror, she realized that three walls were burning as well as the roof. She raced for the open door, heedless of the scalding heat, and screamed for Duncan. She could barely make him out through the smoke. He was struggling to carry another canvas across the floor.

A terrible roar filled her ears and she looked up to see a massive roof timber giving way. She screamed and screamed again, just the way she did in her nightmare. But this time she knew that she shouted at the heedless sky.

"Duncan! Duncan! Duncan!"

The first timber missed him, and for a second, she thought he had a chance. He looked up at the ceiling, obviously aware of the danger, but he didn't abandon the canvas he carried.

She heard the terrible sound again as a second viga broke from the ceiling. She edged as close as she dared and cried out his name again and again and again.

"Duncan! Duncaan! Duuuncaaaan!"

Her cry was still echoing through the clearing as the falling beam struck Duncan and knocked him to the floor. Before she could move, the rest of the roof came crashing down, hurling a fountain of flame into the indigo sky.

CHAPTER 26

Rancho Cielo
May 11, 1930

In the flash point of time between sleeping and waking, Jade had no conscious memory of what had happened in the still of the night. But her unconscious mind knew every detail and recoiled in horror. It urged her to return to the safe cocoon of slumber. She tried. Dear God, how she tried.

In the end her body betrayed her. She hurt, all over. Her lungs ached, her throat burned, and her left hand felt as if it had been flayed. She came fully awake as pain sent urgent messages to her brain. Then she smelled the reassuring aroma of fresh coffee. Duncan must have gotten up and put a pot on to brew.

She tried to push the aura of impending doom aside, but it wouldn't budge. She couldn't dispel the feeling that something unspeakable, unthinkable, had happened. Must be the pregnancy blues, she thought, prying her eyes open.

To her surprise she saw Dulce Ortiz sitting by the bed, running her rosary through her fingers as her mouth moved in silent prayer. Although Duncan drove to Truchas to visit the Ortizes from time to time, Jade hadn't seen Dulce for months.

"Dulce?" she said hoarsely.

The housekeeper looked up. "You're awake, señora." Her voice had a strange catch in it.

"What in the world are you doing here?"

"Oh, señora, I am so sorry." Dulce's olive skin looked preternaturally pale.

Deep down, Jade knew why Dulce was there. Pushing the truth away with every ounce of determination she possessed, she swung her legs over the side of the bed, as if pretending this was a normal day would make it so. "What time is it?"

"It's one in the afternoon." Tears had left watery tracks on Dulce's weatherworn face.

"It can't be. I never sleep this late." She struggled to her feet, feeling dizzy and disoriented.

"The doctor came and gave you something to make you sleep."

Jade swayed as horrific visions overpowered her need to forget what had happened the night before. The fire. Duncan. Oh God. It hadn't been a dream. She remembered it all. The collapse of the ceiling. Trying to get inside the studio and being driven back by the flames. The volunteer fire company arriving too late—more than an hour after the fire began—to do anything but hose down the smoking ruin and call the doctor to care for her injuries.

"Duncan?" She had to ask, had to hear the words even though she already knew the answer.

Dulce used the hem of her apron to wipe her streaming eyes. "Señor Carlisle is dead."

Jade's legs could no longer support her. She reached back and feebly lowered herself onto the bed like an old woman. "Where is he?"

"Dr. Adelman said he would take care of everything until you felt stronger."

Felt stronger? She wanted to tear her hair, to howl her anguish to the sky, to rend her clothes. She wanted to die. She pressed the back of her hand to her mouth to stifle a scream. Duncan was dead. She had watched it happen, had been powerless to save him. How could she live? How could she go on?

"Will you be all right while I see who's there?" Dulce asked.

Jade didn't hear Dulce's question any more than she heard the doorbell ringing. A wrenching cry was rising from her gut. It grew inside her, filling her, and then it burst from her mouth. A pain so deep that it was beyond tears found its home in her chest.

"Oh God, no," she moaned. "Not Duncan." If only she had been brave enough to throw herself into the fire and die too. She couldn't endure life without him.

She reached across the bed for his pillow and cradled it against her body, burying her face in its downy depths. It smelled of him. He had laid his head on it just two nights ago. She closed her eyes against the tears, knowing she might never stop if she began to weep.

She looked up to see Gabriel Natseway standing in front of her, as if her need had materialized him out of thin air. He seemed to have aged a decade since she last saw him. New lines stitched his face and his shoulders hunched under some insupportable burden.

"You know?" Her throat was so raw, she didn't recognize the sound of her own voice.

"Something woke me out of a sound sleep last night. I thought I heard Duncan's voice saying good-bye and asking me to come to you."

He sat next to her and offered the comfort of his arms. "Cry with me. We'll both feel better afterward."

She collapsed into his embrace and felt his body heave, felt the damp of his tears on her own cheek. A tormented wail echoed through the room, then another. But Gabe hadn't made the sound. The wail had been torn from the center of her being. Hot tears scalded her eyes. She wept as she never had before while Gabe cradled her in his arms.

At times she cursed God. At others she begged him to bring Duncan back. She bit her lips until blood mingled with her tears. If Gabe hadn't continued to hold her, to soothe her, she might have gone mad. But he never left her side during the long hours while she spent the first coin of her unendurable grief.

By the time the storm in her soul ebbed, the sun was settling in the western sky. She felt drained, almost cleansed, as if she too had come through a fire and emerged on the other side. She finally retreated from the shelter of Gabe's arms and fell back against the pillows, too weak to sit up.

"Are you all right?" he asked.

"No. I'll never be all right again."

"Do you want to talk about what happened?"

"Yes. No. Oh hell, I don't know." She looked around the room with unseeing eyes. "I guess I should get dressed and wash up."

"Only if it will make you feel better. There's really no need. It's almost evening. Dr. Adelman will be here soon to check on you. Have you had anything to eat today?"

She shook her head. Her stomach seemed to rise up in her throat at the thought of trying to put anything in it. "No. I don't want anything."

He ignored what she had said. "A pregnant woman must eat regularly. I'll ask Dulce to fix something."

"How did you know about the baby?"

"Dulce told me. She's very worried about you. So is Dr. Adelman. He asked her to be sure you took care of yourself until he returned."

After Gabe left for the kitchen, Jade got out of bed. Her legs shook and she had to hold on to the furniture like an invalid, but she finally made it across the floor to the closet. She stared at the clothes inside, utterly unable to do something as prosaic as choosing something to wear. In a way, getting dressed affirmed the fact that life would go on, a life without Duncan.

No. Please God, no.

She finally plucked her blue velvet robe from a hanger and put it on. Then she went into the bathroom to wash. The face she saw in the mirror was gaunt and pale—the face of a stranger. Now she knew what she would look like in old age. Old age. Dear heaven, did she have the courage to live all those years without Duncan? She choked on tears as she thought of raising his child without him.

Five minutes later she made her halting way to the living room in search of Gabe. He stood by a window, staring outside.

Her eyes tracked his gaze, across the clearing to the skeletal remains of the studio. She gasped and turned away. "Please, close the curtains."

"I'm so sorry. I should have done it sooner."

Just then, Dulce arrived carrying a tray. "It's something light. Tea and toast. If you want anything else, just ask." She put the tray down on the coffee table and left as quickly as she had come.

Jade was grateful that Gabe made no attempt at small talk while they ate. She forced herself to eat and drink for the baby's sake. When she finished she felt more ready to confront the myriad tasks that are born of sudden death. She got up, walking more steadily now that she had something in her stomach, and retrieved a pencil and a notepad from the drum-table drawer.

"We need to make plans," she said.

"Are you sure you feel up to it?"

"No. I don't. But I need to keep busy or I'll lose my mind."

He nodded his understanding. "Then we'll make plans."

While Jade and Gabe talked, she became acquainted with the topography of grief, its peaks and valleys. There seemed to be no end to her stock of tears, and she spent them with profligate abandon. She made lists and wept; divided tasks and wept. Gabe volunteered to go to town in the morning to deal with the funeral arrangements, and to bring Blackjack back to be buried at Rancho Cielo. Jade would stay behind telephoning friends, and writing an obituary for the *Santa Fe New Mexican* and *The New York Times*.

At seven Dulce turned on the lights and removed the tray. Dr. Adelman came at eight, expressed his condolences, and gave Jade some sleeping pills. At nine, Gabe insisted they call it a day.

"I know you're tired but don't go to bed yet," Jade said. "I don't want to be alone."

"I don't either."

"Would you like a glass of sherry?"

He smiled for the first time since his arrival. "Didn't you know it's against the law to give an Indian a drink?"

She shook her head.

"It's a silly law," he added. "When I taught at Yale, my wife and I had a glass of sherry before dinner every night."

She walked to the buffet, filled two glasses with amontillado, and carried them back to the sofa. "How did you get over losing her?" she asked, handing one of the glasses to him.

He sipped the amber liquid thoughtfully. "I never did. Not a day goes by when I don't think of her. It's been more than twenty years and I still catch myself saving up things to tell her at the end of the day."

"You mean I'm going to feel this miserable forever?"

"Of course not. The pain will pass. A time will come when you won't need to hide from memories. You will welcome them like an old and cherished friend." He paused and stared off into a time and place that only his eyes could see. "Scientists tell us that matter cannot be destroyed, that it can only be changed. I think it is the same with love. Men dwell too much on the hate that is in them, and the evil they do in its name. But I believe love is the most powerful force in the universe. That—like matter—it cannot be destroyed. Only changed."

He paused to drink his sherry.

"Please don't stop," she said.

He nodded. A world of kindness brimmed in his eyes. "The love I feel for my wife is not the same love I knew in the springtime of my life. But it is just as powerful. It can make the coldest winter day at Acoma seem like summer. You and Duncan shared a very special love. You found your way to him. Perhaps someday in the future, he will find his way back to you."

"Can you be sure?"

"I have thought long and hard about what happened to you since the evening when the three of us traveled through the *shipop* together. I'm not wise enough . . ." He shook his head and looked down at his hands. "Only God has the answers you seek. I am just an old and weary man with a heavy heart. But I have spent most of my life trying to understand the nature of our earthly existence. I view time as a river. We can drink from its headwaters, stand in it at full flood, or turn our faces to the sky and feel it as rain.

"The river exists forever. You and Duncan have drunk from it many times. I believe you will drink from it again."

Jade's parents hadn't believed in funerals. Their wills specified cremation, and their ashes had been scattered over the field behind their house. Their lives had been terminated so abruptly, and so little notice had been given to their passing, that it had taken Jade years to deal with their absence. As she said good-bye to the last of

303

the guests who had come to Rancho Cielo for Duncan's funeral, she realized that a proper burial, complete with flowers and oratory, could be a final act of grace.

Duncan had been laid to rest at the crest of the rise overlooking Rancho Cielo. Blackjack had been buried not ten feet away a couple of days earlier. It seemed fitting that they would watch over Rancho Cielo together.

After bidding good-bye to the last mourner, Jade returned to the three men who waited for her in the living room. Ralph Braithwaite and David Max had arrived two days after the fire, fatigued by their eighteen-hour flight from New York. That afternoon they still seemed to carry a world of woe in the dark pouches under their eyes.

Gabriel Natseway seemed positively chipper by contrast, although she knew his easy smile hid the still-fresh wound of Duncan's loss. He had been a rock, an island fortress in the midst of her grief.

All three men had eulogized Duncan at the service, sharing memories of happier days. At his own request, David had been the last to speak. When he closed by saying, " 'Good night, sweet prince, And flights of angels sing thee to thy rest,' " Jade had almost broken down. But Gabe never left her side, giving freely of his strength.

Now it seemed natural to walk to him and slip her arm through his. "How can I thank the three of you?" she said, looking from man to man. How different they were from one another, and yet utterly alike in their unswerving devotion to Duncan. "I wouldn't have made it without you."

"We did him proud, didn't we?" David's voice had a husky rasp. Of the three, he seemed the most exhausted. "I didn't know there were that many people in Santa Fe. They all cared for Duncan."

Ralph had been pacing restlessly. He seemed enervated and edgy. "Nothing unites people like a reminder of their own frailty." His eyes burned bright against his pallor. "I still can't believe someone set that fire deliberately. Who the hell hated Duncan enough to pour gasoline on the studio in the middle of the night?" He turned to Gabe. "Have the police come up with any suspects?"

"Not yet. But I don't think this is the time to discuss it."

"It's all right," Jade said. She knew Gabe wanted to protect her but it was far too late for that. "I know it won't bring Duncan back but I want to see the arsonist caught and punished. I want it more than anything."

"We all do," Gabe said. "Unfortunately the police don't have much to go on."

"Oh hell," Ralph muttered.

Hell indeed, Jade thought. She had spent the four days since Duncan's death in hell, an eternity of seconds, minutes, hours. The nights had been the worst. She had slept in snatches, jolting awake, her heart thudding, her pulse racing as if the horror was yet to come instead of behind her.

Dulce's appearance interrupted her unhappy musing. "Do you want me to start clearing?" she asked, her gesture indicating the dirty dishes, used glasses, and overflowing ashtrays left by the half a hundred people who had stayed after the funeral.

"Why don't you leave it until morning?" Jade suggested.

"I feel better when I'm busy."

Jade understood perfectly. She dreaded the future, dreaded living out her life in an alien time with nothing but regret to fill her days. "All right, Dulce. We'll get out of your way."

The three men followed her down the hall to Duncan's study. The room still resonated with his presence. Mementos of his existence were everywhere—an old sweater hooked on the back of a chair, his rack of pipes sitting on the desk, an open book he had been reading.

David walked to the wall of photographs, taking his time looking at them, although Jade knew he must have seen them many times before. He didn't utter a word but his heavy sigh told how much he suffered. Ralph went to the window and gazed out, seemingly riveted by the sun-dappled forest beyond the clearing. Gabe busied himself building a fire.

Jade sat down behind the desk, feeling the way Duncan's long, lean body had contoured the chair. It was as close as she would ever come to having his arms around her again.

A collective silence settled over all of them.

Finally, Ralph cleared his throat and turned from the window. "I thought we might go over Duncan's will while the four of us are together."

"Must we?" Jade asked.

"This is as good a time as any. We don't have to have a formal reading—nothing like that—but I wanted to make you aware of a few things. If you'll excuse me for a moment, I'll go get my briefcase."

He reappeared minutes later, pulled a chair up to the desk, and indicated that he wanted the others to join him. When Gabe and David were seated, Ralph opened his briefcase and removed a slender document.

"Megan," he asked, "were you aware that Duncan wrote a new will when the two of you were in New York?"

"He didn't mention it." What next? she thought in anguish.

"The new will reflects the fact that he converted most of his holdings, bank accounts, stocks, et cetera, to more tangible assets. The basic provisions of the new will don't differ from the old one—with one exception that I'll get to in a minute." He looked up, his gaze briefly resting on David and Gabe. "Duncan wanted the three of us to take our pick from his personal possessions—cuff links, watches, things like that. We were to get certain paintings as well but . . ."

A terrible sadness swept over his face and his voice cracked. He cleared his throat. "The Ortizes are to receive twenty thousand dollars. In addition, there are other smaller bequests." He looked at Jade. "Duncan left the bulk of his estate, the diamonds and gold, the cars, the contents of the house, to you. He named Gabe, David, and me as his trustees. But here's the part I don't understand, and believe me, I begged Duncan to explain it. In essence, Megan, you have what's known as a life estate in Rancho Cielo. However, you can't dispose of the property. At your death, Rancho Cielo is to go to a woman called Jade Howard."

Ralph's face betrayed his bewilderment and concern. "Can anyone tell me who the hell Jade Howard is, and why Duncan would leave her the thing he valued most?"

Jade swallowed hard. Her eyes moistened but she refused to weep. How like Duncan to try to look after her, no matter the circum-

306

stances. He must have feared that she would be pulled the wrong way through the *shipop* and he had done his best to make sure she still inherited Rancho Cielo.

"I repeat," Ralph said, "who the hell is this Jade Howard?"

Gabe answered. "She is," he said, gesturing to Jade.

David had been slouching in his chair. Now he sat bolt upright. "This isn't the time for jokes."

"It's no joke," Gabe replied. "With Jade's permission, I have a story to tell you." He cut a glance in her direction.

She knew him well enough to trust him implicitly. He must have a good reason for choosing this time and place to make a clean breast of the truth.

"Go ahead," she said, surprised at the steadiness of her voice.

She closed her eyes against David's and Ralph's inquisitive glances while Gabe launched into the story of her appearance in Santa Fe. Although the events were completely familiar to her, Gabe's recounting held her interest. He was a born storyteller, the sort who would make a superb writer. A few minutes after he began, she reopened her eyes to see David and Ralph sitting on the edge of their seats, giving Gabe their full attention.

"I know you believe what you're saying," Ralph said after Gabe had finished, "but the only proof you've given is hearsay. I'd hate to take a case in front of a jury with such flimsy evidence."

"Would you believe physical evidence?" Jade asked.

Still cautious, Ralph replied, "That depends."

She left them to retrieve her digital watch and her lingerie from their hiding place. She couldn't help smiling as the three men handled them with mingled expressions of confusion and embarrassment on their faces.

Ralph, who seemed to have appointed himself as David's spokesman, finally said, "This is pretty persuasive. But I'd like to hear what happened again, from beginning to end, in your own words, Jade."

David and Ralph interrupted her from time to time, asking for clarification of certain events. They nodded as things that must have puzzled them during the previous year were finally explained. The conversation lasted through the dinner hour and on into the evening as questions were asked and answered and information exchanged.

When the men were satisfied with her story, Jade gave the three of them a thumbnail sketch of the future. She was rewarded by the smile on David's face as he learned of his own longevity and his son's accomplishments.

"To think you held the little pisher on your lap," he said with such genuine pleasure, they all laughed. "And," he added, winking at her, "when we meet fifty years from now, I'll know who you are."

Jade blinked in shock as she realized he was right. No wonder she and David had gotten on so well when they first met in 1979.

As the evening wore on, Jade thought of how wise Gabe had been to reveal the truth. It served as a catharsis for them all, a chance to look forward rather than back. But she didn't realize the full extent of his purpose until he interrupted the give-and-take of conversation and asked for their attention.

"I for one," he said, "could question Jade for a week and not learn all I want to know. But I had a reason for revealing the truth today."

Ralph, with a lawyer's quick mind, came instantly alert. "What might that be?"

"First, I didn't want Jade to have to carry the burden of the truth alone, now that she no longer shares it with Duncan. Second, I was hoping the two of you would help me convince her to attempt to return to her own time."

"But how? And why?" Bewilderment widened David's eyes.

"The why is simple," Gabe replied. "Jade doesn't belong here now that Duncan is gone. The how may be a bit more complicated. I think I know the way to accomplish it, but I can't be certain it will work."

"Is it dangerous?" Ralph asked.

"No more dangerous than it was the first time."

Jade had been listening quietly. She had spent the last few days trying to accept the fact that she would go on living at Rancho Cielo without Duncan. Now a wave of longing swept through her at the thought of returning to her own time. She knew, better than any of those present, that the future was truly a better place to raise a child. Not because of the gadgets, the electronic games, the toys that would be regarded as miraculous in 1930. Hers was, in her opinion, a better era, an age when equality was more than a word in the Constitution.

"Well, Jade, what do you think?" Ralph asked.

She turned to Gabe. "Would it really be possible?"

"I can't be sure, but I think so. Some philosophers see the universe as a chaotic place of random events. I believe there is a pattern, an order to the way things happen. You came through the *shipop* a year ago on May 17. Now that your love for Duncan and his for you no longer holds you here, I believe you have the opportunity to return to your own time."

"When?"

"In three days—on May 17."

"But I can't leave so quickly."

"Why? What is there to keep you here?"

"I want to see justice done. I want to see Duncan's murderer punished."

Gabe's eyes caught and held hers. "Justice will be done, by God if not by man."

Jade could almost feel the tension in the room. "What will happen to Megan if your theory is right?"

"She will return to her own time."

"I know it's selfish, but I'd rather have Jade stay," David interjected. "Besides, think of Megan's shock when she finds out that Duncan is dead."

"I have thought of it," Gabe said. "That's why I want you and Ralph to stay here until Jade makes the attempt. If it works, Megan is going to need the three of us. If it doesn't . . ." He shrugged.

"Suppose I say yes. Then what?" Jade was painfully aware of the hard beating of her own heart. She still wasn't sure she could leave Rancho Cielo, with its reminders of the life she and Duncan had shared.

"On May 17," Gabe said solemnly, as if he were repeating an incantation, "you will recreate the day you came through the *shipop*. You will check into the same suite at La Fonda. You will put on the red dress at the exact time you put it on one year ago . . ."

CHAPTER 27

Santa Fe
May 17, 1990

Jade squeezed her eyes shut and kept her hands protectively clenched over her stomach until the dizziness and nausea passed. Then ever so slowly, fearing what she might see, she opened her eyes and looked around. The lump of fear deep in her gut began to dissolve. She had spent less than twenty-four hours in this room, but every detail, the placement of the furniture, the color of the bedspreads, the size of the prints hanging on the walls, had been indelibly inscribed in her memory.

She didn't need the sound of Tom Brokaw's voice emanating from the sitting room television set to know she had returned to her own time. Weak-kneed, she collapsed on the bed. A week had passed since Duncan's death, but now she had put sixty years between herself and her memories. And yet her grief was as fresh as today's news. It hurt. God, how it hurt.

Truly, the time was out of joint. If Gabe's plan had failed, she would be taking the elevator down to the lobby right now to meet him and Ralph and David. Was Megan making that trip in her place?

She caught a glimpse of her pale face in the mirror over the dresser and saw the red dress gleaming against her flesh. The lovely garment suddenly seemed malevolent. She quickly shucked it off, holding it at arm's length as she carried it to the closet.

The decision to return to her own time had been made so hastily, she hadn't thought about what she would do if she succeeded. Had Megan occupied this room just moments ago, or would some other woman walk in demanding to know what Jade was doing there?

She half expected to find her own jeans and sweaters in the closet, but it was full of high-style fashions. She hung the Molyneux up and began a quick examination of the clothes, not quite knowing what she was searching for. Tucked in a suit jacket pocket, she came across a cryptic note that read, "Harry/seven/Spagos." She hastily returned the note to its place, then chose something to wear and put it on, her nerves so taut, her hands shook.

Too spooked to stay another minute, she hurried from the suite. Taking an elevator down to the lobby, she made a beeline for the registration desk. "Could you tell me who is staying in 310?" she asked the clerk.

The young man looked at her as if she had lost her mind. "That's your suite, Miss Howard. Is something wrong?"

"No. Everything's fine." She tried to control the quiver in her voice and failed. "What's the date?"

"It's May 17."

"And the year?"

The man's elevated brows showed his surprise, but he was too polite to do anything other than reply. "Why, it's 1990, Miss Howard."

Gabe had speculated that she might return on the day she left. But a year had passed. What had happened to her life during that year? So many questions teamed through her mind that they almost filled the aching void created by Duncan's death.

She took the elevator back up to the third floor and began a systematic inventory of the things the previous occupant had left behind. The living room yielded nothing more personal than magazines, but Jade thumbed through them carefully. The May issue of the *Beverly Hills* magazine had been left open at an advertisement for Attitude, a women's store on Rodeo Drive. Jade knew of it, although she herself had never shopped there. Was that where the fashionable outfits in the closet had been purchased?

She returned to the bedroom and began going through the dresser drawers. The top three contained lingerie, the sort of sexy, feminine undergarments a woman wore for her lover. The bottom drawer held purses. The first two were empty, but the third contained a ring of keys, a wallet, and a checkbook. She opened the wallet first and gasped when she saw her own driver's license and credit cards. For a moment the shock of it made her unable to get another breath. She took the license from its plastic pocket and pressed it against her chest like a talisman.

She didn't have the temerity to open the checkbook until the frantic beating of her heart returned to normal. The checkbook had been issued by the bank she used. She read the name printed on the top left corner, blinked, and read it again.

Jade Megan Howard.

Not only had she and Megan changed places, but Megan had found a way to use her own name. When Jade saw the Hollywood address under the name, she felt a shiver of worry. What had Megan done with the Malibu house? It had been comforting to imagine herself raising Duncan's child there. She crossed her arms over her stomach. Sweet heaven. Duncan was gone. Had she lost her house too?

She returned to the sitting room and collapsed onto the sofa, her head in her hands. Her temples throbbed. She still had no idea what had happened during the year Megan had taken her place.

Ira. Had she managed to fool Ira? And who was Harry? Had Megan worn the lingerie for him? Did this Harry think he had been sleeping with her, with Jade Howard?

Only Megan could give her the answers. Perhaps she was grasping at straws, but Jade picked up the slender Santa Fe phone book and opened it at the C's. She gasped out loud when she saw the name Megan Carlisle halfway down the page.

Megan sat in front of the living room television set, but she paid no attention to the action on the screen. Her eyes kept straying to the phone at her elbow. What could be taking Jade so long? Had she made it safely through the *shipop?*

She reached for her cigarettes, lit one, and inhaled deeply. The damn things were supposed to kill you but she was still here. She wouldn't have missed this day for anything in the world—including a jaunt to the Pearly Gates, although she was dying to know what she would find on the other side. Now there's a play on words, she thought.

Although she had been anticipating the call, the ringing of the telephone made her jump. The sudden motion sent spurts of pain through her arthritic joints. She grimaced, then shifted in her chair and reached for the phone.

"Hello."

"Is Megan Carlisle at home?" asked a female voice.

"You're talking to her."

"Oh my God—"

"Is that you, Jade?"

"How did you know?"

"I knew you would call as soon as you figured a few things out."

"Then it really is you, Megan?"

"None other." Megan smiled into the dark room.

"I have a lot of questions."

"And I suspect I have most of the answers. How soon can you get here?"

"Where are you?"

"Rancho Cielo." Megan laughed throatily. "I assume you know the way. The area has built up quite a bit since you were here. Make sure to take the old highway rather than the Interstate. My name is on the mailbox. And Jade—" She paused for breath. A woman her age had no business trying to string so many words together.

"What is it, Megan? Are you all right?"

"As right as a ninety-year-old can be. Now, what was I saying? Oh yes. If memory serves me, you'll find the keys to a white Hertz Ford in my black alligator bag. The car is on the first floor of the hotel parking lot."

"It's seven-thirty. Perhaps we should wait until tomorrow to see each other."

"You'd better make it tonight," Megan replied, trying to keep her voice steady. Considering the way her angina had been acting up, she wasn't sure she'd be there in the morning. She reached for the vial of pills in her dress pocket, took one out, and slipped it under her tongue.

"I'll be there as soon as I can," Jade said.

"There's one more thing. I haven't seen that white Donna Karan suit in sixty years. It would please me if you wore it."

"Anything else?"

"That's it."

When Jade hung up without another word, Megan rapped her cane on the floor. One of the Ortiz women, a Serafina this time, hurried into the room. Megan no longer remembered whether Serafina was Dulce's great- or great-great-niece, but she was a fine girl. Serafina seemed to think she was duty bound to take care of Megan just because Megan had helped with the tuition for her nursing degree. Not many young women would be so loyal these days.

In any case, there wasn't anything wrong with her that nursing or doctoring could fix. Her body was worn out, used up like a dress that's seen too many years or a car that's run too many miles.

"Are you all right, Megan?" Serafina asked, her fine dark eyes barely visible in the gloom. "And why are you sitting here in the dark?"

"I was watching television. Not that there's anything worth a second look since they took "Miami Vice" off the air. Now that Don Johnson was a sight for sore eyes. Reminded me of Harry." Megan knew she was wandering, having what she thought of as an attack of verbal diarrhea. She'd been doing too much of it lately. "Anyway, I'm expecting some company so I want you to turn on the lights and fix a tray with some sherry and a pot of tea."

"You know the doctor doesn't want you to drink."

"Or smoke either. I know. It will kill me one of these days." Megan's laughter was as full bodied as a young woman's. She laughed a lot because the sound reminded her of the time when her skin hadn't looked like the crushed velvet of a Navajo squaw skirt.

Serafina walked across the room, took the cigarette from Megan's hand and stubbed it out. "I'll be back in a few minutes," she said. "In the meantime, try to behave yourself."

Megan waited until she heard Serafina's footsteps retreating down the hall before she lit up again. She ignored the way her heart bumped as the nicotine hit her bloodstream. She wished she were still healthy, young, and beautiful. She wished Jade could have seen her in her prime.

Things were happening too fast, Jade thought as she turned the rented Ford onto what was now called the Old Las Vegas Highway. Events had been crowding each other without giving her a chance to catch her breath. Duncan's death was still an open wound that bled every time she permitted herself to think about him. Now she was on her way to meet the woman who had been his legal wife.

She gazed out the car windows and willed herself to concentrate on the scenery. To her right, a busy four-lane highway paralleled the old road. To her left, the once empty foothills of the Sangre De Cristos were dotted with large homes. She passed so many unpaved drives leading to them, she almost missed the one to Rancho Cielo.

Moments later she stood at the front door, gathering her courage before she rang the bell.

"Just a second," a woman called.

The young woman who answered Jade's summons quickly identified herself. "I'm Serafina Ortiz, Mrs. Carlisle's nurse. She's expecting you but she really isn't up to company. Please don't let her get too tired."

The name Ortiz registered with Jade, but she was too anxious to meet Megan to make any comment. She followed the young nurse to the living room. An old woman was standing in front of the sofa, leaning on a cane and looking their way expectantly. It was almost impossible to equate this ancient dowager with the vibrant beauty Jade knew from photographs.

"Is that you, Jade?" Megan knuckled away the tears that blurred her vision. She had been waiting sixty years for this moment and now she'd be damned if she'd let herself ruin things by acting like a sentimental old fool.

"It's me."

"Come closer. I want to get a good look at you."

When they were face to face, Megan studied the younger woman with unbridled curiosity. "You're prettier than I was," she said bluntly.

"You're very kind to say so." She's so old, Jade thought. She should have realized how much Megan would have aged. But the sixty years that had always separated them still had no reality for Jade, while Megan looked as if she had lived through every one.

Megan laughed. "At my age, I'm beyond being kind. I can afford to be frank." She continued to study Jade. "But that suit looked better on me. The trick of wearing clothes well is to make sure you don't let them wear you." Before Jade could react, Megan reached out and readjusted the jacket collar so that it framed Jade's face. "There, that's better."

Serafina, who had been watching the exchange, hurried to Megan's side and helped her back onto the sofa.

"I'll bet she told you not to tire me," Megan said, frowning at the nurse. "Be off with you, child. Miss Howard and I have a great deal to discuss."

Serafina retreated to the door. "Don't stay up too late," she said before disappearing down the hall.

"Please sit down." Megan patted the cushion next to her. "I know you have a lot on your mind. And I can see you're still grieving. You look like you could use a stiff drink. Or would you rather have tea?"

"Tea."

"Of course. The baby. How silly of me to forget."

"Who told you?"

"Gabe. Sixty years ago. I was sick with jealousy at the time. But you know what they say about water under the bridge." She indicated the tray on the coffee table. "I'm a little shaky from all the excitement. Would you pour? Sherry for me, please." She waited until Jade handed her a glass of wine, then she said, "What do you want to know?"

"Everything," Jade replied. "Everything that happened while you lived my life. Why don't you start by telling me what you did with my house?"

"I sold it."

"You what?"

"After living in it for a few weeks, I realized you couldn't afford it. Neither could I." Megan paused as her eyes searched Jade's face. "You said you wanted to know everything and I won't keep secrets.

But you're going to have to let me tell you in my own way, at my own speed. Is it a deal?"

"It's a deal," Jade said, feeling oddly chastened. Despite her obvious frailty, Megan was very much a power to reckon with. Jade sat back, prepared to listen for as long as Megan could talk.

As a storyteller, Megan lacked organizational skills. She leapfrogged from one subject to another, pausing to light a cigarette, sip her wine, or catch her breath. But Jade had never been more spellbound. She leaned forward intently as she learned of Megan's trip through the *shipop* and how the months that followed had changed her. Jade found herself liking and even admiring Megan. She couldn't help but feel that they would have been friends if they had met under other circumstances.

At nine, Serafina returned and insisted that Megan retire for the night. Although the effort to tell her story was obviously taxing Megan's small reserves of energy, she ordered the nurse to bed with an imperious wave of her hand and simply continued talking. Two hours later, she reached the end of her story.

"I guess you could call it temporary insanity, me thinking I could save Duncan's life." Megan smiled ruefully.

Jade fought back her tears. Damn. She had already wept enough for one lifetime. "I don't know what to say, except to thank you from the bottom of my heart for trying."

"The truth is, I didn't think it would work. When I told Harry I was leaving Los Angeles, I really thought I'd be back."

"How did he take it?"

"Pretty well, all things considered. But I know he'll try to get in touch with me—that is with you—sooner or later. And if he finds out you're pregnant, he may think the baby is his."

Jade didn't know whether to laugh or cry. She hadn't counted on that complication. "Don't worry. I'll find a way to let him down easy. When did you say you talked to Ira last?"

"I didn't. But it was about six months ago, your time. I finally managed to convince him that my writer's block wasn't going away and that talking to him was too painful for me. He'll be delighted to hear that you've recovered, assuming that you do plan to write again."

"I haven't had a chance to think that far ahead."

Megan had grown visibly paler, but she pressed on. "There's one more thing we need to discuss. The money, the half million you left here. There were so many people who needed help during the Depression, and afterward too. So many good people who just needed a little money to tide them over, someone to care if they lived or died. Maybe I was buying friendship. God knows I didn't have any friends at first. In any case, I couldn't turn anyone down."

Jade lightly touched the older woman's hand. "I wish Duncan could have known what you did."

"Hell, Jade, don't make me out to be a plaster saint. I did what I could, but I managed to have fun too. I went to New York once a year in those days, took in the shows, did some shopping, met some interesting men along the way too. When the money ran out a few years ago, I began selling things, Duncan's paintings, the Indian arts and crafts he collected, even my own clothes, although I saved the Molyneux until I knew you would be going to Aurora's Borealis."

Jade tried not to show how much the news upset her. She hated the thought of this dignified woman being forced to live hand to mouth.

Megan surprised her by laughing. "Don't look so worried."

"I wasn't thinking about me. I was thinking about you, how hard the last few years must have been."

"They weren't that bad. When you get to be my age your priorities change. I had a roof over my head, food on the table. And beautiful memories. I just wish . . ." She stopped in midsentence. "Hell, if there's one thing I should have learned long ago, it's not to wish. I always had the feeling that's what started all this in the first place. You—Duncan—me. All wishing for things we didn't have. Now, what was I talking about?"

Jade still had questions. But she had promised to let Megan tell the story her way. "You were saying something about money."

"I guess I forgot to mention that I never did buy an interest in Attitude. There's a couple hundred thousand in your savings account in Los Angeles."

"Dollars?"

Megan nodded.

"Again, I don't know what to say, or how to thank you. When I think of how hard it must have been for you, leaving Harry, going through all that, and then waiting sixty years . . ."

To Jade's dismay, Megan's eyes filled with tears. "I miss them both, Duncan and Harry. Gabe, Ralph, David—they're all gone. So many ghosts." She looked around the shadowed room. "There's one thing I never understood. I'm sure I read the right date in the art catalogue. It said Duncan died on May 17, 1930. I got to La Fonda on the thirteenth and put that damn dress on every night, thinking I could save him. But when I got back to my own time, Gabe told me that Duncan had already died." Megan's eyes blazed. "You're the writer, Jade. Tell me how a writer could have made a mistake like that."

"It must have been a typo. Someone—the writer, the printer—typed the wrong number. It happens all the time. I'm so sorry."

"It's not your fault." All the anger had fled Megan's face. She reached for Jade's hand and gave it a quick pat.

"I just have one last question," Jade said. "Did the police ever find out who set the fire?"

Megan smiled with grim satisfaction. "They didn't, but I did. Don't ask me how. You don't want to know and I wouldn't tell you anyway. It was Hilary. She said she didn't know anyone was in the studio. She just wanted to destroy Duncan's paintings to keep him from having a show that year."

"Did you believe her?"

"Yes. She knew what his work meant better than I did. It was his whole life until you came along. And she was right, wasn't she? He died trying to save his paintings. By the way, Hilary poisoned Blackjack so he wouldn't bark and wake you up while she was pouring gasoline on the studio."

"Did she go to jail?"

"No. I didn't have a shred of proof, nothing you could take into court. As it turned out it didn't matter. Dulce put a curse on her. I don't know if you believe in that sort of thing, but it worked. Hilary died a few years later in a New Orleans whorehouse. Committed suicide, they said."

Jade sat back, badly shaken. "How she must have hated us. Gabe once said that love was the most powerful force in the universe. Knowing what Hilary did, I'm not so sure."

Again, Megan patted her hand. "Gabe was right, you know. Poor Hilary has been dead and gone all these years, and her hatred with her. But Duncan lives on in your memories, in your child, and in his art." She sagged against the sofa. "And now, my dear, I'm terribly tired. Will you help me to my room?"

Jade checked her watch and saw that it was almost midnight. The evening had taxed her. She could only imagine what it must have done to Megan. "I'd like to see you tomorrow."

"It's much too late to drive back to Santa Fe. I want you to spend the night."

"I couldn't impose. Besides, I didn't bring any clothes with me."

"It's no imposition. Don't forget, this place will belong to you when I go." Megan laughed again, that wonderful, throaty young-woman's laugh. "As for the problem of clothes, I believe we're still the same size."

Megan had never been so weary. Her bones felt brittle. Just breathing in and out was an effort. She leaned heavily on Jade as they made their way down the hall. After they said good night, she barely had the strength to shut the bedroom door and walk across the floor to the bed.

Too tired to undress, she stretched out on the spread. She hadn't talked so much in years. It had been good to unburden herself to Jade, to weave together the last threads of their twined lives. But the cost had been high. She felt it in the erratic beat of her heart, the tightness in her chest. She reached in her pocket for her pills and realized she had left them on the coffee table. She thought about trying to get them, but she didn't have the strength.

She felt a swift, sharp pain that took her breath away. It's time, she thought, time to find out what's on the other side. She wasn't afraid, because she saw it ahead.

The *shipop*.

EPILOGUE

Rancho Cielo
May 16, 1991

Jade paused, inhaling the fragrant scent of the bouquet in her arms before making her way across the clearing to the rise where she had buried Duncan. How she missed him. Even now, she felt incomplete, as if half her soul were missing.

It didn't seem possible a year had passed since she had returned to her own time. At first she'd kept busy picking up the pieces of her life, flying to New York to see Ira and then to L.A. to see Harrison Denby. Poor Harrison. He'd been shocked by her revelation, disbelieving, had even wanted to marry her. She'd talked to him for seemingly endless hours, telling and retelling the story, trying to convince him she wasn't Megan.

Ira's reaction to her story had been completely different. He hadn't argued, equivocated, or urged her to consult a psychiatrist. Instead he'd encouraged her to get it all down on paper. Eight months later he'd auctioned the resulting book. Funny how things worked out, Jade mused. Now Harrison, a believer at last, was making the book into a movie.

Throughout the writing, Duncan's child had been growing inside her. She smiled as she recalled how proud Duncan had been when he found out he was going to be a father. They hadn't had a chance to pick a name, but she felt certain he would have agreed with her choice. The first time she held their daughter in her arms, she had known no other name would do.

Megan. She had named the baby Megan. Even though Megan was only three months old, at times Jade saw Duncan in her diminutive features. And her eyes were blue-gray, just like his.

Ahead, sunshine glinted off the simple marble stones that marked Duncan's and Megan's graves. Jade spread the blossoms across both of them. Then she knelt, bowed her head, and said a prayer before heading back to the house.

Serafina was waiting in the shelter of the *portal*, an expression of concern on her face. "Acoma has been there for hundreds of years," she said. "I'm sure it will be there for a few more. Do you really have to go today?"

Jade smiled at her, thinking what remarkable women the Ortiz family had produced. For the past twelve months, she had leaned on Serafina, borrowing her strength. But the time had come to stand on her own two feet, to take life into her own hands. Excitement and apprehension bubbled inside her as she thought of the trip ahead.

When she'd left Los Angeles in what now seemed like another life, she had hoped her travels would help her produce a salable novel. That hope had been richly fulfilled. She had written the manuscript in Duncan's den, sitting in his chair, feeling him so very close. Their story had virtually told itself. All she'd had to do was change the names. But having written a potential best-selling novel wasn't enough to make her happy or even content.

Gabe had suggested that Duncan might find his way to her. She couldn't just sit and wait, though. She had to try to find her way back to him. She had passed through the *shipop* twice in La Fonda, then the door had closed. But there had to be others. She wouldn't rest until she found her way back to Duncan.

Considering what Gabe had told her of his people's legends, Acoma seemed like the logical place to begin her search. "I know you mean well, Serafina," she said, "and I appreciate your concern. But I have to go to Acoma. Did you put my bags in the car?"

Serafina nodded. "Everything's in the trunk—the baby bag, the box of diapers, even that old red dress."

They're coming, Elena Natseway thought as the image of a dark-haired woman with a baby in her arms flashed into her mind. She smiled with satisfaction. Gabe had been right all those years ago when he first began training her, passing on his knowledge in preparation for Jade Howard's arrival.

Elena put aside the pottery piece she had been working on, washed the clay from her hands, and set the CLOSED sign by her front door. Although it was still early in the season, tourists were already making their way to Acoma and she didn't want any customers taking up her time today. She had far too much to do.

As she began readying her home for Jade and the baby, her mind drifted back to the years she had spent with her great-uncle. Gabe had been a brilliant man. He had read the most difficult scientific treatises dealing with time and space in his search for the *shipop*. Perhaps that was why its location had eluded him.

It was Elena's experience that learned men like Gabe tended to overlook the obvious, to make things more complex than they needed to be. She hadn't needed to drink datura to find the *shipop*. It was as real as the floor under her feet and the roof over her head.

She paused a moment to gaze out the window toward Enchanted Mesa. Gabe had known the legends about Enchanted Mesa, yet he had ignored them. A shiver ran the full length of Elena's spine as she thought about what she had discovered on top of the mesa's brooding ramparts.

Jade's heart thudded heavily as she pulled up to the visitor's center below Acoma. Nothing looked familiar. She had expected some changes, but she was unprepared for a full-scale tourist operation.

Six decades ago she and Duncan had hiked a steep trail to the top of the mesa. Now a narrow road wound its way up to the village. Signs warned that cars were not allowed to use the road. Her hope of exploring on her own vanished as she realized that visitors were bused up to Acoma, escorted by Indian tour guides. If only Gabe were still alive, she thought. But he must have died years ago. She was on her own.

Sighing heavily, she turned to the backseat, where Megan slept in her car bed. The baby stirred, opening her eyes. She smiled at Jade as if to say, *Don't worry, Mom. It will all work out.*

Jade leaned toward her daughter and stroked her velvet cheek. When she straightened up again, an Indian woman stood by her car's open window. Apprehension raced through Jade as she realized the woman was staring at her.

There was something disturbingly familiar about her. As they gazed at each other, Jade suddenly realized the woman looked just like Gabe. For a fleeting moment, she felt his presence as surely as if he were there.

She opened the car door, slid from the seat, and held out her hand. "I'm Jade Howard."

"I know who you are," Elena Natseway replied. "I've been expecting you."